Auld Licht Idylls
*and*
A Window in Thrums

# Auld Licht Idylls
## *and*
# A Window in Thrums

## *J.M.Barrie*

WITH AN INTRODUCTION BY
ANDREW NASH

Kennedy & Boyd
an imprint of
Zeticula Ltd
Unit 13
196 Rose Street
Edinburgh
EH2 4AT
Scotland

http://www.kennedyandboyd.co.uk
admin@kennedyandboyd.co.uk

First published in 2015
Copyright ©Zeticula Ltd 2015
Introduction © Andrew P. Nash 2015
Cover painting, *The Keeper's Cottage, Cosyglen* © John Halliday 2015

ISBN  978-1-84921-137-6

# CONTENTS

# Introduction

'The kail grows brittle from the snow in my dank and cheerless garden.'

For the student of Scottish literature today, this line from the opening of J.M. Barrie's *Auld Licht Idylls* (first published in 1888) carries an unintended irony. Although the term Kailyard did not enter Scottish cultural discourse until seven years later in 1895, Barrie has come to be seen as the founder of an influential – and highly damaging – movement in late nineteenth-century Scottish literature. The critic who first applied the term, J.H. Millar, while conceding Barrie's 'genius', declared him 'the founder of a special and notable department in the "parochial" school of fiction' and 'the *pars magna*, if not the *pars maxima*, of the Great Kailyard Movement.'[1] Millar's Latin tongue was probably half-in-cheek, and the main target of his mildly scurrilous attack was not Barrie but the fiction of Ian Maclaren (Rev. John Watson) and S.R. Crockett, whose hugely successful books were widely seen as having been inspired by Barrie's early works. The unintended irony in the line about the kail growing 'brittle' in the schoolmaster's 'dank and cheerless garden' is thus double-edged. For not only did Barrie's writing become trapped within a critical context that owed less to his own writing and more to that of his imitators, but 'Kailyard' came to be seen as a literary style that wilfully evaded anything 'dank and cheerless' about Scottish life.

It is only in recent years that the negative associations surrounding Barrie's early works have been fully scrutinised and destabilised.[2] The reader approaching *Auld Licht Idylls* for the first time may struggle to find evidence for the numerous sins which critics such as George Blake have laid at Barrie's door.[3] Indeed, contemporary reviewers recognised an artistry and fidelity to truth that is wildly at odds with twentieth-century judgements. The opinions of the *Spectator*, which judged the work 'the most truly literary, and the most realistic attempt that has been made for years – if not for generations – to reproduce humble Scotch life', and of the *Aberdeen Free Press*, which claimed that 'nothing has appeared for a long time so vivid and expressive in the way of description of Scottish social existence', are representative of the work's critical reception both within and beyond Scotland.[4] The publication of *A Window in Thrums* the following year drew even greater acclaim. Here was 'the art of a writer of the rarest insight, and genuine mastery of style' observed the *Glasgow Herald*.[5] Barrie's older contemporaries in Scottish fiction were equally taken aback. Writing in *Blackwood's Magazine*, Margaret Oliphant eulogised 'the extraordinary literal truth of this little interior [...] no book could be more deeply instinct with the poetry of real feeling';[6] while Robert Louis Stevenson told Barrie after reading *A Window in Thrums* that his work was 'a source of living pleasure and heartfelt national pride. There are two of us now that the Shirra might have patted on the head.'[7]

One of the reasons for this critical excitement was the keenness among contemporary writers and critics to stimulate a new 'national school' of Scottish literature. Oliphant saw in Barrie's writing the potential for Scottish fiction to be lifted from what she termed the 'poor little local separateness' into which, she claimed, it had fallen since the days of Walter Scott.[8] It is thus again ironic that in the twentieth century, mainly through the influence of Hugh MacDiarmid, Barrie came to be seen as having founded in the Kailyard a national school which only perpetuated 'little local separateness', and impeded the expression of Scottish nationalism and internationalism.[9] That contemporary readers could find a universality in these two short volumes suggests a fundamental difference between Victorian and modern sensibilities. And with this in mind, it is important to remember that *Auld Licht Idylls* and *A Window in Thrums* are apprentice works. In 1895, when J.H. Millar invented the Kailyard context, Barrie had begun his successful career in the theatre, and was hard at work on *Sentimental Tommy* (1896), a novel which, along with its sequel *Tommy and Grizel* (1900), revealed more ambitious artistic intentions than the early 'Thrums' stories.[10] With hindsight, we can view *Auld Licht Idylls* and *A Window in Thrums* as works that captured a late nineteenth-century popular taste for regional fiction which soon passed under the weight of modernist literary forms. They remain, however, an indelible part of the Scottish literary tradition; in their contrasting ways they offer sharp and distinctive perspectives on social and cultural aspects of nineteenth-century Scotland, as well as demonstrating – in embryo – many of the author's distinctive literary concerns. They can also be seen as characteristic works of the late nineteenth-century in their comparison of past and present and their literary evocation of the theme of nostalgia.

The sketches in *Auld Licht Idylls* grew out of material that had first appeared in various newspapers and magazines. Having spent almost two years working in Nottingham as a leader writer for the *Nottingham Journal*, Barrie returned to his home town of Kirriemuir in late October 1884. A few weeks later, on 17 November 1884, a sketch entitled 'An Auld Licht Community' appeared anonymously in the *St. James's Gazette*. The *Gazette*'s editor, Frederick Greenwood, detected a market. When he returned the manuscript of a rejected article on a different topic, he scribbled on the margins: 'But I liked that Scotch thing[.] Any more of those?'[11] For the next four months Barrie lived with his father, mother and sister in Kirriemuir and wrote about the Auld Lichts. A total of nine sketches on the topic appeared in the *St James's Gazette* with five more published in *Home Chimes*. Then, when he moved to London on 28 March 1885, Barrie all but gave up the theme. As Denis Mackail observes, 'there was a break in this kind of output for more than two years. He shook off Scotland when he plunged into London'.[12] In May 1885 he submitted the articles to the publishing firm of Macmillan but was advised there was 'no likelihood of even a small book proving attractive enough to an English audience to give any hope of an adequate sale.'[13] Barrie did not revive the theme until 1887 when he began writing for the *British Weekly*, the liberal nonconformist newspaper edited by William Robertson Nicoll, who was also literary advisor to the publishing firm of Hodder & Stoughton.[14] After two more Auld Licht pieces had appeared in the *British Weekly*, Nicoll persuaded Barrie to reshape the sketches into a book to be published by Hodder.

Confronted with the task of transforming his material into a book, it is often thought that Barrie made only minor changes. Harry Geduld argues that 'the reworking was never taken beyond the stage of improving individual chapters. There was no refashioning of the book as a whole in order to give it even a semblance of structural unity.'[15] This criticism is too extreme, however. A good deal of new matter was included and the scale and nature of the 'improving' was not insignificant. Significantly, Barrie removed some of the traces of a journalist's pandering to audience expectations of life in Scotland. References to tourists visiting Balmoral were omitted, and the narrator's schoolhouse is no longer a 'Highland' one. Barrie also loosened the historical and factual framework of the articles. The original sketch of 'An Old Dominie', for example, had been presented as 'no exaggerated picture, but a true flash into conditions of Scottish education twenty years ago', a line Barrie omitted in the book. Similarly, in the account of the 'Battle of Cabbylatch' in Chapter 5, two paragraphs from the original sketch which had referred directly to real places and historical events were cut.[16]

Barrie also extended his use of his native dialect when revising the material. Several sketches were augmented by inserted passages of dialogue in Scots. For example, the section in 'Little Rathie's Bural' (Chapter 11) where members of the community discuss the deceased farmer and death in general was added to material from the sketch 'An Auld Licht Funeral'. In a preface to an American edition of his works, Barrie recalled that Frederick

Greenwood was one of the few editors at the time who was willing to print Scots dialect. He claimed to have 'tried them all' with 'The Courting of T'nowhead's Bell' – a sketch that depends for its effects upon the evocation of plot and character through dialogue – 'but it never found shelter until it got within book-covers.'[17] Clearly Barrie felt that volume publication offered him greater license to write in Scots, and to do so in a less decorative and cosmetic way than in the newspaper articles. The success of the book gave him more freedom in this area, and several of the chapters in *A Window in Thrums* rely almost entirely for their effects upon the evocation of the vocabulary and pronunciation of the Forfarshire dialect.

The most significant alteration Barrie made, however, was to use his recently invented idea of 'Thrums' as an organising principle for the book. In most of the original sketches Barrie's fictional town is called 'Wheens', although often the articles refer simply to 'Scotland'. 'Thrums' is mentioned only in the last sketch published before the book appeared. The long second chapter, which surveys the town and its inhabitants and customs, was almost entirely original material – little of it can be traced to earlier articles. The opening paragraph, which provides a topographical description of the town of Thrums, was actually drawn from the first instalment of *When a Man's Single*, the serial story Barrie published in the *British Weekly* from October 1887 to March 1888. When he came to issue this novel in volume form later in 1888, Barrie omitted all the descriptions he had by then transported into *Auld Licht Idylls*. This was the work Barrie was undertaking when, writing from Kirriemuir on 4 January 1888, he told his friend Thomas Gilmour: 'I have been devoting all my spare time since I came here to the Auld Licht papers, two thirds of which require rewriting.'[18]

The process of revising the Auld Licht articles, therefore, involved a new focus on the imaginative construction of a fictional place, something which demanded a shift in the narrative perspective. As R.D.S. Jack has observed, Thrums is constructed in *Auld Licht Idylls* – and elsewhere in Barrie's writing – as a region of the mind.[19] When the narrator introduces us to his fictional town he draws attention to his act of describing: 'Thrums is the name I give here to the handful of houses jumbled together in a cup' (6). In this context, Barrie's decision to delay the lengthy account of the social and religious life of the town until the second chapter is telling. The striking opening chapter of *Auld Licht Idylls* is based in part on a sketch entitled 'From a Snowed-up Schoolhouse'.[20] When compiling the book, however, Barrie substantially rewrote the final paragraph, placing greater emphasis on the narrator's solitude. Confronted first by his isolated wintry life in the glen, where the 'road to Thrums has lost itself miles down the valley' (5) and the 'shutter bars the outer world from the schoolhouse' (5) (lines that are original to the book), we are encouraged to look upon the narrator's subsequent visualisation of the town as an act of imagination. As Cairns Craig argues, the opening and closing chapters of the book 'offer a self-conscious commentary on the nature of Barrie's own art and its relationship with its subject matter.'[21] The narrator goes on to relate in Chapter 2 how he sees Thrums literally through a mist:

> I like to linger over the square, for it was from an upper window in it that I got to know Thrums … In my schoolhouse, however, I seem to see the square most readily in the Scotch mist which so often filled it, loosening the stones and choking the drains. (7-8)

This element of self-consciousness about the imaginative painting of the scene becomes more pronounced in *A Window in Thrums* where the narrator frequently draws attention to his efforts to make the reader visualise the scene. In Barrie's writing, narrative is never a transparent window onto life.

Although Barrie conspicuously loosened the social and historical references in his material when compiling the book, *Auld Licht Idylls* can still profitably be read as a sharp and ironic commentary on aspects of nineteenth-century Scottish life. Although the narrator writes from the present – he places the 1733 secession in the Kirk 'a hundred and fifty years ago' (24) – the stories are set in the early nineteenth century. As Eric Anderson notes, the book is 'a series of vignettes illustrative of social change' and 'Barrie goes out of his way to remind the reader that the world being described is past.'[22] This applies both to the religious traditions – 'There are few Auld Licht communities in Scotland nowadays' (6) – and to the depiction of the handloom industry which shapes the life of the community: 'Until twenty years ago' a handloom filled 'every other room' in Thrums, but though its 'clatter can still be heard', the industry and its way of life have gradually been displaced by 'the two factories in the town' (7). Thrums, we are told, 'is nowadays an agricultural centre of some importance' (16), and as Leonee Ormond notes, Barrie's early works are 'in some ways a lament for the hand-loom weaver'.[23] The image of a pre-industrial subsistence way of life is presented in the character of Cree Queery, who takes to the loom and weaves far into the night to earn sufficient money to keep his mother from the poorhouse. By the time we reach *A Window in Thrums*, the image of the 'hand-loom in the house' (100) belongs so much to the past that it can only be imagined by the narrator; and the picture of

Hendry McQumpha, leant forward dead on his silent loom having spent the final moments of his life weaving, signals the passing of more than just an individual.

Barrie's choice of name for his fictional town was not an arbitrary one. Thrums are the fringes of the warp threads left on the loom after the cloth has been removed, and *Auld Licht Idylls* and *A Window in Thrums* are about the fringes and remnants of past ways of life which are left hanging in the present, as the description of the houses in the glen attests:

> The glen was but sparsely dotted with houses even in those days; a number of them inhabited by farmer-weavers, who combined two trades and just managed to live. One would have a plough, another a horse, and so in Glen Quharity they helped each other. Without a loom in addition many of them would have starved, and on Saturdays the big farmer and his wife, driving home in a gig, would pass the little farmer carrying or wheeling his wob to Thrums. When there was no longer a market for the produce of the handloom these farms had to be given up, and thus it is that the old school is not the only house in our weary glen around which gooseberry and currant bushes, once tended by careful hands, now grow wild. (51)

Much of the long second chapter is concerned with the effects of the passing of old habits and customs, such as the 'sensational days of the post office', when the postmistress surreptitiously steamed open the letters and spread gossip around the town. The lengthy account of the farm bothy is presented through a comparison of past and present, as the narrator enters 'a bothy of to-day' and looks back on a pre-mechanical past when 'hands' were 'huddled together … in squalid barns more like cattle than men and women' (20). The description of the old 'bothy system at its worst' is unflinching in its realism, but once again the emphasis is on the traces ('thrums') of a near vanished world that are still visible in the present and which point up the process of change. The reference here (as in the first chapter) to Darwin is not incidental.

Along with the handloom industry, life in Thrums is shaped by its religious traditions. Barrie was himself brought up in the Free Church of Scotland but his mother's family had belonged to the Auld Lichts, and his main source was her stories of her own childhood. Barrie makes few concessions to his reader's knowledge of Scottish ecclesiastical history. Thrums, with its 'four kirks in all before the Disruption, and then another, which split into two immediately afterwards' (10), is riven with denominational rivalry.

Barrie does not feel the need to explain the Disruption to his readers, nor does he trouble them with a genealogical outline of the church in Scotland. The Auld Lichts were part of the body that seceded from the Established Church in 1733, and which remained independent from the various mergers and unions of presbyteries that followed on after this body itself split at various points in history over details of theology and Church governance. Barrie slyly refers to the splintering tendency of Scottish Presbyterianism when the narrator writes of 'the split in the kirk … that comes once at least to every Auld Licht minister.' (31) The division between the 'New Lights' and 'Old Lights' which the narrator mentions at the beginning of Chapter 3 refers to the consequences of the 1820 merger between the Original Burger Church and the Original Secession Church, out of which formed the United Secession Church and later, in 1847, the United Presbyterian Church (members of which are referred to in *Auld Licht Idylls* simply as the U.P.s). In resisting these and other unions, the Auld Lichts looked upon themselves as the true descendants of the original secession. Calvinist in theology, they were uncompromising in upholding the rights of the parish to choose its own minister, and held to the obligations of the Solemn League and Convenant of 1643, which established the grounds for a Presbyterian form of Church government in Scotland. As the narrator comments when recounting how the Auld Licht congregation would scrutinise trial ministers for unsound doctrine: 'It was the Covenanters come back to life.' (29) The theological principles of the Auld Lichts generate a peculiar power dynamic between the minister and his congregation which Barrie exploits for comic effect. We are told that 'for the first year or more of his ministry an Auld Licht minister was a mouse among cats', but in the pulpit the roles had to be reversed. Mr Dishart is 'uncomfortably loved' (28) by his parish because even a 'sweet and pure woman' (6) like the schoolmaster's old landlady seeks a perverse 'pleasure' in being denounced and bewailed by her minister.

Barrie's humour has been attacked by some critics. Geduld argues that 'when laughter is invited it is at the Auld Lichts and not with them'.[24] Certainly there is little piety in his presentation, as the image of the flying Bible in 'A Literary Club' attests, and the characteristics of the Auld Lichts – the reticent, matter-of-fact approach to courtship; the ironic taste for burials – may seem exaggerated. As J.A. Hammerton notes, however, characters such as Tibbie McQuhatty, the woman who 'nearly split the Auld Licht kirk' (24) over the minister's introduction of the 'run line' method of reading out the psalm, have a basis in historical reality and are 'no invention of Barrie's fancy'.[25] The Rev. Alexander Whyte, Principal of New College, Edinburgh and a native of Kirriemuir, witnessed to the accuracy of Barrie's portraits when he wrote: 'All of us in the town know the characters Mr Barrie describes … [he] has thoroughly grasped the characters of the little community, with all their humour and pathos. "Thrums" is a true picture of my native place.'[26]

*A Window in Thrums* is less easy to defend in this context. The authenticity of the picture is not in question – Margaret Oliphant referred to 'the absolute truth of the Scotch village set before us … which is simple matter of fact'[27] – but Barrie's attitude towards his characters has been widely criticised. The enclosed world of Jess and Leeby, obsessively keeping up with the local gossip from behind the window in Thrums, can appear miniaturised and small-minded. Blake concludes that 'Barrie was consciously guying his own people. He was incapable of pity for his fictional victims.'[28] Allen Wright is less harsh, finding 'affectionate amusement' in Barrie's studies: 'He could appear to be patronising but was more often penetrating in his observation. *Auld Licht Idylls* and *A Window in Thrums* are examples of a curious hybrid – sympathetic satire.'[29] The position of the narrator is crucial in this context. In both texts he is presented as both insider and outsider. He points up the characters' eccentricities but also defends their profundities. In *A Window in Thrums* this mediating role becomes more important and the narrator's defence of the provincial world of Thrums is more explicit. 'To those who dwell in great cities Thrums is only a small place, but what a clatter of life it has for me when I come to it from my school-house in the glen.' (101) When he refers at the start of his story to the 'history of tragic little Thrums' (100), the oxymoron, with its self-conscious literary terminology, serves as a vindication of the profundity of the small-town life he will go to describe.

There is a marked shift in tone between *Auld Licht Idylls* and *A Window in Thrums*. In the first text Barrie cannot be accused – as he often has been – of sacrificing realism for sentiment. Clearly the word 'idyll' in the title is ironic since there is nothing idyllic about Thrums or about Barrie's manner of presentation. Life for the Auld Lichts is one of poverty – 'their last years were generally a grim struggle with the workhouse' (7) – and the narrator's descriptions in Chapter 5 of the meal mob riots and the bloodthirsty battles with the neighbouring town, which leave the street littered with 'prostrate lumps of humanity from which all shape had departed' (46), are unsparing. In *A Window in Thrums* the attitude towards the poor is more self-consciously literary. The narrator positions himself against 'cruel writers of these days' (99) and cautions his readers against accompanying him into the 'humble abode' of the house on the brae 'in a contemptuous mood.' (99) The new element of pathos involves a shift in the position of the narrator and the way a picture of the past is presented to the reader.

Unlike *Auld Licht Idylls*, *A Window in Thrums* was substantially composed from original material and planned as a book from the outset. The chapters that are based on previously published sketches were heavily revised and threaded into the main story of Jess and her family. This gives the book a disparate structure which some critics have judged harshly. Geduld is especially unforgiving, judging the book 'a collection of journalistic sketches struggling to become a novel and failing miserably in the attempt.'[30] Some early American editions removed the stand-alone sections and issued the book under the title *Jess*, a move which may have been prompted by the heavy use of Scots in these chapters as much as a desire to tighten the plot – why else, for example, would Jess's story of 'The Ghost Cradle' be omitted, a fine example of supernatural oral folklore that recalls the work of James Hogg? *A Window in Thrums*, in fact, makes no pretension to intricacy of plot. A number of contemporary reviewers linked the work to the Dutch school of painting, a genre which several Victorian novelists, including George Eliot and Thomas Hardy (whose *Under the Greenwood Tree* (1872) is subtitled 'A Rural Painting of the Dutch School'), took as a model for their fictional constructions of rural, peasant life. Barrie's story can profitably be read within the tradition of pastoral idyll to which some of Eliot's and Hardy's early works belong.[31] In such a tradition plot is subordinate to a 'play of the timeless against the here and now'.[32] Change is pointed out in the opening sentences when the narrator juxtaposes the 'old days' of Thrums alongside a 'now' where there is 'the making of a suburb'. But while we are encouraged to enter a world that has passed we are also told that 'the world remains as young as ever':

> The lovers that met on the commonty in the gloaming are gone, but there are other lovers to take their place, and still the commonty is here. [...] The world does not age. The hearse passes over the brae and up the straight burying-ground road, but still there is a cry for the christening robe. (102)

This play between the timeless and the here and now entails an emphasis on the fictionality of the picture, as only memory and imagination can effect a balance between the temporal and the eternal. In this crucial opening chapter the narrator draws attention to his effort to 'bring back' (100) the past, leading his reader into the world of the story by underlining the process of imaginative reconstruction:

I speak of the chairs, but if we go together into the "room" they will not be visible to you. […] You can scarcely stand upright beneath the decaying ceiling. Worn boards and ragged walls, and the rusty ribs fallen from the fireplace, are all that meet your eyes, but I see a round, unsteady, waxcloth-covered table, with four books lying at equal distances on it. There are six prim chairs, two of them not to be sat upon, backed against the walls, and between the window and the fireplace a chest of drawers, with a snowy-coverlet. On the drawers stands a board with coloured marbles for the game of solitaire, and I have only to open the drawer with the loose handle to bring out the dambrod. (99)

The literary method here is sentimental (to use the phrase non-pejoratively) in the way the narrator establishes a relationship with his audience and charges objects with emotional content. It is also elegiac in the way he addresses his readers as if they are at the end of their life, and encourages them to pick up the remembered scenes and images of the past:

We have all found the brae long and steep in the spring of life. Do you remember how the child you once were sat at the foot of it and wondered if a new world began at the top? It climbs from a shallow burn, and we used to sit on the brig a long time before venturing to climb. As boys we ran up the brae. As men and women, young and in our prime, we almost forgot that it was there. But the autumn of life comes, and the brae grows steeper; then the winter, and once again we are as the child pausing apprehensively on the brig. Yet are we no longer the child; we look now for no new world at the top, only for a little garden and a tiny house, and a hand-loom in the house. […] Life is not always hard, even after backs grow bent, and we know that all braes lead only to the grave. (100)

There is an unmistakeable flavour of *fin de siècle* here. The overwhelming emphasis on ageing and the anticipation of death would seem odd in a work by an author not yet out of his twenties. But the 'lingering nostalgia'[33] in the narrator's voice is typical of the literary milieu of the late nineteenth century. It is probably this characteristic of Barrie's writing that prompted Robert Louis Stevenson to tell his fellow author that he had 'the glamour of twilight' on his pen.[34] To a modern audience the style and mood of *A Window in Thrums* may seem dated, but it indicates a characteristically late-Victorian taste for the emotional tug and glamour of a metaphorical twilight. The OED defines glamour as 'magic, enchantment, spell' and 'a magical or fictitious beauty ... a delusive or alluring charm', and Barrie's ability to enchant the reader with seemingly disenchanting scenes of death, loss, grief and regret undoubtedly explains why *A Window in Thrums* was so lauded by contemporary critics.

It is within this 'fictitious' framework of the 'glamour of twilight' that the main story of Jess and her son Jamie is played out. The choice of name has lured some critics into reading the text autobiographically as an exploration of Barrie's supposed mother-fixation. Geduld sees a 'prototypic' Oedipal story as 'patently the basis' for *A Window in Thrums*: Jess is a 'fictional equivalent' of Barrie's own mother, and Joey is Barrie's brother, David, who was indeed at the time of Barrie's writing 'Dead This Twenty Years'.[35] Written during a period when Barrie was mostly resident in London, it is easy to look upon Jamie's fate as a dramatisation of the author's uncertain feelings of separation from his own family. As R.D.S. Jack has argued, however, Oedipal readings fail to get to grips with the actual text.[36] Why is Jamie turned into a barber who 'cared little to read books' (178)? And is there significance in the fact that the (failed) author in 'A Magnum Opus' is also called James? If we must think within a Freudian framework then the most uncanny aspect of the autobiographical component in *A Window in Thrums* is the fact that Barrie's sister and parents were not dead at this time, and yet six years later the imagined narrative of Jamie McQumpha became real when Barrie received a telegram in London informing him that his sister had died. Before he had arrived home in Kirrieumuir his mother had also died.[37] In *A Window in Thrums*, it seems, Barrie had written the future.

What the autobiographical context thus really demands is close attention to the way our response to the story of Jamie is controlled by the narrative perspective, because *A Window in Thrums* is concerned in no small part with the process of telling a story and the construction of emotion through art. The narrator hints in the opening chapter at the 'awful ordeal' (102) Jamie will go through when he returns to Thrums, and throughout the text he uses prolepsis to anticipate the 'dire day of which I shall have to tell' (100). A key to understanding his character as a narrator comes in his account of the battle between Jess and Jamie for the lady's glove that she finds in his pocket. As he reconstructs how he watched the scene unfold the narrator comments: 'At the time I looked on as at play-acting, rejoicing in the happy ending. Alas! In real life how are we to know when we have reached an end?' (177). The reference to 'play-acting' hints at the interest in theatre and theatrical illusion that would soon take over Barrie's career.

Looking on the scene as a play or fiction enables the narrator to make-believe a happy ending, one that will be supplanted, however, by 'real life'. And this interaction between reality and 'play-acting' is what characterises the narrator's story-telling and what links *A Window in Thrums* to Barrie's mature prose and drama. In the closing chapters the narrator repeatedly draws attention to the different ways in which his story might be told. He acknowledges that in his lonely schoolhouse he has spent many hours 'mapping out' (175) happy endings for Leeby and Jamie, and confesses that he 'could not, even at this day, have told any episodes in the life of Jess had it ended in the poorhouse'. (185) As storyteller he is acutely conscious of his power to manipulate our view of the tale through the window of the narrative, something which should make us look at the final depiction of Jess's death and Jamie's homecoming with a close critical eye. In *Auld Licht Idylls* and *A Window in Thrums* we can observe the beginnings of Barrie's distinctive creative interest in the interaction between storytelling – or fantasy – and reality. Apprentice works they may be, but they need to be read with the same kind of perspectival awareness that novels like *Tommy and Grizel* and plays like *Peter Pan* demand.

1   J.H. Millar, 'The Literature of the Kailyard', *New Review*, XII (1895), 384-94, p. 384.
2   See Andrew Nash, *Kailyard and Scottish Literature* (Amsterdam & New York: Rodopi, 2007); R.D.S. Jack, *Myths and the Mythmaker: A Literary Account of J.M. Barrie's Formative Years* (Amsterdam & New York: Rodopi, 2010).
3   See George Blake, *Barrie and the Kailyard School* (London: Arthur Barker, 1951).
4   See Nash, *Kailyard and Scottish Literature*, pp. 17-22, 31-2.
5   Ibid., p. 32.
6   [Margaret Oliphant], 'The Old Saloon', *Blackwood's Magazine* (August 1889), 254-75, p. 264.
7   *The Letters of Robert Louis Stevenson*, ed. Bradford A. Booth and Ernest Mehew, 7 vols (New Haven and London, Yale University Press), VII, 447.
8   [Oliphant], p. 266.
9   See Nash, *Kailyard and Scottish Literature*, pp. 207-17.
10  See Caroline McCracken Flesher's introductions to the recent reprints of *Sentimental Tommy* and *Tommy and Grizel* published in The Kailyard Authors series (Glasgow: Kennedy and Boyd, 2011).
11  Denis Mackail, *The Story of J.M.B.* (London: Peter Davies, 1941), p. 98.
12  Mackail, p. 99.
13  Alexander Macmillan to J.M. Barrie, British Library Add. MS. 55419, fol. 1122.
14  See Keith A. Ives, *Voice of Nonconformity: William Robertson Nicoll and The*

*British Weekly* (Cambridge: Lutterworth Press, 2011).

15 Harry M. Geduld, *Sir James Barrie* (New York: Twayne, 1971), p. 18.

16 For a fuller discussion of the process of revision, see Andrew Nash, 'The Compilation of J.M. Barrie's *Auld Licht Idylls*', *The Bibliotheck*, 23 (1998), 85-96.

17 *The Novels, Tales and Sketches of J.M. Barrie: Auld Licht Idylls and Better Dead* (New York: Charles Scribner's Sons, 1896), p. viii.

18 J.M. Barrie to Thomas Gilmour, 4 January 1888. J.M. Barrie Collection, A3. Beinecke Rare Book and Manuscript Library, Yale University.

19 See R.D.S. Jack, 'Art, Nature and Thrums', in *Literature in Context*, ed. Joachim Schwend et al (Frankfurt am Main: Peter Lang, 1992), 155-64.

20 Published in the *St James's Gazette* on 28 January 1885, this article is missing from Henry Garland's *Bibliography of the Writings of Sir James Barrie* (London: The Bookman's Journal, 1928).

21 Cairns Craig, *The Modern Scottish Novel: Narrative and the National Imagination* (Edinburgh: Edinburgh University Press, 1999), p. 58.

22 Eric Anderson, 'The Kailyard Revisited', in *Nineteenth-Century Scottish Fiction: Critical Essays* ed Ian Campbell (Manchester: Carcanet, 1979), 130-47, p. 132.

23 Leonee Ormond, *J.M. Barrie* (Edinburgh: Scottish Academic Press, 1987), p. 29.

24 Geduld, p. 17.

25 J.A. Hammerton, *Barrieland: a Thrums Pilgrimage* (London: Sampson Low, Marston & Co., [1929]), p. 130.

26 Quoted by James A. Roy, *James Matthew Barrie: an appreciation* (London: Jarrolds, 1937), pp. 88-9.

27 Oliphant, p. 262.

28 Blake, p. 72.

29 Allen Wright, *J.M. Barrie: Glamour of Twilight* (Edinburgh: Ramsay Head Press, 1976), p. 33

30 Geduld, p. 36.

31 For an extended reading of the book along these lines, see Nash, *Kailyard and Scottish Literature*, pp. 63-70.

32 Shelagh Hunter, *Victorian Idyllic Fiction: Pastoral Strategies* (Basingstoke: Macmillan, 1984), p. 5.

33 Craig, p. 59.

34 *The Letters of Robert Louis Stevenson*, VII, 447.

35 Geduld, p. 36.

36 Jack, *Myths and the Mythmaker*, p. 74.

37 See Mackail, pp. 231-2.

# FURTHER READING

Barrie's three longer novels, *The Little Minister* (1891), *Sentimental Tommy* (1896), and *Tommy and Grizel* (1900), are all available from Kennedy & Boyd in The Kailyard Authors series. The most recent biography is by Lisa Chaney, *Hide-and-Seek with Angels* (2005). The first authorised biography, *The Story of J.M.B.* (1941) by Denis Mackail, is idiosyncratic but essential in its detail. Another important study is Andrew Birkin's *J.M. Barrie & the Lost Boys* (1979, repr. 2003). *J.M. Barrie: An Annotated Secondary Bibliography* (1989) by Carl Markgraf, provides a wealth of references for *Auld Licht Idylls* and *A Window in Thrums*.

Critical studies of the Kailyard include Ian Campbell, *Kailyard* (1981), Thomas Knowles, *Ideology, Art & Commerce* (1983) and Andrew Nash, *Kailyard and Scottish Literature* (2007). The latter has a lengthy chapter on Barrie's prose works. George Blake's *Barrie and the Kailyard School* (1951) is oversimplified but essential for understanding the Kailyard debate.

Relevant introductory studies of Barrie include Leonee Ormond's *J.M. Barrie* (1987) and Allen Wright's *J.M. Barrie: Glamour of Twilight* (1976). Cairns Craig's *The Modern Scottish Novel: Narrative and the National Imagination* (1999) has a brief but insightful discussion of *Auld Licht Idylls*. Harry M. Geduld's *Sir James Barrie* (1971) is a merciless invective, and only briefly insightful, but remains important in understanding the Oedipal terms upon which Barrie's writing has frequently been attacked. R.D.S. Jack's *Myths and the mythmaker: a Literary Account of J.M. Barrie's Formative Years* (2010) offers an exploration of, and a corrective to, these attacks. The recent collection *Gateway to the Modern: Resituating J.M. Barrie* (2014), edited by Valentina Bold and Andrew Nash, contains essays covering the full range of Barrie's *oeuvre*. In addition, the essays by Anderson and Jack referred to in the notes should be consulted for specific discussion of *Auld Licht Idylls* and *A Window in Thrums*. Among earlier studies, two books by J.A. Hammerton are worth consulting: *Barrie: the Story of a Genius* (1929) is a readable supplement to Mackail, and *Barrieland: a Thrums Pilgrimage* provides a historical and topographical survey of Kirriemuir with an especially useful chapter on 'The Auld Lichts in Reality'.

# Auld Licht idylls

To
Frederick Greenwood

# I

## THE SCHOOLHOUSE

EARLY this morning I opened a window in my schoolhouse in the glen of Quharity, awakened by the shivering of a starving sparrow against the frosted glass. As the snowy sash creaked in my hand, he made off to the waterspout that suspends its "tangles" of ice over a gaping tank, and, rebounding from that, with a quiver of his little black breast, bobbed through the network of wire and joined a few of his fellows in a forlorn hop round the henhouse in search of food. Two days ago my hilarious bantam-cock, saucy to the last, my cheeriest companion, was found frozen in his own water-trough, the corn-saucer in three pieces by his side. Since then I have taken the hens into the house. At meal-times they litter the hearth with each other's feathers; but for the most part they give little trouble, roosting on the rafters of the low-roofed kitchen among staves and fishing-rods.

Another white blanket has been spread upon the glen since I looked out last night; for over the same wilderness of snow that has met my gaze for a week, I see the steading of Waster Lunny sunk deeper into the waste. The schoolhouse, I suppose, serves similarly as a snowmark for the people at the farm. Unless that is Waster Lunny's grieve foddering the cattle in the snow, not a living thing is visible. The ghostlike hills that pen in the glen have ceased to echo to the sharp crack of the sportsman's gun (so clear in the frosty air as to be a warning to every rabbit and partridge in the valley); and only giant Catlaw shows here and there a black ridge, rearing his head at the entrance to the glen and struggling ineffectually to cast off his shroud. Most wintry sign of all, I think as I close the window hastily, is the open farm-stile, its poles lying embedded in the snow where they were last flung by Waster Lunny's herd. Through the still air comes from a distance a vibration as of a tuning-fork: a robin, perhaps, alighting on the wire of a broken fence.

In the warm kitchen, where I dawdle over my breakfast, the widowed bantam-hen has perched on the back of my drowsy cat. It is needless to go through the form of opening the school to-day; for, with the exception of Waster Lunny's girl, I have had no scholars for nine days. Yesterday she announced that there would be no more schooling till it was fresh, "as she wasna comin';" and indeed, though the smoke from the farm chimneys is a pretty prospect for a snowed-up schoolmaster, the trudge between the two houses must be weary work for a bairn. As for the other children, who have to come from all parts of the hills and glen, I may not see them for weeks. Last year the school was practically deserted for a month. A pleasant outlook, with the March examinations staring me in the face, and an inspector fresh from Oxford. I wonder what he would say if he saw me to-day digging myself out of the schoolhouse with the spade I now keep for the purpose in my bedroom.

The kail grows brittle from the snow in my dank and cheerless garden. A crust of bread gathers timid pheasants round me. The robins, I see, have made the coalhouse their home. Waster Lunny's dog never barks without rousing my sluggish cat to a joyful response. It is Dutch courage with the birds and beasts of the glen, hard driven for food; but I look attentively for them in these long forenoons, and they have begun to regard me as one of themselves. My breath freezes, despite my pipe, as I peer from the door; and with a fortnight-old newspaper I retire to the ingle-nook. The friendliest thing I have seen to-day is the well-smoked ham suspended from my kitchen rafters. It was a gift from the farm of Tullin, with a load of peats, the day before the snow began to fall. I doubt if I have seen a cart since.

This afternoon I was the not altogether passive spectator of a curious scene in natural history. My feet encased in stout "tackety" boots, I had waded down two of Waster Lunny's fields to the glen burn: in summer the never-failing larder from which, with wriggling worm or garish fly, I can any morning whip a savoury breakfast; in the winter-time the only thing in the valley that defies the ice-king's chloroform. I watched the water twisting black and solemn through the snow, the ragged ice on its edge proof of the toughness of the struggle with the frost, from which it has, after all, crept only half victorious. A bare wild rose-bush on the farther bank was violently agitated, and then there ran from its root a black-headed rat with wings. Such was the general effect. I was not less interested when my startled eyes divided this phenomenon into its component parts, and recognised in the disturbance on the opposite bank only another fierce struggle among the hungry animals for existence; they need no professor to teach them the doctrine of the survival of the fittest. A weasel had gripped a water-hen (whit-rit and beltie they are called in these parts) cowering at the root of the rose-bush, and was being dragged down the bank by the terrified bird, which made for the water as its only chance of escape. In less disadvantageous circumstances the weasel would have made short work of his victim; but as he only had the bird by the tail, the prospects of the combatants were equalised. It was the tug-of-war being played with a life as the stakes. "If I do not reach the water," was the argument that went on in the heaving little breast of the one, "I am a dead bird." "If this water-hen," reasoned the other, "reaches the burn, my supper vanishes with her." Down the sloping bank the hen had distinctly the best of it, but after that came a yard of level snow, and here she tugged and screamed in vain. I had so far been an unobserved spectator; but my sympathies were with the beltie, and, thinking it high time to interfere, I jumped into the water. The water-hen gave one mighty final tug and toppled into the burn; while the weasel viciously showed me his teeth, and then stole slowly up the bank to the rose-bush, whence, "girning," he watched me lift his exhausted victim from the water, and set off with her for the schoolhouse. Except for her draggled tail, she already looks wonderfully composed, and so long as the frost holds I shall have little difficulty in keeping her with me. On Sunday I found a frozen sparrow, whose heart had almost ceased to beat, in the disused pigsty, and put him for warmth into my breast-pocket. The ungrateful little scrub bolted without a word of thanks about ten minutes afterwards to the alarm of my cat, which had not known his whereabouts.

I am alone in the schoolhouse. On just such an evening as this last year my desolation drove me to Waster Lunny, where I was storm-staid for the night. The recollection decides me to court my own warm hearth, to challenge my right hand again to a game at the "dambrod" against my left. I do not lock the schoolhouse door at nights; for even a highwayman (there is no such luck) would be received with open arms, and I doubt if there be a barred door in all the glen. But it is cosier to put on the shutters. The road to Thrums has lost itself miles down the valley. I wonder what they are doing out in the world. Though I am the Free Church precentor in Thrums (ten pounds a year, and the little town is five miles away), they have not seen me for three weeks. A packman whom I thawed yesterday at my kitchen fire tells me, that last Sabbath only the Auld Lichts held service. Other people realised that they were snowed up. Far up the glen, after it twists out of view, a manse and half a dozen thatched cottages that are there may still show a candle light, and the crumbling gravestones keep cold vigil round the grey old kirk. Heavy shadows fade into the sky to the north. A flake trembles against the window; but it is too cold for much snow to-night. The shutter bars the outer world from the schoolhouse.

# II

## THRUMS

THRUMS is the name I give here to the handful of houses jumbled together in a cup, which is the town nearest the schoolhouse. Until twenty years ago its every other room, earthen-floored and showing the rafters overhead, had a handloom, and hundreds of weavers lived and died Thoreaus "ben the hoose" without knowing it. In those days the cup overflowed and left several houses on the top of the hill, where their cold skeletons still stand. The road that climbs from the square, which is Thrums's heart, to the north is so steep and straight, that in a sharp frost children hunker at the top and are blown down with a roar and a rush on rails of ice. At such times, when viewed from the cemetery where the traveller from the schoolhouse gets his first glimpse of the little town, Thrums is but two church steeples and a dozen red stone patches standing out of a snow-heap. One of the steeples belongs to the new Free Kirk, and the other to the parish church, both of which the first Auld Licht minister I knew ran past when he had not time to avoid them by taking a back wynd. He was but a pocket edition of a man, who grew two inches after he was called; but he was so full of the cure of souls, that he usually scudded to it with his coat-tails quarrelling behind him. His successor, whom I knew better, was a greater scholar, and said, "Let us see what this is in the original Greek," as an ordinary man might invite a friend to dinner; but he never wrestled as Mr. Dishart, his successor, did with the pulpit cushions, nor flung himself at the pulpit door. Nor was he so "hard on the Book," as Lang Tammas, the precentor, expressed it, meaning that he did not bang the Bible with his fist as much as might have been wished.

Thrums had been known to me for years before I succeeded the captious dominie at the schoolhouse in the glen. The dear old soul who originally induced me to enter the Auld Licht kirk by lamenting the "want of Christ" in the minister's discourses was my first landlady. For the last ten years of her life she was bedridden, and only her interest in the kirk kept her alive. Her case against the minister was that he did not call to denounce her sufficiently often for her sins, her pleasure being to hear him bewailing her on his knees as one who was probably past praying for. She was as sweet and pure a woman as I ever knew, and had her wishes been horses, she would have sold them and kept (and looked after) a minister herself.

There are few Auld Licht communities in Scotland nowadays—perhaps because people are now so well off, for the most devout Auld Lichts were always poor, and their last years were generally a grim struggle with the workhouse. Many a heavy-eyed, back-bent weaver has won his Waterloo in Thrums fighting on his stumps. There are a score or two of them left still, for, though there are now two factories in the town the clatter of the handloom can yet be heard, and they have been starving themselves of late until they have saved up enough money to get another minister.

The square is packed away in the centre of Thrums, and irregularly built little houses squeeze close to it like chickens clustering round a hen. Once the Auld Lichts held property in the square, but other denominations have bought them out of it, and now few of them are even to be found in the main streets that make for the rim of the cup. They live in the kirk-wynd, or in retiring little houses the builder of which does not seem to have remembered that it is a good plan to have a road leading to houses until after they were finished. Narrow paths straggling round gardens, some of them with stunted gates, which it is commoner to step over than to open, have been formed to reach these dwellings, but in winter they are running streams, and then the best way to reach a house such as that of Tammy Mealmaker the wright, pronounced wir-icht, is over a broken dyke and a pigsty. Tammy, who died a bachelor, had been soured in his youth by a disappointment in love, of which he spoke but seldom. She lived far away in a town to which he had wandered in the days when his blood ran hot, and they became engaged. Unfortunately, however, Tammy forgot her name, and he never knew the address; so there the affair ended, to his silent grief. He admitted himself, over his snuff-mull of an evening, that he was a very ordinary character, but a certain halo of horror was cast over the whole family by their connection with little Joey Sutie, who was pointed at in Thrums as the laddie that whistled when he went past the minister. Joey became a pedlar, and was found dead one raw morning dangling over a high wall within a few miles of Thrums. When climbing the dyke his pack had slipped back, the strap round his neck, and choked him.

You could generally tell an Auld Licht in Thrums when you passed him, his dull vacant face wrinkled over a heavy wob. He wore tags of yarn round his trousers beneath the knee, that looked like ostentatious garters, and frequently his jacket of corduroy was put on beneath his waistcoat. If he was too old to carry his load on his back, he wheeled it on a creaking barrow, and when he met a friend they said, "Ay, Jeames," and "Ay, Davit," and then could think of nothing else. At long intervals they passed through the square, disappearing or coming into sight round the town-house which stands on the south side of it, and guards the entrance to a steep brae that leads down and then twists up on its lonely way to the county town. I like to linger over the square, for it was from an upper window in it that I got to know Thrums. On Saturday nights, when the Auld Licht young men came into the square dressed and washed to look at the young women errand-going, and to laugh sometime afterwards to each other, it presented a glare of light; and here even came the cheap jacks and the Fair Circassian, and the showman, who, besides playing "The Mountain Maid and the Shepherd's Bride," exhibited part of the tail of Balaam's ass, the helm of Noah's ark, and the tartan plaid in which Flora Macdonald wrapped Prince Charlie. More select entertainment, such as Shuffle Kitty's waxwork, whose motto was, "A rag to pay, and in you go," was given in a hall whose approach was by an outside stair. On the Muckle Friday, the fair for which children storing their pocket money would accumulate sevenpence-halfpenny in less than six months, the square was crammed with gingerbread stalls, bag-pipers, fiddlers, and monstrosities who were gifted with second sight. There was a bearded man, who had neither legs nor arms, and was drawn through the streets in a small cart by four dogs. By looking at you he could see all the clockwork inside, as could a boy who was led about by his mother at the end of a string. Every Friday there was the market, when a dozen ramshackle carts containing vegetables and cheap crockery filled the centre of the square, resting in line on their shafts. A score of farmers' wives or daughters in old-world garments squatted against the town-house within walls of butter on cabbage-leaves, eggs and chickens. Towards evening the voice of the buckie-man shook the square, and rival fish-cadgers, terrible characters who ran races on horseback, screamed libels at each other over a fruiterer's barrow. Then it was time for douce Auld Lichts to go home, draw their stools near the fire, spread their red handkerchiefs over their legs to prevent their trousers getting singed, and read their *Pilgrim's Progress*.

In my schoolhouse, however, I seem to see the square most readily in the Scotch mist which so often filled it, loosening the stones and choking the drains. There was then no rattle of rain against my window-sill, nor dancing of diamond drops on the roofs, but blobs of water grew on the panes of glass to reel heavily down them. Then the sodden square would have shed abundant tears if you could have taken it in your hands and wrung it like a dripping cloth. At such a time the square would be empty but for one vegetable cart left in the care of a lean collie, which, tied to the wheel, whined and shivered underneath. Pools of water gather in the coarse sacks, that have been spread over the potatoes and bundles of greens, which turn to manure in their lidless barrels. The eyes of the whimpering dog never leave a black close over which hangs the sign of the Bull, probably the refuge of the hawker. At long intervals a farmer's gig rumbles over the bumpy, ill-paved square, or a native, with his head buried in his coat, peeps out of doors, skurries across the way, and vanishes. Most of the leading shops are here, and the decorous draper ventures a few yards from the pavement to scan the sky, or note the effect of his new arrangement in scarves. Planted against his door is the butcher, Henders Todd, white-aproned, and with a knife in his hand, gazing interestedly at the draper, for a mere man may look at an elder. The tinsmith brings out his steps, and, mounting them, stealthily removes the saucepans and pepper-pots that dangle on a wire above his sign-board. Pulling to his door he shuts out the foggy light that showed in his solder-strewn workshop. The square is deserted again. A bundle of sloppy parsley slips from the hawker's cart and topples over the wheel in driblets. The puddles in the sacks overflow and run together. The dog has twisted his chain round a barrel and yelps sharply. As if in response comes a rush of other dogs. A terrified fox terrier tears across the square with half a score of mongrels, the butcher's mastiff and some collies at his heels; he is doubtless a stranger who has insulted them by his glossy coat. For two seconds the square shakes to an invasion of dogs, and then, again, there is only one dog in sight.

No one will admit the Scotch mist. It "looks saft." The tinsmith "wudna wonder but what it was makkin for rain." Tammas Haggart and Pete Lunan dander into sight bareheaded, and have to stretch out their hands to discover what the weather is like. By and by they come to a standstill to discuss the immortality of the soul, and then they are looking silently at the Bull. Neither speaks, but they begin to move toward the inn at the same time, and its door closes on them before they know what they are doing. A few minutes afterwards Jinny Dundas, who is Pete's wife, runs straight for the Bull in her short gown, which is tucked up very high, and emerges with her husband soon afterwards. Jinny is voluble, But Pete says nothing. Tammas follows later, putting his head out at the door first, and looking cautiously about him to see if any one is in sight. Pete is a U.P., and may be left to his fate, but the Auld Licht minister thinks that though it be hard work, Tammas is worth saving.

To the Auld Licht of the, past there were three degrees of damnation—auld kirk, play-acting, chapel. Chapel was the name always given to the English Church, of which I am too much an Auld Licht myself to care to write even now. To belong to the chapel was, in Thrums, to be a Roman Catholic, and the boy who flung a clod of earth at the English minister—who called the Sabbath Sunday—or dropped a "divet" down his chimney was held to be in the right way. The only pleasant story Thrums could tell of the chapel was that its steeple once fell. It is surprising that an English church was ever suffered to be built in such a place; though probably the county gentry had something to do with it. They travelled about too much to be good men. Small though Thrums used to be, it had four kirks in all before the Disruption, and then another, which split into two immediately afterwards. The spire of the parish church, known as the auld kirk, commands a view of the square, from which the entrance to the kirkyard would be visible, if it were not hidden by the town-house. The kirkyard has long been crammed, and is not now in use, but the church is sufficiently large to hold nearly all the congregations in Thrums. Just at the gate lived Pete Todd, the father of Sam'l, a man of whom the Auld Lichts had reason to be proud. Pete was an everyday man at ordinary times, and was even said, when his wife, who had been long ill, died, to have clapped his hands and exclaimed, "Hip, hip, hurrah!" adding only as an afterthought, "The Lord's will be done." But midsummer was his great opportunity. Then took place the rouping of the seats in the parish church. The scene was the kirk itself, and the seats being put up to auction were knocked down to the highest bidder. This sometimes led to the breaking of the peace. Every person was present who was at all particular as to where he sat, and an auctioneer was engaged for the day. He rouped the kirk-seats like potato-drills, beginning by asking for a bid. Every seat was put up to auction separately; for some were much more run after than others, and the men were instructed by their wives what to bid for. Often the women joined in, and as they bid excitedly against each other the church rang with opprobrious epithets. A man would come to the roup late, and learn that the seat he wanted had been knocked down. He maintained that he had been unfairly treated, or denounced the local laird to whom the seat-rents went. If he did not get the seat he would leave the kirk. Then the woman who had forestalled him wanted to know what he meant by glaring at her so, and the auction was interrupted. Another member would "threip down the throat" of the auctioneer that he had a right to his former seat if he continued to pay the same price for it. The auctioneer was screamed at for favouring his friends, and at times the roup became so noisy that men and women had to be forcibly ejected. Then was Pete's chance. Hovering at the gate, he caught the angry people on their way home and took them into his workshop by an outside stair. There he assisted them in denouncing the parish kirk, with the view of getting them to forswear it. Pete made a good many Auld Lichts in his time out of unpromising material.

Sights were to be witnessed in the parish church at times that could not have been made more impressive by the Auld Lichts themselves. Here sinful women were grimly taken to task by the minister, who, having thundered for a time against adultery in general, called upon one sinner in particular to stand forth. She had to step forward into a pew near the pulpit, where, alone and friendless, and stared at by the congregation, she cowered in tears beneath his denunciations. In that seat she had to remain during the forenoon service. She returned home alone, and had to come back alone to her solitary seat in the afternoon. All day no one dared speak to her. She was as much an object of contumely as the thieves and smugglers whom, in the end of last century, it was the privilege of Feudal Bailie Wood (as he was called) to whip round the square.

It is nearly twenty years since the gardeners had their last "walk" in Thrums, and they survived all the other benefit societies that walked once every summer. There was a "weavers' walk" and five or six others, the "women's walk" being the most picturesque. These were processions of the members of benefit societies through the square and wynds, and all the women walked in white, to the number of a hundred or more, behind the Tilliedrum band, Thrums having in those days no band of its own.

From the north-west corner of the square a narrow street sets off, jerking this way and that, as if uncertain what point to make for. Here lurks the post-office, which had once the reputation of being as crooked in its ways as the street itself.

A railway line runs into Thrums now. The sensational days of the post-office were when the letters were conveyed officially in a creaking old cart from Tilliedrum. The "pony" had seen better days than the cart, and always looked as if he were just on the point of succeeding in running away from it. Hookey Crewe was driver; so-called because an iron hook was his substitute for a right arm: Robbie Proctor, the blacksmith, made the hook and fixed it in. Crewe suffered from rheumatism, and when he felt it coming on he stayed at home. Sometimes his cart came undone in a snowdrift; when Hookey, extricated from the fragments by some chance wayfarer, was deposited with his mail-bag (of which he always kept a grip by the hook) in a farmhouse. It was his boast that his letters always reached their destination eventually. They might be a long time about it, but "slow *and* sure" was his motto. Hookey emphasised his "slow *and* sure" by taking a snuff. He was a godsend to the postmistress, for to his failings or the infirmities of his gig were charged all delays.

At the time I write of, the posting of the letter took as long and was as serious an undertaking as the writing. That means a good deal, for many of the letters were written to dictation by the Thrums schoolmaster, Mr. Fleemister, who belonged to the Auld Kirk. He was one of the few persons in the community who looked upon the despatch of his letters by the postmistress as his right, and not a favour on her part; there was a longstanding feud between them accordingly. After a few tumblers of Widow Stables's treacle-beer—in the concoction of which she was the acknowledged mistress for miles around—the schoolmaster would sometimes go the length of hinting that he could get the postmistress dismissed any day. This mighty power seemed to rest on a knowledge of "steamed" letters. Thrums had a high respect for the schoolmaster; but among themselves the weavers agreed that, even if he did write to the Government, Lizzie Harrison, the postmistress, would refuse to transmit the letter. The more shrewd ones among us kept friends with both parties; for, unless you could write "writ-hand," you could not compose a letter without the schoolmaster's assistance; and, unless Lizzie was so courteous as to send it to its destination, it might lie—or so it was thought—much too long in the box. A letter addressed by the schoolmaster found great disfavour in Lizzie's eyes. You might explain to her that you had merely called in his assistance because you were a poor hand at writing yourself, but that was held no excuse. Some addressed their own envelopes with much labour, and sought to palm off the whole as their handiwork. It reflects on the postmistress somewhat that she had generally found them out by next day, when, if in a specially vixenish mood, she did not hesitate to upbraid them for their perfidy.

To post a letter you did not merely saunter to the post-office and drop it into the box. The cautious correspondent first went into the shop and explained to Lizzie how matters stood. She kept what she called a bookseller's shop as well as the post-office; but the supply of books corresponded exactly to the lack of demand for them, and her chief trade was in nicknacks, from marbles and money-boxes up to concertinas. If he found the postmistress in an amiable mood, which was only now and then, the caller led up craftily to the object of his visit. Having discussed the weather and the potato-disease, he explained that his sister Mary, whom Lizzie would remember, had married a fishmonger in Dundee. The fishmonger had lately started on himself and was doing well. They had four children. The youngest had had a severe attack of measles. No news had been got of Mary for twelve months; and Annie, his other sister, who lived in Thrums, had been at him of late for not writing. So he had written a few lines; and, in fact, he had the letter with him. The letter was then produced, and examined by the postmistress. If the address was in the schoolmaster's handwriting, she professed her inability to read it. Was this a *t* or an *l* or an *i*? was that a *b* or a *d*? This was a cruel revenge on Lizzie's part; for the sender of the letter was completely at her mercy. The schoolmaster's name being tabooed in her presence, he was unable to explain that the writing was not his own; and as for deciding between the $t$'s and $l$'s, he could not do it. Eventually he would be directed to put the letter into the box. They would do their best with it, Lizzie said, but in a voice that suggested how little hope she had of her efforts to decipher it proving successful.

There was an opinion among some of the people that the letter should not be stamped by the sender. The proper thing to do was to drop a penny for the stamp into the box along with the letter, and then Lizzie would see that it was all right. Lizzie's acquaintance with the handwriting of every person in the place who could write gave her a great advantage. You would perhaps drop into her shop some day to make a purchase, when she would calmly produce a letter you had posted several days before. In explanation she would tell you that you had not put a stamp on it, or that she suspected there was money in it, or that you had addressed it to the wrong place. I remember an old man, a relative of my own, who happened for once in his life to have several letters to post at one time. The circumstance was so out of the common that he considered it only reasonable to make Lizzie a small present.

Perhaps the postmistress was belied; but if she did not "steam" the letters and confide their titbits to favoured friends of her own sex, it is difficult to see how all the gossip got out. The schoolmaster once played an unmanly trick on her, with the view of catching her in the act. He was a bachelor who had long been given up by all the maids in the town. One day, however, he wrote a letter to an imaginary lady in the county town, asking her to be his, and going into full particulars about his income, his age, and his prospects. A male friend in the secret, at the other end, was to reply, in a lady's handwriting, accepting him, and also giving personal particulars. The first letter was written; and an answer arrived in due course—two days, the schoolmaster said, after date. No other person knew of this scheme for the undoing of the postmistress, yet in a very short time the schoolmaster's coming marriage was the talk of Thrums. Everybody became suddenly aware of the lady's name, of her abode, and of the sum of money she was to bring her husband. It was even noised abroad that the schoolmaster had represented his age as a good ten years less than it was. Then the schoolmaster divulged everything. To his mortification, he was not quite believed. All the proof he could bring forward to support his story was this: that time would show whether he got married or not. Foolish man! this argument was met by another, which was accepted at once. The lady had jilted the schoolmaster. Whether this explanation came from the post-office, who shall say? But so long as he lived the schoolmaster was twitted about the lady who threw him over. He took his revenge in two ways. He wrote and posted letters exceedingly abusive of the postmistress. The matter might be libellous; but then, as he pointed out, she would incriminate herself if she "brought him up" about it. Probably Lizzie felt his other insult more. By publishing his suspicions of her on every possible occasion he got a few people to seal their letters. So bitter was his feeling against her that he was even willing to supply the wax.

They know all about post-offices in Thrums now, and even jeer at the telegraph-boy's uniform. In the old days they gathered round him when he was seen in the street, and escorted him to his destination in triumph. That, too, was after Lizzie had gone the way of all the earth. But perhaps they are not even yet as knowing as they think themselves. I was told the other day that one of them took out a postal order, meaning to send the money to a relative, and kept the order as a receipt.

I have said that the town is sometimes full of snow. One frosty Saturday, seven years ago, I trudged into it from the schoolhouse, and on the Monday morning we could not see Thrums anywhere.

I was in one of the proud two-storied houses in the place, and could have shaken hands with my friends without from the upper windows. To get out of doors you had to walk upstairs. The outlook was a sea of snow fading into white hills and sky with the quarry standing out red and ragged to the right like a rock in the ocean. The Auld Licht manse was gone, but had left its garden-trees behind, their lean branches soft with snow. Roofs were humps in the white blanket. The spire of the Established Kirk stood up cold and stiff, like a monument to the buried inhabitants.

Those of the natives who had taken the precaution of conveying spades into their houses the night before, which is my plan at the schoolhouse, dug themselves out. They hobbled cautiously over the snow, sometimes sinking into it to their knees, when they stood still and slowly took in the situation. It had been snowing more or less for a week, but in a commonplace kind of way, and they had gone to bed thinking all was well. This night the snow must have fallen as if the heavens had opened up, determined to shake themselves free of it for ever.

The man who first came to himself and saw what was to be done was young Henders Ramsay. Henders had no fixed occupation, being but an "orra man" about the place, and the best thing known of him is that his mother's sister was a Baptist. He feared God, man, nor the minister; and all the learning he had was obtained from assiduous study of a grocer's window. But for one brief day he had things his own way in the town, or, speaking strictly, on the top of it. With a spade, a broom, and a pickaxe, which sat lightly on his broad shoulders (he was not even back-bent, and that showed him no respectable weaver), Henders delved his way to the nearest house, which formed one of a row, and addressed the inmates down the chimney. They had already been clearing it at the other end, or his words would have been choked. "You're snawed up, Davit," cried Henders, in a voice that was entirely businesslike; "hae ye a spade?" A conversation ensued up and down this unusual channel of communication. The unlucky householder, taking no thought of the morrow, was without a spade. But if Henders would clear away the snow from his door he would be "varra obleeged." Henders, however, had to come to terms first. "The chairge is saxpence, Davit," he shouted. Then a haggling ensued. Henders must be neighbourly. A plate of broth, now—or, say, twopence. But Henders was obdurate. "I'se nae time to argy-bargy wi' ye, Davit. Gin ye're no willin' to say saxpence, I'm aff to Will'um Pyatt's. He's buried too." So the victim had to make up his mind to one of two things: he must either say saxpence or remain where he was.

If Henders was "promised," he took good care that no snowed-up inhabitant should perjure himself. He made his way to a window first, and, clearing the snow from the top of it, pointed out that he could not conscientiously proceed further until the debt had been paid. "Money doon," he cried, as soon as he reached a pane of glass; or, "Come awa wi' my saxpence noo."

The belief that this day had not come to Henders unexpectedly was borne out by the method of the crafty callant. His charges varied from sixpence to half-a-crown, according to the wealth and status of his victims; and when, later on, there were rivals in the snow, he had the discrimination to reduce his minimum fee to threepence. He had the honour of digging out three ministers at one shilling, one and threepence, and two shillings respectively.

Half a dozen times within the next fortnight the town was reburied in snow. This generally happened in the night-time; but the inhabitants were not to be caught unprepared again. Spades stood ready to their hands in the morning, and they fought their way above ground without Henders Ramsay's assistance. To clear the snow from the narrow wynds and pends, however, was a task not to be attempted; and the Auld Lichts, at least, rested content when enough light got into their workshops to let them see where their looms stood. Wading through beds of snow they did not much mind; but they wondered what would happen to their houses when the thaw came.

The thaw was slow in coming. Snow during the night and several degrees of frost by day were what Thrums began to accept as a revised order of nature. Vainly the Thrums doctor, whose practice extends into the glens, made repeated attempts to reach his distant patients, twice driving so far into the dreary waste that he could neither go on nor turn back. A ploughman who contrived to gallop ten miles for him did not get home for a week. Between the town, which is nowadays an agricultural centre of some importance, and the outlying farms communication was cut off for a month; and I heard subsequently of one farmer who did not see a human being, unconnected with his own farm, for seven weeks. The schoolhouse, which I managed to reach only two days behind time, was closed for a fortnight, and even in Thrums there was only a sprinkling of scholars.

On Sundays the feeling between the different denominations ran high, and the middling good folk who did not go to church counted those who did. In the Established Church there was a sparse gathering, who waited in vain for the minister. After a time it got abroad that a flag of distress was flying from the manse, and then they saw that the minister was storm-staid. An office-bearer offered to conduct service; but the others present thought they had done their duty and went home. The U.P. bell did not ring at all, and the kirk gates were not opened. The Free Kirk did bravely, however. The attendance in the forenoon amounted to seven, including the minister; but in the afternoon there was a turn-out of upwards of fifty. How much denominational competition had to do with this, none can say; but the general opinion was that this muster to afternoon service was a piece of vainglory. Next Sunday all the kirks were on their mettle, and, though the snow was drifting the whole day, services were general. It was felt that after the action of the Free Kirk the Establisheds and the U.P.'s must show what they too were capable of. So, when the bells rang at eleven o'clock and two, church-goers began to pour out of every close. If I remember aright, the victory lay with the U.P.'s by two women and a boy. Of course the Auld Lichts mustered in as great force as ever. The other kirks never dreamt of competing with them. What was regarded as a judgment on the Free Kirk for its boastfulness of spirit on the preceding Sunday happened during the forenoon. While the service was taking place a huge clod of snow slipped from the roof and fell right against the church door. It was some time before the prisoners could make up their minds to leave by the windows. What the Auld Lichts would have done in a similar predicament I cannot even conjecture.

That was the first warning of the thaw. It froze again; there was more snow; the thaw began in earnest; and then the streets were a sight to see. There was no traffic to turn the snow to slush, and, where it had not been piled up in walls a few feet from the houses, it remained in the narrow ways till it became a lake. It tried to escape through doorways, when it sank slowly into the floors. Gentle breezes created a ripple on its surface, and strong winds lifted it into the air and flung it against the houses. It undermined the heaps of clotted snow till they tottered like icebergs and fell to pieces. Men made their way through it on stilts. Had a frost followed, the result would have been appalling; but there was no more frost that winter. A fortnight passed before the place looked itself again, and even then congealed snow stood doggedly in the streets, while the country roads were like newly ploughed fields after rain. The heat from large fires soon penetrated through roofs of slate and thatch; and it was quite a common thing for a man to be flattened to the ground by a slithering of snow from above just as he opened his door. But it had seldom more than ten feet to fall. Most interesting of all was the novel sensation experienced as Thrums began to assume its familiar aspect, and objects so long buried that they had been half forgotten came back to view and use.

Storm-stead shows used to emphasise the severity of a Thrums winter. As the name indicates, these were gatherings of travelling booths in the winter-time. Half a century ago the country was overrun by itinerant showmen, who went their different ways in summer, but formed little colonies in the cold weather, when they pitched their tents in any empty field or disused quarry and huddled together for the sake of warmth: not that they got much of it. Not more than five winters ago we had a storm-stead show on a small scale; but nowadays the farmers are less willing to give these wanderers a camping-place, and the people are less easily drawn to the entertainments provided, by fife and drum. The colony hung together until it was starved out, when it trailed itself elsewhere. I have often seen it forming. The first arrival would be what was popularly known as "Sam'l Mann's Tumbling-Booth," with its tumblers, jugglers, sword-swallowers, and balancers. This travelling show visited us regularly twice a year: once in summer for the Muckle Friday, when the performers were gay and stout, and even the horses had flesh on their bones; and again in the "back-end" of the year, when cold and hunger had taken the blood from their faces, and the scraggy dogs that whined at their side were lashed for licking the paint off the caravans. While the storm-stead show was in the vicinity the villages suffered from an invasion of these dogs. Nothing told more truly the dreadful tale of the showman's life in winter. Sam'l Mann's was a big show, and half a dozen smaller ones, most of which were familiar to us, crawled in its wake. Others heard of its whereabouts and came in from distant parts. There was the well-known Gubbins with his "A' the World in a Box": a halfpenny peepshow, in which all the world was represented by Joseph and his Brethren (with pit and coat), the bombardment of Copenhagen, the Battle of the Nile, Daniel in the Den of Lions, and Mount Etna in eruption. "Aunty Maggy's Whirligig" could be enjoyed on payment of an old pair of boots, a collection of rags, or the like. Besides these and other shows, there were the wandering minstrels, most of whom were "Waterloo veterans" wanting arms or a leg. I remember one whose arms had been "smashed by a thunderbolt at Jamaica." Queer bent old dames, who superintended "lucky bags" or told fortunes, supplied the uncanny element, but hesitated to call themselves witches, for there can still be seen near Thrums the pool where these unfortunates used to be drowned, and in the session book of the Glen Quharity kirk can be read an old minute announcing that on a certain Sabbath there was no preaching because "the minister was away at the burning of a witch." To the storm-stead shows came the gypsies in great numbers. Claypots (which is a corruption of Claypits) was their headquarters hear Thrums, and it is still sacred to their memory. It was a clachan of miserable little huts built entirely of clay from the dreary and sticky pit in which they had been flung together. A shapeless hole on one side was the doorway, and a little hole, stuffed with straw in winter, the window. Some of the remnants of these hovels still stand. Their occupants, though they went by the name of gypsies among themselves, were known to the weavers as the Claypots beggars; and their King was Jimmy Pawse. His regal dignity gave Jimmy the right to seek alms first when he chose to do so; thus he got the cream of a place before his subjects set to work. He was rather foppish in his dress; generally affecting a suit of grey cloth with showy metal buttons on it, and a broad blue bonnet. His wife was a little body like himself; and when they went a-begging, Jimmy with a meal-bag for alms on his back, she always took her husband's arm. Jimmy was the legal adviser of his subjects; his decision was considered final on all question, and he guided them in their courtships as well as on their death-beds. He christened their children and officiated at their weddings, marrying them over the tongs.

The storm-stead show attracted old and young—to looking on from the outside. In the daytime the wagons and tents presented a dreary appearance, sunk in snow, the dogs shivering between the wheels, and but little other sign of life visible. When dusk came the lights were lit, and the drummer and fifer from the booth of tumblers were sent into the town to entice an audience. They marched quickly through the nipping, windy streets, and then returned with two or three score of men, women, and children, plunging through the snow or mud at their heavy heels. It was Orpheus fallen from his high estate. What a mockery the glare of the lamps and the capers of the mountebacks were, and how satisfied were we to enjoy it all without going inside. I hear the "Waterloo veterans" still, and remember their patriotic outbursts:—

On the sixteenth day of June, brave boys, while cannon loud did roar,
We being short of cavalry they pressed on us full sore;
But British steel soon made them yield, though our numbers was
but few,
And death or victory was the word on the plains of Waterloo.

The storm-stead shows often found it easier to sink to rest in a field than to leave it. For weeks at a time they were snowed up, sufficiently to prevent any one from Thrums going near them, though not sufficiently to keep the pallid mummers indoors. That would in many cases have meant starvation. They managed to fight their way through storm and snowdrift to the high road and thence to the town, where they got meal and sometimes broth. The tumblers and jugglers used occasionally to hire an outhouse in the town at these times—you may be sure they did not pay for it in advance— and give performances there. It is a curious thing, but true, that our herd-boys and others were sometimes struck with the stage-fever. Thrums lost boys to the showmen even in winter.

On the whole, the farmers and the people generally were wonderfully long-suffering with these wanderers, who I believe were more honest than was to be expected. They stole, certainly; but seldom did they steal anything more valuable than turnips. Sam'l Mann himself flushed proudly over the effect his show once had on an irate farmer. The farmer appeared in the encampment, whip in hand and furious. They must get off his land before nightfall. The crafty showman, however, prevailed upon him to take a look at the acrobats, and he enjoyed the performance so much that he offered to let them stay until the end of the week. Before that time came there was such a fall of snow that departure was out of the question; and it is to the farmer's credit that he sent Sam'l a bag of meal to tide him and his actors over the storm.

There were times when the showmen made a tour of the bothies, where they slung their poles and ropes and gave their poor performances to audiences that were not critical. The bothy being strictly the "man's" castle, the farmer never interfered; indeed, he was sometimes glad to see the show. Every other weaver in Thrums used to have a son a ploughman, and it was the men from the bothies who filled the square on the muckly. "Hands" are not huddled together nowadays in squalid barns more like cattle than men and women, but bothies in the neighbourhood of Thrums are not yet things of the past. Many a ploughman delves his way to and from them still in all weathers, when the snow is on the ground; at the time of "hairst," and when the turnip "shaws" have just forced themselves through the earth, looking like straight rows of green needles. Here is a picture of a bothy of to-day that I visited recently. Over the door there is a waterspout that has given way, and as I entered I got a rush of rain down my neck. The passage was so small that one could easily have stepped from the doorway on to the ladder standing against the wall, which was there in lieu of a staircase. "Upstairs" was a mere garret, where a man could not stand erect even in the centre. It was entered by a square hole in the ceiling, at present closed by a clap-door in no way dissimilar to the trap-doors on a theatre stage. I climbed into this garret, which is at present used as a store-room for agricultural odds and ends. At harvest-time, however, it is inhabited—full to overflowing. A few decades ago as many as fifty labourers engaged for the harvest had to be housed in the farm out-houses on beds of straw. There was no help for it, and men and women had to congregate in these barns together. Up as early as five in the morning, they were generally dead tired by night; and, miserable though this system of herding them together was, they took it like stoics, and their very number served as a moral safeguard. Nowadays the harvest is gathered in so quickly, and machinery does so much that used to be done by hand, that this crowding of labourers together, which was the bothy system at its worst, is nothing like what it was. As many as six or eight men, however, are put up in the garret referred to during "hairst"-time, and the female labourers have to make the best of it in the barn. There is no doubt that on many farms the two sexes have still at this busy time to herd together even at night.

The bothy was but scantily furnished, though it consisted of two rooms. In the one, which was used almost solely as a sleeping apartment, there was no furniture to speak of, beyond two closet beds, and its bumpy earthen floor gave it a cheerless look. The other, which had a single bed, was floored with wood. It was not badly lit by two very small windows that faced each other, and, besides several stools, there was a long form against one of the walls. A bright fire of peat and coal—nothing in the world makes such a cheerful red fire as this combination—burned beneath a big kettle ("boiler" they called it), and there was a "press" or cupboard containing a fair assortment of cooking utensils. Of these some belonged to the bothy, while others were the private property of the tenants. A tin "pan" and "pitcher" of water stood near the door, and the table in the middle of the room was covered with oilcloth.

Four men and a boy inhabited this bothy, and the rain had driven them all indoors. In better weather they spend the leisure of the evening at the game of quoits, which is the standard pastime among Scottish ploughmen. They fish the neighbouring streams, too, and have burn-trout for supper several times a week. When I entered, two of them were sitting by the fire playing draughts, or, as they called it, "the dam-brod." The dam-brod is the Scottish labourer's billiards; and he often attains to a remarkable proficiency at the game. Wylie, the champion draught-player, was once a herd-boy; and wonderful stories are current in all bothies of the times when his master called him into the farm-parlour to show his skill. A third man, who seemed the elder by quite twenty years, was at the window reading a newspaper; and I got no shock when I saw that it was the *Saturday Review*, which he and a labourer on an adjoining farm took in weekly between them. There was a copy of a local newspaper—the *People's Journal*—also lying about, and some books, including one of Darwin's. These were all the property of this man, however, who did the reading for the bothy.

They did all the cooking for themselves, living largely on milk. In the old days, which the senior could remember, porridge was so universally the morning meal that they called it by that name instead of breakfast. They still breakfast on porridge, but often take tea "above it." Generally milk is taken with the porridge; but "porter" or stout in a bowl is no uncommon substitute. Potatoes at twelve o'clock—seldom "brose" nowadays—are the staple dinner dish, and the tinned meats have become very popular. There are bothies where each man makes his own food; but of course the more satisfactory plan is for them to club together. Sometimes they get their food in the farm-kitchen; but this is only when there are few of them and the farmer and his family do not think it beneath them to dine with the men. Broth, too, may be made in the kitchen and sent down to the bothy. At harvest-time the workers take their food in the fields, when great quantities of milk are provided. There is very little beer drunk, and whisky is only consumed in privacy.

Life in the bothies is not, I should say, so lonely as life at the schoolhouse, for the hands have at least each other's company. The hawker visits them frequently still, though the itinerant tailor, once a familiar figure, has almost vanished. Their great place of congregating is still some country smiddy, which is also their frequent meeting-place when bent on black-fishing. The flare of the black-fisher's torch still attracts salmon to their death in the rivers near Thrums; and you may hear in the glens on a dark night the rattle of the spears on the wet stones. Twenty or thirty years ago, however, the sport was much more common. After the farmer had gone to bed, some half-dozen ploughmen and a few other poachers from Thrums would set out for the meeting-place.

The smithy on these occasions must have been a weird sight; though one did not mark that at the time. The poacher crept from the darkness into the glaring smithy light; for in country parts the anvil might sometimes be heard clanging at all hours of the night. As a rule, every face was blackened; and it was this, I suppose, rather than the fact that dark nights were chosen that gave the gangs the name of black-fishers. Other disguises were resorted to; one of the commonest being to change clothes or to turn your corduroys outside in. The country-folk of those days were more superstitious than they are now, and it did not take much to turn the black-fishers back. There was not a barn or byre in the district that had not its horseshoe over the door. Another popular device for frightening away witches and fairies was to hang bunches of garlic about the farms. I have known a black-fishing expedition stopped because a "yellow yite," or yellowhammer, hovered round the gang when they were setting out. Still more ominous was the "péat" when it appeared with one or three companions. An old rhyme about this bird runs—"One is joy, two is grief, three's a bridal, four is death." Such snatches of superstition are still to be heard amidst the gossip of a north-country smithy.

Each black-fisher brought his own spear and torch, both more or less home-made. The spears were in many cases "gully-knives," fastened to staves with twine land resin, called "rozet." The torches were very rough-and-ready things—rope and tar, or even rotten roots dug from broken trees—in fact, anything that would flare. The black-fishers seldom journeyed far from home, confining themselves to the rivers within a radius of three or four miles. There were many reasons for this: one of them being that the hands had to be at their work on the farm by five o'clock in the morning; another, that so they poached and let poach. Except when in spate, the river I specially refer to offered no attractions to the black-fishers. Heavy rains, however, swell it much more quickly than most rivers into a turbulent rush of water; the part of it affected by the black-fishers being banked in with rocks that prevent the water's spreading. Above these rocks, again, are heavy green banks, from which stunted trees grow aslant across the river. The effect is fearsome at some points where the trees run into each other, as it were, from opposite banks. However, the black-fishers thought nothing of these things. They took a turnip lantern with them—that is, a lantern hollowed out of a turnip, with a piece of candle inside—but no lights were shown on the road. Every one knew his way to the river blindfold; so that the darker the night the better. On reaching the water there was a pause.

One or two of the gang climbed the banks to discover if any bailiffs were on the watch; while the others sat down, and with the help of the turnip lantern "busked" their spears; in other words, fastened on the steel—or, it might be, merely pieces of rusty iron sharpened into a point at home—to the staves. Some had them busked before they set out, but that was not considered prudent; for of course there was always a risk of meeting spoil-sports on the way, to whom the spears would tell a tale that could not be learned from ordinary staves. Nevertheless little time was lost. Five or six of the gang waded into the water, torch in one hand and spear in the other; and the object now was to catch some salmon with the least possible delay, and hurry away. Windy nights were good for the sport, and I can still see the river lit up with the lumps of light that a torch makes in a high wind. The torches, of course, were used to attract the fish, which came swimming to the sheen, and were then speared. As little noise as possible was made; but though the men bit their lips instead of crying out when they missed their fish, there was a continuous ring of their weapons on the stones, and every irrepressible imprecation was echoed up and down the black glen. Two or three of the gang were told off to land the salmon, and they had to work smartly and deftly. They kept by the side of the spearsman, and the moment he struck a fish they grabbed at it with their hands. When the spear had a barb there was less chance of the fish's being lost; but often this was not the case, and probably not more than two-thirds of the salmon speared were got safely to the bank. The takes of course varied; sometimes, indeed, the black-fishers returned home empty-handed.

Encounters with the bailiffs were not infrequent, though they seldom took place at the water's edge. When the poachers were caught in the act, and had their blood up with the excitement of the sport, they were ugly customers. Spears were used and heads were broken. Struggles even took place in the water, when there was always a chance of somebody's being drowned. Where the bailiffs gave the black-fishers an opportunity of escaping without a fight it was nearly always taken; the booty being left behind. As a rule, when the "water-watchers," as the bailiffs were sometimes called, had an inkling of what was to take place, they reinforced themselves with a constable or two and waited on the road to catch the poachers on their way home. One black-fisher, a noted character, was nicknamed the "Deil o' Glen Quharity." He was said to have gone to the houses of the bailiffs and offered to sell them the fish stolen from the streams over which they kept guard. The "Deil" was never imprisoned—partly, perhaps, because he was too eccentric to be taken seriously.

# III

## THE AULD LICHT KIRK

ONE Sabbath day in the beginning of the century the Auld Licht minister at Thrums walked out of his battered, ramshackle, earthen-floored kirk with a following and never returned. The last words he uttered in it were: "Follow me to the commonty, all you persons who want to hear the Word of God properly preached; and James Duphie and his two sons will answer for this on the Day of Judgment." The congregation, which belonged to the body who seceded from the Established Church a hundred and fifty years ago, had split, and as the New Lights (now the U.P.'s) were in the majority, the Old Lights, with the minister at their head, had to retire to the commonty (or common) and hold service in the open air until they had saved up money for a church. They kept possession, however, of the white manse among the trees. Their kirk has but a cluster of members now, most of them old and done, but each is equal to a dozen ordinary church-goers, and there have been men and women among them on whom the memory loves to linger. For forty years they have been dying out, but their cold, stiff pews still echo the Psalms of David, and the Auld Licht kirk will remain open so long as it has one member and a minister.

The church stands round the corner from the square, with only a large door to distinguish it from the other buildings in the short street. Children who want to do a brave thing hit this door with their fists, when there is no one near, and then run away scared. The door, however, is sacred to the memory of a white-haired old lady who, not so long ago, used to march out of the kirk and remain on the pavement until the psalm which had just been given out was sung. Of Thrums's pavement it may here be said that when you come, even to this day, to a level slab you feel reluctant to leave it. The old lady was Mistress (which is Miss) Tibbie McQuhatty, and she nearly split the Auld Licht kirk over "run line." This conspicuous innovation was introduced by Mr. Dishart, the minister, when he was young and audacious. The old, reverent custom in the kirk was for the precentor to read out the psalm a line at a time. Having then sung that line he read out the next one, led the singing of it, and so worked his way on to line three. Where run line holds, however, the psalm is read out first, and forthwith sung. This is not only a flighty way of doing things, which may lead to greater scandals, but has its practical disadvantages, for the precentor always starts singing in advance of the congregation (Auld Lichts never being able to begin to do anything all at once), and, increasing the distance with every line, leaves them hopelessly behind at the finish. Miss McQuhatty protested against this change, as meeting the devil half way, but the minister carried his point, and ever after that she rushed ostentatiously from the church the moment a psalm was given out, and remained behind the door until the singing was finished, when she returned, with a rustle, to her seat. Run line had on her the effect of the reading of the Riot Act. Once some men, capable of anything, held the door from the outside, and the congregation heard Tibbie rampaging in the passage. Bursting into the kirk she called the office-bearers to her assistance, whereupon the minister in miniature raised his voice and demanded the why and wherefore of the ungodly disturbance. Great was the hubbub, but the door was fast, and a compromise had to be arrived at. The old lady consented for once to stand in the passage, but not without pressing her hands to her ears. You may smile at Tibbie, but ah! I know what she was at a sick bedside. I have seen her when the hard look had gone from her eyes, and it would ill become me to smile too.

As with all the churches in Thrums, care had been taken to make the Auld Licht one much too large. The stair to the "laft" or gallery, which was originally little more than a ladder, is ready for you as soon as you enter the doorway, but it is best to sit in the body of the kirk. The plate for collections is inside the church, so that the whole congregation can give a guess at what you give. If it is something very stingy or very liberal, all Thrums knows of it within a few hours; indeed, this holds good of all the churches, especially perhaps of the Free one, which has been called the bawbee kirk, because so many halfpennies find their way into the plate. On Saturday nights the Thrums shops are besieged for coppers by housewives of all denominations, who would as soon think of dropping a threepenny bit into the plate as of giving nothing. Tammy Todd had a curious way of tipping his penny into the Auld Licht plate while still keeping his hand to his side. He did it much as a boy fires a marble, and there was quite a talk in the congregation the first time he missed. A devout plan was to carry your penny in your hand all the way to church, but to appear to take it out of your pocket on entering, and some plumped it down noisily like men paying their way. I believe old Snecky Hobart, who was a canty stock but obstinate, once dropped a penny into the plate and took out a halfpenny as change, but the only untoward thing that happened to the plate was once when the lassie from the farm of Curly Bog capsized it in passing. Mr. Dishart, who was always a ready man, introduced something into his sermon that day about women's dress, which every one hoped Christy Lundy, the lassie in question, would remember.

Nevertheless, the minister sometimes came to a sudden stop himself when passing from the vestry to the pulpit. The passage being narrow, his rigging would catch in a pew as he sailed down the aisle. Even then, however, Mr. Dishart remembered that he was not as other men.

White is not a religious colour, and the walls of the kirk were of a dull grey. A cushion was allowed to the manse pew, but merely as a symbol of office, and this was the only pew in the church that had a door. It was and is the pew nearest to the pulpit on the minister's right, and one day it contained a bonnet which Mr. Dishart's predecessor preached at for one hour and ten minutes. From the pulpit, which was swaddled in black, the minister had a fine sweep of all the congregation except those in the back pews downstairs, who were lost in the shadow of the laft. Here sat Whinny Webster, so called because, having an inexplicable passion against them, he devoted his life to the extermination of whins. Whinny for years ate peppermint lozenges with impunity in his back seat, safe in the certainty that the minister, however much he might try, could not possibly see him. But his day came. One afternoon the kirk smelt of peppermints, and Mr. Dishart could rebuke no one, for the defaulter was not in sight. Whinny's cheek was working up and down in quiet enjoyment of its lozenge, when he started, noticing that the preaching had stopped. Then he heard a sepulchral voice say "Charles Webster!" Whinny's eyes turned to the pulpit, only part of which was visible to him, and to his horror they encountered the minister's head coming down the stairs. This took place after I had ceased to attend the Auld Licht kirk regularly; but I am told that as Whinny gave one wild scream the peppermint dropped from his mouth. The minister had got him by leaning over the pulpit door until, had he given himself only another inch, his feet would have gone into the air. As for Whinny, he became a Godfearing man.

The most uncanny thing about the kirk was the precentor's box beneath the pulpit. Three Auld Licht ministers I have known, but I can only conceive one precentor. Lang Tammas's box was much too small for him. Since his disappearance from Thrums I believe they have paid him the compliment of enlarging it for a smaller man—no doubt with the feeling that Tammas alone could look like a Christian in it. Like the whole congregation, of course, he had to stand during the prayers—the first of which averaged half an hour in length. If he stood erect his head and shoulders vanished beneath funereal trappings, when he seemed decapitated, and if he stretched his neck the pulpit tottered. He looked like the pillar on which it rested, or he balanced it on his head like a baker's tray. Sometimes he leaned forward as reverently as he could, and then, with his long lean arms dangling over the side of his box, he might have been a suit of "blacks" hung up to dry. Once I was talking with Cree Queery in a sober, respectable manner, when all at once a light broke out on his face. I asked him what he was laughing at, and he said it was at Lang Tammas. He got grave again when I asked him what there was in Lang Tammas to smile at, and admitted that he could not tell me. However, I have always been of opinion that the thought of the precentor in his box gave Cree a fleeting sense of humour.

Tammas and Hendry Munn were the two paid officials of the church, Hendry being kirk-officer; but poverty was among the few points they had in common. The precentor was a cobbler, though he never knew it, shoemaker being the name in those parts, and his dwelling-room was also his workshop. There he sat in his "brot," or apron, from early morning to far on to midnight, and contrived to make his six or eight shillings a week. I have often sat with him in the darkness that his "cruizey" lamp could not pierce, while his mutterings to himself of "ay, ay, yes, umpha, oh ay, ay man," came as regularly and monotonously as the tick of his "wag-at-the-wa'" clock. Hendry and he were paid no fixed sum for their services in the Auld Licht kirk, but once a year there was a collection for each of them, and so they jogged along. Though not the only kirk-officer of my time Hendry made the most lasting impression. He was, I think, the only man in Thrums who did not quake when the minister looked at him. A wild story, never authenticated, says that Hendry once offered Mr. Dishart a snuff from his mull. In the streets Lang Tammas was more stern and dreaded by evildoers, but Hendry had first place in the kirk. One of his duties was to precede the minister from the session-house to the pulpit and open the door for him. Having shut Mr. Dishart in he strolled away to his seat. When a strange minister preached, Hendry was, if possible, still more at his ease. This will not be believed, but I have seen him give the pulpit-door on these occasions a fling-to with his feet. However ill an ordinary member of the congregation might become in the kirk he sat on till the service ended, but Hendry would wander to the door and shut it if he noticed that the wind was playing irreverent tricks with the pages of Bibles, and proof could still be brought forward that he would stop deliberately in the aisle to lift up a piece of paper, say, that had floated there. After the first psalm had been sung it was Hendry's part to lift up the plate and carry its tinkling contents to the session-house. On the greatest occasions he remained so calm, so indifferent, so expressionless, that he might have been present the night before at a rehearsal.

When there was preaching at night the church was lit by tallow candles, which also gave out all the artificial heat provided. Two candles stood on each side of the pulpit, and others were scattered over the church, some of them fixed into holes on rough brackets, and some merely sticking in their own grease on the pews. Hendry superintended the lighting of the candles, and frequently hobbled through the church to snuff them. Mr. Dishart was a man who could do anything except snuff a candle, but when he stopped in his sermon to do that he as often as not knocked the candle over. In vain he sought to refix it in its proper place, and then all eyes turned to Hendry. As coolly as though he were in a public hall or place of entertainment, the kirk-officer arose and, mounting the stair, took the candle from the minister's reluctant hands and put it right. Then he returned to his seat, not apparently puffed up, yet perhaps satisfied with himself; while Mr. Dishart, glaring after him to see if he was carrying his head high, resumed his wordy way.

Never was there a man more uncomfortably loved than Mr. Dishart. Easie Haggart, his maid-servant, reproved him at the breakfast-table. Lang Tammas and Sam'l Mealmaker crouched for five successive Sabbath nights on his manse wall to catch him smoking (and got him). Old wives grumbled by their hearths when he did not look in to despair of their salvation. He told the maidens of his congregation not to make an idol of him. His session saw him (from behind a haystack) in conversation with a strange woman, and asked grimly if he remembered that he had a wife. Twenty were his years when he came to Thrums, and on the very first Sabbath he knocked a board out of the pulpit. Before beginning his trial sermon he handed down the big Bible to the precentor, to give his arms freer swing. The congregation, trembling with exhilaration, probed his meaning. Not a square inch of paper, they saw, could be concealed there. Mr. Dishart had scarcely any hope for the Auld Lichts; he had none for any other denomination. Davit Lunan got behind his handkerchief to think for a moment, and the minister was on him like a tiger. The call was unanimous. Davit proposed him.

Every few years, as one might say, the Auld Licht kirk gave way and buried its minister. The congregation turned their empty pockets inside out, and the minister departed in a farmer's cart. The scene was not an amusing one to those who looked on at it. To the Auld Lichts was then the humiliation of seeing their pulpit "supplied" on alternate Sabbaths by itinerant probationers or stickit ministers. When they were not starving themselves to support a pastor the Auld Lichts were saving up for a stipend. They retired with compressed lips to their looms, and weaved and weaved till they weaved another minister. Without the grief of parting with one minister there could not have been the transport of choosing another. To have had a pastor always might have made them vainglorious.

They were seldom longer than twelve months in making a selection, and in their haste they would have passed over Mr. Dishart and mated with a monster. Many years have elapsed since Providence flung Mr. Watts out of the Auld Licht kirk. Mr. Watts was a probationer who was tried before Mr. Dishart, and, though not so young as might have been wished, he found favour in many eyes. "Sluggard in the laft, awake!" he cried to Bell Whamond, who had forgotten herself, and it was felt that there must be good stuff in him. A breeze from Heaven exposed him on Communion Sabbath.

On the evening of this solemn day the door of the Auld Licht kirk was sometimes locked, and the congregation repaired, Bible in hand, to the commonty. They had a right to this common on the Communion Sabbath, but only took advantage of it when it was believed that more persons intended witnessing the evening service than the kirk would hold. On this day the attendance was always very great.

It was the Covenanters come back to life. To the summit of the slope a wooden box was slowly hurled by Hendry Munn and others, and round this the congregation quietly grouped to the tinkle of the cracked Auld Licht bell. With slow majestic tread the session advanced up the steep common with the little minister in their midst. He had the people in his hands now, and the more he squeezed them the better they were pleased. The travelling pulpit consisted of two compartments, the one for the minister and the other for Lang Tammas, but no Auld Licht thought that it looked like a Punch and Judy puppet show. This service on the common was known as the "tent preaching," owing to a tent's being frequently used instead of the box.

Mr. Watts was conducting the service on the commonty. It was a fine, still summer evening, and loud above the whisper of the burn from which the common climbs, and the laboured "pechs" of the listeners, rose the preacher's voice. The Auld Lichts in their rusty blacks (they must have been a more artistic sight in the olden days of blue bonnets and knee-breeches) nodded their heads in sharp approval, for though they could swoop down on a heretic like an eagle on carrion, they scented no prey. Even Lang Tammas, on whose nose a drop of water gathered when he was in his greatest fettle, thought that all was fair and above-board. Suddenly a rush of wind tore up the common, and ran straight at the pulpit. It formed in a sieve, and passed over the heads of the congregation, who felt it as a fan, and looked up in awe. Lang Tammas, feeling himself all at once grow clammy, distinctly heard the leaves of the pulpit Bible shiver. Mr. Watts's hands, outstretched to prevent a catastrophe, were blown against his side, and then some twenty sheets of closely-written paper floated into the air. There was a horrible, dead silence. The burn was roaring now. The minister, if such he can be called, shrunk back in his box, and, as if they had seen it printed in letters of fire on the heavens, the congregation realised that Mr. Watts, whom they had been on the point of calling, read his sermon. He wrote it out on pages the exact size of those in the Bible, and did not scruple to fasten these into the Holy Book itself. At theatres a sullen thunder of angry voices behind the scene represents a crowd in a rage, and such a low, long-drawn howl swept the common when Mr. Watts was found out. To follow a pastor who "read" seemed to the Auld Lichts like claiming heaven on false pretences. In ten minutes the session alone, with Lang Tammas and Hendry, were on the common. They were watched by many from afar off, and (when one comes to think of it now) looked a little curious jumping, like trout at flies, at the damning papers still fluttering in the air. The minister was never seen in our parts again, but he is still remembered as "Paper Watts."

Mr. Dishart in the pulpit was the reward of his upbringing. At ten he had entered the university. Before he was in his teens he was practising the art of gesticulation in his father's gallery pew. From distant congregations people came to marvel at him. He was never more than comparatively young. So long as the pulpit trappings of the kirk at Thrums lasted he could be seen, once he was fairly under weigh with his sermon, but dimly in a cloud of dust. He introduced headaches. In a grand transport of enthusiasm he once flung his arms over the pulpit and caught Lang Tammas on the forehead. Leaning forward, with his chest on the cushions, he would pommel the Evil One with both hands, and then, whirling round to the left, shake his fist at Bell Whamond's neckerchief. With a sudden jump he would fix Pete Todd's youngest boy catching flies at the laft window. Stiffening unexpectedly, he would leap three times in the air, and then gather himself in a corner for a fearsome spring. When he wept he seemed to be laughing, and he laughed in a paroxysm of tears. He tried to tear the devil out of the pulpit rails. When he was not a teetotum he was a windmill. His pump position was the most appalling. Then he glared motionless at his admiring listeners, as if he had fallen into a trance with his arm upraised. The hurricane broke next moment. Nanny Sutie bore up under the shadow of the windmill—which would have been heavier had Auld Licht ministers worn gowns—but the pump affected her to tears. She was stone-deaf.

For the first year or more of his ministry an Auld Licht minister was a mouse among cats. Both in the pulpit and out of it they watched for unsound doctrine, and when he strayed they took him by the neck. Mr. Dishart, however, had been brought up in the true way, and seldom gave his people a chance. In time, it may be said, they grew despondent, and settled in their uncomfortable pews with all suspicion of lurking heresy allayed. It was only on such Sabbaths as Mr. Dishart changed pulpits with another minister that they cocked their ears and leant forward eagerly to snap the preacher up.

Mr. Dishart had his trials. There was the split in the kirk, too, that comes once at least to every Auld Licht minister. He was long in marrying. The congregation were thinking of approaching him, through the medium of his servant, Easie Haggart, on the subject of matrimony; for a bachelor coming on for twenty-two, with an income of eighty pounds per annum, seemed an anomaly, when one day he took the canal for Edinburgh and returned with his bride. His people nodded their heads, but said nothing to the minister. If he did not choose to take them into his confidence, it was no affair of theirs. That there was something queer about the marriage, however, seemed certain. Sandy Whamond, who was a soured man after losing his eldership, said that he believed she had been an "Englishy"—in other words, had belonged to the English Church; but it is not probable that Mr. Dishart would have gone the length of that. The secret is buried in his grave.

Easie Haggart jagged the minister sorely. She grew loquacious with years, and when he had company would stand at the door joining in the conversation. If the company was another minister, she would take a chair and discuss Mr. Dishart's infirmities with him. The Auld Lichts loved their minister, but they saw even more clearly than himself the necessity for his humiliation. His wife made all her children's clothes, but Sanders Gow complained that she looked too like their sister. In one week three of the children died, and on the Sabbath following it rained. Mr. Dishart preached, twice breaking down altogether and gaping strangely round the kirk (there was no dust flying that day), and spoke of the rain as angels' tears for three little girls. The Auld Lichts let it pass, but, as Lang Tammas said in private (for, of course, the thing was much discussed at the looms), if you materialise angels in that way, where are you going to stop?

It was on the Fast Days that the Auld Licht kirk showed what it was capable of, and, so to speak, left all the other churches in Thrums far behind. The Fast came round once every summer, beginning on a Thursday, when all the looms were hushed, and two services were held in the kirk of about three hours' length each. A minister from another town assisted at these times, and when the service ended the members filed in at one door and out at another, passing on their way Mr. Dishart and his elders, who dispensed "tokens" at the foot of the pulpit. Without a token, which was a metal lozenge, no one could take the sacrament on the coming Sabbath, and many a member has Mr. Dishart made miserable by refusing him his token for gathering wild-flowers, say, on a Lord's Day (as testified to by another member). Women were lost who cooked dinners on the Sabbath, or took to coloured ribbons, or absented themselves from church without sufficient cause. On the Fast Day fists were shaken at Mr. Dishart as he walked sternly homewards, but he was undismayed. Next day there were no services in the kirk, for Auld Lichts could not afford many holidays, but they weaved solemnly, with Saturday and the Sabbath and Monday to think of. On Saturday service began at two and lasted until nearly seven. Two sermons were preached, but there was no interval. The sacrament was dispensed on the Sabbath. Nowadays the "tables" in the Auld Licht kirk are soon "served," for the attendance has decayed, and most of the pews in the body of the church are made use of. In the days of which I speak, however, the front pews alone were hung with white, and it was in them only that the sacrament was administered. As many members as could get into them delivered up their tokens and took the first table. Then they made room for others, who sat in their pews awaiting their turn. What with tables, the preaching, and unusually long prayers, the service lasted from eleven to six. At half-past six a two hours' service began, either in the kirk or on the common, from which no one who thought much about his immortal soul would have dared (or cared) to absent himself. A four hours' service on the Monday, which, like that of the Saturday, consisted of two services in one, but began at eleven instead of two, completed the programme.

On those days, if you were a poor creature and wanted to acknowledge it, you could leave the church for a few minutes and return to it, but the creditable thing was to sit on. Even among the children there was a keen competition, fostered by their parents, to sit each other out, and be in at the death.

The other Thrums kirks held the sacrament at the same time, but not with the same vehemence. As far north from the schoolhouse as Thrums is south of it, nestles the little village of Quharity, and there the Fast Day was not a day of fasting. In most cases the people had to go many miles to church. They drove or rode (two on a horse), or walked in from other glens. Without "the tents," therefore, the congregation, with a long day before them, would have been badly off. Sometimes one tent sufficed; at other times rival publicans were on the ground. The tents were those in use at the feeing and other markets, and you could get anything inside them, from broth made in a "boiler" to the finest whisky. They were planted just outside the kirk-gate—long, low tents of dirty white canvas—so that when passing into the church or out of it you inhaled their odours. The congregation emerged austerely from the church, shaking their heads solemnly over the minister's remarks, and their feet carried them into the tent. There was no mirth, no unseemly revelry, but there was a great deal of hard drinking. Eventually the tents were done away with, but not until the services on the Fast Days were shortened. The Auld Licht ministers were the only ones who preached against the tents with any heart, and since the old dominie, my predecessor at the schoolhouse, died, there has not been an Auld Licht permanently resident in the glen of Quharity.

Perhaps nothing took it out of the Auld Licht males so much as a christening. Then alone they showed symptoms of nervousness, more especially after the remarkable baptism of Eppie Whamond. I could tell of several scandals in connection with the kirk. There was, for instance, the time when Easie Haggart saved the minister. In a fit of temporary mental derangement the misguided man had one Sabbath day, despite the entreaties of his affrighted spouse, called at the post-office, and was on the point of reading the letter there received, when Easie, who had slipped on her bonnet and followed him, snatched the secular thing from his hands. There was the story that ran like fire through Thrums and crushed an innocent man to the effect that Pete Todd had been in an Edinburgh theatre countenancing the play-actors. Something could be made, too, of the retribution that came to Chairlie Ramsay, who woke in his pew to discover that its other occupant, his little son Jamie, was standing on the seat divesting himself of his clothes in presence of a horrified congregation. Jamie had begun stealthily, and had very little on when Chairlie seized him. But having my choice of scandals I prefer the christening one—the unique case of Eppie Whamond, who was born late on Saturday night and baptized in the kirk on the following forenoon.

To the casual observer the Auld Licht always looked as if he were returning from burying a near relative. Yet when I met him hobbling down the street, preternaturally grave and occupied, experience taught me that he was preparing for a christening. How the minister would have borne himself in the event of a member of his congregation's wanting the baptism to take place at home it is not easy to say; but I shudder to think of the public prayers for the parents that would certainly have followed. The child was carried to the kirk through rain, or snow, or sleet, or wind, the father took his seat alone in the front pew, under the minister's eye, and the service was prolonged far on into the afternoon. But though the references in the sermon to that unhappy object of interest in the front pew were many and pointed, his time had not really come until the minister signed to him to advance as far as the second step of the pulpit stairs. The nervous father clenched the railing in a daze, and cowered before the ministerial heckling. From warning the minister passed to exhortation, from exhortation to admonition, from admonition to searching questioning, from questioning to prayer and wailing. When the father glanced up, there was the radiant boy in the pulpit looking as if he would like to jump down his throat. If he hung his head the minister would ask, with a groan, whether he was unprepared; and the whole congregation would sigh out the response that Mr. Dishart had hit it. When he replied audibly to the minister's uncomfortable questions, a pained look at his flippancy travelled from the pulpit all round the pews; and when he only bowed his head in answer, the minister paused sternly, and the congregation wondered what the man meant. Little wonder that Davie Haggart took to drinking when his turn came for occupying that front pew.

If wee Eppie Whamond's birth had been deferred until the beginning of the week, or humility had shown more prominently among her mother's virtues, the kirk would have been saved a painful scandal, and Sandy Whamond might have retained his eldership. Yet it was a foolish but wifely pride in her husband's official position that turned Bell Dundas's head—a wild ambition to beat all baptismal record.

Among the wives she was esteemed a poor body whose infant did not see the inside of the kirk within a fortnight of its birth. Forty years ago it was an accepted superstition in Thrums that the ghosts of children who had died before they were baptized went wailing and wringing their hands round the kirkyard at nights, and that they would continue to do this until the crack of doom. When the Auld Licht children grew up, too, they crowed over those of their fellows whose christening had been deferred until a comparatively late date, and the mothers who had needlessly missed a Sabbath for long afterwards hung their heads. That was a good and creditable birth which took place early in the week, thus allowing time for suitable christening preparations; while to be born on a Friday or a Saturday was to humiliate your parents, besides being an extremely ominous beginning for yourself. Without seeking to vindicate Bell Dundas's behaviour, I may note, as an act of ordinary fairness, that being the leading elder's wife, she was sorely tempted. Eppie made her appearance at 9.45 on a Saturday night.

In the hurry and skurry that ensued, Sandy escaped sadly to the square. His infant would be baptized eight days old, one of the longest-deferred christenings of the year. Sandy was shivering under the clock when I met him accidentally, and took him home. But by that time the harm had been done. Several of the congregation had been roused from their beds to hear his lamentations, of whom the men sympathized with him, while the wives triumphed austerely over Bell Dundas. As I wrung poor Sandy's hand, I hardly noticed that a bright light showed distinctly between the shutters of his kitchen-window; but the elder himself turned pale and breathed quickly. It was then fourteen minutes past twelve.

My heart sank within me on the following forenoon, when Sandy Whamond walked, with a queer twitching face, into the front pew under a glare of eyes from the body of the kirk and the laft. An amazed buzz went round the church, followed by a pursing up of lips and hurried whisperings. Evidently Sandy had been driven to it against his own judgment. The scene is still vivid before me: the minister suspecting no guile, and omitting the admonitory stage out of compliment to the elder's standing; Sandy's ghastly face; the proud godmother (aged twelve) with the squalling baby in her arms; the horror of the congregation to a man and woman. A slate fell from Sandy's house even as he held up the babe to the minister to receive a "droukin'" of water, and Eppie cried so vigorously that her shamed godmother had to rush with her to the vestry. Now things are not as they should be when an Auld Licht infant does not quietly sit out her first service.

Bell tried for a time to carry her head high; but Sandy ceased to whistle at his loom, and the scandal was a rolling stone that soon passed over him. Briefly it amounted to this: that a bairn born within two hours of midnight on Saturday could not have been ready for christening at the kirk next day without the breaking of the Sabbath. Had the secret of the nocturnal light been mine alone all might have been well; but Betsy Munn's evidence was irrefutable. Great had been Bell's cunning, but Betsy had outwitted her. Passing the house on the eventful night, Betsy had observed Marget Dundas, Bell's sister, open the door and creep cautiously to the window, the chinks in the outside shutters of which she cunningly closed up with "tow." As in a flash the disgusted Betsy saw what Bell was up to, and, removing the tow, planted herself behind the dilapidated dyke opposite, and awaited events. Questioned at a special meeting of the office-bearers in the vestry, she admitted that the lamp was extinguished soon after twelve o'clock, though the fire burned brightly all night. There had been unnecessary feasting during the night, and six eggs were consumed before breakfast-time. Asked how she knew this, she admitted having counted the egg-shells that Marget had thrown out of doors in the morning. This, with the testimony of the persons from whom Sandy had sought condolence on the Saturday night, was the case for the prosecution. For the defence, Bell maintained that all preparations stopped when the clock struck twelve, and even hinted that the bairn had been born on Saturday afternoon. But Sandy knew that he and his had got a fall. In the forenoon of the following Sabbath the minister preached from the text, "Be sure your sin will find you out;" and in the afternoon from "Pride goeth before a fall." He was grand. In the evening Sandy tendered his resignation of office, which was at once accepted. Wobs were behindhand for a week owing to the length of the prayers offered up for Bell; and Lang Tammas ruled in Sandy's stead.

# IV

## LADS AND LASSES

WITH the severe Auld Lichts the Sabbath began at six o'clock on Saturday evening. By that time the gleaming shuttle was at rest, Davie Haggart had strolled into the village from his pile of stones on the Whunny road; Hendry Robb, the "dummy," had sold his last barrowful of "rozetty (resiny) roots" for firewood; and the people, having tranquilly supped and soused their faces in their water-pails, slowly donned their Sunday clothes. This ceremony was common to all; but here divergence set in. The grey Auld Licht, to whom love was not even a name, sat in his high-backed arm-chair by the hearth, Bible or *Pilgrim's Progress* in hand, occasionally lapsing into slumber. But—though, when they got the chance, they went willingly three times to the kirk—there were young men in the community so flighty that, instead of dozing at home on Saturday night, they dandered casually into the square, and, forming into knots at the corners, talked solemnly and mysteriously of women.

Not even on the night preceding his wedding was an Auld Licht ever known to stay out after ten o'clock. So weekly conclaves at street-corners came to an end at a comparatively early hour, one Cœlebs after another shuffling silently from the square until it echoed, deserted, to the town house clock. The last of the gallants, gradually discovering that he was alone, would look around him musingly, and, taking in the situation, slowly, wend his way home. On no other night of the week was frivolous talk about the softer sex indulged in, the Auld Lichts being creatures of habit who never thought of smiling on a Monday. Long before they reached their teens they were earning their keep as herds in the surrounding glens or filling "pirns" for their parents; but they were generally on the brink of twenty before they thought seriously of matrimony. Up to that time they only trifled with the other sex's affections at a distance—filling a maid's water-pails, perhaps, when no one was looking, or carrying her wob; at the recollection of which they would slap their knees almost jovially on Saturday night. A wife was expected to assist at the loom as well as to be cunning in the making of marmalade and the firing of bannocks, and there was consequently some heartburning among the lads for maids of skill and muscle. The Auld Licht, however, who meant marriage seldom loitered in the streets. By and by there came a time when the clock looked down through its cracked glass upon the hemmed in square and saw him not. His companions, gazing at each other's boots, felt that something was going on, but made no remark.

A month ago, passing through the shabby familiar square, I brushed against a withered old man tottering down the street under a load of yarn. It was piled on a wheelbarrow which his feeble hands could not have raised but for the rope of yarn that supported it from his shoulders; and though Auld Licht was written on his patient eyes, I did not immediately recognise Jamie Whamond. Years ago Jamie was a sturdy weaver and fervent lover whom I had the right to call my friend. Turn back the century a few decades, and we are together on a moonlight night, taking a short cut through the fields from the farm of Craigiebuckle. Buxom were Craigiebuckle's "dochters," and Jamie was Janet's accepted suitor. It was a muddy road through damp grass, and we picked our way silently over its ruts and pools. "I'm thinkin'," Jamie said at last, a little, wistfully, "that I micht hae been as weel wi' Chirsty." Chirsty was Janet's sister, and Jamie had first thought of her. Craigiebuckle, however, strongly advised him to take Janet instead, and he consented. Alack! heavy wobs have taken all the grace from Janet's shoulders this many a year, though she and Jamie go bravely down the hill together. Unless they pass the allotted span of life, the "poorshouse" will never know them. As for bonny Chirsty, she proved a flighty thing, and married a deacon in the Established Church. The Auld Lichts groaned over her fall, Craigiebuckle hung his head, and the minister told her sternly to go her way. But a few weeks afterwards Lang Tammas, the chief elder, was observed talking with her for an hour in Gowrie's close; and the very next Sabbath Chirsty pushed her husband in triumph into her father's pew. The minister, though completely taken by surprise, at once referred to the stranger, in a prayer of great length, as a brand that might yet be plucked from the burning. Changing his text, he preached at him; Lang Tammas, the precentor, and the whole congregation (Chirsty included), sang at him; and before he exactly realised his position he had become an Auld Licht for life. Chirsty's triumph was complete when, next week, in broad daylight, too, the minister's wife called, and (in the presence of Betsy Munn, who vouches for the truth of the story) graciously asked her to come up to the manse on Thursday, at 4 p.m., and drink a dish of tea. Chirsty, who knew her position, of course begged modestly to be excused; but a coolness arose over the invitation between her and Janet—who felt slighted—that was only made up at the laying-out of Chirsty's father-in-law, to which Janet was pleasantly invited.

When they had redd up the house, the Auld Licht lassies sat in the gloaming at their doors on three-legged stools, patiently knitting stockings. To them came stiff-limbed youths who, with a "Blawy nicht, Jeanie" (to which the inevitable answer was, "It is so, Cha-rles"), rested their shoulders on the doorpost, and silently followed with their eyes the flashing needles. Thus the courtship began—often to ripen promptly into marriage, at other times to go no further. The smooth-haired maids, neat in their simple wrappers, knew they were on their trial and that it behoved them to be wary. They had not compassed twenty winters without knowing that Marget Todd lost Davie Haggart because she "fittit" a black stocking with brown worsted, and that Finny's grieve turned from Bell Whamond on account of the frivolous flowers in her bonnet: and yet Bell's prospects, as I happen to know, at one time looked bright and promising. Sitting over her father's peat-fire one night gossiping with him about fishing-flies and tackle, I noticed the grieve, who had dropped in by appointment with some ducks' eggs on which Bell's clockin hen was to sit, performing some sleight-of-hand trick with his coat-sleeve. Craftily he jerked and twisted it, till his own photograph (a black smudge on white) gradually appeared to view. This he gravely slipped into the hands of the maid of his choice, and then took his departure, apparently much relieved. Had not Bell's light-headedness driven him away, the grieve would have soon followed up his gift with an offer of his hand. Some night Bell would have "seen him to the door," and they would have stared sheepishly at each other before saying good-night. The parting salutation given, the grieve would still have stood his ground, and Bell would have waited with him. At last, "Will ye hae's, Bell?" would have dropped from his half-reluctant lips; and Bell would have mumbled, "Ay," with her thumb in her mouth. "Guid nicht to ye, Bell," would be the next remark—"Guid nicht to ye, Jeames," the answer; the humble door would close softly, and Bell and her lad would have been engaged. But, as it was, their attachment never got beyond the silhouette stage, from which, in the ethics of the Auld Lichts, a man can draw back in certain circumstances, without loss of honour. The only really tender thing I ever heard an Auld Licht lover say to his sweetheart was when Gowrie's brother looked softly into Easie Tamson's eyes and whispered, "Do you swite (sweat)?" Even then the effect was produced more by the loving cast in Gowrie's eye than by the tenderness of the words themselves.

The courtships were sometimes of long duration, but as soon as the young man realised that he was courting he proposed. Cases were not wanting in which he realised this for himself, but as a rule he had to be told of it.

There were a few instances of weddings among the Auld Lichts that did not take place on Friday. Betsy Munn's brother thought to assert his two coal-carts, about which he was sinfully puffed up, by getting married early in the week; but he was a pragmatical feckless body, Jamie. The foreigner from York that Finny's grieve after disappointing Jinny Whamond took, sought to sow the seeds of strife by urging that Friday was an unlucky day; and I remember how the minister, who was always great in a crisis, nipped the bickering in the bud by adducing the conclusive fact that he had been married on the sixth day of the week himself. It was a judicious policy on Mr. Dishart's part to take vigorous action at once and insist on the solemnisation of the marriage on a Friday or not at all, for he best kept superstition out of the congregation by branding it as heresy. Perhaps the Auld Lichts were only ignorant of the grieve's lass's theory because they had not thought of it. Friday's claims, too, were incontrovertible; for the Saturday's being a slack day gave the couple an opportunity to put their but and ben in order, and on Sabbath they had a gay day of it, three times at the kirk. The honeymoon over, the racket of the loom began again on the Monday.

The natural politeness of the Allardice family gave me my invitation to Tibbie's wedding. I was taking tea and cheese early one wintry afternoon with the smith and his wife, when little Joey Todd in his Sabbath clothes peered in at the passage, and then knocked primly at the door. Andra forgot himself, and called out to him to come in by; but Jess frowned him into silence, and, hastily donning her black mutch, received Willie on the threshold. Both halves of the door were open, and the visitor had looked us over carefully before knocking; but he had come with the compliments of Tibbie's mother, requesting the pleasure of Jess and her man that evening to the lassie's marriage with Sam'l Todd, and the knocking at the door was part of the ceremony. Five minutes afterwards Joey returned to beg a moment of me in the passage; when I, too, got my invitation. The lad had just received, with an expression of polite surprise, though he knew he could claim it as his right, a slice of crumbling shortbread, and taken his staid departure, when Jess cleared the tea-things off the table, remarking simply that it was a mercy we had not got beyond the first cup. We then retired to dress.

About six o'clock, the time announced for the ceremony, I elbowed my way through the expectant throng of men, women, and children that already besieged the smith's door. Shrill demands of "Toss, toss!" rent the air every time Jess's head showed on the window-blind, and Andra hoped, as I pushed open the door, "that I hadna forgotten my bawbees." Weddings were celebrated among the Auld Lichts by showers of ha'pence, and the guests on their way to the bride's house had to scatter to the hungry rabble like housewives feeding poultry. Willie Todd, the best man, who had never come out so strong in his life before, slipped through the back window, while the crowd, led on by Kitty McQueen, seethed in front, and making a bolt for it to the " 'Sosh," was back in a moment with a handful of small change. "Dinna toss ower lavishly at first," the smith whispered me nervously, as we followed Jess and Willie into the darkening wynd.

The guests were packed hot and solemn in Johnny Allardice's "room": the men anxious to surrender their seats to the ladies who happened to be standing, but too bashful to propose it; the ham and the fish frizzling noisily side by side but the house, and hissing out every now and then to let all whom it might concern know that Janet Craik was adding more water to the gravy. A better woman never lived; but, oh, the hypocrisy of the face that beamed greeting to the guests as if it had nothing to do but politely show them in, and gasped next moment with upraised arms, over what was nearly a fall in crockery. When Janet sped to the door her "spleet new" merino dress fell, to the pulling of a string, over her homemade petticoat, like the drop-scene in a theatre, and rose as promptly when she returned to slice the bacon. The murmur of admiration that filled the room when she entered with the minister was an involuntary tribute to the spotlessness of her wrapper and a great triumph for Janet. If there is an impression that the dress of the Auld Lichts was on all occasions as sombre as their faces, let it be known that the bride was but one of several in "whites," and that Mag Munn had only at the last moment been dissuaded from wearing flowers. The minister, the Auld Lichts congratulated themselves, disapproved of all such decking of the person and bowing of the head to idols; but on such an occasion he was not expected to observe it. Bell Whamond, however, has reason for knowing that, marriages or no marriages, he drew the line at curls.

By and by Sam'l Todd, looking a little dazed, was pushed into the middle of the room to Tibbie's side, and the minister raised his voice in prayer. All eyes closed reverently, except perhaps the bridegroom's, which seemed glazed and vacant. It was an open question in the community whether Mr. Dishart did not miss his chance at weddings; the men shaking their heads over the comparative brevity of the ceremony, the women worshipping him (though he never hesitated to rebuke them when they showed it too openly) for the urbanity of his manners. At that time, however, only a minister of such experience as Mr. Dishart's predecessor could lead up to a marriage in prayer without inadvertently joining the couple; and the catechising was mercifully brief. Another prayer followed the union; the minister waived his right to kiss the bride; every one looked at every other one, as if he had for the moment forgotten what he was on the point of saying and found it very annoying; and Janet signed frantically to Willie Todd, who nodded intelligently in reply, but evidently had no idea what she meant. In time Johnny Allardice, our host, who became more and more doited as the night proceeded, remembered his instructions, and led the way to the kitchen, where the guests, having politely informed their hostess that they were not hungry, partook of a hearty tea. Mr. Dishart presided with the bride and bridegroom near him; but though he tried to give an agreeable turn to the conversation by describing the extensions at the cemetery, his personality oppressed us, and we only breathed freely when he rose to go. Yet we marvelled at his versatility. In shaking hands with the newly-married couple the minister reminded them that it was leap-year, and wished them "three hundred and sixty-six happy and God-fearing days."

Saml's station being too high for it, Tibbie did not have a penny wedding, which her thrifty mother bewailed, penny weddings starting a couple in life. I can recall nothing more characteristic of the nation from which the Auld Lichts sprung than the penny wedding, where the only revellers that were not out of pocket by it were the couple who gave the entertainment. The more the guests ate and drank the better, pecuniarily, for their hosts. The charge for admission to the penny wedding (practically to the feast that followed it) varied in different districts, but with us it was generally a shilling. Perhaps the penny extra to the fiddler accounts for the name penny wedding. The ceremony having been gone through in the bride's house, there was an adjournment to a barn or other convenient place of meeting, where was held the nuptial feast; long white boards from Rob Angus's sawmill, supported on trestles, stood in lieu of tables; and those of the company who could not find a seat waited patiently against the wall for a vacancy. The shilling gave every guest the free run of the groaning board, but though fowls were plentiful, and even white bread too, little had been spent on them. The farmers of the neighbourhood, who looked forward to providing the young people with drills of potatoes for the coming winter, made a bid for their custom by sending them a fowl gratis for the marriage supper. It was popularly understood to be the oldest cock of the farmyard, but for all that it made a brave appearance in a shallow sea of soup. The fowls were always boiled—without exception, so far as my memory carries me; the guid-wife never having the heart to roast them, and so lose the broth. One round of whisky-and-water was all the drink to which his shilling entitled the guest. If he wanted more he had to pay for it. There was much revelry, with song and dance, that no stranger could have thought those stiff-limbed weavers capable of; and the more they shouted and whirled through the barn, the more their host smiled and rubbed his hands. He presided at the bar improvised for the occasion, and if the thing was conducted with spirit, his bride flung an apron over her gown and helped him. I remember one elderly bridegroom, who, having married a blind woman, had to do double work at his penny wedding. It was a sight to see him flitting about the torch-lit barn, with a kettle of hot water in one hand and a besom to sweep up crumbs in the other.

Though Sam'l had no penny wedding, however, we made a night of it at his marriage.

Wedding chariots were not in those days, though I know of Auld Lichts being conveyed to marriages nowadays by horses with white ears. The tea over, we formed in couples, and—the best man with the bride, the bridegroom with the best maid, leading the way—marched in slow procession in the moonlight night to Tibbie's new home, between lines of hoarse and eager onlookers. An attempt was made by an itinerant musician to head the company with his fiddle; but instrumental music, even in the streets, was abhorrent to sound Auld Lichts, and the minister had spoken privately to Willie Todd on the subject. As a consequence, Peter was driven from the ranks. The last thing I saw that night, as we filed, bare-headed and solemn, into the newly-married couple's house, was Kitty McQueen's vigorous arm, in a dishevelled sleeve, pounding a pair of urchins who had got between her and a muddy ha'penny.

That night there was revelry and boisterous mirth (or what the Auld Lichts took for such) in Tibbie's kitchen. At eleven o'clock Davit Lunan cracked a joke. Davie Haggart, in reply to Bell Dundas's request, gave a song of distinctly secular tendencies. The bride (who had carefully taken off her wedding gown on getting home and donned a wrapper) coquettishly let the bridegroom's father hold her hand. In Auld Licht circles, when one of the company was offered whisky and refused it, the others, as if pained even at the offer, pushed it from them as a thing abhorred. But Davie Haggart set another example on this occasion, and no one had the courage to refuse to follow it. We sat late round the dying fire, and it was only Willie Todd's scandalous assertion (he was but a boy) about his being able to dance that induced us to think of moving. In the community, I understand, this marriage is still memorable as the occasion on which Bell Whamond laughed in the minister's face.

# V

## THE AULD LICHTS IN ARMS

ARMS and men I sing: douce Jeemsy Todd, rushing from his loom, armed with a bedpost; Lisbeth Whamond, an avenging whirlwind; Neil Haggart, pausing in his thanks-offerings to smite and slay; the impious foe scudding up the bleeding Brae-head with Nemesis at their flashing heels; the minister holding it a nice question whether the carnage was not justified. Then came the two hours' sermons of the following Sabbath, when Mr. Dishart, revolving like a teetotum in the pulpit, damned every bandaged person present, individually and collectively; and Lang Tammas, in the precentor's box with a plaster on his cheek, included any one the minister might have by chance omitted, and the congregation, with most of their eyes bunged up, burst into psalms of praise.

Twice a year the Auld Lichts went demented. The occasion was the Fast Day at Tilliedrum; when its inhabitants, instead of crowding reverently to the kirk, swooped profanely down in their scores and tens of scores on our God-fearing town, intent on making a day of it. Then did the weavers rise as one man, and go forth to show the ribald crew the errors of their way. All denominations were represented, but Auld Lichts led. An Auld Licht would have taken no man's blood without the conviction that he would be the better morally for the bleeding; and if Tammas Lunan's case gave an impetus to the blows, it can only have been because it opened wider Auld Licht eyes to Tilliedrum's desperate condition. Mr. Dishart's predecessor more than once remarked, that at the Creation the devil put forward a claim for Thrums, but said he would take his chance of Tilliedrum; and the statement was generally understood to be made on the authority of the original Hebrew.

The mustard-seed of a feud between the two parishes shot into a tall tree in a single night, when Davit Lunan's father went to a tattie roup at Tilliedrum and thoughtlessly died there. Twenty-four hours afterwards a small party of staid Auld Lichts, carrying long white poles, stepped out of various wynds and closes and picked their solemn way to the house of mourning. Nanny Low, the widow, received them dejectedly, as one oppressed by the knowledge that her man's death at such an inopportune place did not fulfil the promise of his youth; and her guests admitted bluntly that they were disappointed in Tammas. Snecky Hobart's father's unusually long and impressive prayer was an official intimation that the deceased, in the opinion of the session, sorely needed everything of the kind he could get; and then the silent driblet of Auld Lichts in black stalked off in the direction of Tilliedrum. Women left their spinning-wheels and pirns to follow them with their eyes along the Tenements, and the minister was known to be holding an extra service at the manse. When the little procession reached the boundary-line between the two parishes, they sat down on a dyke and waited.

By and by half a dozen men drew near from the opposite direction, bearing on poles the remains of Tammas Lunan in a closed coffin. The coffin was brought to within thirty yards of those who awaited it, and then roughly lowered to the ground. Its bearers rested morosely on their poles. In conveying Lunan's remains to the borders of his own parish they were only conforming to custom; but Thrums and Tilliedrum differed as to where the boundary-line was drawn, and not a foot would either advance into the other's territory. For half a day the coffin lay unclaimed, and the two parties sat scowling at each other. Neither dared move. Gloaming had stolen into the valley when Dite Deuchars of Tilliedrum rose to his feet and deliberately spat upon the coffin. A stone whizzed through the air; and then the ugly spectacle was presented, in the grey night, of a dozen mutes fighting with their poles over a coffin. There was blood on the shoulders that bore Tammas's remains to Thrums.

After that meeting Tilliedrum lived for the Fast Day. Never, perhaps, was there a community more given up to sin, and Thrums felt "called" to its chastisement. The insult to Lunan's coffin, however, dispirited their weavers for a time, and not until the suicide of Pitlums did they put much fervour into their prayers. It made new men of them. Tilliedrum's sins had found it out. Pitlums was a farmer in the parish of Thrums, but he had been born at Tilliedrum; and Thrums thanked Providence for that, when it saw him suspended between two hams from his kitchen rafters. The custom was to cart suicides to the quarry at the Galla pond and bury them near the cairn that had supported the gallows; but on this occasion not a farmer in the parish would lend a cart, and for a week the corpse lay on the sanded floor as it had been cut down—an object of awe-struck interest to boys who knew no better than to peep, through the darkened window. Tilliedrum bit its lips at home. The Auld Licht minister, it was said, had been approached on the subject; but, after serious consideration, did not see his way to offering up a prayer. Finally old Hobart and two others tied a rope round the body, and dragged it from the farm to the cairn, a distance of four miles. Instead of this incident's humbling Tilliedrum into attending church, the next Fast Day saw its streets deserted. As for the Thrums Auld Lichts, only heavy wobs prevented their walking erect like men who had done their duty. If no prayer was volunteered for Pitlums before his burial, there was a great deal of psalm-singing after it.

By early morn on their Fast Day the Tilliedrummers were straggling into Thrums, and the weavers, already at their looms, read the clattering of feet and carts aright. To convince themselves, all they had to do was to raise their eyes; but the first triumph would have been to Tilliedrum if they had done that. The invaders—the men in Aberdeen blue serge coats, velvet knee-breeches, and broad blue bonnets, and the wincey gowns of the women set off with hooded cloaks of red or tartan—tapped at the windows and shouted insultingly as they passed; but, with pursed lips, Thrums bent fiercely over its wobs, and not an Auld Licht showed outside his door. The day wore on to noon, and still ribaldry was master of the wynds. But there was a change inside the houses. The minister had pulled down his blinds; moody men had left their looms for stools by the fire; there were rumours of a conflict in Andra Gowrie's close, from which Kitty McQueen had emerged with her short gown in rags; and Lang Tammas was going from door to door. The austere precentor admonished fiery youth to beware of giving way to passion; and it was a proud day for the Auld Lichts to find their leading elder so conversant with apt Scripture texts. They bowed their heads reverently while he thundered forth that those who lived by the sword would perish by the sword; and when he had finished they took him ben to inspect their bludgeons. I have a vivid recollection of going the round of the Auld Licht and other houses to see the sticks and the wrists in coils of wire.

A stranger in the Tenements in the afternoon would have noted more than one draggled youth, in holiday attire, sitting on a doorstep with a wet cloth to his nose; and, passing down the Commonty, he would have had to step over prostrate lumps of humanity from which all shape had departed. Gavin Ogilvy limped heavily after his encounter with Thrummy Tosh—a struggle that was looked forward to eagerly as a bi-yearly event; Christy Davie's development of muscle had not prevented her going down before the terrible onslaught of Joe the miller, and Lang Tammas's plasters told a tale. It was in the square that the two parties, leading their maimed and blind, formed in force; Tilliedrum thirsting for its opponents' blood, and Thrums humbly accepting the responsibility of punching the Fast Day breakers into the ways of rectitude. In the small ill-kept square the invaders, to the number of about a hundred, were wedged together at its upper end, while the Thrums people formed in a thick line at the foot. For its inhabitants the way to Tilliedrum lay through this threatening mass of armed weavers. No words were bandied between the two forces; the centre of the square was left open, and nearly every eye was fixed on the town-house clock. It directed operations and gave the signal to charge. The moment six o'clock struck, the upper mass broke its bonds and flung itself on the living barricade. There was a clatter of heads and sticks, a yelling and a groaning, and then the invaders, bursting through the opposing ranks, fled for Tilliedrum. Down the Tanage brae and up the Brae-head they scurried, half a hundred avenging spirits in pursuit. On the Tilliedrum Fast Day I have tasted blood myself. In the godless place there is no Auld Licht kirk, but there are two Auld Lichts in it now who walk to Thrums to church every Sabbath, blow or rain as it lists. They are making their influence felt in Tilliedrum.

The Auld Lichts also did valorous deeds at the Battle of Cabbylatch. The farm land so named lies a mile or more to the south of Thrums. You have to go over the rim of the cup to reach it. It is low-lying and uninteresting to the eye, except for some giant stones scattered cold and naked through the fields. No human hands reared these boulders, but they might be looked upon as tombstones to the heroes who fell (to rise hurriedly) on the plain of Cabbylatch.

The fight of Cabbylatch belongs to the days of what are now but dimly remembered as the Meal Mobs. Then there was a wild cry all over the country for bread (not the fine loaves that we know, but something very much coarser), and hungry men and women, prematurely shrunken, began to forget the taste of meal. Potatoes were their chief sustenance, and, when the crop failed, starvation gripped them. At that time the farmers, having control of the meal, had the small towns at their mercy, and they increased its cost. The price of the meal went up and up, until the famishing people swarmed up the sides of the carts in which it was conveyed to the towns, and, tearing open the sacks, devoured it in handfuls. In Thrums they had a stern sense of justice, and for a time, after taking possession of the meal, they carried it to the square and sold it at what they considered a reasonable price. The money was handed over to the farmers. The honesty of this is worth thinking about, but it seems to have only incensed the farmers the more; and when they saw that to send their meal to the town was not to get high prices for it, they laid their heads together and then gave notice that the people who wanted meal and were able to pay for it must come to the farms. In Thrums no one who cared to live on porridge and bannocks had money to satisfy the farmers; but, on the other hand, none of them grudged going for it, and go they did. They went in numbers from farm to farm, like bands of hungry rats, and throttled the opposition they not infrequently encountered. The raging farmers at last met in council and, noting that they were lusty men and brave, resolved to march in armed force upon the erring people and burn their town. Now we come to the Battle of Cabbylatch.

The farmers were not less than eighty strong, and chiefly consisted of cavalry. Armed with pitchforks and cumbrous scythes where they were not able to lay their hands on the more orthodox weapons of war, they presented a determined appearance; the few foot-soldiers who had no cart-horses at their disposal bearing in their arms bundles of firewood. One memorable morning they set out to avenge their losses; and by and by a halt was called, when each man bowed his head to listen. In Thrums, pipe and drum were calling the inhabitants to arms. Scouts rushed in with the news that the farmers were advancing rapidly upon the town, and soon the streets were clattering with feet. At that time Thrums had its piper and drummer (the bellman of a later and more degenerate age); and on this occasion they marched together through the narrow wynds, firing the blood of haggard men and summoning them to the square. According to my informant's father, the gathering of these angry and startled weavers, when he thrust his blue bonnet on his head and rushed out to join them, was an impressive and solemn spectacle. That bloodshed was meant there can be no doubt; for starving men do not see the ludicrous side of things. The difference between the farmers and the town had resolved itself into an ugly and sullen hate, and the wealthier townsmen who would have come between the people and the bread were fiercely pushed aside. There was no nominal leader, but every man in the ranks meant to fight for himself and his belongings; and they are said to have sallied out to meet the foe in no disorder. The women they would fain have left behind them; but these had their own injuries to redress, and they followed in their husbands' wake carrying bags of stones. The men, who were of various denominations, were armed with sticks, blunderbusses, anything they could snatch up at a moment's notice; and some of them were not unacquainted with fighting. Dire silence prevailed among the men, but the women shouted as they ran, and the curious army moved forward to the drone and squall of drum and pipe. The enemy was sighted on the level land of Cabbylatch; and here, while the intending combatants glared at each other, a well-known local magnate galloped his horse between them and ordered them in the name of the King to return to their homes. But for the farmers that meant further depredation at the people's hands, and the townsmen would not go back to their gloomy homes to sit down and wait for sunshine. Soon stones (the first, it is said, cast by a woman) darkened the air. The farmers got the word to charge, but their horses, with the best intentions, did not know the way. There was a stampeding in different directions, a blind rushing of one frightened steed against another; and then the townspeople, breaking any ranks they had hitherto managed to keep, rushed vindictively forward. The struggle at Cabbylatch itself was not of long duration; for their own horses proved the farmers' worst enemies, except in the cases where these sagacious animals took matters into their own ordering and bolted judiciously for their stables. The day was to Thrums.

Individual deeds of prowess were done that day. Of these not the least fondly remembered by her descendants were those of the gallant matron who pursued the most obnoxious farmer in the district even to his very porch with heavy stones and opprobrious epithets. Once when he thought he had left her far behind did he alight to draw breath and take a pinch of snuff, and she was upon him like a flail. With a terror-stricken cry he leapt once more upon his horse and fled, but not without leaving his snuff-box in the hands of the derisive enemy. Meggy has long gone to the kirkyard, but the snuff-mull is still preserved.

Some ugly cuts were given and received, and heads as well as ribs were broken; but the townsmen's triumph was short-lived. The ringleaders were whipped through the streets of Perth, as a warning to persons thinking of taking the law into their own hands; and all the lasting consolation they got was that, some time afterwards, the chief witness against them, the parish minister, met with a mysterious death. They said it was evidently the hand of God; but some people looked suspiciously at them when they said it.

# VI

## THE OLD DOMINIE

From the new cemetery, which is the highest point in Thrums, you just fail to catch sight of the red schoolhouse that nestles between two bare trees, some five miles up the glen of Quharity. This was proved by Davit Lunan, tinsmith, whom I have heard tell the story. It was in the time when the cemetery gates were locked to keep the bodies of suicides out, but men who cared to risk the consequences could get the coffin over the high dyke and bury it themselves. Peter Lundy's coffin broke, as one might say, into the churchyard in this way, Peter having hanged himself in the Whunny wood when he saw that work he must. The general feeling among the intimates of the deceased was expressed by Davit when he said:

"It may do the crittur nae guid i' the tail o' the day, but he paid for 's bit o' ground, an he's in 's richt to occupy it."

The custom was to push the coffin on to the wall up a plank, and then let it drop less carefully into the cemetery. Some of the mourners were dragging the plank over the wall, with Davit Lunan on the top directing them, when they seem to have let go and sent the tinsmith suddenly into the air. A week afterwards it struck Davit, when in the act of soldering a hole in Leeby Wheens's flagon (here he branched off to explain that he had made the flagon years before, and that Leeby was sister to Tammas Wheens, and married one Baker Robbie, who died of chicken-pox in his forty-fourth year), that when "up there" he had a view of Quharity schoolhouse. Davit was as truthful as a man who tells the same story more than once can be expected to be, and it is far from a suspicious circumstance that he did not remember seeing the schoolhouse all at once. In Thrums things only struck them gradually. The new cemetery, for instance, was only so called because it had been new once.

In this red stone school, full of the modern improvements that he detested, the old dominie whom I succeeded taught, and sometimes slept, during the last five years of his cantankerous life. It was in a little thatched school, consisting of but one room, that he did his best work, some five hundred yards away from the edifice that was reared in its stead. Now dismally fallen into disrepute, often indeed a domicile for cattle, the ragged academy of Glen Quharity, where he held despotic sway for nearly half a century, is falling to pieces slowly in a howe that conceals it from the high road. Even in its best scholastic days, when it sent barefooted lads to college who helped to hasten the Disruption, it was but a pile of ungainly stones, such as Scott's Black Dwarf flung together in a night, with holes in its broken roof of thatch where the rain trickled through, and never with less than two of its knotted little window-panes stopped with brown paper. The twelve or twenty pupils of both sexes who constituted the attendance sat at the two loose desks, which never fell unless you leaned on them, with an eye on the corner of the earthen floor where the worms came out, and on cold days they liked the wind to turn the peat smoke into the room. One boy, who was supposed to wash it out, got his education free for keeping the schoolhouse dirty, and the others paid their way with peats, which they brought in their hands, just as wealthier school-children carry books, and with pence which the dominie collected regularly every Monday morning. The attendance on Monday mornings was often small.

Once a year the dominie added to his income by holding cockfights in the old school. This was at Yule, and the same practice held in the parish school of Thrums. It must have been a strange sight. Every male scholar was expected to bring a cock to the school, and to pay a shilling to the dominie for the privilege of seeing it killed there. The dominie was the master of the sports, assisted by the neighbouring farmers, some of whom might be elders of the church. Three rounds were fought. By the end of the first round all the cocks had fought, and the victors were then pitted against each other. The cocks that survived the second round were eligible for the third, and the dominie, besides his shilling, got every cock killed. Sometimes, if all stories be true, the spectators were fighting with each other before the third round concluded.

The glen was but sparsely dotted with houses even in those days; a number of them inhabited by farmer-weavers, who combined two trades and just managed to live. One would have a plough, another a horse, and so in Glen Quharity they helped each other. Without a loom in addition many of them would have starved, and on Saturdays the big farmer and his wife, driving home in a gig, would pass the little farmer carrying or wheeling his wob to Thrums. When there was no longer a market for the produce of the handloom these farms had to be given up, and thus it is that the old school is not the only house in our weary glen around which gooseberry and currant bushes, once tended by careful hands, now grow wild.

In heavy spates the children were conveyed to the old school, as they are still to the new one, in carts, and between it and the dominie's white-washed dwelling-house swirled in winter a torrent of water that often carried lumps of the land along with it. This burn he had at times to ford on stilts.

Before the Education Act passed the dominie was not much troubled by the school inspector, who appeared in great splendour every year at Thrums. Fifteen years ago, however, Glen Quharity resolved itself into a School Board, and marched down the glen, with the minister at its head, to condemn the school. When the dominie, who had heard of their design, saw the Board approaching, he sent one of his scholars, who enjoyed making a mess of himself, wading across the burn to bring over the stilts which were lying on the other side. The Board were thus unable to send across a spokesman, and after they had harangued the dominie, who was in the best of tempers, from the wrong side of the stream, the siege was raised by their returning home, this time with the minister in the rear. So far as is known this was the only occasion on which the dominie ever lifted his hat to the minister. He was the Established Church minister at the top of the glen, but the dominie was an Auld Licht, and trudged into Thrums to church nearly every Sunday with his daughter.

The farm of Little Tilly lay so close to the dominie's house that from one window he could see through a telescope whether the farmer was going to church, owing to Little Tilly's habit of never shaving except with that intention, and of always doing it at a looking-glass which he hung on a nail in his door. The farmer was Established Church, and when the dominie saw him in his shirt-sleeves with a razor in his hand, he called for his black clothes. If he did not see him it is undeniable that the dominie sent his daughter to Thrums, but remained at home himself. Possibly, therefore, the dominie sometimes went to church, because he did not want to give Little Tilly and the Established minister the satisfaction of knowing that he was not devout to-day, and it is even conceivable that had Little Tilly had a telescope and an intellect as well as his neighbour, he would have spied on the dominie in return. He sent the teacher a load of potatoes every year, and the recipient rated him soundly if they did not turn out as well as the ones he had got the autumn before. Little Tilly was rather in awe of the dominie, and had an idea that he was a Freethinker, because he played the fiddle and wore a black cap.

The dominie was a wizened-looking little man, with sharp eyes that pierced you when they thought they were unobserved, and if any visitor drew near who might be a member of the Board, he disappeared into his house much as a startled weasel makes for its hole. The most striking thing about him was his walk, which to the casual observer seemed a limp. The glen in our part is marshy, and to progress along it you have to jump from one little island of grass or heather to another. Perhaps it was this that made the dominie take the main road and even the streets of Thrums in leaps, as if there were boulders or puddles in the way. It is, however, currently believed among those who knew him best that he jerked himself along in that way when he applied for the vacancy in Glen Quharity school, and that he was therefore chosen from among the candidates by the committee of farmers, who saw that he was specially constructed for the district.

In the spring the inspector was sent to report on the school, and, of course, he said, with a wave of his hand, that this would never do. So a new school was built, and the ramshackle little academy that had done good service in its day was closed for the last time. For years it had been without a lock; ever since a blatter of wind and rain drove the door against the fireplace. After that it was the dominie's custom, on seeing the room cleared, to send in a smart boy—a dux was always chosen—who wedged a clod of earth or peat between doorpost and door. Thus the school was locked up for the night. The boy came out by the window, where he entered to open the door next morning. In time grass hid the little path from view that led to the old school, and a dozen years ago every particle of wood about the building, including the door and the framework of the windows, had been burned by travelling tinkers.

The Board would have liked to leave the dominie in his white-washed dwelling-house to enjoy his old age comfortably, and until he learned that he had intended to retire. Then he changed his tactics and removed his beard. Instead of railing at the new school, he began to approve of it, and it soon came to the ears of the horrified Established minister, who had a man (Established) in his eye for the appointment, that the dominie was looking ten years younger. As he spurned a pension he had to get the place, and then began a warfare of bickerings between the Board and him that lasted until within a few weeks of his death. In his scholastic barn the dominie had thumped the Latin grammar into his scholars till they became university bursars to escape him. In the new school, with maps (which he hid in the hen-house) and every other modern appliance for making teaching easy, he was the scandal of the glen. He snapped at the clerk of the Board's throat, and barred his door in the minister's face. It was one of his favourite relaxations to peregrinate the district, telling the farmers who were not on the Board themselves, but were given to gossiping with those who were, that though he could slumber pleasantly in the school so long as the hum of the standards was kept up, he immediately woke if it ceased.

Having settled himself in his new quarters, the dominie seems to have read over the code, and come at once to the conclusion that it would be idle to think of straightforwardly fulfilling its requirements. The inspector he regarded as a natural enemy, who was to be circumvented by much guile.

One year that admirable Oxford don arrived at the school, to find that all the children, except two girls—one of whom had her face tied up with red flannel—were away for the harvest. On another occasion the dominie met the inspector's trap some distance from the school, and explained that he would guide him by a short cut, leaving the driver to take the dog-cart to a farm where it could be put up. The unsuspecting inspector agreed, and they set off, the obsequious dominie carrying his bag. He led his victim into another glen, the hills round which had hidden their heads in mist, and then slyly remarked that he was afraid they had lost their way. The minister, who liked to attend the examination, reproved the dominie for providing no luncheon, but turned pale when his enemy suggested that he should examine the boys in Latin.

For some reason that I could never discover, the dominie had all his life refused to teach his scholars geography. The inspector and many others asked him why there was no geography class, and his invariable answer was to point to his pupils collectively, and reply in an impressive whisper—

"They winna hae her."

This story, too, seems to reflect against the dominie's views on cleanliness. One examination day the minister attended to open the inspection with prayer. Just as he was finishing, a scholar entered who had a reputation for dirt.

"Michty!" cried a little pupil, as his opening eyes fell on the apparition at the door; "there's Jocky Tamson wi' his face washed!"

When the dominie was a younger man he had first clashed with the minister during Mr. Rattray's attempts to do away with some old customs that were already dying by inches. One was the selection of a queen of beauty from among the young women at the annual Thrums fair. The judges, who were selected from the better known farmers as a rule, sat at the door of a tent that reeked of whisky, and regarded the competitors filing by much as they selected prize sheep, with a stolid stare. There was much giggling and blushing on these occasions among the maidens, and shouts from their relatives and friends to "Haud yer head up, Jean," and "Lat them see yer een, Jess." The dominie enjoyed this, and was one time chosen a judge, when he insisted on the prize's being bestowed on his own daughter, Marget. The other judges demurred, but the dominie remained firm and won the day.

"She wasna the best-faured amon them," he admitted afterwards, "but a man maun mak the maist o' his ain."

The dominie, too, would not shake his head with Mr. Rattray over the apple and loaf bread raffles in the smithy, nor even at the Daft Days, the black week of glum debauch that ushered in the year, a period when the whole countryside rumbled to the farmers "kebec" laden cart.

For the great part of his career the dominie had not made forty pounds a year, but he "died worth" about three hundred pounds. The moral of his life came in just as he was leaving it, for he rose from his deathbed to hide a whisky bottle from his wife.

# VII

## CREE QUEERY AND MYSY DROLLY

THE children used to fling stones at Grinder Queery because he loved his mother. I never heard the Grinder's real name. He and his mother were Queery and Drolly, contemptuously so called, and they answered to these names. I remember Cree best as a battered old weaver, who bent forward as he walked, with his arms hanging limp as if ready to grasp the shafts of the barrow behind which it was his life to totter uphill and downhill, a rope of yarn suspended round his shaking neck, and fastened to the shafts, assisting him to bear the yoke and slowly strangling him. By and by there came a time when the barrow and the weaver seemed both palsy-stricken, and Cree, gasping for breath, would stop in the middle of a brae, unable to push his load over a stone. Then he laid himself down behind it to prevent the barrow's slipping back. On those occasions only the barefooted boys who jeered at the panting weaver could put new strength into his shrivelled arms. They did it by telling him that he and Mysy would have to go to the "poorshouse" after all, at which the grey old man would wince, as if "joukin" from a blow, and, shuddering, rise and, with a desperate effort, gain the top of the incline. Small blame perhaps attached to Cree if, as he neared his grave, he grew a little dottle. His loads of yarn frequently took him past the workhouse, and his eyelids quivered as he drew near. Boys used to gather round the gate in anticipation of his coming, and make a feint of driving him inside. Cree, when he observed them, sat down on his barrow-shafts terrified to approach, and I see them now pointing to the workhouse till he left his barrow on the road and hobbled away, his legs cracking as he ran.

It is strange to know that there was once a time when Cree was young and straight, a callant who wore a flower in his buttonhole, and tried to be a hero for a maiden's sake.

Before Cree settled down as a weaver, he was knife and scissor-grinder for three counties, and Mysy, his mother, accompanied him wherever he went. Mysy trudged alongside him till her eyes grew dim and her limbs failed her, and then Cree was told that she must be sent to the pauper's home. After that a pitiable and beautiful sight was to be seen. Grinder Queery, already a feeble man, would wheel his grindstone along the long high road, leaving Mysy behind. He took the stone on a few hundred yards, and then, hiding it by the roadside in a ditch or behind a paling, returned for his mother. Her he led—sometimes he almost carried her—to the place where the grindstone lay, and thus by double journeys kept her with him. Every one said that Mysy's death would be a merciful release—every one but Cree.

Cree had been a grinder from his youth, having learned the trade from his father, but he gave it up when Mysy became almost blind. For a time he had to leave her in Thrums with Dan'l Wilkie's wife, and find employment himself in Tilliedrum. Mysy got me to write several letters for her to Cree, and she cried while telling me what to say. I never heard either of them use a term of endearment to the other, but all Mysy could tell me to put in writing was—"Oh, my son Cree; oh, my beloved son; oh, I have no one but you; oh, thou God watch over my Cree!" On one of these occasions Mysy put into my hands a paper, which, she said, would perhaps help me to write the letter. It had been drawn up by Cree many years before, when he and his mother had been compelled to part for a time, and I saw from it that he had been trying to teach Mysy to write. The paper consisted of phrases such as "Dear son Cree," "Loving mother," "I am takin' my food weel," "Yesterday," "Blankets," "The peats is near done," "Mr. Dishart," "Come home, Cree." The Grinder had left this paper with his mother, and she had written letters to him from it.

When Dan'l Wilkie objected to keeping a cranky old body like Mysy in his house Cree came back to Thrums and took a single room with a hand-loom in it. The flooring was only lumpy earth, with sacks spread over it to protect Mysy's feet. The room contained two dilapidated old coffin-beds, a dresser, a high-backed arm-chair, several three-legged stools, and two tables, of which one could be packed away beneath the other. In one corner stood the wheel at which Cree had to fill his own pirns. There was a plate-rack on one wall, and near the chimney-piece hung the wag-at-the-wall clock, the timepiece that was commonest in Thrums at that time, and that got this name because its exposed pendulum swung along the wall. The two windows in the room faced each other on opposite walls, and were so small that even a child might have stuck in trying to crawl through them. They opened on hinges, like a door. In the wall of the dark passage leading from the outer door into the room was a recess where a pan and pitcher of water always stood wedded, as it were, and a little hole, known as the "bole," in the wall opposite the fireplace contained Cree's library. It consisted of Baxter's *Saints' Rest*, Harvey's *Meditations*, the *Pilgrim's Progress*, a work on folk-lore, and several Bibles. The saut-backet, or salt- bucket, stood at the end of the fender, which was half of an old cart-wheel. Here Cree worked, whistling "Ower the watter for Chairlie" to make Mysy think that he was as gay as a mavis. Mysy grew querulous in her old age, and up to the end she thought of poor, done Cree as a handsome gallant. Only by weaving far on into the night could Cree earn as much as six shillings a week. He began at six o'clock in the morning, and worked until midnight by the light of his cruizey. The cruizey was all the lamp Thrums had in those days, though it is only to be seen in use now in a few old-world houses in the glens. It is an ungainly thing in iron, the size of a man's palm, and shaped not unlike the palm when contracted, and deepened to hold a liquid. Whale-oil, lying open in the mould, was used, and the wick was a rash with the green skin peeled off. These rashes were sold by herd-boys at a halfpenny the bundle, but Cree gathered his own wicks. The rashes skin readily when you know how to do it. The iron mould was placed inside another of the same shape, but slightly larger, for in time the oil dripped through the iron, and the whole was then hung by a cleek or hook close to the person using it. Even with three wicks it gave but a stime of light, and never allowed the weaver to see more than the half of his loom at a time. Sometimes Cree used threads for wicks. He was too dull a man to have many visitors, but Mr. Dishart called occasionally and reproved him for telling his mother lies. The lies Cree told Mysy were that he was sharing the meals he won for her, and that he wore the overcoat which he had exchanged years before for a blanket to keep her warm.

There was a terrible want of spirit about Grinder Queery. Boys used to climb on to his stone roof with clods of damp earth in their hands, which they dropped down the chimney. Mysy was bed-ridden by this time, and the smoke threatened to choke her; so Cree, instead of chasing his persecutors, bargained with them. He gave them fly-hooks which he had busked himself, and when he had nothing left to give he tried to flatter them into dealing gently with Mysy by talking to them as men. One night it went through the town that Mysy now lay in bed all day listening for her summons to depart. According to her ideas this would come in the form of a tapping at the window, and their intention was to forestall the spirit. Dite Gow's boy, who is now a grown man, was hoisted up to one of the little windows, and he has always thought of Mysy since as he saw her then for the last time. She lay sleeping, so far as he could see, and Cree sat by the fireside looking at her.

Every one knew that there was seldom a fire in that house unless Mysy was cold. Cree seemed to think that the fire was getting low. In the little closet, which, with the kitchen, made up his house, was a corner shut off from the rest of the room by a few boards, and behind this he kept his peats. There was a similar receptacle for potatoes in the kitchen. Cree wanted to get another peat for the fire without disturbing Mysy. First he took off his boots, and made for the peats on tip-toe. His shadow was cast on the bed, however, so he next got down on his knees and crawled softly into the closet. With the peat in his hands, he returned in the same way, glancing every moment at the bed where Mysy lay. Though Tammy Gow's face was pressed against a broken window he did not hear Cree putting that peat on the fire. Some say that Mysy heard, but pretended not to do so for her son's sake, that she realised the deception he played on her, and had not the heart to undeceive him. But it would be too sad to believe that. The boys left Cree alone that night.

The old weaver lived on alone in that solitary house after Mysy left him, and by and by the story went abroad that he was saving money. At first no one believed this except the man who told it, but there seemed after all to be something in it. You had only to hit Cree's trouser pocket to hear the money chinking, for he was afraid to let it out of his clutch. Those who sat on dykes with him when his day's labour was over said that the weaver kept his hand all the time in his pocket, and that they saw his lips move as he counted his hoard by letting it slip through his fingers. So there were boys who called "Miser Query" after him instead of Grinder, and asked him whether he was saving up to keep himself from the workhouse.

But we had all done Cree wrong. It came out on his deathbed what he had been storing up his money for. Grinder, according to the doctor, died of getting a good meal from a friend of his earlier days after being accustomed to starve on potatoes and a very little oatmeal indeed. The day before he died this friend sent him half a sovereign, and when Grinder saw it he sat up excitedly in his bed and pulled his corduroys from beneath his pillow. The woman who, out of kindness, attended him in his last illness, looked on curiously, while Cree added the sixpences and coppers in his pocket to the half-sovereign. After all they only made some two pounds, but a look of peace came into Cree's eyes as he told the woman to take it all to a shop in the town. Nearly twelve years previously Jamie Lownie had lent him two pounds, and though the money was never asked for, it preyed on Cree's mind that he was in debt. He paid off all he owed, and so Cree's life was not, I think, a failure.

# VIII

## THE COURTING OF T'NOWHEAD'S BELL

FOR two years it had been notorious in the square that Sam'l Dickie was thinking of courting T'nowhead's Bell, and that if little Sanders Elshioner (which is the Thrums pronunciation of Alexander Alexander) went in for her he might prove a formidable rival. Sam'l was a weaver in the Tenements, and Sanders a coal-carter whose trade mark was a bell on his horse's neck that told when coals were coming. Being something of a public man, Sanders had not perhaps so high a social position as Sam'l, but he had succeeded his father on the coal-cart, while the weaver had already tried several trades. It had always been against Sam'l, too, that once when the kirk was vacant he had advised the selection of the third minister who preached for it on the ground that it came expensive to pay a large number of candidates. The scandal of the thing was hushed up, out of respect for his father, who was a God-fearing man, but Sam'l was known by it in Lang Tammas's circle. The coal-carter was called Little Sanders to distinguish him from his father, who was not much more than half his size. He had grown up with the name, and its inapplicability now came home to nobody. Sam'l's mother had been more far-seeing than Sanders's. Her man had been called Sammy all his life because it was the name he got as a boy, so when their eldest son was born she spoke of him as Sam'l while still in his cradle. The neighbours imitated her, and thus the young man had a better start in life than had been granted to Sammy, his father.

It was Saturday evening—the night in the week when Auld Licht young men fell in love. Sam'l Dickie, wearing a blue glengarry bonnet with a red ball on the top, came to the door of a one-storey house in the Tenements and stood there wriggling, for he was in a suit of tweed for the first time that week, and did not feel at one with them. When his feeling of being a stranger to himself wore off he looked up and down the road, which straggles between houses and gardens, and then, picking his way over the puddles, crossed to his father's hen-house and sat down on it. He was now on his way to the square.

Eppie Fargus was sitting on an adjoining dyke knitting stockings, and Sam'l looked at her for a time.

"Is't yersel', Eppie?" he said at last.

"It's a' that," said Eppie.

"Hoo's a' wi' ye?" asked Sam'l.

"We're juist aff an' on," replied Eppie, cautiously.

There was not much more to say, but as Sam'l sidled off the henhouse he murmured politely, "Ay, ay." In another minute he would have been fairly started, but Eppie resumed the conversation.

"Sam'l,", she said, with a twinkle in her eye, "ye can tell Lisbeth Fargus I'll likely be drappin' in on her aboot Mununday or Teisday."

Lisbeth was sister to Eppie, and wife of Tammas McQuhatty, better known as T'nowhead, which was the name of his farm. She was thus Bell's mistress.

Sam'l leant against the henhouse as if all his desire to depart had gone.

"Hoo d' ye kin I'll be at the T'nowhead the nicht?" he asked, grinning in anticipation.

"Ou, I'se warrant ye'll be after Bell," said Eppie.

"A'm no sae sure o' that," said Sam'l, trying to leer. He was enjoying himself now.

"A'm no sure o' that," he repeated, for Eppie seemed lost in stitches.

"Sam'l?"

"Ay."

"Ye'll be speirin' her sune noo, I dinna doot?"

This took Sam'l, who had only been courting Bell for a year or two, a little aback.

"Hoo d' ye mean, Eppie?" he asked.

"Maybe ye'll do 't the nicht."

"Na, there's nae hurry," said Sam'l.

"Weel, we're a' coontin' on't, Sam'l."

"Gae wa wi' ye."

"What for no?"

"Gae wa wi' ye," said Sam'l again.

"Bell's gei an' fond o' ye, Sam'l."

"Ay," said Sam'l.

"But a'm dootin' ye're a fell billy wi' the lasses."

"Ay, oh, I d'na kin, moderate, moderate," said Sam'l, in high delight.

"I saw ye," said Eppie, speaking with a wire in her mouth, "gae'in on terr'ble wi' Mysy Haggart at the pump last Saturday."

"We was juist amoosin' oorsels," said Sam'l.

"It'll be nae amoosement to Mysy," said Eppie, "gin ye brak her heart."

"Losh, Eppie," said Sam'l, "I didna think o' that."

"Ye maun kin weel, Sam'l, 'at there's mony a lass wid jump at ye."

"Ou, weel," said Sam'l, implying that a man must take these things as they come.

"For ye're a dainty chield to look at, Sam'l."

"Do ye think so, Eppie? Ay, ay; oh, I d'na kin a'm onything by the ordinar."

"Ye mayna be," said Eppie, "but lasses doesna do to be ower partikler."

Sam'l resented this, and prepared to depart again.

"Ye'll no tell Bell that?" he asked, anxiously.

"Tell her what?"

"Aboot me an Mysy."

"We'll see hoo ye behave yersel, Sam'l."

"No 'at I care, Eppie; ye can tell her gin ye like. I widna think twice o' tellin her mysel."

"The Lord forgie ye for leein', Sam'l," said Eppie, as he disappeared down Tammy Tosh's close. Here he came upon Henders Webster.

"Ye're late, Sam'l," said Henders.

"What for?"

"Ou, I was thinkin' ye wid be gaen the length o' T'nowhead the nicht, an' I saw Sanders Elshioner makkin's wy there an oor syne."

"Did ye?" cried Sam'l, adding craftily, "but it's naething to me."

"Tod, lad," said Henders, "gin ye dinna buckle to, Sanders'll be carryin' her off."

Sam'l flung back his head and passed on.

" Sam'l!" cried Henders after him.

"Ay," said Sam'l, wheeling round.

"Gie Bell a kiss frae me."

The full force of this joke struck neither all at once. Sam'l began to smile at it as he turned down the school-wynd, and it came upon Henders while he was in his garden feeding his ferret. Then he slapped his legs gleefully, and explained the conceit to Will'um Byars, who went into the house and thought it over.

There were twelve or twenty little groups of men in the square, which was lit by a flare of oil suspended over a cadger's cart. Now and again a staid young woman passed through the square with a basket on her arm, and if she had lingered long enough to give them time, some of the idlers would have addressed her. As it was, they gazed after her, and then grinned to each other.

"Ay, Sam'l," said two or three young men, as Sam'l joined them beneath the town clock.

"Ay, Davit," replied Sam'l.

This group was composed of some of the sharpest wits in Thrums, and it was not to be expected that they would let this opportunity pass. Perhaps when Sam'l joined them he knew what was in store for him.

"Was ye lookin' for T'nowhead's Bell, Sam'l?" asked one.

"Or mebbe ye was wantin' the minister?" suggested another, the same who had walked out twice with Chirsty Duff and not married her after all.

Sam'l could not think of a good reply at the moment, so he laughed good-naturedly.

"Ondoobtedly she's a snod bit crittur," said Davit, archly.

"An' michty clever wi' her fingers," added Jamie Deuchars.

"Man, I've thocht o' makkin' up to Bell mysel," said Pete Ogle. "Wid there be ony chance, think ye, Sam'l?"

"I'm thinkin' she widna hae ye for her first, Pete," replied Sam'l, in one of those happy flashes that come to some men, "but there's nae sayin' but what she micht tak ye to finish up wi'."

The unexpectedness of this sally startled every one. Though Sam'l did not set up for a wit, however, like Davit, it was notorious that he could say a cutting thing once in a way.

"Did ye ever see Bell reddin up?" asked Pete, recovering from his overthrow. He was a man who bore no malice.

"It's a sicht," said Sam'l, solemnly.

"Hoo will that be?" asked Jamie Deuchars.

"It's weel worth yer while," said Pete, "to ging atower to the T'nowhead an' see. Ye'll mind the closed-in beds i' the kitchen? Ay, weel, they're a fell spoilt crew, T'nowhead's litlins, an' no that aisy to manage. Th'ither lasses Lisbeth's hae'n had a michty trouble wi' them. When they war i' the middle of their reddin up the bairns wid come tumlin' about the floor, but, sal, I assure ye, Bell didna fash lang wi' them. Did she, Sam'l?"

"She did not," said Sam'l, dropping into a fine mode of speech to add emphasis to his remark.

"I'll tell ye what she did," said Pete to the others. "She juist lifted up the litlins, twa at a time, an' flung them into the coffin-beds. Syne she snibbit the doors on them, an' keepit them there till the floor was dry."

"Ay, man, did she so?" said Davit, admiringly.

"I've seen her do't mysel," said Sam'l.

"There's no a lassie maks better bannocks this side o' Fetter Lums," continued Pete.

"Her mither tocht her that," said Sam'l; "she was a gran' han' at the bakin', Kitty Ogilvy."

"I've heard say," remarked Jamie, putting it this way so as not to tie himself down to anything, "'at Bell's scones is equal to Mag Lunan's."

"So they are," said Sam'l, almost fiercely.

"I kin she's a neat han' at singein' a hen," said Pete.

"An' wi 't a'," said Davit, "she's a snod, canty bit stocky in her Sabbath claes."

"If onything, thick in the waist," suggested Jamie.

"I dinna see that," said Sam'l.

"I d'na care for her hair either," continued Jamie, who was very nice in his tastes; "something mair yallowchy wid be an improvement."

"A'body kins," growled Sam'l, "'at black hair's the bonniest."

The others chuckled.

"Puir Sam'l!" Pete said.

Sam'l not being certain whether this should be received with a smile or a frown, opened his mouth wide as a kind of compromise. This was position one with him for thinking things over.

Few Auld Lichts, as I have said, went the length of choosing a helpmate for themselves. One day a young man's friends would see him mending the washing tub of a maiden's mother. They kept the joke until Saturday night, and then he learned from them what he had been after. It dazed him for a time, but in a year or so he grew accustomed to the idea, and they were then married. With a little help he fell in love just like other people.

Sam'l was going the way of the others, but he found it difficult to come to the point. He only went courting once a week, and he could never take up the running at the place where he left off the Saturday before. Thus he had not, so far, made great headway. His method of making up to Bell had been to drop in at T'nowhead on Saturday nights and talk with the farmer about the rinderpest.

The farm kitchen was Bell's testimonial. Its chairs, tables, and stools were scoured by her to the whiteness of Rob Angus's sawmill boards, and the muslin blind on the window was starched like a child's pinafore. Bell was brave, too, as well as energetic. Once Thrums had been overrun with thieves. It is now thought that there may have been only one, but he had the wicked cleverness of a gang. Such was his repute that there were weavers who spoke of locking their doors when they went from home. He was not very skilful, however, being generally caught, and when they said they knew he was a robber he gave them their things back and went away. If they had given him time there is no doubt that he would have gone off with his plunder. One night he went to T'nowhead, and Bell, who slept in the kitchen, was wakened by the noise. She knew who it would be, so she rose and dressed herself, and went to look for him with a candle. The thief had not known what to do when he got in, and as it was very lonely he was glad to see Bell. She told him he ought to be ashamed of himself, and would not let him out by the door until he had taken off his boots so as not to soil the carpet.

On this Saturday evening Sam'l stood his ground in the square, until by and by he found himself alone. There were other groups there still, but his circle had melted away. They went separately, and no one said good-night. Each took himself off slowly, backing out of the group until he was fairly started.

Sam'l looked about him, and then, seeing that the others had gone, walked round the town-house into the darkness of the brae that leads down and then up to the farm of T'nowhead.

To get into the good graces of Lisbeth Fargus you had to know her ways and humour them. Sam'l, who was a student of women, knew this, and so, instead of pushing the door open and walking in, he went through the rather ridiculous ceremony of knocking. Sanders Elshioner was also aware of this weakness of Lisbeth's, but, though he often made up his mind to knock, the absurdity of the thing prevented his doing so when he reached the door. T'nowhead himself had never got used to his wife's refined notions, and when any one knocked he always started to his feet, thinking there must be something wrong.

Lisbeth came to the door, her expansive figure blocking the way in.

"Sam'l," she said.

"Lisbeth," said Sam'l.

He shook hands with the farmer's wife, knowing that she liked it, but only said, "Ay, Bell," to his sweetheart, "Ay, T'nowhead," to McQuhatty, and "It's yersel, Sanders," to his rival.

They were all sitting round the fire, T'nowhead, with his feet on the ribs, wondering why he felt so warm, and Bell darned a stocking, while Lisbeth kept an eye on a goblet full of potatoes.

"Sit into the fire, Sam'l," said the farmer, not, however, making way for him.

"Na, na," said Sam'l, "I'm to bide nae time." Then he sat into the fire. His face was turned away from Bell, and when she spoke he answered her without looking round. Sam'l felt a little anxious. Sanders Elshioner, who had one leg shorter than the other, but looked well when sitting, seemed suspiciously at home. He asked Bell questions out of his own head, which was beyond Sam'l, and once he said something to her in such a low voice that the others could not catch it. T'nowhead asked curiously what it was, and Sanders explained that he had only said, "Ay, Bell, the morn's the Sabbath." There was nothing startling in this, but Sam'l did not like it. He began to wonder if he was too late, and had he seen his opportunity would have told Bell of a nasty rumour that Sanders intended to go over to the Free Church if they would make him kirk-officer.

Sam'l had the good-will of T'nowhead's wife, who liked a polite man. Sanders did his best, but from want of practice he constantly made mistakes. To-night, for instance, he wore his hat in the house because he did not like to put up his hand and take it off. T'nowhead had not taken his off either, but that was because he meant to go out by and by and lock the byre door. It was impossible to say which of her lovers Bell preferred. The proper course with an Auld Licht lassie was to prefer the man who proposed to her.

"Ye'll bide a wee, an' hae something to eat?" Lisbeth asked Sam'l, with her eyes on the goblet.

"No, I thank ye" said Sam'l, with true genteelity.

"Ye'll better?"

"I dinna think it."

"Hoots aye; What's to hender ye?"

"Weel, since ye're sae pressin' I'll bide."

No one asked Sanders to stay. Bell could not, for she was but the servant, and T'nowhead knew that the kick his wife had given him meant that he was not to do so either. Sanders whistled to show that he was not uncomfortable.

"Ay, then, I'll be stappin' ower the brae," he said at last.

He did not go, however. There was sufficient pride in him to get him off his chair, but only slowly, for he had to get accustomed to the notion of going. At intervals of two or three minutes he remarked that he must now be going. In the same circumstances Sam'l would have acted similarly. For a Thrums man it is one of the hardest things in life to get away from anywhere.

At last Lisbeth saw that something must be done. The potatoes were burning, and T'nowhead had an invitation on his tongue.

"Yes, I'll hae to be movin'," said Sanders, hopelessly, for the fifth time.

"Guid nicht to ye, then, Sanders," said Lisbeth. "Gie the door a fling-to, ahent ye."

Sanders, with a mighty effort, pulled himself together. He looked boldly at Bell, and then took off his hat carefully. Sam'l saw with misgivings that there was something in it which was not a handkerchief. It was a paper bag glittering with gold braid, and contained such an assortment of sweets as lads bought for their lasses on the Muckle Friday.

"Hae, Bell," said Sanders, handing the bag to Bell in an off-hand way as if it were but a trifle. Nevertheless he was a little excited, for he went off without saying good-night.

No one spoke. Bell's face was crimson. T'nowhead fidgeted on his chair, and Lisbeth looked at Sam'l. The weaver was strangely calm and collected, though he would have liked to know whether this was a proposal.

"Sit in by to the table, Sam'l," said Lisbeth, trying to look as if things were as they had been before.

She put a saucerful of butter, salt, and pepper near the fire to melt, for melted butter is the shoeing-horn that helps over a meal of potatoes. Sam'l, however, saw what the hour required, and jumping up, he seized his bonnet.

"Hing the tatties higher up the joist, Lisbeth," he said with dignity; "I'se be back in ten meenits."

He hurried out of the house, leaving the others looking at each other.

"What do ye think?" asked Lisbeth.

"I d'na kin," faltered Bell.

"Thae tatties is lang o' comin' to the boil," said T'nowhead.

In some circles a lover who behaved like Sam'l would have been suspected of intent upon his rival's life, but neither Bell nor Lisbeth did the weaver that injustice. In a case of this kind it does not much matter what T'nowhead thought.

The ten minutes had barely passed when Sam'l was back in the farm kitchen. He was too flurried to knock this time, and, indeed, Lisbeth did not expect it of him.

"Bell, hae!" he cried, handing his sweetheart a tinsel bag twice the size of Sanders's gift.

"Losh preserve's!" exclaimed Lisbeth; "I'se warrant there's a shillin's worth."

"There's a' that, Lisbeth—an' mair," said Sam'l, firmly.

"I thank ye, Sam'l," said Bell, feeling an unwonted elation as she gazed at the two paper bags in her lap.

"Ye're ower extravegint, Sam'l," Lisbeth said.

"Not at all," said Sam'l; "not at all. But I widna advise ye to eat thae ither anes, Bell—they're second quality."

Bell drew back a step from Sam'l.

"How do ye kin?" asked the farmer shortly, for he liked Sanders.

"I spiered i' the shop," said Sam'l.

The goblet was placed on a broken plate on the table with the saucer beside it, and Sam'l, like the others, helped himself. What he did was to take potatoes from the pot with his fingers, peel off their coats, and then dip them into the butter. Lisbeth would have liked to provide knives and forks, but she knew that beyond a certain point T'nowhead was master in his own house. As for Sam'l, he felt victory in his hands, and began to think that he had gone too far.

In the meantime Sanders, little witting that Sam'l had trumped his trick, was sauntering along the kirk-wynd with his hat on the side of his head. Fortunately he did not meet the minister.

The courting of T'nowhead's Bell reached its crisis one Sabbath about a month after the events above recorded. The minister was in great force that day, but it is no part of mine to tell how he bore himself. I was there, and am not likely to forget the scene. It was a fateful Sabbath for T'nowhead's Bell and her swains, and destined to be remembered for the painful scandal which they perpetrated in their passion.

Bell was not in the kirk. There being an infant of six months in the house it was a question of either Lisbeth or the lassie's staying at home with him, and though Lisbeth was unselfish in a general way, she could not resist the delight of going to church. She had nine children besides the baby, and being but a woman, it was the pride of her life to march them into the T'nowhead pew, so well watched that they dared not misbehave, and so tightly packed that they could not fall. The congregation looked at that pew, the mothers enviously, when they sang the lines—

"Jerusalem like a city is
Compactly built together."

The first half of the service had been gone through on this particular Sunday without anything remarkable happening. It was at the end of the psalm which preceded the sermon that Sanders Elshioner, who sat near the door, lowered his head until it was no higher than the pews, and in that attitude, looking almost like a four-footed animal, slipped out of the church. In their eagerness to be at the sermon many of the congregation did not notice him, and those who did put the matter by in their minds for future investigation. Sam'l, however, could not take it so coolly. From his seat in the gallery he saw Sanders disappear, and his mind misgave him. With the true lover's instinct he understood it all. Sanders had been struck by the fine turn-out in the T'nowhead pew. Bell was alone at the farm. What an opportunity to work one's way up to a proposal. T'nowhead was so overrun with children that such a chance seldom occurred, except on a Sabbath. Sanders, doubtless, was off to propose, and he, Sam'l, was left behind.

The suspense was terrible. Sam'l and Sanders had both known all along that Bell would take the first of the two who asked her. Even those who thought her proud admitted that she was modest. Bitterly the weaver repented having waited so long. Now it was too late. In ten minutes Sanders would be at T'nowhead; in an hour all would be over. Sam'l rose to his feet in a daze. His mother pulled him down by the coat-tail, and his father shook him, thinking he was walking in his sleep. He tottered past them, however, hurried up the aisle, which was so narrow that Dan'l Ross could only reach his seat by walking sideways, and was gone before the minister could do more than stop in the middle of a whirl and gape in horror after him.

A number of the congregation felt that day the advantage of sitting in the laft. What was a mystery to those downstairs was revealed to them. From the gallery windows they had a fine open view to the south; and as Sam'l took the common, which was a short cut though a steep ascent, to T'nowhead, he was never out of their line of vision. Sanders was not to be seen, but they guessed rightly the reason why. Thinking he had ample time, he had gone round by the main road to save his boots—perhaps a little scared by what was coming. Sam'l's design was to forestall him by taking the shorter path over the burn and up the commonty.

It was a race for a wife, and several on lookers in the gallery braved the minister's displeasure to see who won. Those who favoured Sam'l's suit exultingly saw him leap the stream, while the friends of Sanders fixed their eyes on the top of the common where it ran into the road. Sanders must come into sight there, and the one who reached this point first would get Bell.

As Auld Lichts do not walk abroad on the Sabbath, Sanders would probably not be delayed. The chances were in his favour. Had it been any other day in the week Sam'l might have run. So some of the congregation in the gallery were thinking, when suddenly they saw him bend low and then take to his heels. He had caught sight of Sanders's head bobbing over the hedge that separated the road from the common, and feared that Sanders might see him. The congregation who could crane their necks sufficiently saw a black object, which they guessed to be the carter's hat, crawling along the hedge-top. For a moment it was motionless, and then it shot ahead. The rivals had seen each other. It was now a hot race. Sam'l, dissembling no longer, clattered up the common, becoming smaller and smaller to the onlookers as he neared the top. More than one person in the gallery almost rose to their feet in their excitement. Sam'l had it. No,

Sanders was in front. Then the two figures disappeared from view. They seemed to run into each other at the top of the brae, and no one could say who was first. The congregation looked at one another. Some of them perspired. But the minister held on his course.

Sam'l had just been in time to cut Sanders out. It was the weaver's saving that Sanders saw this when his rival turned the corner; for Sam'l was sadly blown. Sanders took in the situation and gave in at once. The last hundred yards of the distance he covered at his leisure, and when he arrived at his destination he did not go in. It was a fine afternoon for the time of year, and he went round to have a look at the pig, about which T'nowhead was a little sinfully puffed up.

"Ay," said Sanders, digging his fingers critically into the grunting animal; "quite so."

"Grumph," said the pig, getting reluctantly to his feet.

"Ou ay; yes," said Sanders, thoughtfully.

Then he sat down on the edge of the sty, and looked long and silently at an empty bucket. But whether his thoughts were of T'nowhead's Bell, whom he had lost for ever, or of the food the farmer fed his pig on, is not known.

"Lord preserve 's! Are ye no at the kirk?" cried Bell, nearly dropping the baby as Sam'l broke into the room.

"Bell!" cried Sam'l.

Then T'nowhead's Bell knew that her hour had come.

"Sam'l," she faltered.

"Will ye hae's Bell?" demanded Sam'l, glaring at her sheepishly.

"Ay," answered Bell.

Sam'l fell into a chair.

"Bring's a drink o' water Bell," he said.

But Bell thought the occasion required milk, and there was none in the kitchen. She went out to the byre, still with the baby in her arms, and saw Sanders Elshioner sitting gloomily on the pigsty.

"Weel, Bell," said Sanders.

"I thocht ye'd been at the kirk, Sanders," said Bell.

Then there was a silence between them.

"Has Sam'l spiered ye, Bell?" asked Sanders, stolidly.

"Ay," said Bell again, and this time there was a tear in her eye. Sanders was little better than an "orra man," and Sam'l was a weaver, and yet—— But it was too late now. Sanders gave the pig a vicious poke with a stick, and when it had ceased to grunt, Bell was back in the kitchen. She had forgotten about the milk, however, and Sam'l only got water after all.

In after days, when the story of Bell's wooing was told, there were some who held that the circumstances would have almost justified the lassie in giving Sam'l the go-by. But these perhaps forgot that her other lover was in the same predicament as the accepted one—that of the two, indeed, he was the more to blame, for he set off to T'nowhead on the Sabbath of his own accord, while Sam'l only ran after him. And then there is no one to say for certain whether Bell heard of her suitors' delinquencies until Lisbeth's return from the kirk. Sam'l could never remember whether he told her, and Bell was not sure whether, if he did, she took it in. Sanders was greatly in demand for weeks after to tell what he knew of the affair, but though he was twice asked to tea to the manse among the trees, and subjected thereafter to ministerial cross-examinations, this is all he told. He remained at the pigsty until Sam'l left the farm, when he joined him at the top of the brae, and they went home together.

"It's yersel, Sanders," said Sam'l.

"It is so, Sam'l," said Sanders.

"Very cauld," said Sam'l.

"Blawy," assented Sanders.

After a pause—

"Sam'l," said Sanders.

"Ay."

"I'm hearin' yer to be mairit."

"Ay."

"Weel, Sam'l, she's a snod bit lassie."

"Thank ye," said Sam'l.

"I had ance a kin' o' notion o' Bell mysel' continued Sanders.

"Ye had?"

"Yes, Sam'l; but I thocht better o't."

"Hoo d' ye mean?" asked Sam'l, a little anxiously.

"Weel, Sam'l, mairitch is a terrible responsibeelity."

"It is so," said Sam'l, wincing.

"An' no the thing to tak up withoot conseederation."

"But it's a blessed and honourable state, Sanders; ye've heard the minister on't."

"They say," continued the relentless Sanders, "'at the minister doesna get on sair wi' the wife himsel."

"So they do," cried Sam'l, with a sinking at the heart.

"I've been telt," Sanders went on, "'at gin ye can get the upper han' o' the wife for a while at first, there's the mair chance o' a harmonious exeestence."

"Bell's no the lassie," said Sam'l, appealingly, "to thwart her man."

Sanders smiled.

"D' ye think she is, Sanders?"

"Weel, Sam'l, I d'na want to fluster ye, but she's been ower lang wi' Lisbeth Fargus no to hae learnt her ways. An a'body kins what a life T'nowhead has wi' her."

"Guid sake, Sanders, hoo did ye no speak o' this afore?"

"I thocht ye kent o't, Sam'l."

They had now reached the square, and the U.P. kirk was coming out. The Auld Licht kirk would be half an hour yet.

"But, Sanders," said Sam'l, brightening up, "ye was on yer wy to spier her yersel."

"I was, Sam'l," said Sanders, "and I canna but be thankfu' ye was ower quick for 's."

"Gin 't hadna been you,' said Sam'l, "I wid never hae thocht o't."

"I'm sayin' naething agin Bell," pursued the other, "but, man Sam'l, a body should be mair deleeberate in a thing o' the kind."

"It was michty hurried," said Sam'l, woefully.

"It's a serious thing to spier a lassie," said Sanders.

"It's an awfu' thing," said Sam'l.

"But we'll hope for the best," added Sanders, in a hopeless voice.

They were close to the Tenements now, and Sam'l looked as if he were on his way to be hanged.

"Sam'l?"

"Ay, Sanders."

"Did ye—did ye kiss her, Sam'l?"

"Na."

"Hoo?"

"There was varra little time, Sanders."

"Half an 'oor," said Sanders.

"Was there? Man Sanders, to tell ye the truth, I never thoct o't."

Then the soul of Sanders Elshioner was filled with contempt for Sam'l Dickie.

The scandal blew over. At first it was expected that the minister would interfere to prevent the union, but beyond intimating from the pulpit that the souls of Sabbath-breakers were beyond praying for, and then praying for Sam'l and Sanders at great length, with a word thrown in for Bell, he let things take their course. Some said it was because he was always frightened lest his young men should intermarry with other denominations, but Sanders explained it differently to Sam'l.

"I hav'na a word to say agin the minister," he said; "they're gran' prayers, but Sam'l, he's a mairit man himsel."

"He's a' the better for that, Sanders, isna he?"

"Do ye no see," asked Sanders, compassionately, " 'at he's tryin' to mak the best o't?"

"Oh, Sanders, man!" said Sam'l.

"Cheer up, Sam'l," said Sanders, "it'll sune be ower."

Their having been rival suitors had not interfered with their friendship. On the contrary, while they had hitherto been mere acquaintances, they became inseparables as the wedding-day drew near. It was noticed that they had much to say to each other, and that when they could not get a room to themselves they wandered about together in the churchyard. When Sam'l had anything to tell Bell he sent Sanders to tell it, and Sanders did as he was bid. There was nothing that he would not have done for Sam'l.

The more obliging Sanders was, however, the sadder Sam'l grew. He never laughed now on Saturdays, and sometimes his loom was silent half the day. Sam'l felt that Sanders's was the kindness of a friend for a dying man.

It was to be a penny wedding, and Lisbeth Fargus said it was delicacy that made Sam'l superintend the fitting-up of the barn by deputy. Once he came to see it in person, but he looked so ill that Sanders had to see him home. This was on the Thursday afternoon, and the wedding was fixed for Friday.

"Sanders, Sanders," said Sam'l, in a voice strangely unlike his own, "it'll a' be ower by this time the morn."

"It will," said Sanders.

"If I had only kent her langer," continued Sam'l.

"It wid hae been safer," said Sanders.

"Did ye see the yallow floor in Bell's bonnet?" asked the accepted swain.

"Ay," said Sanders, reluctantly.

"I'm dootin'—I'm sair dootin' she's but a flichty, licht-hearted crittur after a'."

"I had ay my suspeecions o't," said Sanders.

"Ye hae kent her langer than me," said Sam'l.

"Yes," said Sanders, "but there's nae gettin' at the heart o' women. Man, Sam'l, they're desperate cunnin'."

"I'm dootin 't; I'm sair dootin 't."

"It'll be a warnin' to ye, Sam'l, no to be in sic a hurry i' the futur," said Sanders.

Sam'l groaned.

"Ye'll be gaein up to the manse to arrange wi' the minister the morn's mornin'," continued Sanders, in a subdued voice.

Sam'l looked wistfully at his friend.

"I canna do't, Sanders," he said, "I canna do't."

"Ye maun," said Sanders.

"It's aisy to speak," retorted Sam'l, bitterly.

"We have a' oor troubles, Sam'l," said Sanders, soothingly, "an' every man maun bear his ain burdens. Johnny Davie's wife's dead, an' he's no repinin'."

"Ay," said Sam'l, "but a death's no a mairitch. We hae haen deaths in our family too."

"It may a' be for the best," added Sanders, "an' there wid be a michty talk i' the hale country-side gin ye didna ging to the minister like a man."

"I maun hae langer to think o't," said Sam'l.

"Bell's mairitch is the morn," said Sanders, decisively.

Sam'l glanced up with a wild look in his eyes.

"Sanders," he cried.

"Sam'l?"

"Ye hae been a guid friend to me, Sanders, in this sair affliction."

"Nothing ava," said Sanders; "dount mention'd."

"But, Sanders, ye canna deny but what your rinnin oot o' the kirk that awfu' day was at the bottom o'd a'."

"It was so," said Sanders, bravely.

"An' ye used to be fond o' Bell, Sanders."

"I dinna deny 't."

"Sanders, laddie," said Sam'l, bending forward and speaking in a wheedling voice, "I aye thocht it was you she likeit."

"I had some sic idea mysel," said Sanders.

"Sanders, I canna think to pairt twa fowk sae weel suited to ane anither as you an' Bell."

"Canna ye, Sam'l?"

"She wid mak ye a guid wife, Sanders. I hae studied her weel, and she's a thrifty, douce, clever lassie. Sanders, there's no the like o' her. Mony a time, Sanders, I hae said to mysel, There's a lass ony man micht be prood to tak. A'body says the same, Sanders. There's nae risk ava, man: nane to speak o'. Tak her, laddie, tak her, Sanders; it's a grand chance, Sanders. She's yours for the spierin. I'll gie her up, Sanders."

"Will ye, though?" said Sanders.

"What d' ye think?" asked Sam'l.

"If ye wid rayther," said Sanders, politely.

"There's my han' on't," said Sam'l. "Bless ye, Sanders; ye've been a true frien' to me."

Then they shook hands for the first time in their lives; and soon afterwards Sanders struck up the brae to T'nowhead.

Next morning Sanders Elshioner, who had been very busy the night before, put on his Sabbath clothes and strolled up to the manse.

"But—but where is Sam'l?" asked the minister; "I must see himself."

"It's a new arrangement," said Sanders.

"What do you mean, Sanders?"

"Bell's to marry me," explained Sanders.

"But—but what does Sam'l say?"

"He's willin'," said Sanders.

"And Bell?"

"She's willin', too. She prefers 't."

"It is unusual," said the minister.

"It's a' richt," said Sanders.

"Well, you know best," said the minister.

"You see the hoose was taen, at ony rate," continued Sanders. "An I'll juist ging in til't instead o' Sam'l."

"Quite so."

"An' I cudna think to disappoint the lassie."

"Your sentiments do you credit, Sanders," said the minister; "but I hope you do not enter upon the blessed state of matrimony without full consideration of its responsibilities. It is a serious business marriage."

"It's a' that," said Sanders, "but I'm willin' to stan' the risk."

So, as soon as it could be done, Sanders Elshioner took to wife T'nowhead's Bell, and I remember seeing Sam'l Dickie trying to dance at the penny wedding.

Years afterwards it was said in Thrums that Sam'l had treated Bell badly, but he was never sure about it himself.

"It was a near thing—a michty near thing," he admitted in the square.

"They say," some other weaver would remark, " 'at it was you Bell liked best."

"I d'na kin," Sam'l would reply, "but there's nae doot the lassie was fell fond o'me. Ou, a mere passin' fancy's ye micht say."

## DAVIT LUNAN'S POLITICAL REMINISCENCES

WHEN an election-day comes round now, it takes me back to the time of 1832. I would be eight or ten year old at that time. James Strachan was at the door by five o'clock in the morning in his Sabbath clothes, by arrangement. We was to go up to the hill to see them building the bonfire. Moreover, there was word that Mr. Scrimgour was to be there tossing pennies, just like at a marriage. I was wakened before that by my mother at the pans and bowls. I have always associated elections since that time with jelly-making; for just as my mother would fill the cups and tankers and bowls with jelly to save cans, she was emptying the pots and pans to make way for the ale and porter. James and me was to help to carry it home from the square—him in the pitcher and me in a flagon, because I was silly for my age and not strong in the arms.

It was a very blowy morning, though the rain kept off, and what part of the bonfire had been built already was found scattered to the winds. Before we rose a great mass of folk was getting the barrels and things together again; but some of them was never recovered, and suspicion pointed to William Geddes, it being well known that William would not hesitate to carry off anything if unobserved. More by token Chirsty Lamby had seen him rolling home a barrowful of firewood early in the morning, her having risen to hold cold water in her mouth, being down with the toothache. When we got up to the hill everybody was making for the quarry, which being more sheltered was now thought to be a better place for the bonfire. The masons had struck work, it being a general holiday in the whole country-side. There was a great commotion of people, all fine dressed and mostly with glengarry bonnets; and me and James was well acquaint with them, though mostly weavers and the like and not my father's equal. Mr. Scrimgour was not there himself; but there was a small active body in his room as tossed the money for him fair enough; though not so liberally as was expected, being mostly ha'pence where pennies was looked for. Such was not my father's opinion, and him and a few others only had a vote. He considered it was a waste of money giving to them that had no vote and so taking out of other folks' mouths, but the little man said it kept everybody in good-humour and made Mr. Scrimgour popular. He was an extraordinary affable man and very spirity, running about to waste no time in walking, and gave me a shilling, saying to me to be a truthful boy and tell my father. He did not give James anything, him being an orphan, but clapped his head and said he was a fine boy.

The Captain was to vote for the Bill if he got in, the which he did. It was the Captain was to give the ale and porter in the square like a true gentleman. My father gave a kind of laugh when I let him see my shilling, and said he would keep care of it for me; and sorry I was I let him get it, me never seeing the face of it again to this day. Me and James was much annoyed with the women, especially Kitty Davie, always pushing in when there was tossing, and tearing the very ha'pence out of our hands: us not caring so much about the money, but humiliated to see women mixing up in politics. By the time the topmost barrel was on the bonfire there was a great smell of whisky in the quarry, it being a confined place. My father had been against the bonfire being in the quarry, arguing that the wind on the hill would have carried off the smell of the whisky; but Peter Tosh said they did not want the smell carried off; it would be agreeable to the masons for weeks to come. Except among the women there was no fighting nor wrangling at the quarry but all in fine spirits.

I misremember now whether it was Mr. Scrimgour or the Captain that took the fancy to my father's pigs; but it was this day, at any rate, that the Captain sent him the gamecock. Whichever one it was that fancied the litter of pigs, nothing would content him but to buy them, which he did at thirty shillings each, being the best bargain ever my father made. Nevertheless I'm thinking he was windier of the cock. The Captain, who was a local man when not with his regiment, had the grandest collection of fighting-cocks in the county, and sometimes came into the town to try them against the town cocks. I mind well the large wicker cage in which they were conveyed from place to place, and never without the Captain near at hand. My father had a cock that beat all the other town cocks at the cock fight at our school, which was superintended by the elder of the kirk to see fair play; but the which died of its wounds the next day but one. This was a great grief to my father, it having been challenged to fight the Captain's cock. Therefore it was very considerate of the Captain to make my father a present of his bird; father, in compliment to him, changing its name from the "Deil" to the "Captain."

During the forenoon, and I think until well on in the day, James and me was busy with the pitcher and the flagon. The proceedings in the square, however, was not so well conducted as in the quarry, many of the folk there assembled showing a mean and grasping spirit. The Captain had given orders that there was to be no stint of ale and porter, and neither there was; but much of it lost through hastiness. Great barrels was hurled into the middle of the square, where the country wives sat with their eggs and butter on market-day, and was quickly stove in with an axe or paving-stone or whatever came handy. Sometimes they would break into the barrel at different points; and then, when they tilted it up to get the ale out at one hole, it gushed out at the bottom till the square was flooded. My mother was fair disgusted when told by me and James of the waste of good liquor. It is gospel truth I speak when I say I mind well of seeing Singer Davie catching the porter in a pan as it ran down the sire, and, when the pan was full to overflowing, putting his mouth to the stream and drinking till he was as full as the pan. Most of the men, however, stuck to the barrels, the drink running in the street being ale and porter mixed, and left it to the women and the young folk to do the carrying. Susy M'Queen brought as many pans as she could collect on a barrow, and was filling them all with porter, rejecting the ale; but indignation was aroused against her, and as fast as she filled, the others emptied.

My father scorned to go to the square to drink ale and porter with the crowd, having the election on his mind and him to vote. Nevertheless he instructed me and James to keep up a brisk trade with the pans, and run back across the gardens in case we met dishonest folk in the streets who might drink the ale. Also, said my father, we was to let the excesses of our neighbours be a warning in sobriety to us; enough being as good as a feast, except when you can store it up for the winter. By and by my mother thought it was not safe me being in the streets with so many wild men about, and would have sent James himself, him being an orphan and hardier; but this I did not like, but, running out, did not come back for long enough. There is no doubt that the music was to blame for firing the men's blood, and the result most disgraceful fighting with no object in view. There was three fiddlers and two at the flute, most of them blind, but not the less dangerous on that account; and they kept the town in a ferment, even playing the countryfolk home to the farms, followed by bands of townsfolk. They were a quarrelsome set, the ploughmen and others; and it was generally admitted in the town that their overbearing behaviour was responsible for the fights. I mind them being driven out of the square, stones flying thick; also some stand-up fights with sticks, and others fair enough with fists. The worst fight I did not see. It took place in a field. At first it was only between two who had been miscalling one another; but there was many looking on, and when the town man was like getting the worst of it the others set to, and a most heathenish fray with no sense in it ensued. One man had his arm broken. I mind Hobart the bellman going about ringing his bell and telling all persons to get within doors; but little attention was paid to him, it being notorious that Snecky had had a fight earlier in the day himself.

When James was fighting in the field, according to his own account, I had the honour of dining with the electors who voted for the Captain, him paying all expenses. It was a lucky accident my mother sending me to the town-house, where the dinner came off, to try to get my father home at a decent hour, me having a remarkable power over him when in liquor but at no other time. They were very jolly, however, and insisted on my drinking the Captain's health and eating more than was safe. My father got it next day from my mother for this; and so would I myself, but it was several days before I left my bed, completely knocked up as I was with the excitement and one thing or another. The bonfire, which was built to celebrate the election of Mr. Scrimgour, was set ablaze, though I did not see it, in honour of the election of the Captain; it being thought a pity to lose it, as no doubt it would have been. That is about all I remember of the celebrated election of '32 when the Reform Bill was passed.

# X

## A VERY OLD FAMILY

THEY were a very old family with whom Snecky Hobart, the bellman, lodged. Their favourite dissipation, when their looms had come to rest, was a dander through the kirkyard. They dressed for it: the three young ones in their rusty blacks; the patriarch in his old blue coat, velvet kneebreeches, and broad blue bonnet; and often of an evening I have met them moving from grave to grave. By this time the old man was nearly ninety, and the young ones averaged sixty. They read out the inscriptions on the tombstones in a solemn drone, and their father added his reminiscences. He never failed them. Since the beginning of the century he had not missed a funeral, and his children felt that he was a great example. Sire and sons returned from the cemetery invigorated for their daily labours. If one of them happened to start a dozen yards behind the others, he never thought of making up the distance. If his foot struck against a stone, he came to a dead-stop; when he discovered that he had stopped, he set off again.

A high wall shut off this old family's house and garden from the clatter of Thrums, a wall that gave Snecky some trouble before he went to live within it. I speak from personal knowledge. One spring morning, before the schoolhouse was built, I was assisting the patriarch to divest the gaunt garden pump of its winter suit of straw. I was taking a drink, I remember, my palm over the mouth of the wooden spout and my mouth at the gimlet hole above, when a leg appeared above the corner of the wall against which the henhouse was built. Two hands followed clutching desperately at the uneven stones. Then the leg worked as if it were turning a grindstone, and next moment Snecky was sitting breathlessly on the dyke. From this to the henhouse, whose roof was of "divets," the descent was comparatively easy, and a slanting board allowed the daring bellman to slide thence to the ground. He had come on business, and having talked it over slowly with the old man he turned to depart. Though he was a genteel man, I heard him sigh heavily as, with the remark, "Ay, weel, I'll be movin' again," he began to rescale the wall. The patriarch, twisted round the pump, made no reply, so I ventured to suggest to the bellman that he might find the gate easier. "Is there a gate?" said Snecky, in surprise at the resources of civilisation. I pointed it out to him, and he went his way chuckling. The old man told me that he had sometimes wondered at Snecky's mode of approach, but it had not struck him to say anything. Afterwards, when the bellman took up his abode there, they discussed the matter heavily.

Hobart inherited both his bell and his nickname from his father, who was not a native of Thrums. He came from some distant part where the people speak of snecking the door, meaning shut it. In Thrums the word used is steek, and sneck seemed to the inhabitants so droll and ridiculous that Hobart got the name of Snecky. His son left Thrums at the age of ten for the distant farm of Tirl, and did not return until the old bellman's death, twenty years afterwards; but the first remark he overheard on entering the kirk-wynd was a conjecture flung across the street by a grey-haired crone, that he would be "little Snecky come to bury auld Snecky."

The father had a reputation in his day for "crying" crimes he was suspected of having committed himself, but the Snecky I knew had too high a sense of his own importance for that. On great occasions, such as the loss of little Davy Dundas, or when a tattie roup had to be cried, he was even offensively inflated; but ordinary announcements, such as the approach of a flying stationer, the roup of a deceased weaver's loom, or the arrival in Thrums of a cart-load of fine "kebec" cheeses, he treated as the merest trifles. I see still the bent legs of the snuffy old man straightening to the tinkle of his bell, and the smirk with which he let the curious populace gather round him. In one hand he ostentatiously displayed the paper on which what he had to cry was written, but, like the minister, he scorned to "read." With the bell carefully tucked under his oxter he gave forth his news in a rasping voice that broke now and again into a squeal. Though Scotch in his unofficial conversation, he was believed to deliver himself on public occasions in the finest English. When trotting from place to place with his news he carried his bell by the tongue as cautiously as if it were a flagon of milk.

Snecky never allowed himself to degenerate into a mere machine. His proclamations were provided by those who employed him, but his soul was his own. Having cried a potato roup he would sometimes add a word of warning, such as, "I wudna advise ye, lads, to hae onything to do wi' thae tatties; they're diseased." Once, just before the cattle market, he was sent round by a local laird to announce that "any drover found taking the short cut to the hill through the grounds of Muckle Plowy would be prosecuted to the utmost limits of the law. The people were aghast. "Hoots, lads," Snecky said; "dinna fash yoursels. It's juist a haver o' the grieve's." One of Hobart's ways of striking terror into evildoers was to announce, when crying a crime, that he himself knew perfectly well who the culprit was. "I see him brawly," he would say, "standing afore me, an' if he disna instantly mak retribution, I am determined this very day to mak a public example of him."

Before the time of the Burke and Hare murders Snecky's father was sent round Thrums to proclaim the startling news that a grave in the kirkyard had been tampered with. The "resurrectionist" scare was at its height then, and the patriarch, who was one of the men in Thrums paid to watch new graves in the night-time, has often told the story. The town was in a ferment as the news spread, and there were fierce suspicious men among Hobart's hearers who already had the rifler of graves in their eye.

He was a man who worked for the farmers when they required an extra hand, and loafed about the square when they could do without him. No one had a good word for him, and lately he had been flush of money. That was sufficient. There was a rush of angry men through the "pend" that led to his habitation, and he was dragged, panting and terrified, to the kirkyard before he understood what it all meant. To the grave they hurried him, and almost without a word handed him a spade. The whole town gathered round the spot—a sullen crowd, the women only breaking the silence with their sobs, and the children clinging to their gowns. The suspected resurrectionist understood what was wanted of him, and, flinging off his jacket, began to reopen the grave. Presently the spade struck upon wood, and by and by part of the coffin came in view. That was nothing, for the resurrectionists had a way of breaking the coffin at one end and drawing out the body with tongs. The digger knew this. He broke the boards with the spade and revealed an arm. The people convinced, he dropped the arm savagely, leapt out of the grave and went his way, leaving them to shovel back the earth themselves.

There was humour in the old family as well as in their lodger. I found this out slowly. They used to gather round their peat fire in the evening, after the poultry had gone to sleep on the kitchen rafters, and take off their neighbours. None of them ever laughed; but their neighbours did afford them subject for gossip, and the old man was very sarcastic over other people's old-fashioned ways. When one of the family wanted to go out he did it gradually. He would be sitting "into the fire" browning his corduroy trousers, and he would get up slowly. Then he gazed solemnly before him for a time, and after that, if you watched him narrowly, you would see that he was really moving to the door. Another member of the family took the vacant seat with the same precautions. Will'um, the eldest, has a gun, which customarily stands behind the old eight-day clock; and he takes it with him to the garden to shoot the blackbirds. Long before Will'um is ready to let fly, the blackbirds have gone away; and so the gun is never, never fired: but there is a determined look on Will'um's face when he returns from the garden.

In the stormy days of his youth the old man had been a "Black Nib." The Black Nibs were the persons who agitated against the French war; and the public feeling against them ran strong and deep. In Thrums the local Black Nibs were burned in effigy, and whenever they put their heads out of doors they risked being stoned. Even where the authorities were unprejudiced they were helpless to interfere; and as a rule they were as bitter against the Black Nibs as the populace themselves. Once the patriarch was running through the street with a score of the enemy at his heels, and the bailie, opening his window, shouted to them, "Stane the Black Nib oot o' the toon!"

When the patriarch was a young man he was a follower of pleasure. This is the one thing about him that his family have never been able to understand. A solemn stroll through the kirkyard was not sufficient relaxation in those riotous times, after a hard day at the loom; and he rarely lost a chance of going to see a man hanged. There was a good deal of hanging in those days; and yet the authorities had an ugly way of reprieving condemned men on whom the sightseers had been counting. An air of gloom would gather on my old friend's countenance when he told how he and his contemporaries in Thrums trudged every Saturday for six weeks to the county town, many miles distant, to witness the execution of some criminal in whom they had a local interest, and who, after disappointing them again and again, was said to have been bought off by a friend. His crime had been stolen entrance into a house in Thrums by the chimney, with intent to rob; and, though this old-fashioned family did not see it, not the least noticeable incident in the scrimmage that followed was the prudence of the canny housewife. When she saw the legs coming down the lum, she rushed to the kail-pot which was on the fire and put on the lid. She confessed that this was not done to prevent the visitor's scalding himself, but to save the broth.

The old man was repeated in his three sons. They told his stories precisely as he did himself, taking as long in the telling, and making the points in exactly the same way. By and by they will come to think that they themselves were of those past times. Already the young ones look like contemporaries of their father.

# XI

## LITTLE RATHIE'S "BURAL"

DEVOUT-UNDER-DIFFICULTIES would have been the name of Lang Tammas had he been of Covenanting times. So I thought one wintry afternoon, years before I went to the schoolhouse, when he dropped in to ask the pleasure of my company to the farmer of Little Rathie's "bural." As a good Auld Licht, Tammas reserved his swallow-tail coat and "lum hat" (chimney pot) for the kirk and funerals; but the coat would have flapped villainously, to Tammas's eternal ignominy, had he for one rash moment relaxed his hold on the bottom button, and it was only by walking sideways, as horses sometimes try to do, that the hat could be kept at the angle of decorum. Let it not be thought that Tammas had asked me to Little Rathie's funeral on his own responsibility. Burals were among the few events to break the monotony of an Auld Licht winter, and invitations were as much sought after as cards to my lady's dances in the south. This had been a fair average season for Tammas, though of his four burials one had been a bairn's—a mere bagatelle; but had it not been for the death of Little Rathie I would probably not have been out that year at all.

The small farm of Little Rathie lies two miles from Thrums, and Tammas and I trudged manfully through the snow, adding to our numbers as we went. The dress of none differed materially from the precentor's, and the general effect was of septuagenarians in each other's best clothes, though living in low-roofed houses had bent most of them before their time. By a rearrangement of garments, such as making Tammas change coat, hat, and trousers with Cragiebuckle, Silva McQueen, and Sam'l Wilkie respectively, a dexterous tailor might perhaps have supplied each with a "fit." The talk was chiefly of Little Rathie, and sometimes threatened to become animated, when another mourner would fall in and restore the more fitting gloom.

"Ay, ay," the new comer would say, by way of responding to the sober salutation, "Ay, Johnny." Then there was silence, but for the "gluck" with which we lifted our feet from the slush.

"So little Rathie's been ta'en awa'," Johnny would venture to say, by and by.

"He's gone, Johnny; ay, man, he is so."

"Death must come to all," some one would waken up to murmur.

"Ay," Lang Tammas would reply, putting on the coping-stone, "in the morning we are strong, and in the evening we are cut down."

"We are so, Tammas; ou ay, we are so; we're here the wan day an' gone the neist."

"Little Rathie wasna a crittur I took till; no, I canna say he was," said Bowie Haggart, so called because his legs described a parabola, "but he maks a vary creeditable corp (corpse). I will say that for him. It's wonderfu' hoo death improves a body. Ye cudna hae said as Little Rathie was a weel-faured man when he was i' the flesh."

Bowie was the wright, and attended burials in his official capacity. He had the gift of words to an uncommon degree, and I do not forget his crushing blow at the reputation of the poet Burns, as delivered under the auspices of the Thrums Literary Society. "I am of opeenion," said Bowie, "that the works of Burns is of an immoral tendency. I have not read them myself, but such is my opeenion."

"He was a queer stock, Little Rathie, michty queer," said Tammas Haggart, Bowie's brother, who was a queer stock himself, but was not aware of it; "but, ou, I'm thinkin' the wife had something to do wi't. She was ill to manage, an' Little Rathie hadna the way o' the women. He hadna the knack o' managin' them 's ye micht say—no, Little Rathie hadna the knack."

"They're kittle cattle, the women," said the farmer of Craigiebuckle—son of the Craigiebuckle mentioned elsewhere—a little gloomily. "I've often thocht maiterimony is no onlike the lucky bags th' auld wifies has at the muckly. There's prizes an' blanks baith inside, but, losh, ye're far frae sure what ye'll draw oot when ye put in yer han'."

"Ou, weel," said Tammas, complacently, "there's truth in what ye say, but the women can be managed if ye have the knack."

"Some o' them," said Cragiebuckle, woefully.

"Ye had yer wark wi' the wife yersel, Tammas, so ye had," observed Lang Tammas, unbending to suit his company.

"Ye're speakin' aboot the bit wife's bural," said Tammas Haggart, with a chuckle, "ay, ay, that brocht her to reason."

Without much pressure Haggart retold a story known to the majority of his hearers. He had not the "knack" of managing women apparently when he married, for he and his gipsy wife "agreed ill thegither" at first. Once Chirsty left him and took up her abode in a house just across the wynd. Instead of routing her out, Tammas, without taking any one into his confidence, determined to treat Chirsty as dead, and celebrate her decease in a "lyke wake"—a last wake. These wakes were very general in Thrums in the old days, though they had ceased to be common by the date of Little Rathie's death. For three days before the burial the friends and neighbours of the mourners were invited into the house to partake of food and drink by the side of the corpse.

The dead lay on chairs covered with a white sheet. Dirges were sung, and the deceased was extolled, but when night came the lights were extinguished, and the corpse was left alone. On the morning of the funeral tables were spread with a white cloth outside the house, and food and drink were placed upon them. No neighbour could pass the tables without paying his respects to the dead; and even when the house was in a busy, narrow thoroughfare, this part of the ceremony was never omitted. Tammas did not give Chirsty a wake inside the house; but one Friday morning—it was market-day, and the square was consequently full—it went through the town that the tables were spread before his door. Young and old collected, wandering round the house, and Tammas stood at the tables in his blacks inviting every one to eat and drink. He was pressed to tell what it meant; but nothing could be got from him except that his wife was dead. At times he pressed his hands to his heart, and then he would make wry faces, trying hard to cry. Chirsty watched from a window across the street, until she perhaps began to fear that she really was dead. Unable to stand it any longer, she rushed out into her husband's arms, and shortly afterwards she could have been seen dismantling the tables.

"She's gone this fower year," Tammas said, when he had finished his story, "but up to the end I had no more trouble wi' Chirsty. No, I had the knack o' her."

"I've heard tell, though," said the sceptical Craigiebuckle, "as Chirsty only cam back to ye because she cudna bear to see the fowk makkin' sae free wi' the whisky."

" I mind hoo she bottled it up at ance, and drove the laddies awa'," said Bowie, "an' I hae seen her after that, Tammas, giein' ye up yer fut an' you no sayin' a word."

"Ou, ay," said the wife-tamer, in the tone of a man who could afford to be generous in trifles, "women maun talk, an' a man hasna aye time to conterdick them, but frae that day I had the knack o' Chirsty."

"Donal Elshioner's was a very seemilar case," broke in Snecky Hobart, shrilly. "Maist o' ye'll mind 'at Donal was michty plague't wi' a drucken wife. Ay, weel, wan day Bowie's man was carryin' a coffin past Donal's door, and Donal an' the wife was there. Says Donal, 'Put doon yer coffin, my man, an' tell's wha it's for.' The laddie rests the coffin on its end, an' says he, 'It's for Davie Fairbrother's guid-wife.' 'Ay, then,' says Donal,' tak it awa', tak it awa' to Davie, an' tell 'im as ye kin a man wi' a wife 'at wid be glad to neifer (exchange) wi' him.' Man, that terrified Donal's wife; it did so."

As we delved up the twisting road between two fields, that leads to the farm of Little Rathie, the talk became less general, and another mourner who joined us there was told that the farmer was gone.

"We must all fade as a leaf," said Lang Tammas.

"So we maun, so we maun," admitted the newcomer. "They say," he added, solemnly, "as Little Rathie has left a full teapot."

The reference was to the safe in which the old people in the district stored their gains.

"He was thrifty," said Tammas Haggart, "an' shrewd, too, was Little Rathie. I mind Mr. Dishart admonishin' him for no attendin' a special weather service i' the kirk, when Finny an' Lintool, the twa adjoinin' farmers, baith attendit. 'Ou,' says Little Rathie, 'I thocht to mysel, thinks I, if they get rain for prayin' for 't on Finny an' Lintool, we're bound to get the benefit o't on Little Rathie.'"

"Tod," said Snecky, "there's some sense in that; an' what says the minister?"

"I d'na kin what he said," admitted Haggart; "but he took Little Rathie up to the manse, an' if ever I saw a man lookin' sma', it was Little Rathie when he cam oot."

The deceased had left behind him a daughter (herself now known as Little Rathie) quite capable of attending to the ramshackle "but and ben"; and I remember how she nipped off Tammas's consolations to go out and feed the hens. To the number of about twenty we assembled round the end of the house to escape the bitter wind, and here I lost the precentor, who, as an Auld Licht elder, joined the chief mourners inside. The post of distinction at a funeral is near the coffin; but it is not given to every one to be a relative of the deceased, and there is always much competition and genteelly concealed disappointment over the few open vacancies. The window of the room was decently veiled, but the mourners outside knew what was happening within, and that it was not all prayer, neither mourning. A few of the more reverent uncovered their heads at intervals; but it would be idle to deny that there was a feeling that Little Rathie's daughter was favouring Tammas and others somewhat invidiously. Indeed, Robbie Gibruth did not scruple to remark that she had made "an inauspeecious beginning." Tammas Haggart, who was melancholy when not sarcastic, though he brightened up wonderfully at funerals, reminded Robbie that disappointment is the lot of man on his earthly pilgrimage; but Haggart knew who were to be invited back after the burial to the farm, and was inclined to make much of his position. The secret would doubtless have been wormed from him had not public attention been directed into another channel. A prayer was certainly being offered up inside; but the voice was not the voice of the minister.

Lang Tammas told me afterwards that it had seemed at one time "vary queistionable" whether Little Rathie would be buried that day at all.

The incomprehensible absence of Mr. Dishart (afterwards satisfactorily explained) had raised the unexpected question of the legality of a burial in a case where the minister had not prayed over the "corp." There had even been an indulgence in hot words, and the Reverend Alexander Kewans, a "stickit minister," but not of the Auld Licht persuasion, had withdrawn in dudgeon on hearing Tammas asked to conduct the ceremony instead of himself. But, great as Tammas was on religious questions, a pillar of the Auld Licht kirk, the Shorter Catechism at his finger-ends, a sad want of words at the very time when he needed them most, incapacitated him for prayer in public, and it was providential that Bowie proved himself a man of parts. But Tammas tells me that the wright grossly abused his position, by praying at such length that Craigiebuckle fell asleep, and the mistress had to rise and hang the pot on the fire higher up the joist, lest its contents should burn before the return from the funeral. Loury grew the sky, and more and more anxious the face of Little Rathie's daughter, and still Bowie prayed on. Had it not been for the impatience of the precentor and the grumbling of the mourners outside, there is no saying when the remains would have been lifted through the "bole," or little window.

Hearses had hardly come in at this time and the coffin was carried by the mourners on long stakes. The straggling procession of pedestrians behind wound its slow way in the waning light to the kirkyard, showing startlingly black against the dazzling snow; and it was not until the earth rattled on the coffin-lid that Little Rathie's nearest male relative seemed to remember his last mournful duty to the dead. Sidling up to the favoured mourners, he remarked casually and in the most emotionless tone he could assume: "They're expec'in ye to stap doon the length o' Little Rathie noo. Ay, ay, he's gone. Na, na, nae refoosal, Da-avit; ye was aye a guid friend till him, an' it's onything a body can do for him noo."

Though the uninvited slunk away sorrowfully, the entertainment provided at Auld Licht houses of mourning was characteristic of a stern and sober sect. They got to eat and to drink to the extent, as a rule, of a "lippy" of shortbread and a "brew" of toddy; but open Bibles lay, on the table, and the eyes of each were on his neighbours to catch them transgressing, and offer up a prayer for them on the spot. Ay me! there is no Bowie nowadays to fill an absent minister's shoes.

# XII

## A LITERARY CLUB

THE ministers in the town did not hold with literature. When the most notorious of the clubs met in the town-house under the presidentship of Gavin Ogilvy, who was no better than a poacher, and was troubled in his mind because writers called Pope a poet, there was frequently a wrangle over the question, Is literature necessarily immoral? It was a fighting club, and on Friday nights the few respectable, god-fearing members dandered to the town-house, as if merely curious to have another look at the building. If Lang Tammas, who was dead against letters, was in sight they wandered off, but when there were no spies abroad they slunk up the stair. The attendance was greatest on dark nights, though Gavin himself and some other characters would have marched straight to the meeting in broad daylight. Tammas Haggart, who did not think much of Milton's devil, had married a gypsy woman for an experiment, and the Coat of Many Colours did not know where his wife was. As a rule, however, the members were wild bachelors. When they married they had to settle down.

Gavin's essay on Will'um Pitt, the Father of the Taxes, led to the club's being bundled out of the town-house, where people said it should never have been allowed to meet. There was a terrible town when Tammas Haggart then disclosed the secret of Mr. Byars's supposed approval of the club. Mr, Byars was the Auld Licht minister whom Mr. Dishart succeeded, and it was well known that he had advised the authorities to grant the use of the little town-house to the club on Friday evenings. As he solemnly warned his congregation against attending the meetings the position he had taken up created talk, and Lang Tammas called at the manse with Sanders Whamond to remonstrate. The minister, however, harangued them on their sinfulness in daring to question the like of him, and they had to retire vanquished though dissatisfied. Then came the disclosures of Tammas Haggart, who was never properly secured by the Auld Lichts until Mr. Dishart took him in hand. It was Tammas who wrote anonymous letters to Mr. Byars about the scarlet woman, and, strange to say, this led to the club's being allowed to meet in the town-house. The minister, after many days, discovered who his correspondent was, and succeeded in inveigling the stone-breaker to the manse. There, with the door snibbed, he opened out on Tammas, who, after his usual manner when hard pressed, pretended to be deaf. This sudden fit of deafness so exasperated the minister that he flung a book at Tammas. The scene that followed was one that few Auld Licht manses can have witnessed. According to Tammas the book had hardly reached the floor when the minister turned white. Tammas picked up the missile. It was a Bible. The two men looked at each other. Beneath the window Mr. Byars's children were prattling. His wife was moving about in the next room, little thinking what had happened. The minister held out his hand for the Bible, but Tammas shook his head, and then Mr. Byars shrank into a chair. Finally, it was arranged that if Tammas kept the affair to himself the minister would say a good word to the Bailie about the literary club. After that the stone-breaker used to go from house to house, twisting his mouth to the side and remarking that he could tell such a tale of Mr. Byars as would lead to a split in the kirk. When the town-house was locked on the club Tammas spoke out, but though the scandal ran from door to door, as I have seen a pig in a fluster do, the minister did not lose his place. Tammas preserved the Bible, and showed it complacently to visitors as the present he got from Mr. Byars. The minister knew this, and it turned his temper sour. Tammas's proud moments, after that, were when he passed the minister.

Driven from the town-house, literature found a table with forms round it in a tavern hard by, where the club, lopped of its most respectable members, kept the blinds down and talked openly of Shakspeare. It was a low-roofed room, with pieces of lime hanging from the ceiling and peeling walls. The floor had a slope that tended to fling the debater forward, and its boards, lying loose on an uneven foundation, rose and looked at you as you crossed the room. In winter, when the meetings were held regularly every fortnight, a fire of peat, sod, and dross lit up the curious company who sat round the table shaking their heads over Shelley's mysticism, or requiring to be called to order because they would not wait their turn to deny an essayist's assertion that Berkeley's style was superior to David Hume's. Davit Hume, they said, and Watty Scott. Burns was simply referred to as Rob or Robbie.

There was little drinking at these meetings for the members knew what they were talking about, and your mind had to galop to keep up with the flow of reasoning. Thrums is rather a remarkable town. There are scores and scores of houses in it that have sent their sons to college (by what a struggle!), some to make their way to the front in their professions, and others, perhaps, despite their broadcloth, never to be a patch on their parents. In that literary club there were men of a reading so wide and catholic that it might put some graduates of the universities to shame, and of an intellect so keen that had it not had a crook in it their fame would have crossed the county. Most of them had but a thread-bare existence, for you weave slower with a Wordsworth open before you, and some were strange Bohemians (which does not do in Thrums), yet others wandered into the world and compelled it to recognise them. There is a London barrister whose father belonged to the club. Not many years ago a man died on the staff of the *Times*, who, when he was a weaver near Thrums, was one of the club's prominent members. He taught himself shorthand by the light of a cruizey, and got a post on a Perth paper, afterwards on the *Scotsman* and the *Witness*, and finally on the *Times*. Several other men of his type had a history worth reading, but it is not for me to write. Yet I may say that there is still at least one of the original members of the club left behind in Thrums to whom some of the literary dandies might lift their hats.

Gavin Ogilvy I only knew as a weaver and a poacher; a lank, long-armed man, much bent from crouching in ditches whence he watched his snares. To the young he was a romantic figure, because they saw him frequently in the fields with his call-birds tempting siskins, yellow yites, and Unties to twigs which he had previously smeared with lime. He made the lime from the tough roots of holly; sometimes from linseed oil, which is boiled until thick, when it is taken out of the pot and drawn and stretched with the hands like elastic. Gavin was also a famous hare-snarer at a time when the ploughman looked upon this form of poaching as his perquisite. The snare was of wire, so constructed that the hare entangled itself the more when trying to escape, and it was placed across the little roads through the fields to which hares confine themselves, with a heavy stone attached to it by a string. Once Gavin caught a toad (fox) instead of a hare, and did not discover his mistake until it had him by the teeth. He was not able to weave for two months. The grouse-netting was more lucrative and more exciting, and women engaged in it with their husbands. It is told of Gavin that he was on one occasion chased by a gamekeeper over moor and hill for twenty miles, and that by and by when the one sank down exhausted so did the other. They would sit fifty yards apart, glaring at each other. The poacher eventually escaped. This, curious as it may seem, is the man whose eloquence at the club has not been forgotten in fifty years. "Thus did he stand," I have been told recently, "exclaiming in language sublime that the soul shall bloom in immortal youth through the ruin and wrack of time."

Another member read to the club an account of his journey to Lochnagar, which was afterwards published in *Chambers's Journal*. He was celebrated for his descriptions of scenery, and was not the only member of the club whose essays got into print. More memorable perhaps was an itinerant match-seller known to Thrums and the surrounding towns as the literary spunk-seller. He was a wizened, shivering old man, often barefooted, wearing at the best a thin ragged coat that had been black but was green-brown with age, and he made his spunks as well as sold them. He brought Bacon and Adam Smith into Thrums, and he loved to recite long screeds from Spenser, with a running commentary on the versification and the luxuriance of the diction. Of Jamie's death I do not care to write. He went without many a dinner in order to buy a book.

The Coat of Many Colours and Silva Robbie were two street preachers who gave the Thrums ministers some work. They occasionally appeared at the club. The Coat of Many Colours was so called because he wore a garment consisting of patches of cloth of various colours sewed together. It hung down to his heels. He may have been cracked rather than inspired, but he was a power in the square where he preached, the women declaring that he was gifted by God. An awe filled even the men, when he admonished them for using strong language, for at such a time he would remind them of the woe which fell upon Tibbie Mason. Tibbie had been notorious in her day for evil-speaking, especially for her free use of the word handless, which she flung a hundred times in a week at her man, and even at her old mother. Her punishment was to have a son born without hands. The Coat of Many Colours also told of the liar who exclaimed, "If this is not gospel true may I stand here for ever," and who is standing on that spot still, only nobody knows where it is. George Wishart was the Coat's hero, and often he has told in the Square how Wishart saved Dundee. It was the time when the plague lay over Scotland, and in Dundee they saw it approaching from the West in the form of a great black cloud. They fell on their knees and prayed, crying to the cloud to pass them by, and while they prayed it came nearer. Then they looked around for the most holy man among them, to intervene with God on their behalf. All eyes turned to George Wishart, and he stood up, stretching his arms to the cloud and prayed, and it rolled back. Thus Dundee was saved from the plague, but when Wishart ended his prayer he was alone, for the people had all returned to their homes. Less of a genuine man than the Coat of Many Colours was Silva Robbie, who had horrid fits of laughing in the middle of his prayers, and even fell in a paroxysm of laughter from the chair on which he stood. In the club he said things not to be borne, though logical up to a certain point.

Tammas Haggart was the most sarcastic member of the club, being celebrated for his sarcasm far and wide. It was a remarkable thing about him, often spoken of, that if you went to Tammas with a stranger and asked him to say a sarcastic thing that the man might take away as a specimen, he could not do it. "Na, na," Tammas would say, after a few trials, referring to sarcasm, "she's no a crittur to force. Ye maun lat her tak her ain time. Sometimes she's dry like the pump, an' syne, again, oot she comes in a gush." The most sarcastic thing the stone-breaker ever said was frequently marvelled over in Thrums, both before and behind his face, but unfortunately no one could ever remember what it was. The subject, however, was Cha Tamson's potato pit. There is little doubt that it was a fit of sarcasm that induced Tammas to marry a gypsy lassie. Mr. Byars would not join them, so Tammas had himself married by Jimmy Pawse, the gay little gypsy king, and after that the minister re-married them. The marriage over the tongs is a thing to scandalise any well-brought up person, for before he joined the couple's hands, Jimmy jumped about in a startling way, uttering wild gibberish, and after the ceremony was over there was rough work, with incantations and blowing on pipes. Tammas always held that this marriage turned out better than he had expected, though he had his trials like other married men. Among them was Chirsty's way of climbing on to the dresser to get at the higher part of the plate-rack. One evening I called in to have a smoke with the stone-breaker, and while we were talking Chirsty climbed the dresser. The next moment she was on the floor on her back, wailing, but Tammas smoked on imperturbably. "Do you not see what has happened, man?" I cried. "Ou," said Tammas, "she's aye fa'in aff the dresser."

Of the schoolmasters who were at times members of the club, Mr. Dickie was the ripest scholar, but my predecessor at the schoolhouse, had a way of sneering at him that was as good as sarcasm. When they were on their legs at the same time, asking each other passionately to be calm, and rolling out lines from Homer, that made the innkeeper look fearfully to the fastenings of the door, their heads very nearly came together although the table was between them. The old dominie had an advantage in being the shorter man, for he could hammer on the table as he spoke, while gaunt Mr. Dickie had to stoop to it. Mr. McRittie's arguments were a series of nails that he knocked into the table, and he did it in a workmanlike manner. Mr. Dickie, though he kept firm on his feet, swayed his body until by and by his head was rotating in a large circle. The mathematical figure he made was a cone revolving on its apex. Gavin's reinstalment in the chair year after year was made by the disappointed dominie the subject of some tart verses which he called an epode, but Gavin crushed him when they were read before the club. "Satire," he said, "is a legitimate weapon, used with michty effect by Swift, Sammy Butler, and others, and I dount object to being made the subject of creeticism. It has often been called a t'nife (knife), but them as is not used to t'nives cuts their hands, and ye'll a' observe that Mr. McRittie's fingers is bleedin'." All eyes were turned upon the dominie's hand, and though he pocketed it smartly several members had seen the blood. The dominie was a rare visitor at the club after that, though he outlived poor Mr. Dickie by many years. Mr. Dickie was a teacher in Tilliedrum, but he was ruined by drink. He wandered from town to town, reciting Greek and Latin poetry to any one who would give him a dram, and sometimes he wept and moaned aloud in the street, crying, "Poor Mr. Dickie! poor Mr. Dickie!"

The leading poet in a club of poets was Dite Walls, who kept a school when there were scholars, and weaved when there were none. He had a song that was published in a half penny leaflet about the famous lawsuit instituted by the farmer of Teuchbusses against the Laird of Drumlee. The laird was alleged to have taken from the land of Teuchbusses sufficient broom to make a besom thereof, and I am not certain that the case is settled to this day. It was Dite or another member of the club, who wrote "The Wife o' Deeside," of all the songs of the period the one that had the greatest vogue in the county at a time when Lord Jeffrey was cursed at every fireside in Thrums. The wife of Deeside was tried for the murder of her servant who had infatuated the young laird, and had it not been that Jeffrey defended her she would, in the words of the song, have "hung like a troot." It is not easy now to conceive the rage against Jeffrey when the woman was acquitted. The song was sung and recited in the streets, at the smiddy, in bothies, and by firesides, to the shaking of fists and the grinding of teeth. It began—

"Ye'll a' hae hear tell o' the wife o' Deeside,
Ye'll a' hae hear tell o' the wife o' Deeside,
She poisoned her maid for to keep up her pride,
Ye'll a' hae hear tell o' the wife o' Deeside."

Before the excitement had abated, Jeffrey was in Tilliedrum for electioneering purposes, and he was mobbed in the streets. Angry crowds pressed close to howl, "Wife o' Deeside!" at him. A contingent from Thrums was there, and it was long afterwards told of Sam'l Todd, by himself, that he hit Jeffrey on the back of the head with a clod of earth.

Johnny McQuhatty, a brother of the T'nowhead farmer, was the one taciturn member of the club, and you had only to look at him to know that he had a secret. He was a great genius at the handloom, and invented a loom for the weaving of linen such as has not been seen before or since. In the day-time he kept guard over his "shop," into which no one was allowed to enter, and the fame of his loom was so great that he had to watch over it with a gun. At night he weaved, and when the result at last pleased him he made the linen into shirts, all of which he stitched together with his own hands, even to the buttonholes. He sent one shirt to the Queen, and another to the Duchess of Athole, mentioning a very large price for them, which he got. Then he destroyed his wonderful loom, and how it was made no one will ever know. Johnny only took to literature after he had made his name, and he seldom spoke at the club except when ghosts and the like were the subject of debate, as they tended to be when the farmer of Muckle Haws could get in a word. Muckle Haws was fascinated by Johnny's sneers at superstition, and sometimes on dark nights the inventor had to make his courage good by seeing the farmer past the doulie yates (ghost gates), which Muckle Haws had to go perilously near on his way home. Johnny was a small man, but it was the burly farmer who shook at sight of the gates standing out white in the night. White gates have an evil name still, and Muckles Haws was full of horrors as he drew near them, clinging to Johnny's arm. It was on such a night, he would remember, that he saw the White Lady go through the gates greeting sorely, with a dead bairn in her arms, while water kelpie laughed and splashed in the pools, and the witches danced in a ring round Broken Buss. That very night twelve months ago the packman was murdered at Broken Buss, and Easie Pettie hanged herself on the stump of a tree. Last night there were ugly sounds from the quarry of Croup, where the bairn lies buried, and it's not mous (canny) to be out at such a time. The farmer had seen spectre maidens walking round the ruined castle of Darg, and the Castle all lit up with flaring torches, and dead knights and ladies sitting in the halls at the wine-cup, and the devil himself flapping his wings on the ramparts.

When the debates were political, two members with the gift of song fired the blood with their own poems about taxation and the depopulation of the Highlands, and by selling these songs from door to door they made their livelihood.

Books and pamphlets were brought into the town by the flying stationers, as they were called, who visited the square periodically carrying their wares on their backs, except at the Muckly, when they had their stall and even sold books by auction. The flying stationer best known to Thrums was Sandersy Riach, who was stricken from head to foot with the palsy, and could only speak with a quaver in consequence. Sandersy brought to the members of the club all the great books he could get second hand, but his stock-in-trade was *Thrummy Cap and Akenstaff*, *The Fishwives of Buckhaven*, *The Devil upon Two Sticks*, *Gilderoy*, *Sir James the Rose*, *The Brownie of Badenoch*,

*The Ghaist of Firenden*, and the like. It was from Sandersy that Tammas Haggart bought his copy of Shakspeare, whom Mr. Dishart could never abide. Tammas kept what he had done from his wife, but Chirsty saw a deterioration setting in and told the minister of her suspicions. Mr. Dishart was newly placed at the time and very vigorous, and the way he shook the truth out of Tammas was grand. The minister pulled Tammas the one way and Gavin pulled him the other, but Mr. Dishart was not the man to be beaten, and he landed Tammas in the Auld Licht kirk before the year was out. Chirsty buried Shakspeare in the yard.

A WINDOW IN THRUMS

# I

## THE HOUSE ON THE BRAE

ON the bump of green round which the brae twists, at the top of the brae, and within cry of T'nowhead Farm, still stands a one-storey house, whose whitewashed walls, streaked with the discoloration that rain leaves, look yellow when the snow comes. In the old days the stiff ascent left Thrums behind, and where is now the making of a suburb was only a poor row of dwellings and a manse, with Hendry's cot to watch the brae. The house stood bare, without a shrub, in a garden whose paling did not go all the way round, the potato pit being only kept out of the road, that here sets off southward, by a broken dyke of stones and earth. On each side of the slate-coloured door was a window of knotted glass. Ropes were flung over the thatch to keep the roof on in wind.

Into this humble abode I would take any one who cares to accompany me. But you must not come in a contemptuous mood, thinking that the poor are but a stage removed from beasts of burden, as some cruel writers of these days say; nor will I have you turn over with your foot the shabby horse-hair chairs that Leeby kept so speckless, and Hendry weaved for years to buy, and Jess so loved to look upon.

I speak of the chairs, but if we go together into the "room" they will not be visible to you. For a long time the house has been to let. Here, on the left of the doorway, as we enter, is the room, without a shred of furniture in it except the boards of two closed-in beds. The flooring is not steady, and here and there holes have been eaten into the planks. You can scarcely stand upright beneath the decaying ceiling. Worn boards and ragged walls, and the rusty ribs fallen from the fireplace, are all that meet your eyes, but I see a round, unsteady, waxcloth-covered table, with four books lying at equal distances on it. There are six prim chairs, two of them not to be sat upon, backed against the walls, and between the window and the fire-place a chest of drawers, with a snowy-coverlet. On the drawers stands a board with coloured marbles for the game of solitaire, and I have only to open the drawer with the loose handle to bring out the dambrod. In the carved wood frame over the window hangs Jamie's portrait; in the only other frame a picture of Daniel in the den of lions, sewn by Leeby in wool. Over the chimney-piece with its shells, in which the roar of the sea can be heard, are strung three rows of birds' eggs. Once again we might be expecting company to tea.

The passage is narrow. There is a square hole between the rafters, and a ladder leading up to it. You may climb and look into the attic, as Jess liked to hear me call my tiny garret-room. I am stiffer now than in the days when I lodged with Jess during the summer holiday I am trying to bring back, and there is no need for me to ascend. Do not laugh at the newspapers with which Leeby papered the garret, nor at the yarn Hendry stuffed into the windy holes. He did it to warm the house for Jess. But the paper must have gone to pieces and the yarn rotted decades ago.

I have kept the kitchen for the last, as Jamie did on the dire day of which I shall have to tell. It has a flooring of stone now, where there used only to be hard earth, and a broken pane in the window is indifferently stuffed with rags. But it is the other window I turn to, with a pain at my heart, and pride and fondness too, the square foot of glass where Jess sat in her chair and looked down the brae.

Ah, that brae! The history of tragic little Thrums is sunk into it like the stones it swallows in the winter. We have all found the brae long and steep in the spring of life. Do you remember how the child you once were sat at the foot of it and wondered if a new world began at the top? It climbs from a shallow burn, and we used to sit on the brig a long time before venturing to climb. As boys we ran up the brae. As men and women, young and in our prime, we almost forgot that it was there. But the autumn of life comes, and the brae grows steeper; then the winter, and once again we are as the child pausing apprehensively on the brig. Yet are we no longer the child; we look now for no new world at the top, only for a little garden and a tiny house, and a hand-loom in the house. It is only a garden of kail and potatoes, but there may be a line of daisies, white and red, on each side of the narrow footpath, and honeysuckle over the door. Life is not always hard, even after backs grow bent, and we know that all braes lead only to the grave.

This is Jess's window. For more than twenty years she had not been able to go so far as the door, and only once while I knew her was she ben in the room. With her husband, Hendry, or their only daughter, Leeby, to lean upon, and her hand clutching her staff, she took twice a day, when she was strong, the journey between her bed and the window where stood her chair. She did not lie there looking at the sparrows or at Leeby redding up the house, and I hardly ever heard her complain. All the sewing was done by her; she often baked on a table pushed close to the window, and by leaning forward she could stir the porridge. Leeby was seldom off her feet, but I do not know that she did more than Jess, who liked to tell me, when she had a moment to spare, that she had a terrible lot to be thankful for.

To those who dwell in great cities Thrums is only a small place, but what a clatter of life it has for me when I come to it from my school-house in the glen. Had my lot been cast in a town I would no doubt have sought country parts during my September holiday, but the school-house is quiet even when the summer takes brakes full of sportsmen and others past the top of my footpath, and I was always light-hearted when Craigiebuckle's cart bore me into the din of Thrums. I only once stayed during the whole of my holiday at the house on the brae, but I knew its inmates for many years, including Jamie, the son, who was a barber in London. Of their ancestry I never heard. With us it was only some of the articles of furniture, or perhaps a snuff-mull, that had a genealogical tree. In the house on the brae was a great kettle, called the boiler, that was said to be fifty years old in the days of Hendry's grandfather, of whom nothing more is known. Jess's chair, which had carved arms and a seat stuffed with rags, had been Snecky Hobart's father's before it was hers, and old Snecky bought it at a roup in the Tenements. Jess's rarest possession was, perhaps, the christening robe that even people at a distance came to borrow. Her mother could count up a hundred persons who had been baptized in it.

Every one of the hundred, I believe, is dead, and even I cannot now pick out Jess and Hendry's grave; but I heard recently that the christening robe is still in use. It is strange that I should still be left after so many changes, one of the three or four who can to-day stand on the brae and point out Jess's window. The little window commands the incline to the point where the brae suddenly jerks out of sight in its climb down into the town. The steep path up the commonty makes for this elbow of the brae, and thus, whichever way the traveller takes, it is here that he comes first into sight of the window. Here, too, those who go to the town from the south get their first glimpse of Thrums.

Carts pass up and down the brae every few minutes, and there comes an occasional gig. Seldom is the brae empty, for many live beyond the top of it now, and men and women go by to their work, children to school or play. Not one of the children I see from the window to-day is known to me, and most of the men and women I only recognize by their likeness to their parents. That sweet-faced old woman with the shawl on her shoulders may be one of the girls who was playing at the game of palaulays when Jamie stole into Thrums for the last time; the man who is leaning on the commonty gate gathering breath for the last quarter of the brae may, as a barefooted callant, have been one of those who chased Cree Queery past the poor-house. I cannot say; but this I know, that the grandparents of most of these boys and girls were once young with me. If I see the sons and daughters of my friends grown old, I also see the grandchildren spinning the peerie and hunkering at I-dree-I-dree—I-droppit-it—as we did so long ago. The world remains as young as ever. The lovers that met on the commonty in the gloaming are gone, but there are other lovers to take their place, and still the commonty is here. The sun had sunk on a fine day in June, early in the century, when Hendry and Jess, newly married, he in a rich moleskin waistcoat, she in a white net cap, walked to the house on the brae that was to be their home. So Jess has told me. Here again has been just such a day, and somewhere in Thrums there may be just such a couple; setting out for their home behind a horse with white ears instead of walking, but with the same hopes and fears, and the same love light in their eyes. The world does not age. The hearse passes over the brae and up the straight burying-ground road, but still, there is a cry for the christening robe.

Jess's window was a beacon by night to travellers in the dark, and it will be so in the future when there are none to remember Jess. There are many such windows still, with loving faces behind them. From them we watch for the friends and relatives who are coming back, and some, alas! watch in vain. Not every one returns who takes the elbow of the brae bravely, or waves his handkerchief to those who watch from the window with wet eyes, and some return too late. To Jess, at her window always when she was not in bed, things happy and mournful and terrible came into view. At this window she sat for twenty years or more looking at the world as through a telescope; and here an awful ordeal was gone through after her sweet untarnished soul had been given back to God.

# II

## ON THE TRACK OF THE MINISTER

On the afternoon of the Saturday that carted me and my two boxes to Thrums, I was ben in the room playing Hendry at the dambrod. I had one of the room chairs, but Leeby brought a chair from the kitchen for her father. Our door stood open, and as Hendry often pondered for two minutes with his hand on a "man," I could have joined in the gossip that was going on but the house.

"Ay, weel, then, Leeby," said Jess, suddenly, "I'll warrant the minister 'll no be preachin' the morn."

This took Leeby to the window.

"Yea, yea," she said (and I knew she was nodding her head sagaciously); I looked out at the room window, but all I could see was a man wheeling an empty barrow down the brae.

"That's Robbie Tosh," continued Leeby; "an' there's nae doot 'at he's makkin for the minister's, for he has on his black coat. He'll be to row the minister's luggage to the post-cart. Ay, an' that's Davit Lunan's barrow. I ken it by the shaft's bein' spliced wi' yarn. Davit broke the shaft at the saw-mill."

"He'll be gaen awa for a curran (number of) days," said Jess, "or he would juist hae taen his bag. Ay, he'll be awa to Edinbory, to see the lass."

"I wonder wha'll be to preach the morn—tod, it'll likely be Mr. Skinner, frae Dundee; him an' the minister's chief, ye ken."

"Ye micht gang up to the attic, Leeby, an' see if the spare bedroom vent (chimney) at the manse is gaen. We're sure, if it's Mr. Skinner, he'll come wi' the post frae Tilliedrum the nicht, an' sleep at the manse."

"Weel, I assure ye," said Leeby, descending from the attic, "it'll no be Mr. Skinner, for no only is the spare bedroom vent no gaen, but the blind's drawn doon frae tap to fut, so they're no even airin' the room. Na, it canna be him; an' what's mair, it'll be naebody 'at's to bide a' nicht at the manse."

"I wouldna say that; na, na. It may only be a student; an' Marget Dundas" (the minister's mother and housekeeper) "michtna think it necessary to put on a fire for him."

"Tod, I'll tell ye wha it'll be. I wonder I didna think o' 'im sooner. It'll be the lad Wilkie; him 'at's mither mairit on Sam'l Duthie's wife's brither. They bide in Cupar, an' I mind 'at when the son was here twa or three year syne he was juist gaen to begin the diveenity classes in Glesca."

"If that's so, Leeby, he would be sure to bide wi' Sam'l. Hendry, hae ye heard 'at Sam'l Duthie's expeckin' a stranger the nicht?"

"Haud yer toague," replied Hendry, who was having the worst of the game.

"Ay, but I ken he is," said Leeby triumphantly to her mother, "for ye mind when I was in at Johnny Watt's (the draper's) Chirsty (Sam'l's wife) was buyin' twa yards o' chintz, an' I couldna think what she would be wantin' 't for!"

"I thocht Johnny said to ye 'at it was for a present to Chirsty's auntie?"

"Ay, but he juist guessed that; for, though he tried to get oot o' Chirsty what she wanted the chintz for, she wouldna tell 'im. But I see noo what she was after. The lad Wilkie 'll be to bide wi' them, and Chirsty had bocht the chintz to cover the airm-chair wi'. It's ane o' thae hair-bottomed chairs, but terrible torn, so she'll hae covered it for 'im to sit on."

"I wouldna wonder but ye're richt, Leeby; for Chirsty would be in an oncommon fluster if she thocht the lad's mither was likely to hear 'at her best chair was torn. Ay, ay, bein' a man, he wouldna think to tak aff the chintz an' hae a look at the chair withoot it."

Here Hendry, who had paid no attention to the conversation, broke in—

"Was ye speirin' had I seen Sam'l Duthie? I saw 'im yesterday buyin' a fender at Will'um Crook's roup."

"A fender! Ay, ay, that settles the queistion," said Leeby; "I'll warrant the fender was for Chirsty's parlour. It's preyed on Chirsty's mind, they say, this fower-and-thirty year 'at she doesna hae a richt parlour fender."

"Leeby, look! That's Robbie Tosh wi' the barrow. He has a michty load o' luggage. A'm thinkin' the minister's bound for Tilliedrum."

"Na, he's no, he's gaen to Edinbory, as ye micht ken by the bandbox. That'll be his mither's bonnet he's takkin' back to get altered. Ye'll mind she was never pleased wi' the set o' the flowers."

"Weel, weel, here comes the minister himsel, an' very snod he is. Ay, Marget's been puttin' new braid on his coat, an' he's carryin' the sma' black bag he bocht in Dundee last year: he'll hae's nicht-shirt an' a comb in't, I dinna doot. Ye micht rin to the corner, Leeby, an' see if he cries in at Jess McTaggart's in passin'."

"It's my opeenion," said Leeby, returning excitedly from the corner, " 'at the lad Wilkie's no to be preachin' the morn, after a'. When I gangs to the corner, at ony rate, what think ye's the first thing I see but the minister an' Sam'l Duthie meetin' face to face? Ay, weel, it's gospel a'm tellin' ye when I say as Sam'l flung back his head an' walkit richt by the minister!"

"Losh keep's a', Leeby; ye say that? They maun hae haen a quarrel."

"I'm thinkin' we'll hae Mr. Skinner i' the poopit the morn after a'."

"It may be, it may be. Ay, ay, look, Leeby, whatna bit kimmer's that wi' the twa jugs in her hand?"

"Eh? Ou, it'll be Lawyer Ogilvy's servant lassieky gaen to the farm o' T'nowhead for the milk. She gangs ilka Saturday nicht. But, what did ye say—twa jugs? Tod, let's see! Ay, she has so, a big jug an' a little ane. The little ane 'll be for cream; an', sal, the big ane's bigger na usual."

"There maun be something gaen on at the lawyer's if they're buyin' cream, Leeby. Their reg'lar thing's twopence worth o' milk."

"Ay, but I assure ye that sma' jug's for cream, an' I dinna doot mysel but 'at there's to be fower-pence worth o' milk this nicht."

"There's to be a puddin' made the morn, Leeby. Ou, ay, a' thing points to that; an' we're very sure there's nae puddins at the lawyer's on the Sabbath onless they hae company."

"I dinna ken wha they can hae, if it be na that brither o' the wife's 'at bides oot by Aberdeen."

"Na, it's no him, Leeby; na, na. He's no weel to do, an' they wouldna be buyin' cream for 'im."

"I'll run up to the attic again, an' see if there's ony stir at the lawyer's hoose."

By and by Leeby returned in triumph.

"Ou, ay," she said, "they're expectin' veesitors at the lawyer's, for I could see twa o' the bairns dressed up to the nines, an' Mistress Ogilvy doesna dress at them in that wy for naething."

"It fair beats me though, Leeby, to guess wha's comin' to them. Ay, but stop a meenute, I wouldna wonder, no, really I would not wonder but what it'll be——"

"The very thing 'at was passin' through my head, mother."

"Ye mean 'at the lad Wilkie 'll be to bide wi' the lawyer i' stead o' wi' Sam'l Duthie? Sal, a'm thinkin' that's it. Ye ken Sam'l an' the lawyer married on cousins; but Mistress Ogilvy ay lookit on Chirsty as dirt aneath her feet. She would be glad to get a minister, though, to the hoose, an' so I warrant the lad Wilkie 'll be to bide a' nicht at the lawyer's."

"But what would Chirsty be doin' gettin' the chintz an' the fender in that case?"

"Ou, she'd been, expeckin' the lad, of course. Sal, she'll be in a michty tantrum aboot this. I wouldna wonder though she gets Sam'l to gang ower to the U. P.'s."

Leeby went once more to the attic.

"Ye're wrang, mother," she cried out "Whaever's to preach the morn is to bide at the manse, for the minister's servant's been at Baker Duff's buyin' short-bread—half a lippy, nae doot."

"Are ye sure o' that, Leeby?"

"Oh, a'm certain. The servant gaed in to Duff's the noo, an', as ye ken fine, the manse fowk doesna deal wi' him, except they're wantin' short-bread. He's Auld Kirk."

Leeby returned to the kitchen, and Jess sat for a time ruminating.

"The lad Wilkie," she said at last, triumphantly, "'ll be to bide at Lawyer Ogilvy's; but he'll be gaen to the manse the morn for a tea-dinner."

"But what," asked Leeby, "aboot the milk an' the cream for the lawyer's?"

"Ou, they'll be hae'n a puddin' for the supper the nicht. That's a michty genteel thing, I've heard."

It turned out that Jess was right in every particular.

# III

## PREPARING TO RECEIVE COMPANY

Leeby was at the fire brandering a quarter of steak on the tongs, when the house was flung into consternation by Hendry's casual remark that he had seen Tibbie Mealmaker in the town with her man.

"The Lord preserve's!" cried Leeby.

Jess looked quickly at the clock.

"Half fower!" she said, excitedly.

"Then it canna be dune," said Leeby, falling despairingly into a chair, "for they may be here ony meenute."

"It's most michty," said Jess, turning on her husband, "'at ye should tak a pleasure in bringin' this hoose to disgrace. Hoo did ye no tell's suner?"

"I fair forgot" Hendry answered, "but what's a' yer steer?"

Jess looked at me (she often did this) in a way that meant, "What a man is this I'm tied to!"

"Steer!" she exclaimed. "Is't no time we was makkin' a steer? They'll be in for their tea ony meenute, an' the room no sae muckle as sweepit. Ay, an' me lookin' like a sweep; an' Tibbie Mealmaker 'at's sae partikler genteel seein' you sic a sicht as ye are!"

Jess shook Hendry out of his chair, while Leeby began to sweep with the one hand, and agitatedly to unbutton her wrapper with the other.

"She didna see me," said Hendry, sitting down forlornly on the table.

"Get aff that table!" cried Jess. "See haud o' the besom," she said to Leeby.

"For mercy's sake, mother," said Leeby, "gie yer face a dicht, an' put on a clean mutch."

"I'll open the door if they come afore you're ready," said Hendry, as Leeby pushed him against the dresser.

"Ye daur to speak aboot openin' the door, an' you a mess!" cried Jess, with pins in her mouth.

"Havers!" retorted Hendry. "A man canna be aye washin' at 'imsel."

Seeing that Hendry was as much in the way as myself, I invited him upstairs to the attic, whence we heard Jess and Leeby upbraiding each other shrilly. I was aware that the room was speckless; but for all that, Leeby was turning it upside down.

"She's aye ta'en like that," Hendry said to me, referring to his wife, "when she's expectin' company. Ay, it's a peety she canna tak things cannier."

"Tibbie Mealmaker must be some one of importance?" I asked.

"Ou, she's naething by the ord'nar'; but ye see she was mairit to a Tilliedrum man no lang syne, an' they're said to hae a michty grand establishment. Ay, they've a wardrobe spleet new; an' what think ye Tibbie wears ilka day?"

I shook my head.

"It was Chirsty Miller 'at put it through the toon," Hendry continued. "Chirsty was in Tilliedrum last Teisday or Wednesday, an' Tibbie gae her a cup o' tea. Ay, weel, Tibbie telt Chirsty 'at she wears hose ilka day."

"Wears hose?"

"Ay. It's some michty grand kind o' stockin'. I never heard o't in this toon. Na, there's naebody in Thrums 'at wears hose."

"And who did Tibbie get?" I asked; for in Thrums they say, "Wha did she get?" and "Wha did he tak?"

"His name's Davit Curly. Ou, a crittur fu' o' maggots, an' nae great match, for he's juist the Tilliedrum bill-sticker."

At this moment Jess shouted from her chair (she was burnishing the society teapot as she spoke), "Mind, Hendry McQumpha, 'at upon nae condition are ye to mention the bill-stickin' afore Tibbie!"

"Tibbie," Hendry explained to me, "is a terrible vain tid, an' doesna think the bill-stickin' genteel. Ay, they say 'at if she meets Davit in the street wi' his paste-pot an' the brush in his hands she pretends no to ken 'im."

Every time Jess paused to think she cried up orders, such as—

"Dinna call her Tibbie, mind ye. Always address her as Mistress Curly."

"Shak' hands wi' baith o' them, an' say ye hope they're in the enjoyment o' guid health."

"Dinna put yer feet on the table."

"Mind, you're no' to mention 'at ye kent they were in the toon."

"When onybody passes ye yer tea say, 'Thank ye.'"

"Dinna stir yer tea as if ye was churnin' butter, nor let on 'at the scones is no our ain bakin'."

"If Tibbie says onything aboot the china yer no' to say 'at we dinna use it ilka day."

"Dinna lean back in the big chair, for it's broken, an' Leeby's gi'en it a lick o' glue this meenute."

"When Leeby gies ye a kick aneath the table that'll be a sign to ye to say grace."

Hendry looked at me apologetically while these instructions came up.

"I winna dive my head wi' sic nonsense," he said; "it's no' for a man body to be sae crammed fu' o' manners."

"Come awa doon," Jess shouted to him, "an' put on a clean dickey."

"I'll better do't to please her," said Hendry, "though for my ain part I dinna like the feel o' a dickey on week-days. Na, they mak's think it's the Sabbath."

Ten minutes afterwards I went downstairs to see how the preparations were progressing. Fresh muslin curtains had been put up in the room. The grand footstool, worked by Leeby, was so placed that Tibbie could not help seeing it; and a fine cambric handkerchief, of which Jess was very proud, was hanging out of a drawer as if by accident. An antimacassar lying carelessly on the seat of a chair concealed a rent in the horse-hair, and the china ornaments on the mantlepiece were so placed that they looked whole. Leeby's black merino was hanging near the window in a good light, and Jess's Sabbath bonnet, which was never worn, occupied a nail beside it. The tea-things stood on a tray in the kitchen bed, whence they could be quickly brought into the room, just as if they were always ready to be used daily. Leeby, as yet in deshabille, was shaving her father at a tremendous rate, and Jess, looking as fresh as a daisy, was ready to receive the visitors. She was peering through the tiny window-blind looking for them.

"Be cautious, Leeby," Hendry was saying, when Jess shook her hand at him. "Wheesht," she whispered; "they're comin'."

Hendry was hustled into his Sabbath coat, and then came a tap at the door, a very genteel tap. Jess nodded to Leeby, who softly shoved Hendry into the room.

The tap was repeated, but Leeby pushed her father into a chair and thrust Barrow's Sermons open into his hand. Then she stole but the house, and swiftly buttoned her wrapper, speaking to Jess by nods the while. There was a third knock, whereupon Jess said, in a loud, Englishy voice—

"Was that not a chap (knock) at the door?"

Hendry was about to reply, but she shook her fist at him. Next moment Leeby opened the door. I was upstairs, but I heard Jess say—

"Dear me, if it's not Mrs. Curly—and Mr. Curly! And hoo are ye? Come in, by. Weel, this is, indeed, a pleasant surprise!"

# IV

## WAITING FOR THE DOCTOR

Jess had gone early to rest, and the door of her bed in the kitchen was pulled to. From her window I saw Hendry buying dulse.

Now and again the dulseman wheeled his slimy boxes to the top of the brae, and sat there stolidly on the shafts of his barrow. Many passed him by, but occasionally some one came to rest by his side. Unless the customer was loquacious, there was no bandying of words, and Hendry merely unbuttoned his east-trouser pocket, giving his body the angle at which the pocket could be most easily filled by the dulseman. He then deposited his halfpenny, and moved on. Neither had spoken; yet in the country they would have roared their predictions about to-morrow to a ploughman half a field away.

Dulse is roasted by twisting it round the tongs fired to a red-heat, and the house was soon heavy with the smell of burning sea-weed. Leeby was at the dresser munching it from a broth-plate, while Hendry, on his knees at the fireplace, gingerly tore off the blades of dulse that were sticking to the tongs, and licked his singed fingers.

"Whaur's yer mother?" he asked Leeby.

"Ou," said Leeby, "whaur would she be but in her bed?"

Hendry took the tongs to the door, and would have cleaned them himself, had not Leeby (who often talked his interfering ways over with her mother) torn them from his hands.

"Leeby!" cried Jess at that moment.

"Ay," answered Leeby, leisurely, not noticing, as I happened to do, that Jess spoke in an agitated voice.

"What is't?" asked Hendry, who liked to be told things.

He opened the door of the bed.

"Yer mother's no weel," he said to Leeby.

Leeby ran to the bed, and I went ben the house.

In another two minutes we were a group of four in the kitchen, staring vacantly. Death could not have startled us more, tapping thrice that quiet night on the window-pane.

"It's diphtheria!" said Jess, her hands trembling as she buttoned her wrapper.

She looked at me, and Leeby looked at me. "It's no, it's no," cried Leeby, and her voice was as a fist shaken at my face. She blamed me for hesitating in my reply. But ever since this malady left me a lonely dominie for life, diphtheria has been a knockdown word for me. Jess had discovered a great white spot on her throat. I knew the symptoms.

"Is't dangerous?" asked Hendry, who once had a headache years before, and could still refer to it as a reminiscence.

"Them 'at has 't never recovers," said Jess, sitting down very quietly. A stick fell from the fire, and she bent forward to replace it.

"They do recover," cried Leeby, again turning angry eyes on me.

I could not face her; I had known so many who did not recover. She put her hand on her mother's shoulder.

"Mebbe ye would be better in yer bed," suggested Hendry,

No one spoke.

"When I had the headache," said Hendry, "I was better in my bed."

Leeby had taken Jess's hand—a worn old hand that had many a time gone out in love and kindness when younger hands were cold. Poets have sung and fighting men have done great deeds for hands that never had such a record.

"If ye could eat something," said Hendry, "I would gae to the flesher's for't. I mind when I had the headache, hoo a small steak——"

"Gae awa for the doctor, rayther," broke in Leeby.

Jess started, for sufferers think there is less hope for them after the doctor has been called in to pronounce sentence.

"I winna hae the doctor," she said, anxiously.

In answer to Leeby's nods, Hendry slowly pulled out his boots from beneath the table, and sat looking at them, preparatory to putting them on. He was beginning at last to be a little scared, though his face did not show it.

"I winna hae ye," cried Jess, getting to her feet, "ga'en to the doctor's sic a sicht. Yer coat's a' yarn."

"Havers," said Hendry, but Jess became frantic. I offered to go for the doctor, but while I was upstairs looking for my bonnet I heard the door slam. Leeby had become impatient, and darted off herself, buttoning her jacket probably as she ran. When I returned to the kitchen, Jess and Hendry were still by the fire. Hendry was beating a charred stick into sparks, and his wife sat with her hands in her lap. I saw Hendry look at her once or twice, but he could think of nothing to say. His terms of endearment had died out thirty-nine years before with his courtship. He had forgotten the words. For his life he could not have crossed over to Jess and put his arm round her. Yet he was uneasy. His eyes wandered round the poorly lit room.

"Will ye hae a drink o' watter?" he asked.

There was a sound of footsteps outside.

"That'll be him," said Hendry in a whisper. Jess started to her feet, and told Hendry to help her ben the house.

The steps died away, but I fancied that Jess, now highly strung, had gone into hiding, and I went after her. I was mistaken. She had lit the room lamp, turning the crack in the globe to the wall. The sheepskin hearthrug, which was generally carefully packed away beneath the bed, had been spread out before the empty fireplace, and Jess was on the arm-chair hurriedly putting on her grand black mutch with the pink flowers.

"I was juist makkin' mysel respectable," she said, but without life in her voice.

This was the only time I ever saw her in the room. Leeby returned panting to say that the doctor might be expected in an hour. He was away among the hills.

The hour passed reluctantly. Leeby lit a fire ben the house, and then put on her Sabbath dress. She sat with her mother in the room. Never before had I seen Jess sit so quietly, for her way was to work until, as she said herself, she was ready "to fall into her bed."

Hendry wandered between the two rooms, always in the way when Leeby ran to the window to see if that was the doctor at last. He would stand gaping in the middle of the room for five minutes, then slowly withdraw to stand as drearily but the house. His face lengthened. At last he sat down by the kitchen fire, a Bible in his hand. It lay open on his knee, but he did not read much. He sat there with his legs outstretched, looking straight before him. I believe he saw Jess young again. His face was very solemn, and his mouth twitched. The fire sank into ashes unheeded.

I sat alone at my attic window for hours, waiting for the doctor. From the attic I could see nearly all Thrums, but, until very late, the night was dark, and the brae, except immediately before the door, was blurred and dim. A sheet of light canopied the square as long as a cheap Jack paraded his goods there. It was gone before the moon came out. Figures tramped, tramped up the brae, passed the house in shadow and stole silently on. A man or boy whistling seemed to fill the valley. The moon arrived too late to be of service to any wayfarer. Everybody in Thrums was asleep but ourselves, and the doctor who never came.

About midnight Hendry climbed the attic stair and joined me at the window. His hand was shaking as he pulled back the blind. I began to realize that his heart could still overflow.

"She's waur," he whispered, like one who had lost his voice.

For a long time he sat silently, his hand on the blind. He was so different from the Hendry I had known, that I felt myself in the presence of a strange man. His eyes were glazed with staring at the turn of the brae where the doctor must first come into sight. His breathing became heavier, till it was a gasp. Then I put my hand on his shoulder, and he stared at me.

"Nine-and-thirty years come June," he said, speaking to himself.

For this length of time, I knew, he and Jess had been married. He repeated the words at intervals.

"I mind—" he began, and stopped. He was thinking of the spring-time of Jess's life.

The night ended as we watched; then came the terrible moment that precedes the day—the moment known to shuddering watchers by sick beds, when a chill wind cuts through the house, and the world without seems cold in death. It is as if the heart of the earth did not mean to continue beating.

"This is a fearsome nicht," Hendry said, hoarsely.

He turned to grope his way to the stairs, but suddenly went down on his knees to pray. . . .

There was a quick step outside. I arose in time to see the doctor on the brae. He tried the latch, but Leeby was there to show him in. The door of the room closed on him.

From the top of the stair I could see into the dark passage, and make out Hendry shaking at the door. I could hear the doctor's voice, but not the words he said. There was a painful silence, and then Leeby laughed joyously.

"It's gone," cried Jess; "the white spot's gone! Ye juist touched it, an' it's gone! Tell Hendry."

But Hendry did not need to be told. As Jess spoke I heard him say, huskily: "Thank God!" and then he tottered back to the kitchen. When the doctor left, Hendry was still on Jess's armchair, trembling like a man with the palsy. Ten minutes afterwards I was preparing for bed, when he cried up the stair—

"Come awa' doon."

I joined the family party in the room: Hendry was sitting close to Jess.

"Let us read," he said, firmly, "in the fourteenth of John."

# V

## A HUMORIST ON HIS CALLING

After the eight o'clock bell had rung, Hendry occasionally crossed over to the farm of T'nowhead and sat on the pig-sty. If no one joined him he scratched the pig, and returned home gradually. Here what was almost a club held informal meetings, at which two or four, or even half a dozen assembled to debate, when there was any one to start them. The meetings were only memorable when Tammas Haggart was in fettle, to pronounce judgments in his well-known sarcastic way. Sometimes we had got off the pig-sty to separate before Tammas was properly yoked. There we might remain a long time, planted round him like trees, for he was a mesmerising talker.

There was a pail belonging to the pig-sty, which some one would turn bottom upwards and sit upon if the attendance was unusually numerous. Tammas liked, however, to put a foot on it now and again in the full swing of a harangue, and when he paused for a sarcasm I have seen the pail kicked toward him. He had the wave of the arm that is so convincing in argument, and such a natural way of asking questions, that an audience not used to public speaking might have thought he wanted them to reply. It is an undoubted fact, that when he went on the platform at the time of the election, to heckle the Colonel, he paused in the middle of his questions to take a drink out of the tumbler of water which stood on the table. As soon as they saw what he was up to, the spectators raised a ringing cheer.

On concluding his perorations, Tammas sent his snuff-mull round, but we had our own way of passing him a vote of thanks. One of the company would express amazement at his gift of words, and the others would add, "Man, man," or, "Ye cow, Tammas," or, "What a crittur ye are!" all which ejaculations meant the same thing. A new subject being thus ingeniously introduced, Tammas again put his foot on the pail.

"I tak no creedit," he said, modestly, on the evening, I remember, of Willie Pyatt's funeral, "in bein' able to speak wi' a sort o' faceelity on topics 'at I've made my ain."

"Ay," said T'nowhead, "but it's no the faceelity o' speakin' 'at taks me. There's Davit Lunan 'at can speak like as if he had learned it aff a paper, an' yet I canna thole 'im."

"Davit," said Hendry, "doesna speak in a wy 'at a body can follow 'im. He doesna gae even on. Jess says he's juist like a man ay at the cross-roads, an' no sure o' his wy. But the stock has words, an' no ilka body has that."

"If I was bidden to put Tammas's gift in a word," said T'nowhead, "I would say 'at he had a wy. That's what I would say."

"Weel, I suppose I have,"Tammas admitted, "but, wy or no wy, I couldna put a point on my words if it wasna for my sense o' humour. Lads, humour's what gies the nip to speakin'."

"It's what maks ye a sarcesticist, Tammas," said Hendry; "but what I wonder at is yer sayin' the humorous things sae aisy like. Some says ye mak them up aforehand, but I ken that's no true."

"No only is't no true," said Tammas, "but it couldna be true. Them 'at says sic things, an', weel I ken you're meanin' Davit Lunan, hasna nae idea o' what humour is. It's a thing 'at spouts oot o' its ain accord. Some o' the maist humorous things I've ever said cam oot, as a body may say, by themsels."

"I suppose that's the case," said T'nowhead, "an' yet it maun be you 'at brings them up?"

"There's no nae doubt aboot its bein' the case," said Tammas, "for I've watched mysel often. There was a vara guid instance occurred sune after I married Easie. The Earl's son met me one day, aboot that time, i' the Tenements, an' he didna ken 'at Chirsty was deid, an' I'd married again. 'Well, Haggart,' he says, in his frank wy, 'and how is your wife?' 'She's vara weel, sir,' I maks answer, 'but she's no the ane you mean.'"

"Na, he meant Chirsty," said Hendry.

"Is that a' the story?" asked T'nowhead.

Tammas had been looking at us queerly.

"There's no nane o' ye lauchin'," he said, "but I can assure ye the Earl's son gaed east the toon lauchin' like onything."

"But what was't he lauched at?"

"Ou," said Tammas, "a humorist doesna tell whaur the humour comes in."

"No, but when you said that, did ye mean it to be humorous?"

"A'm no sayin' I did, but as I've been tellin' ye humour spouts oot by itsel."

"Ay, but do ye ken noo what the Earl's son gaed awa lauchin' at?"

Tammas hesitated.

"I dinna exactly see't," he confessed, "but that's no an oncommon thing. A humorist would often no ken 'at he was ane if it wasna by the wy he maks other fowk lauch. A body canna be expeckit baith to mak the joke an' to see't. Na, that would be doin' twa fowks' wark."

"Weel, that's reasonable enough, but I've often seen ye lauchin'," said Hendry, "lang afore other fowk lauched."

"Nae doubt," Tammas explained, "an' that's because humour has twa sides, juist like a penny piece. When I say a humorous thing mysel I'm dependent on other fowk to tak note o' the humour o't, bein' mysel ta'en up wi' the makkin' o't. Ay, but there's things I see an' hear 'at maks me lauch, an' that's the other side o' humour."

"I never heard it put sae plain afore," said T'nowhead, "an', sal, a'm no nane sure but what a'm a humorist too."

"Na, na, no you, T'nowhead," said Tammas, hotly.

"Weel," continued the farmer, "I never set up for bein' a humorist, but I can juist assure ye 'at I lauch at queer things too. No lang syne I woke up i' my bed lauchin' like onything, an' Lisbeth thocht I wasna weel. It was something I dreamed 'at made me lauch, I couldna think what it was, but I lauched richt. Was that no fell like a humorist?"

"That was neither here nor there," said Tammas. Na, dreams dinna coont, for we're no responsible for them. Ay, an' what's mair, the mere lauchin's no the important side o' humour, even though ye hinna to be telt to lauch. The important side's the other side, the sayin' the humorous things. I'll tell ye what: the humorist's like a man firin' at a target—he doesna ken whether he hits or no till them at the target tells 'im."

"I would be of opeenion," said Hendry, who was one of Tammas's most staunch admirers, " 'at another mark o' the rale humorist was his seein' humour in all things?"

Tammas shook his head—a way he had when Hendry advanced theories.

"I dinna haud wi' that ava," he said. "I ken fine 'at Davit Lunan gaes aboot sayin' he sees humour in everything, but there's nae surer sign 'at he's no a genuine humorist. Na, the rale humorist kens vara weel 'at there's subjects withoot a spark o' humour in them. When a subject rises to the sublime it should be regairded philosophically, an' no humorously. Davit would lauch 'at the grandest thochts, whaur they only fill the true humorist wi' awe. I've found it necessary to rebuke 'im at times whaur his lauchin' was oot o' place. He pretended aince on this vara spot to see humour i' the origin o' cock-fightin'."

"Did he, man?" said Hendry; "I wasna here. But what is the origin o' cock-fechtin'?"

"It was a' i' the Cheap Magazine," said T'nowhead.

"Was I sayin' it wasna?" demanded Tammas. "It was through me readin' the account oot o' the Cheap Magazine 'at the discussion arose."

"But what said the Cheapy was the origin o' cock-fechtin'?"

"T'nowhead 'll tell ye," answered Tammas; "he says I dinna ken."

"I never said naething o' the kind," returned T'nowhead, indignantly; "I mind o' ye readin't oot fine."

"Ay, weel," said Tammas, "that's a' richt. Ou, the origin o' cock-fightin'
gangs back to the time o' the Greek wars, a thoosand or twa years syne,
mair or less. There was ane, Miltiades by name, 'at was the captain o' the
Greek army, an' one day he led them doon the mountains to attack the
biggest army 'at was ever gathered thegither."

"They were Persians," interposed T'nowhead.

"Are you tellin' the story, or am I?" asked Tammas. "I kent fine 'at they
were Persians. Weel, Miltiades had the matter o' twenty thoosand men wi'
'im, and when they got to the foot o' the mountain, behold there was two
cocks fechtin'."

"Man, man," said Hendry, "an' was there cocks in thae days?"

"Ondoubtedly," said Tammas, "or hoo could thae twa hae been fechtin'?"

"Ye have me there, Tammas," admitted Hendry. "Ye're perfectly richt."

"Ay, then," continued the stone-breaker, "when Miltiades saw the cocks
at it wi' all their micht, he stopped the army and addressed it. 'Behold!' he
cried, at the top o' his voice, 'these cocks do not fight for their household
gods, nor for the monuments of their ancestors, nor for glory, nor for
liberty, nor for their children, but only because the one will not give way
unto the other.'"

"It was nobly said," declared Hendry; "na, cocks wouldna hae sae muckle
understandin' as to fecht for thae things. I wouldna wonder but what it was
some laddies 'at set them at ane another."

"Hendry doesna see what Miltydes was after," said T'nowhead.

"Ye've taen't up wrang, Hendry," Tammas explained. "What Miltiades
meant was 'at if cocks could fecht sae weel oot o' mere deviltry, surely the
Greeks would fecht terrible for their gods an' their bairns an' the other
things."

"I see, I see; but what was the monuments o' their ancestors?"

"Ou, that was the gravestanes they put up i' their kirkyards."

"I wonder the other billies would want to tak them awa. They would be
a michty wecht."

"Ay, but they wanted them, an' nat'rally the Greeks stuck to the stanes
they paid for."

"So, so, an' did Davit Lunan mak oot 'at there was humour in that?"

"He do so. He said it was a humorous thing to think o' a hale army lookin'
on at twa cocks fechtin'. I assure ye I telt 'im 'at I saw nae humour in't. It
was ane o' the most impressive sichts ever seen by man, an' the Greeks was
sae inspired by what Miltiades said 'at they sweepit the Persians oot o' their
country."

We all agreed that Tammas's was the genuine humour.

"An' an enviable possession it is," said Hendry.

"In a wy," admitted Tammas, "but no in a' wys."

He hesitated, and then added in a low voice—

"As sure as death, Hendry, it sometimes taks grip o' me i' the kirk itsel, an' I can hardly keep frae lauchin'."

# VI

## DEAD THIS TWENTY YEARS

IN the lustiness of youth there are many who cannot feel that they, too, will die. The first fear stops the heart. Even then they would keep death at arm's length by making believe to disown him. Loved ones are taken away, and the boy, the girl, will not speak of them, as if that made the conqueror's triumph the less. In time the fire in the breast burns low, and then in the last glow of the embers, it is sweeter to hold to what has been than to think of what may be.

Twenty years had passed since Joey ran down the brae to play. Jess, his mother, shook her staff fondly at him. A cart rumbled by, the driver nodding on the shaft. It rounded the corner and stopped suddenly, and then a woman screamed. A handful of men carried Joey's dead body to his mother, and that was the tragedy of Jess's life.

Twenty years ago, and still Jess sat at the window, and still she heard that woman scream. Every other living being had forgotten Joey; even to Hendry he was now scarcely a name, but there were times when Jess's face quivered and her old arms went out for her dead boy.

"God's will be done," she said, "but oh, I grudged Him my bairn terrible sair. I dinna want him back noo, an' ilka day is takkin' me nearer to him, but for mony a lang year I grudged him sair, sair. He was juist five minutes gone, an' they brocht him back deid my Joey."

On the Sabbath day Jess could not go to church, and it was then, I think, that she was with Joey most. There was often a blessed serenity on her face when we returned, that only comes to those who have risen from their knees with their prayers answered. Then she was very close to the boy who died. Long ago she could not look out from her window upon the brae, but now it was her seat in church. There, on the Sabbath evenings she sometimes talked to me of Joey.

"It's been a fine day," she would say, "juist like that day. I thank the Lord for the sunshine noo, but oh, I thocht at the time I couldna look at the sun shinin' again."

"In all Thrums," she has told me, and I know it to be true, "there's no a better man than Hendry. There's them 'at's cleverer in the wys o' the world, but my man, Hendry McQumpha, never did naething in all his life 'at wasna weel intended, an' though his words is common, it's to the Lord he looks. I canna think but what Hendry's pleasin' to God. Oh, I dinna ken what to say wi' thankfulness to Him when I mind hoo guid he's been to me. There's Leeby 'at I couldna hae done withoot, me bein' sae silly (weak bodily), an' ay Leeby's stuck by me an' gien up her life, as ye micht say, for me. Jamie——"

But then Jess sometimes broke down.

"He's so far awa," she said, after a time, "an' aye when he gangs back to London after his holidays he has a fear he'll never see me again, but he's terrified to mention it, an' I juist ken by the wy he taks haud o' me, an' comes runnin' back to tak haud o' me again. I ken fine what he's thinkin', but I daurna speak.

"Guid is no word for what Jamie has been to me, but he wasna born till after Joey died. When we got Jamie, Hendry took to whistlin' again at the loom, an' Jamie juist filled Joey's place to him. Ay, but naebody could fill Joey's place to me. It's different to a man. A bairn's no the same to him, but a fell bit o' me was buried in my laddie's grave.

"Jamie an' Joey was never nane the same nature. It was aye something in a shop, Jamie wanted to be, an' he never cared muckle for his books, but Joey hankered after being a minister, young as he was, an' a minister Hendry an' me would hae done our best to mak him. Mony, mony a time after he came in frae the kirk on the Sabbath he would stand up at this very window and wave his hands in a reverent way, juist like the minister. His first text was to be 'Thou God seest me.'

"Ye'll wonder at me, but I've sat here in the lang fore-nichts dreamin' 'at Joey was a grown man noo, an' 'at I was puttin' on my bonnet to come to the kirk to hear him preach. Even as far back as twenty years an' mair I wasna able to gang aboot, but Joey would say to me, 'We'll get a carriage to ye, mother, so 'at ye can come and hear me preach on "Thou God seest me."' He would say to me, 'It doesna do, mother, for the minister in the pulpit to nod to ony o' the fowk, but I'll gie ye a look an' ye'll ken it's me.' Oh, Joey, I would hae gien you a look too, an' ye would hae kent what I was thinkin'. He often said, 'Ye'll be proud o' me, will ye no', mother, when ye see me comin' sailin' alang to the pulpit in my gown?' So I would hae been proud o' him, an' I was proud to hear him speakin' o't. 'The other fowk,' he said, 'will be sittin' in their seats wonderin' what my text's to be, but you'll ken, mother, an' you'll turn up to "Thou God seest me," afore I gie oot the Chapter.' Ay, but that day he was coffined, for all the minister prayed, I found it hard to say, 'Thou God seest me.' It's the text I like best noo, though, an' when Hendry an' Leeby is at the kirk, I turn't up often, often in the Bible. I read frae the begininn' o' the Chapter, but when I come to 'Thou

God seest me,' I stop. Na, it's no 'at there's ony rebellion to the Lord in my heart noo, for I ken He was lookin' doon when the cart gaed ower Joey, an' He wanted to tak my laddie to Himsel. But juist when I come to 'Thou God seest me,' I let the Book lie in my lap, for aince a body's sure o' that they're sure o' all. Ay, ye'll laugh, but I think, mebbe juist because I was his mother, 'at though Joey never lived to preach in a kirk, he's preached frae 'Thou God seest me' to me. I dinna ken 'at I, would ever hae been sae sure o' that if it hadna been for him, an' so I think I see 'im sailin' doon to the pulpit juist as he said he would do. I seen him gien me the look he spoke o'—ay, he looks my wy first, an' I ken it's him. Naebody sees him but me, but I see him gien me the look he promised. He's so terrible near me, an' him dead, 'at when my time comes I'll be rale willin' to go. I dinna say that to Jamie, because he all trembles; but I'm auld noo, an' I'm no nane loth to gang."

Jess's staff probably had a history before it became hers, for, as known to me, it was always old and black. If we studied them sufficiently we might discover that staves age perceptibly just as the hair turns grey. At the risk of being thought fanciful I dare to say that in inanimate objects, as in ourselves, there is honourable and shameful old age, and that to me Jess's staff was a symbol of the good, the true. It rested against her in the window, and she was so helpless without it when on her feet, that to those who saw much of her it was part of herself. The staff was very short, nearly a foot having been cut, as I think she once told me herself, from the original, of which to make a porridge thieval (or stick with which to stir, porridge), and in moving Jess leant heavily on it. Had she stood erect it would not have touched the floor. This was the staff that Jess shook so joyfully at her boy the forenoon in May when he ran out to his death. Joey, however, was associated in Jess's memory with her staff in less painful ways. When she spoke of him she took the dwarf of a staff in her hands and looked at it softly.

"It's hard to me," she would say, "to believe 'at twa an' twenty years hae come and gone since the nicht Joey hod (hid) my staff. Ay, but Hendry was straucht in thae days by what he is noo, an' Jamie wasna born. Twa an' twenty years come the back end o' the year, an' it wasna thocht 'at I could live through the winter. 'Ye'll no last mair than anither month, Jess,' was what my sister Bell said, when she came to see me, and yet here I am aye sittin' at my window, an' Bell's been i' the kirkyard this dozen years.

"Leeby was saxteen month younger than Joey, an' mair quiet like. Her heart was juist set on helpin' aboot the hoose, an' though she was but fower year auld she could kindle the fire an' red up (clean up) the room. Leeby's been my savin' ever since she was fower year auld. Ay, but it was Joey 'at hung aboot me maist, an' he took notice 'at I wasna gaen out as I used to do. Since sune after my marriage I've needed the stick, but there was days 'at I could gang across the road an' sit on a stane. Joey kent there was something wrang when I had to gie that up, an' syne he noticed 'at I couldna even gang to the window unless Hendry kind o' carried me. Na, ye wouldna think 'at there could hae been days when Hendry did that, but he did. He was a sort o' ashamed if ony o' the neighbours saw him so affectionate like, but he was terrible taen up aboot me. His loom was doon at T'nowhead's Bell's father's, an' often he cam awa up to see if I was ony better. He didna lat on to the other weavers 'at he was comin' to see what like I was. Na, he juist said he'd forgotten a pirn, or his cruizey lamp, or onything. Ah, but he didna mak nae pretence o' no carin' for me aince he was inside the hoose. He came crawlin' to the bed no to wauken me if I was sleepin', an' mony a time I made belief 'at I was, juist to please him. It was an awfu' business on him to hae a young wife sae helpless, but he wasna the man to cast that at me. I mind o' sayin' to him one day in my bed, 'Ye made a poor bargain, Hendry, when ye took me.' But he says, 'Not one soul in Thrums 'll daur say that to me but yersel, Jess. Na, na, my dawty, you're the wuman o' my choice; there's juist one wuman i' the warld to me, an' that's you, my ain Jess.' Twa an' twenty years syne. Ay, Hendry called me fond like names, thae no everyday names. What a straucht man he was!

"The doctor had said he could, do no more for me, an' Hendry was the only ane 'at didna gie me up. The bairns, of course, didna understand and Joey would come into the bed an' play on the top o' me. Hendry would hae ta'en him awa, but I liked to hae 'im. Ye see, we was lang married afore we had a bairn, an' though I couldna bear ony other weight on me, Joey didna hurt me, somehoo. I liked to hae 'im so close to me.

"It was through that 'at he came to bury my staff. I couldna help often thinkin' o' what like the hoose would be when I was gone, an' aboot Leeby an' Joey left so young. So, when I could say it without greetin', I said to Joey 'at I was goin' far awa, an' would he be a terrible guid laddie to his father and Leeby when I was gone? He aye juist said, 'Dinna gang, mother, dinna gang,' but one day Hendry came in frae his loom, and says Joey, 'Father, whaur's my mother gaen to, awa frae us?' I'll never forget Hendry's face. His mooth juist opened an' shut twa or three times, an' he walked quick ben to the room. I cried oot to him to come back, but he didna come, so I sent Joey for him. Joey came runnin' back to me sayin', 'Mother, mother, a'm awfu' fleid (frightened), for my father's greetin' sair.'

"A' thae things took a haud o' Joey, an' he ended in gien us a fleg (fright).
I was sleepin' ill at the time, an' Hendry was ben sleepin' in the room wi'
Leeby, Joey bein' wi' me. Ay, weel, one nicht I woke up in the dark an' put
oot my hand to 'im, an' he wasna there. I sat up wi' a terrible start, an' syne
I kent by the cauld 'at the door maun be open. I cried oot quick to Hendry,
but he was a soond sleeper, an' he didna hear me. Ay, I dinna ken hoo I
did it, but I got ben to the room an' shook him up. I was near daft wi' fear
when I saw Leeby wasna there either. Hendry couldna tak it in a' at aince,
but sune he had his trousers on, an' he made me lie down on his bed. He
said he wouldna move till I did it, or I wouldna hae dune it. As sune as he
was oot o' the hoose crying their names I sat up in my bed listenin'. Sune
I heard speakin', an' in a minute Leeby comes runnin' in to me, roarin' an'
greetin'. She was barefeeted, and had juist her nichtgown on, an' her teeth
was chatterin'. I took her into the bed, but it was an hour afore she could
tell me onything, she was in sic a state.

"Sune after Hendry came in carryin' Joey. Joey was as naked as Leeby,
and as cauld as lead, but he wasna greetin'. Instead o' that he was awfu'
satisfied like, and for all Hendry threatened to lick him he wouldna tell
what he an' Leeby had been doin'. He says, though, says he, 'Ye'll no gang
awa noo, mother; no, ye'll bide noo.' My bonny laddie, I didna fathom him
at the time.

"It was Leeby 'at I got it frae. Ye see, Joey had never seen me gaen ony
gait withoot my staff, an' he thocht if he hod it I wouldna be able to gang
awa. Ay, he planned it all oot, though he was but a bairn, an' lay watchin'
me in my bed till I fell asleep. Syne he creepit oot o' the bed, an' got the
staff, and gaed ben for Leeby. She was fleid, but he said it was the only
wy to mak me 'at I couldna gang awa. It was juist ower there whaur thae
cabbages is 'at he dug the hole wi' a spade, an' buried the staff. Hendry dug
it up next mornin'."

# VII

## THE STATEMENT OF TIBBIE BIRSE

On a Thursday Pete Lownie was buried, and when Hendry returned from the funeral Jess asked if Davit Lunan had been there.

"Na," said Hendry, who was shut up in the closet-bed, taking off his blacks, "I heard tell he wasna bidden."

"Yea, yea," said Jess, nodding to me significantly. "Ay, weel," she added, "we'll be hae'n Tibbie ower here on Saturday to deve's (weary us) to death aboot it."

Tibbie, Davit's wife, was sister to Marget, Pete's widow, and she generally did visit Jess on Saturday night to talk about Marget, who was fast becoming one of the most fashionable persons in Thrums. Tibbie was hopelessly plebeian. She was none of your proud kind, and if I entered the kitchen when she was there she pretended not to see me, so that, if I chose, I might escape without speaking to the like of her. I always grabbed her hand, however in a frank way.

On Saturday Tibbie made her appearance. From the rapidity of her walk, and the way she was sucking in her mouth, I knew that she had strange things to unfold. She had pinned a grey shawl about her shoulders, and wore a black mutch over her dangling grey curls.

"It's you, Tibbie," I heard Jess say, as the door opened.

Tibbie did not knock, not considering herself grand enough for ceremony, and indeed Jess would have resented her knocking. On the other hand, when Leeby visited Tibbie, she knocked as politely as if she were collecting for the precentor's present. All this showed that we were superior socially to Tibbie.

"Ay, hoo are ye, Jess?" Tibbie said.

"Muckle aboot it," answered Jess; "juist aff an' on; ay, an' hoo hae ye been yersel?"

"Ou," said Tibbie.

I wish I could write "ou" as Tibbie said it. With her it was usually a sentence in itself. Sometimes it was a mere bark, again it expressed indignation, surprise, rapture; it might be a check upon emotion or a way of leading up to it, and often it lasted for half a minute. In this instance it was, I should say, an intimation that if Jess was ready Tibbie would begin.

"So Pete Lownie's gone," said Jess, whom I could not see from ben the house. I had a good glimpse of Tibbie, however, through the open door-ways. She had the armchair on the south side, as she would have said, of the fireplace.

"He's awa," assented Tibbie, primly.

I heard the lid of the kettle dancing, and then came a prolonged "ou." Tibbie bent forward to whisper, and if she had anything terrible to tell I was glad of that, for when she whispered I heard her best. For a time only a murmur of words reached me, distant music with an "ou" now and again that fired Tibbie as the beating of his drum may rouse the martial spirit of a drummer. At last our visitor broke into an agitated whisper, and it was only when she stopped whispering, as she did now and again, that I ceased to hear her. Jess evidently put a question at times, but so politely (for she had on her best wrapper) that I did not catch a word.

"Though I should be struck deid this nicht," Tibbie whispered, and the sibilants hissed between her few remaining teeth, "I wasna sae muckle as speired to the layin' oot. There was Mysy Cruickshanks there, an' Kitty Wobster 'at was nae friends to the corpse to speak o', but Marget passed by me, me 'at is her ain flesh an' blood, though it mayna be for the like o' me to say it. It's gospel truth, Jess, I tell ye, when I say 'at, for all I ken officially, as ye micht say, Pete Lownie may be weel and hearty this day. If I was to meet Marget in the face I couldna say he was deid, though I ken 'at the wricht coffined him; na, an' what's mair, I wouldna gie Marget the satisfaction o' hearin' me say it. No, Jess, I tell ye, I dinna pertend to be on an equalty wi' Marget, but equality or no equalty, a body has her feelings, an' lat on 'at I ken Pete's gone I will not. Eh? Ou, weel. . . .

"Na faags a; na, na, I ken my place better than to gang near Marget. I dinna deny 'at she's grand by me, and her keeps a bakehoose o' her ain, an' glad am I to see her doin' sae weel, but let me tell ye this, Jess, 'Pride goeth before a fall.' Yes, it does, it's Scripture; ay, it's nae mak-up o' mine, it's Scripture. And this I will say, though kennin' my place, 'at Davit Lunan is as dainty a man as is in Thrums, an' there's no one 'at's better behaved at a bural, being particularly wise-like (presentable) in's blacks, an' them spleet new. Na, na, Jess, Davit may hae his faults an' tak a dram at times like anither, but he would shame naebody at a bural, an' Marget deleeberately insulted him, no speirin' him to Pete's. What's mair, when the minister cried in to see me yesterday, an' me on the floor washin', says he, 'So Marget's lost her man,' an' I said, 'Say ye so, na?' for let on 'at I kent, and neither me at the layin' oot nor Davit Lunan at the funeral, I would not.

"'David should hae gone to the funeral,' says the minister, 'for I doubt not he was only omitted in the invitations by a mistake.'

"Ay, it was weel meant, but says I, Jess, says I, 'As lang as a'm livin' to tak chairge o' 'im, Davit Lunan gangs to nae burals 'at he's no bidden to. An' I tell ye,' I says to the minister, 'if there was one body 'at had a richt to be at the bural o' Pete Lownie, it was Davit Lunan, him bein' my man an' Marget my ain sister. Yes,' says I, though a'm no o' the boastin' kind, 'Davit had maist richt to be there next to Pete 'imsel.' Ou, Jess. . . .

"This is no a maiter I like to speak aboot; na, I dinna care to mention it, but the neighbours is nat'rally taen up aboot it, and Chirsty Tosh was sayin' what I would wager 'at Marget hadna sent the minister to hint 'at Davit's bein' over-lookit in the invitations was juist an accident? Losh, losh, Jess, to think 'at a woman could hae the michty assurance to mak a tool o' the very minister! But, sal, as far as that gangs, Marget would do it, an' gae twice to the kirk next Sabbath, too; but if she thinks she's to get ower me like that, she taks me for a bigger fule than I tak her for. Na, na, Marget, ye dinna draw my leg (deceive me). Ou, no. . . .

"Mind ye, Jess, I hae no desire to be friends wi' Marget. Naething could be farrer frae my wish than to hae helpit in the layin' oot o' Peter Lownie, an', I assure ye, Davit wasna keen to gang to the bural. ' If they dinna want me to their burals,' Davit says, 'they hae nae mair to do than to say sae. But I warn ye, Tibbie,' he says, 'if there's a bural frae this hoose, be it your bural, or be it my bural, not one o' the family o' Lownies casts their shadows upon the corp.' Thae was the very words Davit said to me as we watched the hearse frae the sky-licht. Ay, he bore up wonderfu', but he felt it, Jess—he felt it, as I could tell by his takkin' to drink again that very nicht Jess, Jess. . . .

"Marget's getting waur an' waur? Ay, ye may say so, though I'll say naething agin her mysel. Of coorse a'm no on equalty wi' her, especially since she had the bell put up in her hoose. Ou, I hinna seen it mysel, na, I never gang near the hoose, an', as mony a body can tell ye, when I do hae to gang that wy I mak my feet my friend. Ay, but as I was sayin', Marget's sae grand noo 'at she has' a bell in the hoose. As I understan', there's a rope in the wast room, an' when ye pu' it a bell rings in the east room. Weel, when Marget has company at their tea in the wast room, an' they need mair watter or scones or onything, she rises an' rings the bell. Syne Jean, the auldest lassie, gets up frae the table an' lifts the jug or the plates an' gaes awa ben to the east room for what's wanted. Ay, it's a wy o' doin' 'at's juist like the gentry, but I'll tell ye, Jess, Pete juist fair hated the soond o' that bell, an' there's them 'at says it was the death o' 'im. To think o' Marget ha'en sic an establishment! . . .

"Na, I hinna seen the mournin', I've heard o't. Na, if Marget doesna tell me naething, a'm no the kind to speir naething, an' though I'll be at the kirk the morn, I winna turn my heid to look at the mournin'. But it's fac as death I ken frae Janet McQuhatty 'at the bonnet's a' crape, an' three yairds o' crape on the dress, the which Marget calls a costume. . . . Ay, I wouldna wonder but what it was hale watter the morn, for it looks michty like rain, an' if it is it'll serve Marget richt, an' mebbe bring doon her pride a wee. No 'at I want to see her humbled, for, in coorse, she's grand by the like o' me. Ou, but . . ."

# VIII

## A CLOAK WITH BEADS

On weekdays the women who passed the window were meagrely dressed; mothers in draggled winsey gowns, carrying infants that were armfuls of grandeur. The Sabbath clothed every one in her best, and then the women went by with their hands spread out. When I was with Hendry cloaks with beads were the fashion, and Jess sighed as she looked at them. They were known in Thrums as the Eleven and a Bits (threepenny bits), that being their price at Kyowowy's in the square. Kyowowy means finicky, and applied to the draper by general consent. No doubt it was very characteristic to call the cloaks by their market value. In the glen my scholars still talk of their school-books as the tupenny, the fowerpenny, the saxpenny. They finish their education with the tenpenny.

Jess's opportunity for handling the garments that others of her sex could finger in shops was when she had guests to tea. Persons who merely dropped in and remained to tea got their meal, as a rule, in the kitchen. They had nothing on that Jess could not easily take in as she talked to them. But when they came by special invitation, the meal was served in the room, the guests' things being left on the kitchen bed. Jess not being able to go ben the house, had to be left with the things. When the time to go arrived, these were found on the bed, just as they had been placed there, but Jess could now tell Leeby whether they were imitation, why Bell Elshioner's feather went far round the bonnet, and Chirsty Lownie's reason for always holding her left arm fast against her side when she went abroad in the black jacket. Ever since My Hobart's eleven and a bit was left on the kitchen bed Jess had hungered for a cloak with beads. My's was the very marrows of the one T'nowhead's wife got in Dundee for ten-and-sixpence; indeed, we would have thought that 'Lisbeth's also came from Kyowowy's had not Sanders Elshioner's sister seen her go into the Dundee shop with T'nowhead (who was loth), and hung about to discover what she was after.

Hendry was not quick at reading faces like Tammas Haggart, but the wistful look on Jess's face when there was talk of eleven and a bits had its meaning for him.

"They're grand to look at, no doubt," I have heard him say to Jess, "but they're richt annoyin'. That new wife o' Peter Dickie's had ane on in the kirk last Sabbath, an' wi' her sittin' juist afore us I couldna listen to the sermon for tryin' to count the beads."

Hendry made his way into these gossips uninvited, for his opinions on dress were considered contemptible, though he was worth consulting on material. Jess and Leeby discussed many things in his presence, confident that his ears were not doing their work; but every now and then it was discovered that he had been hearkening greedily. If the subject was dress, he might then become a little irritating.

"Oh, they're grand," Jess admitted; "they set a body aff oncommon."

"They would be no use to you," said Hendry, "for ye canna wear them except ootside."

"A body doesna buy cloaks to be wearin' at them steady," retorted Jess.

"No, no, but you could never wear yours though ye had ane."

"I dinna want ane. They're far ower grand for the like o' me."

"They're no nae sic thing. A'm thinkin' ye're juist as fit to wear an eleven and a bit as My Hobart."

"Weel, mebbe I am, but it's oot o' the queistion gettin' ane, they're sic a price."

"Ay, an' though we had the siller, it would surely be an awfu' like thing to buy a cloak 'at ye could never wear?"

"Ou, but I dinna want ane."

Jess spoke so mournfully that Hendry became enraged.

"It's most michty," he said, " 'at ye would gang an' set yer heart on sic a completely useless thing."

"I hinna set my heart on't."

"Dinna blether. Ye've been speakin' aboot thae eleven and a bits to Leeby, aff an' on, for twa month."

Then Hendry hobbled off to his loom, and Jess gave me a look which meant that men are trying at the best, once you are tied to them.

The cloaks continued to turn up in conversation, and Hendry poured scorn upon Jess's weakness, telling her she would be better employed mending his trousers than brooding over an eleven and a bit that would have to spend its life in a drawer. An outsider would have thought that Hendry was positively cruel to Jess. He seemed to take a delight in finding that she had neglected to sew a button on his waistcoat. His real joy, however, was the knowledge that she sewed as no other woman in Thrums could sew. Jess had a genius for making new garments out of old ones, and Hendry never tired of gloating over her cleverness so long as she was not present. He was always athirst for fresh proofs of it, and these were forthcoming every day. Sparing were his words of praise to herself, but in the evening he generally had a smoke with me in the attic, and then the thought of Jess made him chuckle till his pipe went out. When he smoked he grunted as if in pain, though this really added to the enjoyment.

"It doesna matter," he would say to me, "what Jess turns her hand to, she can mak ony mortal thing. She doesna need nae teachin'; na, juist gie her a guid look at onything, be it clothes, or furniture, or in the bakin' line, it's all the same to her. She'll mak another exactly like it. Ye canna beat her. Her bannocks is so superior 'at a Tilliedrum woman took to her bed after tastin' them, an' when the lawyer has company his wife gets Jess to mak some bannocks for her an' syne pretends they're her ain bakin'. Ay, there's a story aboot that. One day the auld doctor, him 'at's deid, was at his tea at the lawyer's, an' says the guidwife, 'Try the cakes, Mr. Riach; they're my own bakin'.' Weel, he was a fearsomely outspoken man, the doctor, an' nae suner had he the bannock atween his teeth, for he didna stop to swallow't, than he says, 'Mistress Geddie,' says he, 'I wasna born on a Sabbath. Na, na, you're no the first grand leddy 'at has gien me bannocks as their ain bakin' 'at was baked and fired by Jess Logan, her 'at's Hendry McQumpha's wife.' Ay, they say the lawyer's wife didna ken which wy to look, she was that mortified. It's juist the same wi' sewin'. There's wys o' ornamentin' christenin' robes an' the like 'at's kent to naebody but hersel; an' as for stockin's, weel, though I've seen her mak sae mony, she amazes me yet. I mind o' a furry waistcoat I aince had. Weel, when it was fell dune, do you think she gae it awa to some gaen aboot body (vagrant)? Na, she made it into a richt neat coat to Jamie, wha was a bit laddie at the time. When he grew out o' it, she made a slipbody o't for hersel. Ay, I dinna ken a' the different things it became, but the last time I saw it was ben in the room, whaur she'd covered a footstool wi' 't. Yes, Jess is the cleverest crittur I ever saw. Leeby's handy, but she's no a patch on her mother."

I sometimes repeated these panegyrics to Jess. She merely smiled, and said that men haver most terrible when they are not at their work.

Hendry tried Jess sorely over the cloaks, and a time came when, only by exasperating her, could he get her to reply to his sallies.

"Wha wants an eleven an' a bit?" she retorted now and again.

"It's you 'at wants it," said Hendry, promptly.

"Did I ever say I wanted ane? What use could I hae for't?"

"That's the queistion," said Hendry. "Ye canna gang the length o' the door, so ye would never be able to wear't."

"Ay, weel," replied Jess, "I'll never hae the chance o' no bein' able to wear't, for, hooever muckle I wanted it, I couldna get it."

Jess's infatuation had in time the effect of making Hendry uncomfortable. In the attic he delivered himself of such sentiments as these:

"There's nae understandin' a woman. There's Jess 'at hasna her equal for cleverness in Thrums, man or woman, an' yet she's fair skeered about thae cloaks. Aince a woman sets her mind on something to wear, she's mair onreasonable than the stupidest man. Ay, it micht mak them humble to see hoo foolish they are syne. No, but it doesna do't.

"If it was a thing to be useful noo, I wouldna think the same o't, but she could never wear't. She kens she could never wear't, an' yet she's juist as keen to hae't.

"I dinna like to see her so wantin' a thing, an' no able to get it. But it's an awfu' sum, eleven an' a bit."

He tried to argue with her further.

"If ye had eleven an' a bit to fling awa," he said, "ye dinna mean to tell me 'at ye would buy a cloak instead o' cloth for a gown, or flannel for petticoats, or some useful thing?"

"As sure as death," said Jess, with unwonted vehemence, "if a cloak I could get, a cloak I would buy."

Hendry came up to tell me what Jess had said.

"It's a michty infatooation," he said, "but it shows hoo her heart's set on thae cloaks."

"Aince ye had it," he argued with her, "ye would juist hae to lock it awa in the drawers. Ye would never even be seein't."

"Ay, would I," said Jess. "I would often tak it oot an' look at it. Ay, an' I would aye ken it was there."

"But naebody would ken ye had it but yersel," said Hendry, who had a vague notion that this was a telling objection.

"Would they no?" answered Jess. "It would be a' through the toon afore nicht."

"Weel, all I can say," said Hendry, "is 'at ye're terrible foolish to tak the want o' sic a useless thing to heart."

"A'm no takkin't to heart," retorted Jess, as usual.

Jess needed many things in her days that poverty kept from her to the end, and the cloak was merely a luxury. She would soon have let it slip by as something unattainable, had not Hendry encouraged it to rankle in her mind. I cannot say when he first determined that Jess should have a cloak, come the money as it liked, for he was too ashamed of his weakness to admit his project to me. I remember, however, his saying to Jess one day:

"I'll warrant ye could mak a cloak yersel the marrows o' thae eleven and a bits, at half the price?"

"It would cost," said Jess, "sax an' saxpence, exactly. The cloth would be five shillins, an' the beads a shillin'. I have some braid 'at would do fine for the front, but the buttons would be saxpence."

"Ye're sure o' that?"

"I ken fine, for I got Leeby to price the things in the shop."

"Ay, but it maun be ill to shape the cloaks richt. There was a queer cut aboot that ane Peter Dickie's new wife had on."

"Queer cut or no queer cut," said Jess, "I took the shape o' My Hobart's ane the day she was here at her tea, an' I could mak the identical o't for sax and sax."

"I dinna believe't," said Hendry, but when he and I were alone he told me, "There's no a doubt she could mak it. Ye heard her say she had ta'en the shape? Ay, that shows she's rale set on a cloak."

Had Jess known that Hendry had been saving up for months to buy her material for a cloak, she would not have let him do it. She could not know, however, for all the time he was scraping together his pence, he kept up a ring-ding-dang about her folly. Hendry gave Jess all the wages he weaved, except threepence weekly, most of which went in tobacco and snuff. The dulse-man had perhaps a halfpenny from him in the fortnight. I noticed that for a long time Hendry neither smoked nor snuffed, and I knew that for years he had carried a shilling in his snuff-mull. The remainder of the money he must have made by extra work at his loom, by working harder, for he could scarcely have worked longer.

It was one day shortly before Jamie's return to Thrums that Jess saw Hendry pass the house and go down the brae when he ought to have come in to his brose. She sat at the window watching for him, and by and by he reappeared, carrying a parcel.

"Whaur on earth hae ye been?" she asked, "an' what's that you're carryin'?"

"Did ye think it was an eleven an' a bit?" said Hendry.

"No, I didna," answered Jess, indignantly. Then Hendry slowly undid the knots of the string with which the parcel was tied. He took off the brown paper.

"There's yer cloth," he said, "an' here's one an' saxpence for the beads an' the buttons."

While Jess still stared he followed me ben the house.

"It's a terrible haver," he said, apologetically, "but she had set her heart on't."

# IX

## THE POWER OF BEAUTY

ONE evening there was such a gathering at the pig-sty that Hendry and I could not get a board to lay our backs against. Circumstances had pushed Pete Elshioner into the place of honour that belonged by right of mental powers to Tammas Haggart, and Tammas was sitting rather sullenly on the bucket, boring a hole in the pig with his sarcastic eye. Pete was passing round a card, and in time it reached me. "With Mr. and Mrs. David Alexander's compliments," was printed on it, and Pete leered triumphantly at us as it went the round.

"Weel, what think ye?" he asked, with a pretence at modesty.

"Ou," said T'nowhead, looking at the, others like one who asked a question, "ou, I think; ay, ay."

The others seemed to agree with him, all but Tammas, who did not care to tie himself down to an opinion.

"Ou, ay," T'nowhead continued, more confidently, "it is so, deceededly."

"Ye'll no ken," said Pete, chuckling, "what it means?"

"Na," the farmer admitted, "na, I canna say I exac'ly ken that."

"I ken, though," said Tammas, in his keen way.

"Weel, then, what is't?" demanded Pete, who had never properly come under Tammas's spell.

"I ken," said Tammas.

"Oot wi't then."

"I dinna say it's lyin' on my tongue," Tammas replied, in a tone of reproof, "but if ye'll juist speak awa aboot some other thing for a meenute or twa, I'll tell ye syne."

Hendry said that this was only reasonable, but we could think of no subject at the moment, so we only stared at Tammas, and waited.

"I fathomed it," he said at last, "as sune as my een lichted on't. It's one o' the bit cards 'at grand fowk slip 'aneath doors when they mak calls, an' their friends is no in. Ay, that's what it is."

"I dinna say ye're wrang," Pete answered, a little annoyed. "Ay, weel, lads, of course David Alexander's oor Dite as we called 'im, Dite Elshioner, an' that's his wy o' signifyin' to us 'at he's married."

"I assure ye," said Hendry, "Dite's doin' the thing in style."

"Ay, we said that when the card arrived," Pete admitted.

"I kent," said Tammas, " 'at that was the wy grand fowk did when they got married. I've kent it a lang time. It's no nae surprise to me."

"He's been lang in marryin'," Hookey Crewe said.

"He was thirty at Martinmas," said Pete.

"Thirty, was he?" said Hookey. "Man, I'd buried twa wives by the time I was that age, an' was castin' aboot for a third."

"I mind o' them," Henry interposed.

"Ay," Hookey said, "the first twa was angels." There he paused. "An' so's the third," he added, "in many respects."

"But wha's the woman Dite's ta'en?" T'nowhead or some one of the more silent members of the company asked of Pete.

"Ou, we dinna ken wha she is," answered Pete; "but she'll be some Glasca lassie, for he's there noo. Look, lads, look at this. He sent this at the same time; it's her picture." Pete produced the silhouette of a young lady, and handed it round.

"What do ye think ?" he asked.

"I assure ye!" said Hookey.

"Sal," said Hendry, even more charmed, "Dite's done weel."

"Lat's see her in a better licht," said Tammas.

He stood up and examined the photograph narrowly, while Pete fidgeted with his legs.

"Fairish," said Tammas at last. "Ou, ay; no what I would selec' mysel, but a dainty bit stocky! Ou, a tasty crittury! ay, an' she's weel in order. Lads, she's a fine stoot kimmer."

"I conseeder her a beauty," said Pete, aggressively.

"She's a' that," said Hendry.

"A' I can say," said Hookey, " is 'at she taks me most michty."

"She's no a beauty," Tammas maintained; "na, she doesna juist come up to that; but I dinna deny but what she's weel faured."

"What faut do ye find wi' her, Tammas?" asked Hendry.

"Conseedered critically," said Tammas, holding the photograph at arm's length, "I would say 'at she—let's see noo; ay, I would say 'at she's defeecient in genteelity."

"Havers," said Pete.

"Na," said Tammas, "no when conseedered critically. Ye see she's drawn lauchin'; an' the genteel thing's no to lauch, but juist to put on a bit smirk. Ay, that's the genteel thing."

"A smile, they ca' it," interposed T'nowhead.

"I said a smile," continued Tammas. "Then there's her waist I say naething agin her waist, speakin' in the ord'nar meanin'; but, conseedered critically, there's a want o' suppleness, as ye micht say, aboot it. Ay, it doesna compare wi' the waist o'——" (Here Tammas mentioned a young lady who had recently married into a local county family.)

"That was a pretty tiddy," said Hookey. "Ou, losh, ay! it made me a kind o' queery to look at her."

"Ye're ower kyowowy (particular), Tammas," said Pete.

"I may be, Pete," Tammas admitted; "but I maun say I'm fond o' a bonny-looken wuman, an' no aisy to please: na, I'm nat'rally ane o' the critical kind."

"It's extror'nar," said T'nowhead, "what a poo'er beauty has. I mind when I was a callant readin' aboot Mary Queen o' Scots till I was fair mad, lads; yes, I was fair mad at her bein' deid. Ou, I could hardly sleep at nichts for thinking o' her."

"Mary was spunky as weel as a beauty," said Hookey, "an' that's the kind I like. Lads, what a persuasive tid she was!"

"She got roond the men," said Hendry, "ay, she turned them roond her finger. That's the warst o' thae beauties."

"I dinna gainsay," said T'nowhead, "but what there was a little o' the deevil in Mary, the crittur."

Here T'nowhead chuckled, and then looked scared.

"What Mary needed," said Tammas, "was a strong man to manage her."

"Ay, man, but it's ill to manage thae beauties. They, gie ye a glint o' their een, an' syne whaur are ye?"

"Ah, they can be managed," said Tammas, complacently. "There's naebody nat'rally safter wi' a pretty stocky o' a bit wumany than mysel; but for a' that, if I had been Mary's man I would hae stood nane o' her tantrums. 'Na, Mary, my lass,' I would hae said, 'this winna do; na, na, ye're a bonny body, but ye maun mind 'at man's the superior; ay, man's the lord o' creation, an' so ye maun juist sing sma'.' That's hoo I would hae managed Mary, the speerity crittur 'at she was."

"Ye would hae haen yer wark cut oot for ye, Tammas."

"Ilka mornin'," pursued Tammas, "I would hae said to her, 'Mary,' I would hae said, 'wha's to wear thae breeks the day, you or me?' Ay, syne I would hae ordered her to kindle the fire, or if I had been the king, of coorse I would hae telt her instead to ring the bell an' hae the cloth laid for the breakfast. Ay, that's the wy to mak the like o' Mary respec ye."

Pete and I left them talking. He had written a letter to David Alexander, and wanted me to "back" it.

# X

## A MAGNUM OPUS

Two Bibles, a volume of sermons by the learned Dr. Isaac Barrow, a few numbers of the *Cheap Magazine*, that had strayed from Dunfermline, and a *Pilgrim's Progress*, were the works that lay conspicuous ben in the room. Hendry had also a copy of Burns, whom he always quoted in the complete poem, and a collection of legends in song and prose, that Leeby kept out of sight in a drawer.

The weight of my box of books was a subject Hendry was very willing to shake his head over, but he never showed any desire to take off the lid. Jess, however, was more curious; indeed, she would have been an omnivorous devourer of books had it not been for her conviction that reading was idling. Until I found her out she never allowed to me that Leeby brought her my books one at a time. Some of them were novels, and Jess took about ten minutes to each. She confessed that what she read was only the last Chapter, owing to a consuming curiosity to know whether "she got him."

She read all the London part, however, of *The Heart of Midlothian*, because London was where Jamie lived, and she and I had a discussion about it which ended in her remembering that Thrums once had an author of its own.

"Bring oot the book," she said to Leeby, "it was put awa i' the bottom drawer ben i' the room sax year syne, an' I sepad it's there yet."

Leeby came but with a faded little book, the title already rubbed from its shabby brown covers. I opened it, and then all at once I saw before me again the man who wrote and printed it and died. He came hobbling up the brae, so bent that his body was almost at right angles to his legs, and his broken silk hat was carefully brushed as in the days when Janet, his sister, lived. There he stood at the top of the brae, panting.

I was but a boy when Jimsy Duthie turned the corner of the brae for the last time, with a score of mourners behind him. While I knew him there was no Janet to run to the door to see if he was coming. So occupied was Jimsy with the great affair of his life, which was brewing for thirty years, that his neighbours saw how he missed his sister better than he realized it himself. Only his hat was no longer carefully brushed, and his coat hung awry, and there was sometimes little reason why he should go home to dinner. It is for the sake of Janet who adored him that we should remember Jimsy in the days before she died.

Jimsy was a poet, and for the space of thirty years he lived in a great epic on the Millennium. This is the book presented to me by Jess, that lies so quietly on my topmost shelf now. Open it, however, and you will find that the work is entitled "The Millennium: an Epic Poem, in Twelve Books: by James Duthie." In the little hole in his wall where Jimsy kept his books there was, I have no doubt—for his effects were rouped before I knew him except by name—a well-read copy of *Paradise Lost*. Some people would smile, perhaps, if they read the two epics side by side, and others might sigh, for there is a great deal in "The Millennium" that Milton could take credit for. Jimsy had educated himself, after the idea of writing something that the world would not willingly let die came to him, and he began his book before his education was complete. So far as I know, he never wrote a line that had not to do with "The Millennium." He was ever a man sparing of his plural tenses, and "The Millennium" says "has" for "have"; a vain word, indeed, which Thrums would only have permitted as a poetical licence. The one original character in the poem is the devil, of whom Jimsy gives a picture that is startling and graphic, and received the approval of the Auld Licht minister.

By trade Jimsy was a printer, a master-printer with no one under him, and he printed and bound his book, ten copies in all, as well as wrote it. To print the poem took him, I dare say, nearly as long as to write it, and he set up the pages as they were written, one by one. The book is only printed on one side of the leaf, and each page was produced separately like a little hand-bill. Those who may pick up the book—but who will care to do so?—will think that the author or his printer could not spell—but they would not do Jimsy that injustice if they knew the circumstances in which it was produced. He had but a small stock of type, and on many occasions he ran out of a letter. The letter *e* tried him sorely. Those who knew him best say that he tried to think of words without an *e* in them, but when he was baffled he had to use a little *a* or an o instead. He could print correctly, but in the book there are a good many capital letters in the middle of words, and sometimes there is a note of interrogation after "alas" or "Woes me," because all the notes of exclamation had been used up.

Jimsy never cared to speak about his great poem even to his closest friends, but Janet told how he read it out to her, and that his whole body trembled with excitement while he raised his eyes to heaven as if asking for inspiration that would enable his voice to do justice to his writing. So grand it was, said Janet, that her stocking would slip from her fingers as he read—and Janet's stockings, that she was always knitting when not otherwise engaged, did not slip from her hands readily. After her death he was heard by his neighbours reciting the poem to himself, generally with his door locked. He is said to have declaimed part of it one still evening from the top of the commonty like one addressing a multitude, and the idlers who had crept up to jeer at him fell back when they saw his face. He walked through them, they told, with his old body straight once more, and a queer light playing on his face. His lips are moving as I see him turning the corner of the brae. So he passed from youth to old age, and all his life seemed a dream, except that part of it in which he was writing, or printing, or stitching, or binding "The Millennium." At last the work was completed.

"It is finished," he printed at the end of the last book. "The task of thirty years is over."

It is indeed over. No one ever read "The Millennium." I am not going to sentimentalize over my copy, for how much of it have I read? But neither shall I say that it was written to no end.

You may care to know the last of Jimsy, though in one sense he was blotted out when the last copy was bound. He had saved one hundred pounds by that time, and being now neither able to work nor to live alone, his friends cast about for a home for his remaining years. He was very spent and feeble, yet he had the fear that he might be still alive when all his money was gone. After that was the workhouse. He covered sheets of paper with calculations about how long the hundred pounds would last if he gave away for board and lodgings ten shillings, nine shillings, seven and sixpence a week. At last, with sore misgivings, he went to live with a family who took him for eight shillings. Less than a month afterwards he died.

## THE GHOST CRADLE

OUR dinner-hour was twelve o'clock, and Hendry, for a not incomprehensible reason, called this meal his brose. Frequently, however, while I was there to share the expense, broth was put on the table, with beef to follow in clean plates, much to Hendry's distress, for the comfortable and usual practice was to eat the beef from the broth-plates. Jess, however, having three whole white plates and two cracked ones, insisted on the meals being taken genteelly, and her husband, with a look at me, gave way.

"Half a pound o' boiling beef, an' a penny bone," was Leeby's almost invariable order when she dealt with the flesher, and Jess had always neighbours poorer than herself who got a plateful of the broth. She never had anything without remembering some old body who would be the better of a little of it.

Among those who must have missed Jess sadly after she was gone was Johnny Proctor, a halfwitted man who, because he could not work, remained straight at a time of life when most weavers, male and female, had lost some inches of their stature. For as far back as my memory goes, Johnny had got his brose three times a week from Jess, his custom being to walk in without ceremony, and, drawing a stool to the table, tell Leeby that he was now ready. One day, however, when I was in the garden putting some rings on a fishing-wand, Johnny pushed by me, with no sign of recognition on his face. I addressed him, and, after pausing undecidedly, he ignored me. When he came to the door, instead of flinging it open and walking in, he knocked primly, which surprised me so much that I followed him.

"Is this whaur Mistress McQumpha lives?" he asked, when Leeby, with a face ready to receive the minister himself, came at length to the door.

I knew that the gentility of the knock had taken both her and her mother aback.

"Hoots, Johnny," said Leeby, "what haver's this? Come awa in."

Johnny seemed annoyed.

"Is this whaur Mistress McQumpha lives?" he repeated.

"Say'at it is," cried Jess, who was quicker in the uptake than her daughter.

"Of course this is whaur Mistress McQumpha lives," Leeby then said, "as-weel ye ken, for ye had yer dinner here no twa hours syne."

" Then," said Johnny, "Mistress Tully's compliments to her, and would she kindly lend the christenin' robe, an' also the tea-tray, if the same be na needed?"

Having delivered his message as instructed, Johnny consented to sit down until the famous christening robe and the tray were ready, but he would not talk, for that was not in the bond. Jess's sweet face beamed over the compliment Mrs. Tully, known on ordinary occasions as Jean McTaggart, had paid her, and, after Johnny had departed laden, she told me how the tray, which had a great bump in the middle, came into her possession.

"Ye've often heard me speak aboot the time when I was a lassie workin' at the farm o' the Bog? Ay, that was afore me an' Hendry kent ane anither, an' I was as fleet on my feet in thae days as Leeby is noo. It was Sam'l Fletcher 'at was the farmer, but he maun hae been gone afore you was mair than born. Mebbe, though, ye ken 'at he was a terrible invalid, an' for the hinmost years o' his life he, sat in a muckle chair nicht an' day. Ay, when I took his denner to 'im, on that very tray 'at Johnny cam for, I little thocht 'at by an' by I would be sae keepit in a chair mysel.

"But the thinkin' o' Sam'l Fletcher's case is ane o' the things 'at maks me awfu' thankfu' for the lenient wy the Lord has aye dealt wi' me; for Sam'l couldna move oot o' the chair, aye sleepin' in't at nicht, an' I can come an' gang between mine an' my bed. Mebbe, ye think I'm no much better off than Sam'l, but that's a terrible mistak. What a glory it would hae been to him if he could hae gone frae one end o' the kitchen to the ither. Ay, I'm sure o' that.

"Sam'l was rale weel liked, for he was saft-spoken to everybody, an' fond o' ha'en a gossip wi' ony ane 'at was aboot the farm. We didna care sae muckle for the wife, Eppie Lownie, for she managed the farm, an' she was fell hard an' terrible reserved we thocht, no even likin' ony body to get friendly wi' the mester, as we called Sam'l. Ay, we made a richt mistak."

As I had heard frequently of this queer, mournful mistake made by those who considered Sam'l unfortunate in his wife, I turned Jess on to the main line of her story.

"It was the ghost cradle, as they named it, 'at I meant to tell ye aboot. The Bog was a bigger farm in thae days than noo, but I daursay it has the new steadin' yet. Ay, it winna be new noo, but at the time there was sic a commotion aboot the ghost cradle, they were juist puttin' the new steadin' up. There was sax or mair masons at it, wi' the lads on the farm helpin', an' as they were all sleepin' at the farm, there was great stir aboot the place. I couldna tell ye hoo the story aboot the farm's bein' haunted rose, to begin wi', but I mind fine hoo fleid I was; ay, an' no only me, but every man-body an' woman-body on the farm. It was aye late 'at the soond began, an' we never saw naething, we juist heard it. The masons said they wouldna hae been sae fleid if they could hae seen't, but it never was seen. It had the soond o' a cradle rocking an' when we lay in our beds hearkening it grew louder an' louder till it wasna to be borne, an' the women-folk fair skirled wi' fear. The mester was intimate wi' a' the stories aboot ghosts an' water-kelpies an' sic like, an' we couldna help listenin' to them. But he aye said 'at ghosts 'at was juist heard an' no seen was the maist fearsome an' wicked. For all there was sic fear ower the hale farm-toon 'at naebody would gang ower the door alane after the gloamin' cam, the mester said he wasna fleid to sleep i' the kitchen by 'imsel. We thocht it richt brave o''im, for ye see he was as helpless as a bairn.

"Richt queer stories rose aboot the cradle, an' travelled to the ither farms. The wife didna like them ava, for it was said 'at there maun hae been some awful murder o' an infant on the farm, or we wouldna be haunted by a cradle, Syne folk began to mind 'at there had been nae bairns born on the farm as far back as onybody kent, an' it was said 'at some lang syne crime had made the bog cursed.

"Dinna think 'at we juist lay in our beds or sat round the fire shakkin' wi' fear. Everything 'at could be dune was dune. In the daytime, when naething was heard, the masons explored a place i' the farm, in the hope o' findin' oot 'at the sound was caused by sic a thing as the wind playin' on the wood in the garret. Even at nichts, when they couldna sleep wi' the soond, I've kent them rise in a body an' gang all ower the house wi' lichts. I've seen them climbin' on the new steadin', crawlin' alang the rafters haudin' their cruizey lamps afore them, an' us women-bodies shiverin' wi' fear at the door. It was on ane o' thae nichts 'at a mason fell off the rafters an' broke his leg. Weel, sic a state was the men in to find oot what it was 'at was terrifyin' them sae muckle, 'at the rest o' them climbed up at aince to the place he'd fallen frae, thinkin' there was something there 'at had fleid 'im. But though they crawled back an' forrit there was naething ava.

"The rockin' was louder, we thocht, after that nicht, an' syne the men said it would go on till somebody was killed. That idea took a richt haud o' them, an' twa ran awa back to Tilliedrum, whaur they had come frae. They gaed thegither i' the middle o' the nicht, an' it was thocht next mornin' 'at the ghost had spirited them awa.

"Ye couldna conceive hoo low-spirited we all were after the masons had gien up hope o' findin' a nat'ral cause for the soond. At ord'nar times there's no ony mair lichtsome place than a farm after the men hae come in to their supper, but at the Bog we sat dour an' sullen; an' there wasna a mason or a farm-servant 'at would gang by 'imsel as far as the end o' the hoose whaur the peats was keepit. The mistress maun hae saved some siller that spring through the Egyptians (gypsies) keepin' awa, for the farm had got sic an ill name, 'at nae tinkler would come near't at nicht. The tailor-man an' his laddie, 'at should hae bidden wi' us to sew things for the men, walkit off fair skeered one mornin', an' settled doon at the farm o' Cragiebuckle fower mile awa, whaur our lads had to gae to them. Ay, I mind the tailor's sendin' the laddie for the money owin' him; he hadna the speerit to venture again within soond o' the cradle 'imsel. The men on the farm, though, couldna blame 'im for that. They were juist as flichtered themsels, an' mony a time I saw them hittin' the dogs for whinin' at the soond. The wy the dogs took on was fearsome in itsel, for they seemed to ken, aye when nicht cam on, 'at the rockin' would sune begin, an' if they werena chained they cam runnin' to the hoose. I hae heard the hale glen fu, as ye micht say, wi' the whinin' o' dogs, for the dogs on the other farms took up the cry, an' in a glen ye can hear soonds terrible far awa at nicht.

"As lang as we sat i' the kitchen, listenin' to what the mester had to say aboot the ghosts in his young days, the cradle would be still, but we were nae suner awa speeritless to our beds than it began, an' sometimes it lasted till mornin'. We lookit upon the mester almost wi' awe, sittin' there sae helpless in his chair, an' no fleid to be left alane. He had lang white hair, an' a saft bonny face 'at would hae made 'im respeckit by onybody, an' aye when we speired if he wasna fleid to be left alane, he said, 'Them 'at has a clear conscience has naething to fear frae ghosts.'

"There was some 'at said the curse would never leave the farm till the house was razed to the ground, an' it's the truth I'm tellin' ye when I say there was talk among the men aboot settin't on fire. The mester was richt stern when he heard o' that, quotin' frae Scripture in a solemn wy 'at abashed the masons, but he said 'at in his opeenion there was a bairn buried on the farm, an' till it was found the cradle would go on rockin'. After that the masons dug in a lot o' places lookin' for the body, an' they found some queer things, too, but never nae sign o' a murdered litlin'. Ay, I dinna ken what would hae happened if the commotion had gaen on muckle langer. One thing I'm sure o' is 'at the mistress would hae gaen daft, she took it a' sae terrible to heart.

"I lauch at it noo, but I tell ye I used to tak my heart to my bed in my mooth. If ye hinna heard the story, I dinna think ye'll be able to guess what the ghost cradle was."

I said I had been trying to think what the tray had to do with it.

"It had everything to do wi't," said Jess; "an' if the masons had kent hoo that cradle was rockit, I think they would hae killed the mester. It was Eppie 'at found oot, an' she telt naebody but me, though mony a ane kens noo. I see ye canna mak it oot yet, so I'll tell ye what the cradle was. The tray was keepit against the kitchen wall near the mester, an' he played on't wi' his foot. He made it gang bump bump, an' the soond was juist like a cradle rockin'. Ye could hardly believe sic a thing would hae made that din, but it did, an' ye see we lay in our beds hearkenin' for't. Ay, when Eppie telt me, I could scarce believe 'at that guid devout-lookin' man could hae been sae wicked. Ye see, when he found hoo terrified we a' were, he keepit it up. The wy Eppie found out i' the tail o' the day was by wonderin' at 'im sleepin' sae muckle in the daytime. He did that so as to be fresh for his sport at nicht. What a fine releegious man we thocht 'im, too!

"Eppie couldna bear the very sicht o' the tray after that, an' she telt me to break it up; but I keepit it, ye, see. The lump i' the middle's the mark, as ye may say, o' the auld man's foot."

# XII

### THE TRAGEDY OF A WIFE

Were Jess still alive to tell the life-story of Sam'l Fletcher and his wife, you could not hear it and sit still. The ghost cradle is but a page from the black history of a woman who married, to be blotted out from that hour. One case of the kind I myself have known, of a woman so good mated to a man so selfish that I cannot think of her even now with a steady mouth. Hers was the tragedy of living on, more mournful than the tragedy that kills. In Thrums the weavers spoke of "lousing" from their looms, removing the chains, and there is something woeful in that. But pity poor Nanny Coutts, who took her chains to bed with her.

Nanny was buried a month or more before I came to the house on the brae, and even in Thrums the dead are seldom remembered for so long a time as that. But it was only after Sanders was left alone that we learned what a woman she had been, and how basely we had wronged her. She was an angel, Sanders went about whining when he had no longer a woman to ill-treat. He had this sentimental way with him, but it lost its effect after we knew the man.

"A deevil couldna hae deserved waur treatment," Tammas Haggart said to him; "gang oot o' my sicht, man."

"I'll blame mysel till I die," Jess said, with tears in her eyes, "for no understandin' puir Nanny better."

So Nanny got sympathy at last, but not until her forgiving soul had left her tortured body. There was many a kindly heart in Thrums that would have gone out to her in her lifetime, but we could not have loved her without upbraiding him, and she would not buy sympathy at the price. What a little story it is, and how few words are required to tell it! He was a bad husband to her, and she kept it secret. That is Nanny's life summed up. It is all that was left behind when her coffin went down the brae. Did she love him to the end, or was she only doing what she thought her duty? It is not for me even to guess. A good woman who suffers is altogether beyond man's reckoning. To such heights of self-sacrifice we cannot rise. It crushes us; it ought to crush us on to our knees. For us who saw Nanny, infirm, shrunken, and so weary, yet a type of the noblest womanhood, suffering for years, and misunderstood her to the end, what expiation can there be? I do not want to storm at the man who made her life so burdensome. Too many years have passed for that, nor would Nanny take it kindly if I called her man names.

Sanders worked little after his marriage. He had a sore back, he said, which became a torture if he leant forward at his loom. What truth there was in this I cannot say, but not every weaver in Thrums could "louse" when his back grew sore. Nanny went to the loom in his place, filling as well as weaving, and he walked about, dressed better than the common, and with cheerful words for those who had time to listen. Nanny got no approval even for doing his work as well as her own, for they were understood to have money, and Sanders let us think her merely greedy. We drifted into his opinions.

Had Jess been one of those who could go about, she would, I think, have read Nanny better than the rest of us, for her intellect was bright, and always led her straight to her neighbours' hearts. But Nanny visited no one, and so Jess only knew her by hearsay. Nanny's standoffishness, as it was called, was not a popular virtue, and she was blamed still more for trying to keep her husband out of other people's houses. He was so frank and full of gossip, and she was so reserved. He would go everywhere, and she nowhere. He had been known to ask neighbours to tea, and she had shown that she wanted them away, or even begged them not to come. We were not accustomed to go behind the face of a thing, and so we set down Nanny's inhospitality to churlishness or greed. Only after her death, when other women had to attend him, did we get to know what a tyrant Sanders was at his own hearth. The ambition of Nanny's life was that we should never know it, that we should continue extolling him, and say what we chose about herself. She knew that if we went much about the house and saw how he treated her, Sanders would cease to be a respected man in Thrums.

So neat in his dress was Sanders, that he was seldom seen abroad in corduroys. His blue bonnet for everyday wear was such as even well-to-do farmers only wore at fair-time, and it was said that he had a handkerchief for every day in the week. Jess often held him up to Hendry as a model of courtesy and polite manners.

"Him an' Nanny's no weel matched," she used to say, "for he has grand ideas, an' she's o' the commonest: It maun be a richt trial to a man wi' his fine tastes to hae a wife 'at's wrapper's never even on, an' wha doesna wash her mutch aince in a month."

It is true that Nanny was a slattern, but only because she married into slavery. She was kept so busy washing and ironing for Sanders that she ceased to care how she looked herself. What did it matter whether her mutch was clean? Weaving and washing and cooking, doing the work of a breadwinner as well as of a housewife, hers was soon a body prematurely old, on which no wrapper would sit becomingly. Before her face, Sanders would hint that her slovenly ways and dress tried him sorely, and in company at least she only bowed her head. We were given to respecting those who worked hard, but Nanny, we thought, was a woman of means, and Sanders let us call her a miser. He was always anxious, he said, to be generous, but Nanny would not let him assist a starving child. They had really not a penny beyond what Nanny earned at the loom, and now we know how Sanders shook her if she did not earn enough. His vanity was responsible for the story about her wealth, and she would not have us think him vain.

Because she did so much, we said that she was as strong as a cart-horse. The doctor who attended her during the last week of her life discovered that she had never been well. Yet we had often wondered at her letting Sanders pit his own potatoes when he was so unable.

"Them 'at's strong, ye see," Sanders explained, "doesna ken what illness is, an' so it's nat'ral they shouldna sympathize wi' onweel fowk. Ay, I'm rale thankfu' 'at Nanny keeps her health. I often envy her."

These were considered creditable sentiments, and so they might have been had Nanny uttered them. Thus easily Sanders built up a reputation for never complaining. I know now that he was a hard and cruel man who should have married a shrew; but while Nanny lived I thought he had a beautiful nature. Many a time I have spoken with him at Hendry's gate, and felt the better of his heartiness.

"I mauna complain," he always said; "na, we maun juist fecht awa."

Little, indeed, had he to complain of, and little did he fight away.

Sanders went twice to church every Sabbath, and thrice when he got the chance. There was no man who joined so lustily in the singing or looked straighter at the minister during the prayer. I have heard the minister say that Sanders's constant attendance was an encouragement and a help to him. Nanny had been a great church-goer when she was a maiden, but after her marriage she only went in the afternoons, and a time came when she ceased altogether to attend. The minister admonished her many times, telling her, among other things, that her irreligious ways were a distress to her husband. She never replied that she could not go to church in the forenoon because Sanders insisted on a hot meal being waiting him when the service ended. But it was true that Sanders, for appearance's sake, would have had her go to church in the afternoons. It is now believed that on this point alone did she refuse to do as she was bidden. Nanny was very far from perfect, and the reason she forsook the kirk utterly was because she had no Sabbath clothes.

She died as she had lived, saying not a word when the minister, thinking it his duty, drew a cruel comparison between her life and her husband's.

"I got my first glimpse into the real state of affairs in that house," the doctor told me one night on the brae," the day before she died. 'You're sure there's no hope for me?' she asked wistfully, and when I had to tell the truth she sank back on the pillow with a look of joy."

Nanny died with a lie on her, lips. "Ay," she said, "Sanders has been a guid man to me."

# XIII

## MAKING THE BEST OF IT

Hendry had a way of resuming a conversation where he had left off the night before. He would revolve a topic in his mind, too, and then begin aloud, "He's a queer ane," or, "Say ye so?" which was at times perplexing. With the whole day before them, none of the family was inclined to waste strength in talk; but one morning when he was blowing the steam off his porridge, Hendry said, suddenly—

"He's hame again."

The women-folk gave him time to say to whom he was referring, which he occasionally did as an after-thought. But he began to sup his porridge, making eyes as it went steaming down his throat.

"I dinna ken wha ye mean," Jess said; while Leeby, who was on her knees rubbing the hearthstone a bright blue, paused to catch her father's answer.

"Jeames Geogehan," replied Hendry, with the horn spoon in his mouth.

Leeby turned to Jess for enlightenment.

"Geogehan," repeated Jess; "what, no little Jeames 'at ran awa?"

"Ay, ay, but he's a muckle stoot man noo, an' gey grey."

"Ou, I dinna wonder at that. It's a guid forty year since he ran off."

"I waurant ye couldna say exact hoo lang syne it is?"

Hendry asked this question because Jess was notorious for her memory, and he gloried in putting it to the test.

"Let's see," she said.

"But wha is he?" asked Leeby. "I never kent nae Geogehans in Thrums."

"Weel, it's forty-one years syne come Michaemas," said Jess.

"Hoo do ye ken?"

"I ken fine. Ye mind his father had been lickin' 'im, an' he ran awa in a passion, cryin' oot 'at he would never come back? Ay, then, he had a pair o' boots on at the time, an' his father ran after 'im an' took them aff 'im. The boots was the last 'at Davie Mearns made, an' it's fully ane-an-forty years since Davie fell ower the quarry on the day o' the hill-market. That settles't. Ay, an' Jeames 'll be turned fifty noo, for he was comin' on for ten year auld at that time. Ay, ay, an' he's come back. What a state Eppie 'll be in!"

"Tell's wha he is, mother."

"Od, he's Eppie Guthrie's son. Her man was William Geogehan, but he died afore you was born, an' as Jeames was their only bairn, the name o' Geogehan's been a kind o' lost sicht o'. Hae ye seen him, Hendry? Is't true 'at he made a fortune in thae far-awa countries? Eppie 'll be blawin' aboot him richt?"

"There's nae doubt abbot the siller," said Hendry, "for he drove in a carriage frae Tilliedrum, an' they say he needs a closet to hing his claes in, there's sic a heap o' them. Ay, but that's no a' he's brocht, na, far frae a'."

"Dinna gang awa till ye've telt's a' aboot 'im. What mair has he brocht?"

"He's brocht a wife," said Hendry, twisting his face curiously.

"There's naething surprisin' in that."

"Ay, but there is, though. Ye see, Eppie had a letter frae 'im no mony weeks syne, sayin' 'at he wasna deid, an' he was comin' hame wi' a fortune. He said, too, 'at he was a single man, an' she's been boastin' aboot that, so ye may think 'at she got a surprise when he hands a wuman oot o' the carriage."

"An' no a pleasant ane," said Jess. "Had he been leein'?"

"Na, he was single when he wrote, an' single when he got the length o' Tilliedrum. Ye see, he fell in wi' the lassie there, an' juist gaed clean aft his heid aboot her. After managin' to withstand the women o' foreign lands for a' thae years, he gaed fair skeer aboot this stocky at Tilliedrum. She's juist seventeen year auld, an' the auld fule sits wi' his airm round her in Eppie's hoose, though they've been mairit this fortnicht."

"The doited fule," said Jess.

Jeames Geogehan and his bride became the talk of Thrums, and Jess saw them from her window several times. The first time she had only eyes for the jacket with fur round it worn by Mrs. Geogehan, but subsequently she took in Jeames.

"He's tryin' to carry't aff wi' his heid in the air," she said, "but I can see he's fell shamefaced, an' nae wonder. Ay, I sepad he's mair ashamed o't in his heart than she is. It's an awful like thing o' a lassie to marry an auld man. She had dune't for the siller. Ay, there's pounds' worth o' fur aboot that jacket."

"They say she had siller hersel," said Tibbie Birse.

"Dinna tell me," said Jess. "I ken by her wy o' carryin' hersel 'at she never had a jacket like that afore."

Eppie was not the only person in Thrums whom this marriage enraged. Stories had long been alive of Jeames's fortune, which his cousins' children were some day to divide among themselves, and as a consequence these young men and women looked on Mrs. Geogehan as a thief.

"Dinna bring the wife to our hoose, Jeames," one of them told him, for we would be fair ashamed to hae her. We used to hae a respect for yer name, so we couldna look her i' the face."

"She's mair like yer dochter than yer wife," said another.

"Na," said a third, "naebody could mistak her for yer dochter. She's ower young-like for that."

"Wi' the siller you'll leave her, Jeames," Tammas Haggart told him, "she'll get a younger man for her second venture."

All this was very trying to the newly-married man, who was thirsting for sympathy. Hendry was the person whom he took into his confidence.

"It may hae been foolish at my time o' life," Hendry reported him to have said, "but I couldna help it. If they juist kent her better they couldna but see 'at she's a terrible takkin' crittur."

Jeames was generous; indeed he had come home with the intention of scattering largess. A beggar met him one day on the brae, and got a shilling from him. She was waving her arms triumphantly as she passed Hendry's house, and Leeby got the story from her.

"Eh, he's a fine man that, an' a saft ane," the woman said. "I juist speired at 'im hoo his bonny wife was, an' he oot wi' a shillin'!"

Leeby did not keep this news to herself, and soon it was through the town. Jeames's face began to brighten.

"They're comin' round to a mair sensible wy o' lookin' at things," he told Hendry. "I was walkin' wi' the wife i' the buryin' ground yesterday, an' we met Kitty McQueen. She was ane o' the warst agin me at first, but she telt me i' the buryin' ground 'at when a man mairit he should please 'imsel. Oh, they're comin' round."

What Kitty told Jess was—

"I minded o' the tinkler wuman 'at he gae a shillin' to, so I thocht I would butter up at the auld fule too. Weel, I assure ye, I had nae suner said 'at he was rale wise to marry wha he likit than he slips a pound note into my hand. 'Ou, Jess, we've taen the wrang wy wi' Jeames. I've telt a' my bairns 'at if they meet him they're to praise the wife terrible, an' I'm far mista'en if that doesna mean five shillins to ilka ane o' them."

Jean Whamond got a pound note for saying that Jeames's wife had an uncommon pretty voice, and Davit Lunan had ten shillings for a judicious word about her attractive manners. Tibbie Birse invited the newly-married couple to tea (one pound).

"They're takkin' to her, they're takkin' to her," Jeames said, gleefully. "I kent they would come round in time. Ay, even my mother, 'at was sae mad at first, sits for hours noo aside her, haudin' her hand. They're juist inseparable."

The time came when we had Mr. and Mrs. Geogehan and Eppie to tea.

"It's true enough," Leeby ran ben to tell Jess, " 'at Eppie an' the wife's fond o' ane another. I wouldna hae believed it o' Eppie if I hadna seen it, but I assure ye they sat even at the tea-table haudin' ane another's hands. I waurant they're doin't this meenute."

"I wasna born on a Sabbath," retorted Jess. "Na, na, dinna tell me Eppie's fond o' her. Tell Eppie to come but to the kitchen when the tea's ower."

Jess and Eppie had half an hour's conversation alone, and then our guests left.

"It's a richt guid thing," said Hendry, " 'at Eppie has ta'en sic a notion o' the wife."

"Ou, ay," said Jess.

Then Hendry hobbled out of the house.

"What said Eppie to ye?" Leeby asked her mother.

"Juist what I expeckit," Jess answered. "Ye see she's dependent on Jeames, so she has to butter up 'at 'im."

"Did she say onything aboot haudin' the wife's hand sae fond-like?"

"Ay, she said it was an awfu' trial to her, an' 'at it sickened her to see Jeames an' the wife baith believin' 'at she likit to do't."

# XIV

## VISITORS AT THE MANSE

On bringing home his bride, the minister showed her to us, and we thought she would do when she realized that she was not the minister. She was a grand lady from Edinburgh, though very frank, and we simple folk amused her a good deal, especially when we were sitting cowed in the manse parlour drinking a dish of tea with her, as happened to Leeby, her father, and me, three days before Jamie came home.

Leeby had refused to be drawn into conversation, like one who knew her place, yet all her actions were genteel and her monosyllabic replies in the Englishy tongue, as of one who was, after all, a little above the common. When the minister's wife asked her whether she took sugar and cream, she said politely, "If you please" (though she did not take sugar), a reply that contrasted with Hendry's equally well-intended answer to the same question. "I'm no partikler," was what Hendry said.

Hendry had left home glumly, declaring that the white collar Jess had put on him would throttle him; but her feikieness ended in his surrender, and he was looking unusually perjink. Had not his daughter been present he would have been the most at ease of the company, but her manners were too fine not to make an impression upon one who knew her on her everyday behaviour, and she had also ways of bringing Hendry to himself by a touch beneath the table. It was in church that Leeby brought to perfection her manner of looking after her father. When he had confidence in the preacher's soundness, he would sometimes have slept in his pew if Leeby had not had a watchful foot. She wakened him in an instant, while still looking modestly at the pulpit; however reverently he might try to fall over, Leeby's foot went out. She was such an artist that I never caught her in the act. All I knew for certain was that, now and then, Hendry suddenly sat up.

The ordeal was over when Leeby went upstairs to put on her things. After tea Hendry had become bolder in talk, his subject being ministerial. He had an extraordinary knowledge, got no one knew where, of the matrimonial affairs of all the ministers in these parts, and his stories about them ended frequently with a chuckle. He always took it for granted that a minister's marriage was womanhood's great triumph, and that the particular woman who got him must be very clever. Some of his tales were even more curious than he thought them, such as the one Leeby tried to interrupt by saying we must be going.

"There's Mr. Pennycuick, noo," said Hendry, shaking his head in wonder at what he had to tell; "him 'at's minister at Tilliedrum. Weel, when he was a probationer he was michty poor, an' one day he was walkin' into Thrums frae Glen Quharity, an' he tak's a rest at a little housey on the road. The fowk didna ken him ava, but they saw he was a minister, an' the lassie was sorry to see him wi' sic an auld hat. What think ye she did?"

"Come away, father," said Leeby, re-entering the parlour; but Hendry was now in full pursuit of his story.

"I'll tell ye what she did," he continued. "She juist took his hat awa, an' put her father's new ane in its place, an' Mr. Pennycuick never kent the differ till he landed in Thrums. It was terrible kind o' her. Ay, but the auld man would be in a michty rage when he found she had swappit the hats."

"Come away," said Leeby, still politely, though she was burning to tell her mother how Hendry had disgraced them.

"The minister," said Hendry, turning his back on Leeby, "didna forget the lassie. Na; as sune as he got a kirk, he married her. Ay, she got her reward. He married her. It was rale noble of 'im."

I do not know what Leeby said to Hendry when she got him beyond the manse gate, for I stayed behind to talk to the minister. As it turned out, the minister's wife did most of the talking, smiling good-humouredly at country gawkiness the while.

"Yes," she said, "I am sure I shall like Thrums, though those teas to the congregation are a little trying. Do you know, Thrums is the only place I was ever in where it struck me that the men are cleverer than the women."

She told us why.

"Well, to-night affords a case in point. Mr. McQumpha was quite brilliant, was he not, in comparison with his daughter? Really she seemed so put out at being at the manse that she could not raise her eyes. I question if she would know me again, and I am sure she sat in the room as one blindfolded. I left her in the bedroom a minute, and I assure you, when I returned she was still standing on the same spot in the centre of the floor."

I pointed out that Leeby had been awestruck.

"I suppose so," she said; "but it is a pity she cannot make use of her eyes, if not of her tongue. Ah, the Thrums women are good, I believe, but their wits are sadly in need of sharpening. I daresay it comes of living in so small a place."

I overtook Leeby on the brae, aware, as I saw her alone, that it had been her father whom I passed talking to Tammas Haggart in the Square. Hendry stopped to have what he called a tove with any likely person he encountered, and, indeed, though he and I often took a walk on Saturdays, I generally lost him before we were clear of the town.

In a few moments Leeby and I were at home to give Jess the news.

"Whaur's yer father?" asked Jess, as if Hendry's way of dropping behind was still unknown to her.

"Ou, I left him speakin' to Gavin Birse," said Leeby. "I daursay he's awa to some hoose."

"It's no very silvendy (safe) his comin' ower the brae by himsel'," said Jess, adding in a bitter tone of conviction, "but he'll gang in to no hoose as lang as he's so weel dressed. Na, he would think it boastfu'."

I sat down to a book by the kitchen fire; but, as Leeby became communicative, I read less and less. While she spoke she was baking bannocks with all the might of her, and Jess, leaning forward in her chair, was arranging them in a semicircle round the fire.

"Na," was the first remark of Leeby's that came between me and my book, "it is no new furniture."

"But there was three cart-loads o't, Leeby, sent on frae Edinbory. Tibbie Birse helpit to lift it in, and she said the parlour furniture beat a'."

"Ou, it's substantial, but it is no new. I sepad it had been bocht cheap second-hand, for the chair' I had was terrible scratched like, an', what's mair, the airm-chair was a heap shinnier than the rest."

"Ay, ay, I wager it had been new, stuffed. Tibbie said the carpet cowed for grandeur!"

"Oh, I dinna deny it's a guid carpet; but if it's been turned once it's been turned half a dozen times, so it's far frae new. Ay, an' forby, it was rale threadbare aneath the table, so ye may be sure they've been cuttin't an' puttin' the worn pairt whaur it would be least seen."

"They say 'at there's twa grand gas brackets i' the parlour, an' a wonderfu' gasoliery i' the dinin'-room?"

"We wasna i' the dinin'-room, so I ken naething aboot the gasoliery; but I'll tell ye what the gas brackets is. I recognized them immeditly. Ye mind the auld gasoliery i' the dinin'-room had twa lichts? Ay, then, the parlour brackets is made oot o' the auld gasoliery."

"Weel, Leeby, as sure as ye're standin' there, that passed through my head as sune as Tibbie mentioned them!"

"There's nae doot about it. Ay, I was in ane o' the bedrooms, too!"

"It would be grand?"

"I wouldna say 'at it was partikler grand, but there was a great mask (quantity) o' things in't, an' near everything was covered wi' cretonne. But the chairs dinna match. There was a very bonny-painted cloth alang the chimley—what they call a mantlepiece border, I warrant."

"Sal, I've often wondered what they was."

"Weel, I assure ye they winna be ill to mak, for the border was juist nailed upon a board laid on the chimley. There's naething to hender's makin' ane for the room."

"Ay, we could sew something on the border instead o' paintin't. The room lookit weel, ye say?"

"Yes, but it was economically furnished. There was nae carpet below the wax-cloth; na, there was nane below the bed either."

"Was't a grand bed?"

"It had a fell lot o' brass aboot it, but there was juist one pair o' blankets. I thocht it was gey shabby, hae'n the ewer a different pattern frae the basin; ay, an' there was juist a poker in the fireplace, there was nae tangs."

"Yea, yea; they'll hae but one set o' bedroom fire-irons. The tangs'll be in anither room. Tod, that's no sae michty grand for Edinbory. What like was she hersel?"

"Ou, very ladylike and saft spoken. She's a canty body an' frank. She wears her hair low on the left side to hod (hide) a scar, an' there's twa warts on her richt hand."

"There hadna been a fire i' the parlour?"

"No, but it was ready to licht There was sticks and paper in't. The paper was oot o' a dressmaker's journal."

"Ye say so? She'll mak her ain frocks, I sepad."

When Hendry entered to take off his collar and coat before sitting down to his evening meal of hot water, porter, and bread mixed in a bowl, Jess sent me off to the attic. As I climbed the stairs I remembered that the minister's wife thought Leeby in need of sharpening.

### XV

### HOW GAVIN BIRSE PUT IT TO MAG LOWNIE

In a wet day the rain gathered in blobs on the road that passed our garden. Then it crawled into the cart-tracks until the road was streaked with water. Lastly, the water gathered in heavy yellow pools. If the on-ding still continued, clods of earth toppled from the garden dyke into the ditch.

On such a day, when even the dulseman had gone into shelter, and the women scudded by with their wrappers over their heads, came Gavin Birse to our door. Gavin, who was the Glen Quharity post, was still young, but had never been quite the same man since some amateurs in the glen ironed his back for rheumatism. I thought he had called to have a crack with me. He sent his compliments up to the attic, however, by Leeby, and would I come and be a witness?

Gavin came up and explained. He had taken off his scarf and thrust it into his pocket, lest the rain should take the colour out of it. His boots cheeped, and his shoulders had risen to his ears. He stood steaming before my fire.

"If it's no' ower muckle to ask ye," he said, "I would like ye for a witness."

"A witness! But for what do you need a witness, Gavin?"

"I want ye," he said, "to come wi' me to Mag's, and be a witness."

Gavin and Mag Birse had been engaged for a year or more. Mag was the daughter of Janet Ogilvy, who was best remembered as the body that took the hill (that is, wandered about it) for twelve hours on the day Mr. Dishart, the Auld Licht minister, accepted a call to another church. "You don't mean to tell me, Gavin," I asked, "that your marriage is to take place to-day?"

By the twist of his mouth I saw that he was only deferring a smile.

"Far frae that," he said.

"Ah, then, you, have quarrelled, and I am to speak up for you?"

"Na, na," he said, "I dinna want ye to do that above all things. It would be a favour if ye could gie me a bad character."

This beat me, and, I daresay, my face showed it.

"I'm no' juist what ye would call anxious to marry Mag noo," said Gavin, without a tremor.

I told him to go on.

"There's a lassie oot at Craigiebuckle," he explained, "workin' on the farm—Jeanie Luke by name. Ye may ha'e seen her?"

"What of her?" I asked, severely.

"Weel," said Gavin, still unabashed, "I'm thinkin' noo 'at I would rather ha'e her."

Then he stated his case more fully.

"Ay, I thocht I liked Mag oncommon till I saw Jeanie, an' I like her fine yet, but I prefer the other ane. That state o' matters canna gang on for ever, so I came into Thrums the day to settle't one wy or another."

"And how," I asked, "do you propose going about it? It is a somewhat delicate business."

"Ou, I see nae great difficulty in't. I'll speir at Mag, blunt oot, if she'll let me aff. Yes, I'll put it to her plain."

"You're sure Jeanie would take you?"

"Ay; oh, there's nae fear o' that."

"But if Mag keeps you to your bargain?"

"Weel, in that case there's nae harm done."

"You are in a great hurry, Gavin?"

"Ye may say that; but I want to be married. The wifie I lodge wi' canna last lang, an' I would like to settle doon in some place."

"So you are on your way to Mag's now?"

"Ay, we'll get her in atween twal' and ane."

"Oh, yes; but why do you want me to go with you?"

"I want ye for a witness. If she winna let me aff, weel and guid; and if she will, it's better to hae a witness in case she should go back on her word."

Gavin made his proposal briskly, and as coolly as if he were only asking me to go fishing; but I did not accompany him to Mag's. He left the house to look for another witness, and about an hour afterwards Jess saw him pass with Tammas Haggart. Tammas cried in during the evening to tell us how the mission prospered.

"Mind ye," said Tammas, a drop of water hanging to the point of his nose, "I disclaim all responsibility in the business. I ken Mag weel for a thrifty, respectable woman, as her mither was afore her, and so I said to Gavin when he came to speir me."

"Ay, mony a pirn has 'Lisbeth filled to me," said Hendry, settling down to a reminiscence.

"No to be ower hard on Gavin," continued Tammas, forestalling Hendry, "he took what I said in guid part; but aye when I stopped speakin' to draw breath, he says, 'The queistion is, will ye come wi' me?' He was michty, made up in's mind."

"Weel, ye went wi' him," suggested Jess, who wanted to bring Tammas to the point.

"Ay," said the stone-breaker, "but no in sic a hurry as that."

He worked his mouth round and round, to clear the course, as it were, for a sarcasm.

"Fowk often say," he continued, " 'at a'm quick beyond the ordinar' in seein' the humorous side o' things."

Here Tammas paused, and looked at us.

"So ye are, Tammas," said Hendry. "Losh, ye mind hoo ye saw the humorous side o' me wearin' a pair o' boots 'at wisna marrows! No, the ane had a toe-piece on, an' the other hadna."

"Ye juist wore them sometimes when ye was delvin'," broke in Jess, "ye have as guid a pair o' boots as ony in Thrums."

"Ay, but I had worn them," said Hendry, "at odd times for mair than a year, an' I had never seen the humorous side o' them. Weel, as fac as death (here he addressed me), Tammas had juist seen them twa or three times when he saw the humorous side o' them. Syne I saw their humorous side, too, but no till Tammas pointed it oot."

"That was naething," said Tammas, "naething ava to some things I've done."

"But what aboot Mag?" said Leeby.

"We wasna that length, was we?" said Tammas. "Na, we was speakin' aboot the humorous side. Ay, wait a wee, I didna mention the humorous side for naething."

He paused to reflect.

"Oh, yes," he said at last, brightening up, "I was sayin' to ye hoo quick I was to see the humorous side o' onything. Ay, then, what made me say that was 'at in a clink (flash) I saw the humorous side o' Gavin's position."

"Man, man," said Hendry, admiringly, "and what is't?"

"Oh, it's this, there's something humorous in speirin' a woman to let ye aff so as ye can be married to another woman."

"I daursay there is," said Hendry, doubtfully.

"Did she let him aff?" asked Jess, taking the words out of Leeby's mouth.

"I'm comin' to that," said Tammas. "Gavin proposes to me after I had haen my laugh——"

"Yes," cried Hendry, banging the table with his fist, "it has a humorous side. Ye're richt again, Tammas."

"I wish ye wadna blatter (beat) the table," said Jess, and then Tammas proceeded.

"Gavin wanted me to tak' paper an' ink an' a pen wi' me, to write the proceedins doon, but I said, 'Na, na, I'll tak' paper, but no nae ink nor nae pen, for there'll be ink an' a pen there.' That was what I said."

"An' did she let him aff?" asked Leeby.

"Weel," said Tammas, "aff we goes to Mag's hoose, an' sure enough Mag was in. She was alane, too; so Gavin, no to waste time, juist sat doon for politeness' sake, an' syne rises up again; an' says he, 'Marget Lownie, I ha'e a solemn question to speir at ye, namely this, Will you, Marget Lownie, let me, Gavin Birse, aff?'"

"Mag would start at that?"

"Sal, she was braw an' cool. I thocht she maun ha'e got wind o' his intentions aforehand, for she juist replies, quiet-like, 'Hoo do ye want aff, Gavin?'

"'Because,' says he, like a book, 'my affections has undergone a change.'

"'Ye mean Jean Luke,' says Mag.

"'That is wha I mean,' says Gavin, very straitforrard."

"But she didna let him aff, did she?"

"Na, she wasna the kind. Says she, 'I wonder to hear ye, Gavin, but a'm no goin' to agree to naething o' that sort.'"

"'Think it ower,' says Gavin.

"'Na, my mind's made up,' said she.

"'Ye would sune get anither man,' he says, earnestly.

"'Hoo do I ken that?' she speirs, rale sensibly, I thocht, for men's no sae easy to get.

"'A'm sure o't,' Gavin says, wi' michty conviction in his voice, 'for ye're bonny to look at, an' weel-kent for bein' a guid body.'

"'Ay,' says Mag, 'I'm glad ye like me, Gavin, for ye have to tak me.'"

"That put a clincher on him," interrupted Hendry.

"He was loth to gie in," replied Tammas, "so he says, 'Ye think a'm a fine character, Marget Lownie, but ye're very far mista'en. I wouldna wonder but what I was lossin' my place some o' thae days, an' syne whaur would ye be?—Marget Lownie,' he goes on,' a'm nat'rally lazy an' fond o' the drink. As sure as ye stand there, a'm a reglar deevil!'"

"That was strong language," said Hendry, "but he would be wantin' to fleg (frighten) her?"

"Juist so, but he didna manage't, for Mag says, 'We a' ha'e oor faults, Gavin, an' deevil or no deevil, ye're the man for me!'

"Gavin thocht a bit," continued Tammas, "an' syne he tries her on a new tack. 'Marget Lownie,' he says, 'ye're father's an auld man noo, an' he has naebody but yersel to look after him. I'm thinkin' it would be kind o' cruel o' me to tak ye awa frae him?'"

"Mag wouldna be ta'en in wi' that; she wasna born on a Sawbath," said Jess, using one of her favourite sayings.

"She wasna," answered Tammas. "Says she, 'Hae nae fear on that score, Gavin; my father's fine willin' to spare me!'"

"An' that ended it?"

"Ay, that ended it."

"Did ye tak it doon in writin'?" asked Hendry.

"There was nae need," said Tammas, handing round his snuff-mull. "No, I never touched paper. When I saw the thing was settled, I left them to their coortin'. They're to tak a look at Snecky Hobart's auld hoose the nicht. It's to let."

# XVI

### THE SON FROM LONDON

In the spring of the year there used to come to Thrums a painter from nature whom Hendry spoke of as the drawer. He lodged with Jess in my attic, and when the weavers met him they said, "Weel, drawer," and then passed on, grinning. Tammas Haggart was the first to say this.

The drawer was held a poor man because he straggled about the country looking for subjects for his draws, and Jess, as was her way, gave him many comforts for which she would not charge. That, I daresay, was why he painted for her a little portrait of Jamie. When the drawer came back to Thrums he always found the painting in a frame in the room. Here I must make a confession about Jess. She did not in her secret mind think the portrait quite the thing, and as soon as the drawer departed it was removed from the frame to make way for a calendar. The deception was very innocent, Jess being anxious not to hurt the donor's feelings.

To those who have the artist's eye, the picture, which hangs in my school-house now, does not show a handsome lad, Jamie being short and dapper, with straw-coloured hair, and a chin that ran away into his neck. That is how I once regarded him, but I have little heart for criticism of those I like, and, despite his madness for a season, of which alas, I shall have to tell, I am always Jamie's friend. Even to hear any one disparaging the appearance of Jess's son is to me a pain.

All Jess's acquaintants knew that in the beginning of every month a registered letter reached her from London. To her it was not a matter to keep secret. She was proud that the help she and Hendry needed in the gloaming of their lives should come from her beloved son, and the neighbours esteemed Jamie because he was good to his mother. Jess had more humour than any other woman I have known while Leeby was but sparingly endowed; yet, as the month neared its close, it was the daughter who put on the humorist, Jess thinking money too serious a thing to jest about. Then if Leeby had a moment for gossip, as when ironing a dickey for Hendry, and the iron was a trifle too hot, she would look archly at me before addressing her mother in these words:

"Will he send, think ye?" Jess, who had a conviction that he would send, affected surprise at the question.

"Will Jamie send this month, do ye mean ? Na, oh, losh no! it's no to be expeckit. Na, he couldna do't this time."

"That's what ye aye say, but he aye sends. Yes, an' vara weel ye ken 'at he will send."

"Na, na, Leeby; dinna let me ever think o' sic a thing this month."

"As if ye wasna thinkin' o't day an' nicht!"

"He's terrible mindfu', Leeby, but he doesna hae't. Na, no this month; mebbe next month."

"Do you mean to tell me, mother, 'at ye'll no be up oot o' yer bed on Monunday an hour afore yer usual time, lookin' for the post?"

"Na no this time. I may be up, an' tak a look for 'im, but no expeckin' a registerdy; na na, that wouldna be reasonable."

"Reasonable here, reasonable there, up you'll be, keekin' (peering) through the blind to see if the post's comin', ay, an' what's mair, the post will come, and a registerdy in his hand wi' fifteen shillings in't at the least."

"Dinna say fifteen, Leeby; I would never think o' sic a sum. Mebbe five——"

"Five! I wonder to hear ye. Vera weel you ken 'at since he had twenty-twa shillings in the week he's never sent less than half a sovereign."

"No, but we canna expeck——"

"Expeck ! No, but it's no expeck, it's get."

On the Monday morning when I came downstairs, Jess was in her chair by the window, beaming, a piece of paper in her hand. I did not require to, be told about it, but I was told. Jess had been up before Leeby could get the fire lit, with great difficulty reaching the window in her bare feet, and many a time had she said that the post must be by.

"Havers," said Leeby, "he winna be for an hour yet. Come awa' back to your bed."

"Na, he maun be by," Jess would say in a few minutes; "ou, we couldna expeck this month."

So it went on until Jess's hand shook the blind.

"He's comin', Leeby, he's comin'. He'll no hae naething, na, I couldna expeck—— He's by!"

"I dinna believe it," cried Leeby, running to the window, "he's juist at his tricks again."

This was in reference to a way our saturnine post had of pretending that he brought no letters and passing the door. Then he turned back. "Mistress McQumpha," he cried, and whistled.

"Run, Leeby, run," said Jess, excitedly.

Leeby hastened to the door, and came back with a registered letter.

"Registerdy," she cried in triumph, and Jess, with fond hands, opened the letter. By the time I came down the money was hid away in a box beneath the bed, where not even Leeby could find it, and Jess was on her chair hugging the letter. She preserved all her registered envelopes.

This was the first time I had been in Thrums when Jamie was expected for his ten days' holiday, and for a week we discussed little else. Though he had written saying when he would sail for Dundee, there was quite a possibility of his appearing on the brae at any moment, for he liked to take Jess and Leeby by surprise. Hendry there was no surprising, unless he was in the mood for it, and the coolness of him was one of Jess's grievances. Just two years earlier Jamie came north a week before his time, and his father saw him from the window. Instead of crying out in amazement or hacking his face, for he was shaving at the time, Hendry calmly wiped his razor on the window-sill, and said—

"Ay, there's Jamie."

Jamie was a little disappointed at being seen in this way, for he had been looking forward for four and forty hours to repeating the sensation of the year before. On that occasion he had got to the door unnoticed, where he stopped to listen. I daresay he checked his breath, the better to catch his mother's voice, for Jess being an invalid, Jamie thought of her first. He had Leeby sworn to write the truth about her, but many an anxious hour he had on hearing that she was "complaining fell (considerably) about her back the day," Leeby, as he knew, being frightened to alarm him. Jamie, too, had given his promise to tell exactly how he was keeping, but often he wrote that he was "fine" when Jess had her doubts. When Hendry wrote he spread himself over the table, and said that Jess was "juist about it," or "aff and on," which does not tell much. So Jamie hearkened painfully at the door, and by and by heard his mother say to Leeby that she was sure the teapot was running out. Perhaps that voice was as sweet to him as the music of a maiden to her lover, but Jamie did not rush into his mother's arms. Jess has told me with a beaming face how craftily he behaved. The old man, of lungs that shook Thrums by night, who went from door to door selling firewood, had a way of shoving doors rudely open and crying—

"Ony rozetty roots?" and him Jamie imitated.

"Juist think," Jess said, as she recalled the incident, "what a startle we got. As we think, Pete kicks open the door and cries oot, 'Ony rozetty roots?' and Leeby says 'No,' and gangs to shut the door. Next minute she screeches, 'What, what, what!' and in walks Jamie!"

Jess was never able to decide whether it was more delightful to be taken aback in this way or to prepare for Jamie. Sudden excitement was bad for her according to Hendry, who got his medical knowledge second-hand from persons under treatment, but with Jamie's appearance on the threshold Jess's health began to improve. This time he kept to the appointed day, and the house was turned upside down in his honour. Such a polish did Leeby put on the flagons which hung on the kitchen wall, that, passing between them and the window, I thought once I had been struck by lightning. On the morning of the day that was to bring him, Leeby was up at two o'clock, and eight hours before he could possibly arrive Jess had a night-shirt warming for him at the fire. I was no longer anybody, except as a person who could give Jamie advice. Jess told me what I was to say. The only thing he and his mother quarrelled about was the underclothing she would swaddle him in, and Jess asked me to back her up in her entreaties.

"There's no a doubt," she said, "but what it's a hantle caulder here than in London, an' it would be a terrible business if he was to tak the cauld."

Jamie was to sail from London to Dundee, and come on to Thrums from Tilliedrum in the post-cart. The road at that time, however, avoided the brae, and at a certain point Jamie's custom was to alight, and take the short cut home, along a farm road and up the commonty. Here, too, Hookey Crewe, the post, deposited his passenger's box, which Hendry wheeled home in a barrow. Long before the cart had lost sight of Tilliedrum, Jess was at her window.

"Tell her Hookey's often late on Monundays," Leeby whispered to me, "for she'll gang oot o' her mind if she thinks there's onything wrang."

Soon Jess was painfully excited, though she sat as still as salt.

"It maun be yer time," she said, looking at both Leeby and me, for in Thrums we went out and met our friends.

" Hoots," retorted Leeby, trying to be hardy, "Hookey canna be oot o' Tilliedrum yet."

"He maun hae startit lang syne."

"I wonder at ye, mother, puttin' yersel in sic a state. Ye'll be ill when he comes."

"Na, a'm no in nae state, Leeby, but there'll no be nae accident, will there?"

"It's most provokin' 'at ye will think 'at every time Jamie steps into a machine there'll be an accident. A'm sure if ye would tak mair after my father, it would be a blessin'. Look hoo cool he is."

"Whaur is he, Leeby?"

"Oh, I dinna ken. The henmost time I saw him he was layin' doon the law aboot something to T'nowhead."

"It's an awfu' wy that he has o' ga'en oot withoot a word. I wouldna wonder 'at he's no bein' in time to meet Jamie, an' that would be a pretty business."

"Od, ye're sure he'll be in braw time."

"But he hasna ta'en the barrow wi' him, an' hoo is Jamie's luggage to be brocht up withoot a barrow?"

"Barrow! He took the barrow to the saw-mill an hour syne to pick it up at Rob Angus's on the wy."

Several times Jess was sure she saw the cart in the distance, and implored us to be off.

"I'll tak no settle till ye're awa," she said, her face now flushed and her hands working nervously.

"We've time to gang and come twa or three times yet," remonstrated Leeby; but Jess gave me so beseeching a look that I put on my hat. Then Hendry dandered in to change his coat deliberately, and when the three of us set off, we left Jess with her eye on the door by which Jamie must enter. He was her only son now, and she had not seen him for a year.

On the way down the commonty, Leeby had the honour of being twice addressed as Miss McQumpha, but her father was Hendry to all, which shows that we make our social position for ourselves. Hendry looked forward to Jamie's annual appearance only a little less hungrily than Jess, but his pulse still beat regularly. Leeby would have considered it almost wicked to talk of anything except Jamie now, but Hendry cried out comments on the tatties, yesterday's roup, the fall in jute, to everybody he encountered. When he and a crony had their say and parted, it was their custom to continue the conversation in shouts until they were out of hearing.

Only to Jess at her window was the cart late that afternoon. Jamie jumped from it in the long great-coat that had been new to Thrums the year before, and Hendry said calmly—

"Ay, Jamie."

Leeby and Jamie made signs that they recognized each other as brother and sister, but I was the only one with whom he shook hands. He was smart in his movements and quite the gentleman, but the Thrums ways took hold of him again at once. He even inquired for his mother in a tone that was meant to deceive me into thinking he did not care how she was.

Hendry would have had a talk out of him on the spot, but was reminded of the luggage. We took the heavy farm road, and soon we were at the saw-mill. I am naturally leisurely, but we climbed the commonty at a stride. Jamie pretended to be calm, but in a dark place I saw him take Leeby's hand, and after that he said not a word. His eyes were fixed on the elbow of the brae, where he would come into sight of his mother's window. Many, many a time, I know, that lad had prayed to God for still another sight of the window with his mother at it. So we came to the corner where the stile is that Sam'l Dickie jumped in the race for T'nowhead's Bell, and before Jamie was the house of his childhood and his mother's window, and the fond, anxious face of his mother herself. My eyes are dull, and I did not see her, but suddenly Jamie cried out, "My mother!" and Leeby and I were left behind. When I reached the kitchen Jess was crying, and her son's arms were round her neck. I went away to my attic.

There was only one other memorable event of that day. Jamie had finished his tea, and we all sat round him, listening to his adventures and opinions. He told us how the country should be governed, too, and perhaps put on airs a little. Hendry asked the questions, and Jamie answered them as pat as if he and his father were going through the Shorter Catechism. When Jamie told anything marvellous, as how many towels were used at the shop in a day, or that twopence was the charge for a single shave, his father screwed his mouth together as if preparing to whistle, and then instead made a curious clucking noise with his tongue, which was reserved for the expression of absolute amazement. As for Jess, who was given to making much of me, she ignored my remarks and laughed hilariously at jokes of Jamie's which had been received in silence from me a few minutes before.

Slowly it came to me that Leeby had something on her mind, and that Jamie was talking to her with his eyes. I learned afterwards that they were plotting how to get me out of the kitchen, but were too impatient to wait. Thus it was that the great event happened in my presence. Jamie rose and stood near Jess—I daresay he had planned the scene frequently. Then he produced from his pocket a purse, and coolly opened it. Silence fell upon us as we saw that purse. From it he took a neatly-folded piece of paper, crumpled it into a ball, and flung it into Jess's lap.

I cannot say whether Jess knew what it was. Her hand shook, and for a moment she let the ball of paper lie there.

"Open't up," cried Leeby, who was in the secret.

"What is't?" asked Hendry, drawing nearer.

"It's juist a bit paper Jamie flung at me," said Jess, and then she unfolded it.

"It's a five-pound note!" cried Hendry.

"Na, na; oh keep us, no," said Jess; but she knew it was.

For a time she could not speak.

"I canna tak it, Jamie," she faltered at last.

"But Jamie waved his hand, meaning that it was nothing, and then, lest he should burst, hurried out into the garden, where he walked up and down whistling. May God bless the lad, thought I. I do not know the history of that five-pound note, but well aware I am that it grew slowly out of pence and silver, and that Jamie denied his passions many things for this great hour. His sacrifices watered his young heart and kept it fresh and tender. Let us no longer cheat our consciences by talking of filthy lucre. Money may always be a beautiful thing. It is we who make it grimy.

# XVII

## A HOME FOR GENIUSES

From hints he had let drop at odd times I knew that Tammas Haggart had a scheme for geniuses, but not until the evening after Jamie's arrival did I get it out of him. Hendry was with Jamie at the fishing, and it came about that Tammas and I had the pig-sty to ourselves.

"Of course," he said, when we had got a grip of the subject, "I dount pretend as my ideas is to be followed withoot deeviation, but ondootedly something should be done for geniuses, them bein' aboot the only class as we do naething for. Yet they're fowk to be prood o', an' we shouldna let them overdo the thing, nor run into debt; na, na. There was Robbie Burns, noo, as real a genius as ever——"

At the pig-sty, where we liked to have more than one topic, we had frequently to tempt Tammas away from Burns.

"Your scheme," I interposed, "is for living geniuses, of course?"

"Ay," he said, thoughtfully, "them 'at's gone canna be brocht back. Weel, my idea is 'at a Home should be built for geniuses at the public expense, whaur they could all live thegither, an' be decently looked after. Na, no in London; that's no my plan, but I would hae't within an hour's distance o' London, say five mile frae the market-place, an' standin' in a bit garden, whaur the geniuses could walk aboot arm-in-arm, composin' their minds."

"You would have the grounds walled in, I suppose, so that the public could not intrude?"

"Weel, there's a difficulty there, because, ye'll observe, as the public would support the institootion, they would hae a kind o' richt to look in. How-some-ever, I daur say we could arrange to fling the grounds open to the public once a week on condition 'at they didna speak to the geniuses. I'm thinkin' 'at if there was a small chairge for admission the Home could be made self-supportin'. Losh! to think 'at if there had been sic an institootion in his time a man micht hae sat on the bit dyke and watched Robbie Burns danderin' roond the——"

"You would divide the Home into suites of rooms, so that every inmate would have his own apartments?"

"Not by no means; na, na. The mair I read aboot geniuses the mair clearly I see as their wy o' living alane ower muckle is ane o' the things as breaks doon their health, and makes them meeserable. I' the Home they would hae a bedroom apiece, but the parlour an' the other sittin'-rooms would be for all, so as they could enjoy ane another's company. The management? Oh, that's aisy. The superintendent would be a medical man appointed by Parliament, and he would hae men-servants to do his biddin'."

"Not all men-servants, surely?"

"Every one o' them. Man, geniuses is no to be trusted wi' womenfolk. No, even Robbie Bu——"

"So he did; but would the inmates have to put themselves entirely in the superintendent's hands?"

"Nae doubt; an' they would see it was the wisest, thing they could do. He would be careful o' their health, an' send them early to bed as weel as hap them up at eight sharp. Geniuses' healths is always breakin' doon because of late hours, as in the case o' the lad wha used often to begin his immortal writin's at twal' o'clock at nicht, a thing 'at would ruin ony constitootion. But the superintendent would see as they had a tasty supper at nine o'clock—something as agreed wi' them. Then for half an hour they would quiet their brains readin' oot aloud, time about, frae sic a book as the *Pilgrim's Progress*, an' the gas would be turned aff at ten precisely."

"When would you have them up in the morning?"

"At sax in summer an' seven in winter. The superintendent would see as they were all properly bathed every mornin', cleanliness bein' most important for the preservation o' health."

"This sounds well; but suppose a genius broke the rules—lay in bed, for instance, reading by the light of a candle after hours, or refused to take his bath in the morning?"

"The superintendent would hae to punish him. The genius would be sent back to his bed, maybe. An' if he lay lang i' the mornin' he would hae to gang withoot his breakfast."

"That would be all very well where the inmate only broke the regulations once in a way; but suppose he were to refuse to take his bath day after day (and, you know, geniuses are said to be eccentric in that particular), what would be done? You could not starve him; geniuses are too scarce."

"Na, na; in a case like that he would hae to be reported to the public. The thing would hae to come afore the Hoose of Commons. Ay, the superintendent would get a member o' the Opposeetion to ask a queistion such as 'Can the honourable gentleman, the Secretary of State for Home Affairs, inform the Hoose whether it is a fac that Mr. Sic-a-one, the well-known genius, at present resident in the Home for Geniuses, has, contrairy to regulations, perseestently and obstinately refused to change his linen; and, if so, whether the Government proposes to take any steps in the matter?"The newspapers would report the discussion next mornin', an' so it would be made public withoot onnecessary ootlay."

"In a general way, however, you would give the geniuses perfect freedom? They could work when they liked, and come and go when they liked?"

"Not so. The superintendent would fix the hours o' wark, an' they would all write, or whatever it was, thegither in one large room. Man, man, it would mak a grand draw for a painter-chield, that room, wi' all the geniuses working awa' thegither."

"But when the labours of the day were over the genius would be at liberty to make calls by himself or to run up, say, to London for an hour or two?"

"Hoots no, that would spoil everything. It's the drink, ye see, as does for a terrible lot o' geniuses. Even Rob——"

"Alas! yes. But would you have them all teetotalers?"

"What do ye tak me for? Na, na; the superintendent would allow them one glass o' toddy every nicht, an' mix it himsel; but he would never get the keys o' the press, whaur he kept the drink, oot o' his hands. They would never be allowed oot o' the gairden either, withoot a man to look after them; an' I wouldna burthen them wi' ower muckle pocket-money. Saxpence in the week would be suffeecient."

"How about their clothes?"

"They would get twa suits a year, wi' the letter G sewed on the shoulders, so as if they were lost they could be recognized and brocht back."

"Certainly it is a scheme deserving consideration, and I have no doubt our geniuses would jump at it; but you must remember that some of them would have wives."

"Ay, an' some o' them would hae husbands. I've been thinkin' that oot, an' I daur say the best plan would be to partition aff a pairt o' the Home for female geniuses."

"Would Parliament elect the members?"

"I wouldna trust them. The election would hae to be by competitive examination. Na, I canna say wha would draw up the queistions. The scheme's juist growin' i' my mind, but the mair I think o't the better I like it."

# XVIII

## LEEBY AND JAMIE

By the bank of the Quharity on a summer day I have seen a barefooted girl gaze at the running water until tears filled her eyes. That was the birth of romance. Whether this love be but a beautiful dream I cannot say, but this we see, that it comes to all, and colours the whole future life with gold. Leeby must have dreamt it, but I did not know her then. I have heard of a man who would have taken her far away into a county where the corn is yellow when it is still green with us, but she would not leave her mother, nor was it him she saw in her dream. From her earliest days, when she was still a child staggering round the garden with Jamie in her arms, her duty lay before her, straight as the burying-ground road. Jess had need of her in the little home at the top of the brae, where God, looking down upon her as she scrubbed and gossipped and sat up all night with her ailing mother, and never missed the prayer-meeting, and adored the minister, did not perhaps think her the least of His handmaids. Her years were less than thirty when He took her away, but she had few days that were altogether dark. Those who bring sunshine to the lives of others cannot keep it from themselves.

The love Leeby bore for Jamie was such that in their younger days it shamed him. Other laddies knew of it, and flung it at him until he dared Leeby to let on in public that he and she were related.

"Hoo is your lass?" they used to cry to him, inventing a new game.

"I saw Leeby lookin' for ye," they would say; "she's wearyin' for ye to gang an' play wi' her."

Then if they were not much bigger boys than himself, Jamie got them against the dyke and hit them hard until they publicly owned to knowing that she was his sister, and that he was not fond of her.

"It distressed him mair than ye could believe, though," Jess has told me; "an' when he came hame he would greet an' say 'at Leeby disgraced him."

Leeby, of course, suffered for her too obvious affection.

"I wonder 'at ye dinna try to control yersel," Jamie would say to her, as he grew bigger.

"A'm sure," said Leeby, "I never gie ye a look if there's onybody there."

"A look! You're ay lookin' at me sae fond-like 'at I dinna ken what wy to turn."

"Weel, I canna help it," said Leeby, probably beginning to whimper.

If Jamie was in a very bad temper he left her, after this, to her own reflections; but he was naturally soft-hearted.

"A'm no tellin' ye no to care for me," he told her, "but juist to keep it mair to yersel. Naebody would ken frae me 'at a'm fond o' ye."

"Mebbe ye're no?" said Leeby.

"Ay, am I, but I can keep it secret. When we're in the hoose a'm juist richt fond o' ye."

"Do ye love me, Jamie?"

Jamie waggled his head in irritation.

"Love," he said, "is an awful like word to use when fowk's weel. Ye shouldna spier sic annoyin' queistions."

"But if ye juist say ye love me I'll never let on again afore fowk 'at ye're onything to me ava."

"Ay, ye often say that."

"Do ye no believe my word?"

"I believe fine ye mean what ye say, but ye forget yersel when the time comes."

"Juist try me this time."

"Weel, then, I do."

"Do what?" asked the greedy Leeby.

"What ye said."

"I said love."

"Weel," said Jamie," I do't."

"What do ye do? Say the word."

"Na," said Jamie, "I winna say the word. It's no a word to say, but I do't."

That was all she could get out of him, unless he was stricken with remorse, when he even went the length of saying the word.

"Leeby kent perfectly weel," Jess has said, " 'at it was a trial to Jamie to tak her ony gait, an' I often used to say to her 'at I wondered at her want o' pride in priggin' wi' him. Ay, but if she could juist get a promise wrung oot o' him, she didna care hoo muckle she had to prig. Syne they quarrelled, an' ane or baith o' them grat (cried) afore they made it up. I mind when Jamie went to the fishin' Leeby was aye terrible keen to get wi' him, but ye see he wouldna be seen gaen through the toon wi' her. 'If ye let me gang,' she said to him, 'I'll no seek to go through the toon wi' ye. Na, I'll gang roond by the Roods an' you can tak the buryin'-ground road, so as we can meet on the hill.' Yes, Leeby was willin' to agree wi' a' that, juist to get gaen wi' him. I've seen lassies makkin' themsels sma' for lads often enough, but I never saw ane 'at prigged so muckle wi' her ain brother. Na, it's other lassies' brothers they like as a rule."

"But though Jamie was terrible reserved aboot it," said Leeby, "he was as fond o' me as ever I was o' him. Ye mind the time I had the measles, mother?"

"A'm no likely to forget it, Leeby," said Jess, an' you blind wi' them for three days. Ay, ay, Jamie was richt taen up aboot ye. I mind he broke open his pirly (money-box), an' bocht a ha'penny worth o' something to ye every day."

"An' ye hinna forgotten the stick?"

" 'Deed no, I hinna. Ye see," Jess explained to me, "Leeby was lyin' ben the hoose, an' Jamie wasna allowed to gang near her for fear o' infection. Weel, he got a lang stick—it was a pea-stick—an' put it 'aneath the door an' waggled it. Ay, he did that a curran times every day, juist to let her see he was thinkin' o' her."

"Mair than that," said Leeby, "he cried oot 'at he loved me."

"Ay, but juist aince," Jess said, "I dinna mind o't but aince. It was the time the doctor came late, an' Jamie, being waukened by him, thocht ye was deein'. I mind as if it was yesterday hoo he cam runnin' to the door an' cried oot, 'I do love ye, Leeby; I love ye richt.' The doctor got a start when he heard the voice, but he laughed loud when he unerstood."

"He had nae business, though," said Leeby, "to tell onybody."

"He was a rale clever man, the doctor," Jess explained to me, "ay, he kent me as weel as though he'd gaen through me wi' a lichted candle. It got oot through him, an' the young billies took to sayin' to Jamie, 'Ye do love her, Jamie; ay, ye love her richt.' The only reglar fecht I ever kent Jamie hae was wi' a lad 'at cried that to him. It was Bowlegs Christy's laddie. Ay, but when she got better Jamie blamed Leeby."

"He no only blamed me," said Leeby, "but he wanted me to pay him back a' the bawbees he had spent on me."

"Ay, an' I sepad he got them too," said Jess.

In time Jamie became a barber in Tilliedrum, trudging many heavy miles there and back twice a day that he might sleep at home, trudging bravely I was to, say, but it was what he was born to, and there was hardly an alternative. This was the time I saw most of him, and he and Leeby were often in my thoughts. There is as terrible a bubble in the little kettle as on the cauldron of the world, and some of the scenes between Jamie and Leeby were great tragedies, comedies, what you will, until the kettle was taken off the fire. Hers was the more placid temper; indeed, only in one way could Jamie suddenly rouse her to fury. That was when he hinted that she had a large number of frocks. Leeby knew that there could never be more than a Sabbath frock and an everyday gown for her, both of her mother's making, but Jamie's insinuations were more than she could bear. Then I have seen her seize and shake him. I know from Jess that Leeby cried herself hoarse the day Joey was buried, because her little black frock was not ready for wear.

Until he went to Tilliedrum Jamie had been more a stay-at-home boy than most. The warmth of Jess's love had something to do with keeping his heart aglow, but more, I think, he owed to Leeby. Tilliedrum was his introduction to the world, and for a little it took his head. I was in the house the Sabbath day that he refused to go to church.

He went out in the forenoon to meet the Tilliedrum lads, who were, to take him off for a holiday in a cart. Hendry was more wrathful than I remember ever to have seen him, though I have heard how he did with the lodger who broke the Lord's Day. This lodger was a tourist who thought, in folly surely rather than in hardness of heart, to test the religious convictions of an Auld Licht by insisting on paying his bill on a Sabbath morning. He offered the money to Jess, with the warning that if she did not take it now she might never see it. Jess was so kind and good to her lodgers that he could not have known her long who troubled her with this poor trick. She was sorely in need at the time, and entreated the thoughtless man to have some pity on her.

"Now or never," he said, holding out the money.

"Put it on the dresser," said Jess at last, "an' I'll get it the morn."

The few shillings were laid on the dresser, where they remained unfingered until Hendry, with Leeby and Jamie, came in from church.

"What siller's that?" asked Hendry, and then Jess confessed what she had done.

"I wonder at ye, woman," said Hendry, sternly; and lifting the money he climbed up to the attic with it.

He pushed open the door, and confronted the lodger.

"Take back yer siller," he said, laying it on the table, "an' leave my hoose. Man, you're a pitiable crittur to tak the chance, when I was oot, o' playin' upon the poverty o' an onweel woman."

It was with such unwonted severity as this that Hendry called upon Jamie to follow him to church; but the boy went off, and did not return till dusk, defiant and miserable. Jess had been so terrified that she forgave him everything for sight of his face, and Hendry prayed for him at family worship with too much unction. But Leeby cried as if her tender heart would break. For a long time Jamie refused to look at her, but at last he broke down.

"If ye go on like that," he said, "I'll gang awa oot an' droon mysel, or be a sojer."

This was no uncommon threat of his, and sometimes, when he went off, banging the door violently, she ran after him and brought him back. This time she only wept the more, and so both went to bed in misery. It was after midnight that Jamie rose and crept to Leeby's bedside. Leeby was shaking the bed in her agony. Jess heard what they said.

"Leeby," said Jamie, "dinna greet, an' I'll never do't again."

He put his arms round her, and she kissed him passionately.

"Oh, Jamie," she said, "hae ye prayed to God to forgie ye?"

Jamie did not speak.

"If ye was to die this nicht," cried Leeby, "an' you no made it up wi' God, ye wouldna gang to heaven. Jamie, I canna sleep till ye've made it up wi' God."

But Jamie still hung back. Leeby slipped from her bed, and went down on her knees.

"O God, O dear God," she cried, "mak Jamie to pray to you!"

Then Jamie went down on his knees too, and they made it up with God together.

This is a little thing for me to remember all these years, and yet how fresh and sweet it keeps Leeby in my memory.

Away up in the glen, my lonely schoolhouse lying deep, as one might say, in a sea of snow, I had many hours in the years long by for thinking of my friends in Thrums and mapping out the future of Leeby and Jamie. I saw Hendry and Jess taken to the churchyard, and Leeby left alone in the house. I saw Jamie fulfil his promise to his mother, and take Leeby, that stainless young woman, far away to London, where they had a home together. Ah, but these were only the idle dreams of a dominie. The Lord willed it otherwise.

# XIX

## A TALE OF A GLOVE

So long as Jamie was not the lad, Jess twinkled gleefully over tales of sweethearting. There was little Kitty Lamby who used to skip in of an evening, and, squatting on a stool near the window unwind the roll of her enormities. A wheedling thing she was, with an ambition to drive men crazy, but my presence killed the gossip on her tongue, though I liked to look at her. When I entered, the wag at the wa' clock had again possession of the kitchen. I never heard more than the end of a sentence:

"An' did he really say he would fling himsel into the dam, Kitty?"

Or—"True as death, Jess, he kissed me."

Then I wandered away from the kitchen, where I was not wanted, and marvelled to know that Jess of the tender heart laughed most merrily when he really did say that he was going straight to the dam. As no body was found in the dam in those days, whoever he was he must have thought better of it.

But let Kitty, or any other maid, cast a glinting eye on Jamie, then Jess no longer smiled. If he returned the glance she sat silent in her chair till Leeby laughed away her fears.

"Jamie's no the kind, mother," Leeby would say. "Na, he's quiet, but he sees through them. They dinna draw his leg (get over him)."

"Ye never can tell, Leeby. The laddies 'at's maist ill to get sometimes gangs up in a flame a' at aince, like a bit o' paper."

"Ay, weel, at ony rate Jamie's no on fire yet."

Though clever beyond her neighbours, Jess lost all her sharpness if they spoke of a lassie for Jamie.

"I warrant," Tibbie Birse said one day in my hearing, " 'at there's some leddy in London he's thinkin' o'. Ay, he's been a guid laddie to ye, but i' the coorse o' nature he'll be settlin' dune soon."

Jess did not answer, but she was a picture of woe.

"Ye're lettin' what Tibbie Birse said lie on yer mind," Leeby remarked, when Tibbie was gone. "What can it maiter what she thinks?"

"I canna help it, Leeby," said Jess. "Na, an' I canna bear to think o' Jamie bein' mairit. It would lay me low to loss my laddie. No yet, no yet."

"But, mother," said Leeby, quoting from the minister at weddings, "ye wouldna be lossin' a son, but juist gainin' a dochter."

"Dinna haver, Leeby," answered Jess, "I want nane o' thae dochters; na, na."

This talk took place while we were still awaiting Jamie's coming. He had only been with us one day when Jess made a terrible discovery. She was looking so mournful when I saw her, that I asked Leeby what was wrong.

"She's brocht it on hersel," said Leeby. "Ye see she was up sune i' the mornin' to begin to the darnin' o' Jamie's stockins an' to warm his sark at the fire afore he put it on. He woke up, an' cried to her 'at he wasna accustomed to hae'n his things warmed for him. Ay, he cried it oot fell thrawn, so she took it into her head 'at there was something in his pouch he didna want her to see. She was even onaisy last nicht."

I asked what had aroused Jess's suspicions last night.

"Ou, ye would notice 'at she sat devourin' him wi' her een, she was so lifted up at ha'en 'im again. Weel, she says noo 'at she saw 'im twa or three times put his hand in his pouch as if he was findin' to mak sure 'at something was safe. So when he fell asleep again this mornin' she got haud o' his jacket to see if there was onything in't I advised her no to do't, but she couldna help hersel. She put in her hand, an' pu'd it oot. That's what's makkin' her look sae ill."

"But what was it she found?"

"Did I no tell ye? I'm ga'en dottle, I think. It was a glove, a woman's glove, in a bit paper. Ay, though she's sittin' still she's near frantic."

I said I supposed Jess had put the glove back in Jamie's pocket.

"Na," said Leeby, "'deed no. She wanted to fling it on the back o' the fire, but I wouldna let her. That's it she has aneath her apron."

Later in the day I remarked to Leeby that Jamie was very dull. "He's missed it," she explained. "Has any one mentioned it to him," I asked, "or has he inquired about it?"

"Na," said Leeby, "there hasna been a syllup (syllable) aboot it. My mother's fleid to mention't, an' he doesna like to speak aboot it either."

"Perhaps he thinks he has lost it?"

"Nae fear o' him," Leeby said. "Na, he kens, fine wha has't."

I never knew how Jamie came by the glove, nor whether it had originally belonged to her who made him forget the window at the top of the brae. At the time I looked on as at play-acting, rejoicing in the happy ending. Alas! in the real life how are we to know when we have reached an end?

But this glove, I say, may not have been that woman's, and if it was, she had not then bedevilled him. He was too sheepish to demand it back from his mother, and already he cared for it too much to laugh at Jess's theft with Leeby. So it was that a curious game at chess was played with the glove, the players a silent pair.

Jamie cared little to read books, but on the day following Jess's discovery, I found him on his knees in the attic, looking through mine. A little box, without a lid, held them all, but they seemed a great library to him.

"There's readin' for a lifetime in them," he said. "I was juist takkin' a look through them."

His face was guilty, however, as if his hand had been caught in a money-bag, and I wondered what had enticed the lad to my books. I was still standing pondering when Leeby ran up the stair; she was so active that she generally ran, and she grudged the time lost in recovering her breath.

"I'll put yer books richt," she said, making her word good as she spoke. "I kent Jamie had been ransackin' up here, though he came up rale canny, Ay, ye would notice he was in his stockin' soles."

I had not noticed this, but I remembered, now his slipping from the room very softly. If he wanted a book, I told Leeby, he could have got it without any display of cunning.

"It's no a book he's lookin' for," she said, "na, it's his glove."

The time of day was early for Leeby to gossip, but I detained her for a moment.

"My mother's hodded (hid) it," she explained, "an' he winna speir nae queistions. But he's lookin' for't. He was ben in the room searchin' the drawers when I was up i' the toon in the forenoon. Ye see he pretends no to be carin' afore me, an' though my mother's sittin' sae quiet-like at the window she's hearkenin' a' the time. Ay, an' he thocht I had hod it up here."

But where, I asked, was the glove hid.

"I ken nae mair than yersel," said Leeby. "My mother's gien to hoddin' things. She has a place aneath the bed whaur she keeps the siller, an' she's no speakin' aboot the glove to me noo, because she thinks Jamie an' me's in comp (company). I speired at her whaur she had hod it, but she juist said: 'What would I be doin' hoddin't?' She'll never admit to me 'at she hods the siller either."

Next day Leeby came to me with the latest news.

"He's found it," she said, "ay, he's got the glove again. Ye see what put him on the wrang scent was a notion 'at I had put it some gait. He kent 'at if she'd hod it, the kitchen maun be the place, but he thocht she'd gi'en it to me to hod. He came upon't by accident. It was aneath the paddin' o' her chair."

Here, I thought, was the end of the glove incident, but I was mistaken. There were no presses or drawers with locks in the house, and Jess got hold of the glove again. I suppose she had reasoned out no line of action. She merely hated the thought that Jamie should have a woman's glove in his possession.

"She beats a' wi' cuteness," Leeby said to me. "Jamie didna put the glove back in his pouch. Na, he kens her ower weel by this time. She was up, though, lang afore he was wauken, an' she gaed almost strecht to the place whaur he had hod it. I believe she lay waukin a' nicht thinkin' oot whaur it would be. Ay, it was aneath the mattress. I saw her hodden't i' the back o' the drawer, but I didna let on."

I quite believed Leeby when she told me afterwards that she had watched Jamie feeling beneath the mattress.

"He had a face," she said, "I assure ye, he had a face, when he discovered the glove was gone again."

"He maun be terrible ta'en up aboot it," Jess said to Leeby, "or he wouldna keep it aneath the mattress."

"Od," said Leeby, "it was yersel 'at drove him to't."

Again Jamie recovered his property, and again Jess got hold of it. This time he looked in vain. I learnt the fate of the glove from Leeby.

"Ye mind 'at she keepit him at hame frae the kirk on Sabbath, because he had a cauld?" Leeby, said. "Ay, me or my father would hae a gey ill cauld afore she would let's bide at hame frae the kirk; but Jamie's different. Weel, mair than aince she's been near speakin' to 'im aboot the glove, but she grew fleid aye. She was sae terrified there was something in't.

"On Sabbath, though, she had him to hersel, an' he wasna so bright as usual. She sat wi' the Bible on her lap, pretendin' to read, but a' the time she was takkin' keeks (glances) at him. I dinna ken 'at he was broodin' ower the glove, but she thocht he was, an' juist afore the kirk came oot she couldna stand it nae langer. She put her hand in her pouch, an' pu'd oot the glove, wi' the paper round it, juist as it had been when she came upon't.

"'That's yours, Jamie,' she said; 'it was ill-dune o' me to tak it, but I couldna help it.'

"Jamie put oot his hand, an' syne he drew't back. 'It's no a thing o' nae consequence, mother,' he said.

"'Wha is she, Jamie?' my mother said.

"He turned awa his heid—so she telt me. 'It's a lassie in London,' he said, 'I dinna ken her muckle.'

"'Ye maun ken her weel,' my mother persisted, 'to be carryin' aboot her glove; I'm dootin' yer gey fond o' her, Jamie?'

"'Na,' said Jamie, 'a'm no. There's no naebody I care for like yersel, mother.'

"'Ye wouldna carry aboot onything o' mine, Jamie,' my mother said; but he says, 'Oh, mother, I carry aboot yer face wi' me aye; an' sometimes at nicht I kind o' greet to think o' ye.'

"Ay, after that I've nae doot he was sitting wi' his airms aboot her. She didna tell me that, but weel he kens it's what she likes, an' she maks nae pretence o' it's no bein'. But for a' he said an' did, she noticed him put the glove back in his inside pouch.

"'It's wrang o' me, Jamie,' she said, 'but I canna bear to think o' ye carryin' that aboot sae carefu'. No, I canna help it.'

"Weel, Jamie, the crittur, took it oot o' his pouch, an' kind o' hesitated. Syne he lays't on the back o' the fire, an' they sat thegither glowerin' at it.

"'Noo, mother,' he says, 'you're satisfied, are ye no?'

"Ay," Leeby ended her story, she said she was satisfied. But she saw 'at he laid it on the fire fell fond-like."

# XX

## THE LAST NIGHT

"JUIST another sax nichts, Jamie," Jess would say, sadly. "Juist fower nichts noo, an' you'll be awa." Even as she spoke seemed to come the last night.

The last night! Reserve slipped unheeded to the floor. Hendry wandered ben and but the house, and Jamie sat at the window holding his mother's hand. You must walk softly now if you would cross that humble threshold. I stop at the door. Then, as now, I was a lonely man, and when the last night came the attic was the place for me.

This family affection, how good and beautiful it is. Men and maids love, and after many years they may rise to this. It is the grand proof of the goodness in human nature, for it means that the more we see of each other the more we find that is lovable. If you would cease to dislike a man, try to get nearer his heart.

Leeby had no longer any excuse for bustling about. Everything was ready—too soon. Hendry had been to the fish-cadger in the square to get a bervie for Jamie's supper, and Jamie had eaten it, trying to look as if it made him happier. His little box was packed and strapped, and stood terribly conspicuous against the dresser. Jess had packed it herself.

"Ye mauna trachle (trouble) yersel, mother," Jamie said, when she had the empty box pulled toward her.

Leeby was wiser.

"Let her do't," she whispered, "it'll keep her frae broodin'."

Jess tied ends of yarn round the stockings to keep them in a little bundle by themselves. So she did with all the other articles.

"No 'at it's ony great affair," she said, for on the last night they were all thirsting to do something for Jamie that would be a great affair to him.

"Ah, ye would wonder, mother," Jamie said, "when I open my box an' find a'thing tied up wi' strings sae careful, it a' comes back to me wi' a rush wha did it, an' a'm as fond o' thae strings as though they were a grand present. There's the pocky (bag) ye gae me to keep sewin' things in. I get the wifie I lodge wi' to sew to me, but often when I come upon the pocky I sit an' look at it."

Two chairs were backed to the fire, with underclothing hanging upside down on them. From the string over the fireplace dangled two pairs of much-darned stockings.

"Ye'll put on baith thae pair o' stockin's, Jamie," said Jess, "juist to please me?"

When he arrived he had rebelled against the extra clothing.

"Ay, will I, mother?" he said now.

Jess put her hand fondly through his ugly hair. How handsome she thought him.

"Ye have a fine brow, Jamie," she said. "I mind the day ye was born sayin' to mysel 'at ye had a fine brow."

"But ye thocht he was to be a lassie, mother," said Leeby.

"Na, Leeby, I didna. I kept sayin' I thocht he would be a lassie because I was fleid he would be; but a' the time I had a presentiment he would be a laddie. It was wi' Joey deein' sae sudden, an' I took on sae terrible aboot 'im 'at I thocht all alang the Lord would gie me another laddie."

"Ay, I wanted 'im to be a laddie mysel," said Hendry, so as he could tak Joey's place."

Jess's head jerked back involuntarily, and Jamie may have felt her hand shake, for he said in a voice, out of Hendry's hearing—

"I never took Joey's place wi' ye, mother."

Jess pressed his hand tightly in her two worn palms, but she did not speak.

"Jamie was richt like Joey when he was a bairn," Hendry said.

"Again Jess's head moved, but still she was silent.

"They were sae like," continued Hendry, " 'at often I called Jamie by Joey's name."

Jess looked at her husband, and her mouth opened and shut.

"I canna mind 'at you ever did that?" Hendry said.

She shook her head.

"Na," said Hendry, "you never mixed them up. I dinna think ye ever missed Joey sae sair as I did."

Leeby went ben, and stood in the room in the dark; Jamie knew why.

"I'll just gang ben an' speak to Leeby for a meenute," he said to his mother; "I'll no be lang."

"Ay, do that, Jamie," said Jess. "What Leeby's been to me nae tongue can tell. Ye canna bear to hear me speak, I ken, o' the time when Hendry an' me'll be awa, but, Jamie, when that time comes ye'll no forget Leeby?"

"I winna, mother, I winna," said Jamie. "There'll never be a roof ower me 'at's no hers too."

He went ben and shut the door. I do not know what he and Leeby said. Many a time since their earliest youth had these two been closeted together, often to make up their little quarrels in each other's arms. They remained a long time in the room, the shabby room of which Jess and Leeby were so proud, and whatever might be their fears about their mother they were not anxious for themselves.

Leeby was feeling lusty and well, and she, could not know that Jamie required to be reminded of his duty to the folk at home. Jamie would have laughed at the notion. Yet that woman in London must have been waiting for him even then. Leeby, who was about to die, and Jamie, who was to forget his mother, came back to the kitchen with a happy light on their faces. I have with me still the look of love they gave each other before Jamie crossed over to Jess.

"Ye'll gang anower, noo, mother," Leeby said, meaning that it was Jess's bed-time.

"No yet, Leeby," Jess answered, "I'll sit up till the readin's ower."

"I think ye should gang, mother," Jamie said, "an' I'll come an' sit aside ye after ye're i' yer bed."

"Ay, Jamie, I'll no hae ye to sit aside me the morn's nicht, an' hap (cover) me wi' the claes."

"But ye'll gang suner to yer bed, mother."

"I may gang, but I winna sleep. I'll aye be thinkin' o' ye tossin' on the sea. I pray for ye a lang time ilka nicht, Jamie."

"Ay, I ken."

"An' I pictur ye ilka hour o' the day. Ye never gang hame through thae terrible streets at nicht but I'm thinkin' o' ye."

"I would try no to be sae sad, mother," said Leeby. "We've ha'en a richt fine time, have we no?"

"It's been an awfu' happy time," said Jess. "We've ha'en a pleasantness in oor lives 'at comes to few. I ken naebody 'at's ha'en sae muckle happiness one wy or another."

"It's because ye're sae guid, mother," said Jamie.

"Na, Jamie, a'm no guid ava. It's because my fowk's been sae guid, you an' Hendry an' Leeby an' Joey when he was livin'. I've got a lot mair than my deserts."

"We'll juist look to meetin' next year again, mother. To think o' that keeps me up a' the winter."

"Ay, if it's the Lord's will, Jamie, but a'm gey dune noo, an' Hendry's fell worn too."

Jamie, the boy that he was, said, "Dinna speak like that, mother," and Jess again put her hand on his head.

"Fine I ken, Jamie," she said, "'at all my days on this earth, be they short or lang, I've you for a staff to lean on."

Ah, many years have gone since then, but if Jamie be living now he has still those words to swallow.

By and by Leeby went ben for the Bible, and put it into Hendry's hands. He slowly turned over the leaves to his favourite Chapter, the fourteenth of John's Gospel. Always, on eventful occasions, did Hendry turn to the fourteenth of John.

"Let not your heart be troubled; ye believe in God, believe also in Me.

"In My Father's house are many mansions; if it were not so I would have told you. I go to prepare a place for you."

As Hendry raised his voice to read there was a great stillness in the kitchen. I do not know that I have been able to show in the most imperfect way what kind of man Hendry was. He was dense in many things, and the cleverness that was Jess's had been denied to him. He had less book-learning than most of those with whom he passed his days, and he had little skill in talk. I have not known a man more easily taken in by persons whose speech had two faces. But a more simple, modest, upright man, there never was in Thrums, and I shall always revere his memory.

"And if I go and prepare a place for you, I will come again, and receive you unto Myself; that where I am, there ye may be also."

The voice may have been monotonous. I have always thought that Hendry's reading of the Bible was the most solemn and impressive I have ever heard. He exulted in the fourteenth of John, pouring it forth like one whom it intoxicated while he read. He emphasized every other word; it was so real and grand to him.

We went upon our knees while Hendry prayed, all but Jess, who could not. Jamie buried his face in her lap. The words Hendry said were those he used every night. Some, perhaps, would have smiled at his prayer to God that we be not puffed up with riches nor with the things of this world. His head shook with emotion while he prayed, and he brought us very near to the throne of grace. "Do thou, O our God," he said, in conclusion, "spread Thy guiding hand over him whom in Thy great mercy Thou hast brought to us again, and do Thou guard him through the perils which come unto those that go down to the sea in ships. Let not our hearts be troubled, neither let them be afraid, for this is not our abiding home, and may we all meet in Thy house, where there are many mansions, and where there will be no last night. Amen."

It was a silent kitchen after that, though the lamp burned long in Jess's window. By its meagre light you may take a final glance at the little family; you will never see them together again.

# XXI

## JESS LEFT ALONE

THERE may be a few who care to know how the lives of Jess and Hendry ended. Leeby died in the back-end of the year I have been speaking of, and as I was snowed up in the school-house at the time, I heard the news from Gavin Birse too late to attend her funeral. She got her death on the commonty one day of sudden rain, when she had run out to bring in her washing, for the terrible cold she woke with next morning carried her off very quickly. Leeby did not blame Jamie for not coming to her, nor did I, for I knew that even in the presence of death the poor must drag their chains. He never got Hendry's letter with the news, and we know now that he was already in the hands of her who played the devil with his life. Before the spring came he had been lost to Jess.

"Them 'at has got sae mony blessin's mair than the generality," Hendry said to me one day, when Craigiebuckle had given me a lift into Thrums, "has nae shame if they would pray aye for mair. The Lord has gi'en this hoose sae muckle, 'at to pray for mair looks like no bein' thankfu' for what we've got. Ay, but I canna help prayin' to Him 'at in His great mercy he'll tak Jess afore me. Noo 'at Leeby's gone, an' Jamie never lets us hear frae him, I canna gulp doon the thocht o' Jess bein' left alane."

This was a prayer that Hendry may be pardoned for having so often in his heart, though God did not think fit to grant it. In Thrums, when a weaver died, his womenfolk had to take his seat at the loom, and those who, by reason of infirmities, could not do so, went to a place, the name of which, I thank God, I am not compelled to write in this Chapter. I could not, even at this day, have told any episodes in the life of Jess had it ended in the poorhouse.

Hendry would probably have recovered from the fever had not this terrible dread darkened his intellect when he was still prostrate. He was lying in the kitchen when I saw him last in life, and his parting words must be sadder to the reader than they were to me.

"Ay, richt ye are," he said, in a voice that had become a child's; "I hae muckle, muckle, to be thankfu' for, an' no the least is 'at baith me an' Jess has aye belonged to a bural society. We hae nae cause to be anxious aboot a' thing bein' dune respectable aince we're gone. It was Jess 'at insisted on oor joinin': a' the wisest things I ever did I was put up to by her."

I parted from Hendry, cheered by the doctor's report, but the old weaver died a few days afterwards. His end was mournful, yet I can recall it now as the not unworthy close of a good man's life. One night poor worn Jess had been helped ben into the room, Tibbie Birse having undertaken to sit up with Hendry. Jess slept for the first time for many days, and as the night was dying Tibbie fell asleep too. Hendry had been better than usual, lying quietly, Tibbie said, and the fever was gone. About three o'clock Tibbie woke and rose to mend the fire. Then she saw that Hendry was not in his bed.

Tibbie went ben the house in her stocking-soles, but Jess heard her.

"What is't, Tibbie?" she asked, anxiously.

"Ou, it's no naething," Tibbie said, "he's lyin' rale quiet."

Then she went up to the attic. Hendry was not in the house.

She opened the door gently and stole out. It was not snowing, but there had been a heavy fall two days before, and the night was windy. A tearing gale had blown the upper part of the brae clear, and from T'nowhead's fields the snow was rising like smoke. Tibbie ran to the farm and woke up T'nowhead.

For an hour they looked in vain for Hendry. At last some one asked who was working in Elshioner's shop all night. This was the long earthen-floored room in which Hendry's loom stood with three others.

"It'll be Sanders Whamond likely," T'nowhead said, and the other men nodded.

But it happened that T'nowhead's Bell, who had flung on a wrapper, and hastened across to sit with Jess, heard of the light in Elshioner's shop.

"It's Hendry," she cried, and then every one moved toward the workshop.

The light at the diminutive, yarn-covered window was pale and dim, but Bell, who was at the house first, could make the most of a cruizey's glimmer.

"It's him," she said, and then, with swelling throat, she ran back to Jess.

The door of the workshop was wide open, held against the wall by the wind. T'nowhead and the others went in. The cruizey stood on the little window. Hendry's back was to the door, and he was leaning forward on the silent loom. He had been dead for some time, but his fellow-workers saw that he must have weaved for nearly an hour.

So it came about that for the last few months of her pilgrimage Jess was left alone. Yet I may not say that she was alone. Jamie, who should have been with her, was undergoing his own ordeal far away; where, we did not now even know. But though the poorhouse stands in Thrums, where all may see it, the neighbours did not think only of themselves.

Than Tammas Haggart there can scarcely have been a poorer man, but Tammas was the first to come forward with offer of help. To the day of Jess's death he did not once fail to carry her water to her in the morning, and the luxuriously living men of Thrums in those present days of pumps at every corner, can hardly realize what that meant. Often there were lines of people at the well by three o'clock in the morning, and each had to wait his turn. Tammas filled his own pitcher and pan, and then had to take his place at the end of the line with Jess's pitcher and pan, to wait his turn again. His own house was in the Tenements, far from the brae in winter time, but he always said to Jess it was "naething ava."

Every Saturday old Robbie Angus sent a bag of sticks and shavings from the saw-mill by his little son Rob, who was afterwards to become a man, for speaking about at nights. Of, all the friends that Jess and Hendry had, T'nowhead was the ablest to help, and the sweetest memory I have of the farmer and his wife is the delicate way they offered it. You who read will see Jess wince at the offer of charity. But the poor have fine feelings beneath the grime, as you will discover if you care to look for them, and when Jess said she would bake if any one would buy, you would wonder to hear how many kindly folk came to her door for scones.

She had the house to herself at nights, but Tibbie Birse was with her early in the morning, and other neighbours dropped in. Not for long did she have to wait the summons to the better home.

"Na," she said to the minister, who has told me that he was a better man from knowing her, "my thochts is no nane set on the vanities o' the world noo. I kenna hoo I could ever hae haen sic an ambeetion to hae thae stuff-bottomed chairs."

I have tried to keep away from Jamie, whom the neighbours sometimes upbraided in her presence. It is of him you who read would like to hear, and I cannot pretend that Jess did not sit at her window looking for him.

"Even when she was bakin'," Tibbie told me, "she aye had an eye on the brae. If Jamie had come at any time when it was licht she would hae seen 'im as sune as he turned the corner."

"If he ever comes back, the sacket (rascal)," T'nowhead said to Jess, "we'll show 'im the door gey quick."

Jess just looked, and all the women knew how she would take Jamie to her arms.

We did not know of the London woman then, and Jess never knew of her. Jamie's mother never for an hour allowed that he had become anything but the loving laddie of his youth.

"I ken 'im ower weel," she always said, "my ain Jamie."

Toward the end she was sure he was dead. I do not know when she first made up her mind to this, nor whether it was not merely a phrase for those who wanted to discuss him with her. I know that she still sat at the window looking at the elbow of the brae.

The minister was with her when she died. She was in her chair, and he asked her, as was his custom, if there was any particular which she would like him to read. Since her husband's death she had always asked for the fourteenth of John, "Hendry's Chapter," as it is still called among a very few old people in Thrums. This time she asked him to read the sixteenth of Genesis.

"When I came to the thirteenth verse," the minister told me, "'And she called the name of the Lord that spake unto her, Thou God seest me,' she covered her face with her two hands, and said, 'Joey's text, Joey's text. Oh, but I grudged ye sair, Joey.'"

"I shut the book," the minister said, "when I came to the end of the Chapter, and then I saw that she was dead. It is my belief that her heart broke one-and-twenty years ago."

# XXII

### JAMIE'S HOME-COMING

On a summer day, when the sun was in the weavers' workshops, and bairns hopped solemnly at the game of palaulays, or gaily shook their bottles of sugarelly water into a froth, Jamie came back. The first man to see him was Hookey Crewe, the post.

"When he came frae London," Hookey said afterwards at T'nowhead's pig-sty, "Jamie used to wait for me at Zoar, i' the north end o' Tilliedrum. He carried his box ower the market muir, an' sat on't at Zoar, waitin' for me to catch 'im up. Ay, the day afore yesterday me an' the powny was clatterin' by Zoar, when there was Jamie standin' in his identical place. He hadna nae box to sit upon, an' he was far frae bein' weel in order, but I kent 'im at aince, an' I saw 'at he was waitin' for me. So I drew up, an' waved my hand to 'im."

"I would hae drove straucht by 'im," said T'nowhead; "them 'at leaves their auld mother to want doesna deserve a lift."

"Ay, ye say that sittin' there," Hookey said; "but, lads, I saw his face, an' as sure as death it was sic an' awfu' meeserable face 'at I couldna but pu' the powny up. Weel, he stood for the space o' a meenute lookin' straucht at me, as if he would like to come forrit but dauredna, an' syne he turned an' strided awa ower the muir like a huntit thing. I sat still i' the cart, an' when he was far awa he stoppit an' lookit again, but a' my cryin' wouldna bring him a step back, an' i' the end I drove on. I've thocht since syne 'at he didna ken whether his fowk was livin' or deid, an' was fleid to speir."

"He didna ken," said T'nowhead, "but the faut was his ain. It's ower late to be taen up aboot Jess noo."

"Ay, ay, T'nowhead," said Hookey, "it's aisy to you to speak like that. Ye didna see his face."

It is believed that Jamie walked from Tilliedrum, though no one is known to have met him on the road. Some two hours after the post left him he was seen by old Rob Angus at the sawmill.

"I was sawin' awa wi' a' my micht," Rob said, "an' little Rob was haudin' the booards, for they were silly but things, when something made me look at the window. It couldna hae been a tap on't, for the birds has used me to that, an' it would hardly be a shadow, for little Rob didna look up. Whatever it was I stoppit i' the middle o' a booard, an' lookit up, an' there I saw Jamie McQumpha. He joukit back when our een met, but I saw him weel; ay, it's a queer thing to say, but he had the face o' a man 'at had come straucht frae hell."

"I stood starin' at the window," Angus continued, "after he'd gone, an' Robbie cried oot to ken what was the maiter wi' me. Ay, that brocht me back to mysel, an' I hurried oot to look for Jamie, but he wasna to be seen. That face gae me a turn."

From the saw-mill to the house at the top of the brae, some may remember, the road is up the commonty. I do not think any one saw Jamie on the commonty, though there were those to say they met him.

"He gae me sic a look," a woman said, " 'at I was fleid an' ran hame," but she did not tell the story until Jamie's home-coming had become a legend.

There were many women hanging out their washing on the commonty that day, and none of them saw him. I think Jamie must have approached his old home by the fields, and probably he held back until gloaming.

The young woman who was now mistress of the house at the top of the brae both saw and spoke with Jamie.

"Twa or three times," she said, "I had seen a man walk quick up the brae an' by the door. It was gettin' dark, but I noticed 'at he was short an' thin, an' I would hae said he wasna nane weel if it hadna been 'at he gaed by at sic a steek. He didna look our wy—at least no when he was close up, an' I set 'im doon for some ga'en aboot body. Na, I saw naething aboot 'im to be fleid at.

"The aucht o'clock bell was ringin' when I saw 'im to speak to. My twa-year-auld bairn was standin' aboot the door, an' I was makkin' some porridge for my man's supper when I heard the bairny skirlin'. She came runnin' in to the hoose an' hung i' my wrapper, an' she was hingin' there, when I gaed to the door to see what was wrang.

"It was the man I'd seen passin' the hoose. He was standin' at the gate, which, as a'body kens, is but sax steps frae the hoose, an' I wondered at 'im neither runnin' awa nor comin' forrit. I speired at 'im what he meant by terrifyin' a bairn, but he didna say naething. He juist stood. It was ower dark to see his face richt, an' I wasna nane taen aback yet, no till he spoke. Oh, but he had a fearsome word when he did speak. It was a kind o' like a man hoarse wi' a cauld, an' yet no that either."

"'Wha bides i' this hoose?' he said, ay standin' there.

"'It's Davit Patullo's hoose,' I said, 'an' a'm the wife.'

"'Whaur's Hendry McQumpha?' he speired.

"'He's deid,' I said.

"He stood still for a fell while.

"'An' his wife, Jess?' he said.

"'She's deid, too,' I said.

"I thocht he gae a groan, but it may hae been the gate.

"'There was a dochter, Leeby?' he said.

"'Ay,' I said, 'she was ta'en first.'

"I saw 'im put up his hands to his face, an' he cried oot, 'Leeby too!' an' syne he kind o' fell agin the dyke. I never kent 'im nor nane o' his fowk, but I had heard aboot them, an' I saw 'at it would be the son frae London. It wasna for me to judge 'im, an' I said to 'im would he no come in by an' tak a rest. I was nearer 'im by that time, an' it's an awfu' haver to say 'at he had a face to frichten fowk. It was a rale guid face, but no ava what a body would like to see on a young man. I felt mair like greetin' mysel when I saw his face than drawin' awa frae 'im.

"But he wouldna come in. 'Rest,' he said, like ane speakin' to 'imsel, 'na, there's nae mair rest for me.' I didna weel ken what mair to say to 'im, for he aye stood on, an' I wasna even sure 'at he saw me. He raised his heid when he heard me tellin' the bairn no to tear my wrapper.

"'Dinna set yer heart ower muckle on that bairn,' he cried oot, sharp like. 'I was aince like her, an' I used to hing aboot my mother, too, in that very roady. Ay, I thocht I was fond o' her, an' she thocht it too. Tak' a care, wuman, 'at that bairn doesna grow up to murder ye.'

"He gae a lauch when he saw me tak haud o' the bairn, an' syne a' at aince he gaed awa quick. But he wasna far doon the brae when he turned an' came back.

"'Ye'll, mebbe, tell me,' he said, richt low, 'if ye hae the furniture 'at used to be my mother's?'

"'Na,' I said, 'it was roupit, an' I kenna whaur the things gaed, for me an' my man comes frae Tilliedrum.'

"'Ye wouldna hae heard,' he said, 'wha got the muckle airm-chair 'at used to sit i' the kitchen i' the window 'at looks ower the brae?'

"'I couldna be sure,' I said, 'but there was an airm-chair 'at gaed to Tibbie Birse. If it was the ane ye mean, it a' gaed to bits, an' I think they burned it. It was gey dune.'

"'Ay,' he said, 'it was gey dune.'

"'There was the chairs ben i' the room,' he said, after a while.

"I said I thocht Sanders Elshioner had got them at a bargain because twa o' them was mended wi' glue, an' gey silly.

"'Ay, that's them,' he said, 'they were richt neat mended. It was my mother 'at glued them. I mind o' her makkin' the glue, an' warnin' me an' my father no to sit on them. There was the clock too, an' the stool 'at my mother got oot an' into her bed wi', an' the basket 'at Leeby carried when she gaed the errands. The straw was aff the handle, an' my father mended it wi' strings.'

"'I dinna ken,' I said, 'whaur nane o' thae gaed; but did yer mother hae a staff?'

"A little staff," he said; 'it was near black wi' age. She couldna gang frae the bed to her chair withoot it. It was broadened oot at the foot wi' her leanin' on't sae muckle."

"'I've heard tell,' I said, ' 'at the dominie up i' Glen Quharity took awa the staff.'

"He didna speir for nae other thing. He had the gate in his hand, but I dinna think he kent 'at he was swinging back an' forrit. At last he let it go.

"'That's a',' he said, 'I maun awa. Good-nicht, an' thank ye kindly.'

"I watched 'im till he gaed oot o' sicht. He gaed doon the brae."

We learnt afterwards from the gravedigger that some one spent great part of that night in the graveyard, and we believe it to have been Jamie. He walked up the glen to the school-house next forenoon, and I went out to meet him when I saw him coming down the path.

"Ay," he said, "it's me come back."

I wanted to take him into the house and speak with him of his mother, but he would not cross the threshold.

"I came oot," he said, "to see if ye would gie me her staff—no 'at I deserve't."

I brought out the staff and handed it to him, thinking that he and I would soon meet again. As he took it I saw that his eyes were sunk back into his head. Two great tears hung on his eyelids, and his mouth closed in agony. He stared at me till the tears fell upon his cheeks, and then he went away.

"That evening he was seen by many persons crossing the square. He went up the brae to his old home, and asked leave to go through the house for the last time. First he climbed up into the attic, and stood looking in, his feet still on the stair. Then he came down and stood at the door of the room, but he went into the kitchen.

"'I'll ask one last favour o' ye,' he said to the woman; "I would like ye to leave me here alane for juist a little while."

"I gaed oot," the woman said, "meanin' to leave 'im to 'imsel', but my bairn wouldna come, an' he said, "Never mind her," so I left her wi' 'im, an' closed the door. He was in a lang time, but I never kent what he did, for the bairn juist aye greets when I speir at her.

"I watched 'im frae the corner window gang doon the brae till he came to the corner. I thocht he turned round there an' stood lookin' at the hoose. He would see me better than I saw him for my lamp was i' the window, whaur I've heard tell his mother keepit her cruizey. When my man came in

I speired at 'im if he'd seen onybody standin' at the corner o' the brae, an' he said he thocht he'd seen somebody wi' a little staff in his hand. Davit gaed doon to see if he was aye there after supper-time, but he was gone."

Jamie was never again seen in Thrums.

THE END.